SPECTRES CARRY

WORKIN

STOCK

(The Con ...mg Saga)

By

N R P Wilson

Contents

Dedication

To My wife Sylvia, who has had to tolerate my absence while I have been writing this, yet another attempt at writing novels, (this one now being the eighteenth) which were themselves also partly stimulated in the first place by the 'Lockdown' caused by the Coronavirus problem in 2020 and 2021. I must also include Sylvia's cousin Clare and also my three daughters, Samantha, Caroline & Nicola who have each been reading through various parts (or trying to do so) while I have been writing them, and also Ken Farmer, an author of some Historical Novels of Ancient Rome. It was he who first of all got me to have a go as he told me of some of how he started and has been an ongoing encouragement to me as I have been writing.

The name that I am commonly known by is Ralph Wilson. The first book that I wrote, long ago in the nineteen eighties (about the subject of meat inspection) went to the printers with somehow, a slip of paper carrying my name with initials, N R P Wilson, so, to ensure some continuity, all of my books do show the author as N R P Wilson. I do hope that anyone who reads any of my novels will perhaps think that they are written by Ralph Wilson, that does seem to be a much friendlier thing to do, don't you think? None of the novels that I have written appears to me to have been arrived at with any 'common theme' or any detailed plan. When I make a start, I never have a clue what the story is going to be about. If that is a mistake, my sincere apologies!

My first attempt at a novel came out in the 'Case' series of novels (a series of 4 novels): These were written by me as something of a challenge in 2019. My interest in writing before that effort had all been in the form of the writing of books about meat and the meat industry and it was my firm belief at that time that I didn't have enough, or even any, imagination at all anywhere in me to write a novel, although I had often wanted, or have even longed to do so. However, since then I have had some very encouraging comments from those early days and so, for any future potential authors, if this is, to you a book that is worth reading at all, I would simply say, go on, do have a go. If I can do it, so can you! Remember, if you seek deep inside yourself you may also have some imagination that you can find, somehow, somewhere.

Just as a matter of interest to any readers of this book, I had, I thought, stopped trying to write novels (after the first four, which were about a case being delivered to a man who then opened it and used the contents) and it was followed by the onset of the 'lockdown' due to Coronavirus that I saw a need to do something! The book, *'Toil and Turmoil in the Village'* was started in March of that year to try and fill some time.

That book was followed by a group of three, (rather incongruously about a Burglar in the early 1800s entitled *'Beneath Society's Surface'* the first one included *'London'* in the title, the second, *'Several English Cities'* in the title and the third one *'England'* in the title) all were set in the era of the early to mid-1800s and taking a totally different view of attitudes and time during the nineteenth century. They were started at the beginning of December of the lockdown period and, in the absence of any other interest, it went on almost continuously until its completion.

The series about Alec (and his family) being endowed with a strange 'power' to do things just followed since I just had to find something else to do, and so that novel ran into another series of three.

The lockdown was still going on and I knew that as I got older, and was now supposedly retired I didn't want my brain to just turn into a cabbage (or whatever) so I began yet another one. This time it was set a few decades into the future (we hope) and it somehow followed the early life of some young lads who had been on the brink of entering into a life of crime when he was helped by another man. He was another man who, being a part of a group that was being supported by wealthy businessmen who didn't like the idea of the towns being overrun with criminal elements. So, they funded a group of very fit young men to combat those criminals. As can be expected they do succeed.

Now, it had in some way come to a total of twelve novels (in addition to my other books about meat and the meat industry) and that, to me just seemed to be so wrong so I decided to try for novel number thirteen. That told a strange story of a man who could have a dream and that dream could bounce some things into his real life.

Number fourteen was about two young men, one quite an exceptional woodworker and one an equally exceptional electronics genius. The electronics man created a time gadget to enable his friend to visit his old-time heroes, such as Thomas Chippendale.

Number fifteen did have some of the earlier stories of crime getting out of control. In this case, it was an undercover army group that dealt with the criminals.

Novel, number sixteen is about a group of people who do like to help other people when they have some problems. They are then aided by a Leprechaun who can make many things happen for them all. Number seventeen, well, it's finished and it is a bit different. If anyone has any suggestions for a theme or a title for a future book, do let me know. I would appreciate any comments.

Number seventeen was about a young man who is visited by the ghost of an old pal who had died in a car accident and he wants to get our 'hero' to follow the path that he takes him on which does lead to him becoming the Richest Man in the World.

I have found that doing some writing does appear to occupy me and somehow relaxes me. So, don't despair, if I can do it, you too can do it! Anyway, if it has been worth it for you when you do try, you may even find a need to follow it up with a sequel, as has been the case with several of my efforts. This book, as I have mentioned, follows on from number seventeen as a sequel. Well, the first book turned into a series of four and then the one about our nineteenth-century 'bad lad' did start as just one and it too then went on to become a series of three.

Perhaps, considering all of the novels that I have done, there is some kind of science fiction thing about a good few of them. Definitely, the series about the case of papers does fit into that genre. The one about the young people who have left school and want to progress their careers themselves is looking to the future, but not science fiction. Even the one that goes back to the nineteenth century, yes, that one, it is at least considering what the punishments may be. The one about Alec and the Power certainly looks to what can happen in the future unless things are corrected, while the one about the young lads kept away from a life of crime most certainly does: These latest ones also are certainly slightly different, but I suppose still a bit science-fiction. At least when it gets to ghosts, I think that it is!

When you have finished reading it though, do please give some kind of a review. Once a book has been written, the best opinion of what it's reading of is like is for a reader to make comments, not the author, he can him (or her)self be somewhat biased! As with all of my novels, the names used are fictitious and any resemblance to anyone living or dead is coincidental.

Ralph Wilson - November 2023
(N R P Wilson)

Other books that are written by this author:

Meat & Meat Products – factors affecting quality control
Published 1980 by Applied Science Publishers Ltd (Hardback)

The Meat Hygienists Pocket Book.
Published by Association of Meat Inspectors 1980 (Paperback)

The Meat Hygienists Pocket Book, 2nd edition. (Paperback)
Published by Association of Meat Inspectors 1986

The Meat Hygienists Pocket Book 3rd edition (Kindle & Paperback)
Published by Amazon in Sept. 2021

Meating the American Way – the diary of a Sir Winston Churchill Fellow.
Published by Amazon 2019 Kindle, Paperback and Hardback

Meat as an industry in the UK and elsewhere.
Published by Amazon 2019

Meat Quality, a True Matter of Taste.
Published by Amazon 2019

In this series of novels:

1. A Case to Investigate.
   Published by Amazon 2019 (Book 1 in this series of 'cases')

2. Another case, Another time.
   Published by Amazon 2019 (Book 2 in this series)

3. Just one more case, But was it just in time?
   Published 2019 by Amazon (Book 3 in this series)

4. A case of some dimensions
   Published by Amazon 2020 (Book 4 in this series)

5. Toil and Turmoil in the Village
   Published by Amazon 2020

6. Beneath Society's surface in 1817. London
   Published by Amazon 2020 (Book 1 in the series)

7. Beneath Society's surface during 1817 in several English Cities
   Published by Amazon 2020 (Book 2 in the series)

8. Beneath Society's surface during the mid-1800s in several areas of England.
   Published by Amazon 2020 (Book 3 in the series)

9. Alec discovers how to make good use of the Power.
   Published by Amazon 2021 (book 1 in the series)

10. Alec finds further developments that happen while he is working with the Power.
    Published by Amazon 2021 (book 2 in the series)

11. Alec starts to become a trainer for the Power
    Published by Amazon September 2021 (book 3 in the series)

12. A crime and serving time? Just how can it get worse than it already is?
    Published by Amazon in January 2022

Chapter One

Jack and Jennifer left their house and decided to walk over to see both sets of parents. They both knew that their security-conscious friends (who happened to be the security team that Jack had now employed to keep them safe) would probably say that they were mad to go out like that without at least one of their security team being with them. The pair of them though had been talking after leaving Alec and Ray (their ghostly stock brokers) and they had both decided that yes, they may need some security but, as far as they were concerned, they had not been sentenced to a prison life for the rest of their lives. Some of their neighbours knew who they were and in general, they were usually very friendly towards the pair of them. Now and then they saw a few other people who weren't neighbours but, no one appeared to be taking any massive interest in them so they carried on walking.

They arrived first of all at Jennifer's parents' house and as they got there, they pressed the doorbell. They had both forgotten to bring a key with them and they knew that it was more than likely that they would have been seen approaching by the security people and devices in the house. Hugo had been quite insistent that all of their houses should have some top-quality detection systems in place. Both Jennifer's Dad and Jack's Dad had said that they didn't want to stop working and, there was nothing that Jack or Jennifer could do to make them stop working. They had barely taken their fingers from the doorbell when the door flew open and Jennifer's Mum reached out to get hold of Jennifer and give her a huge hug.

"My goodness Jennifer," her Mum said, "It's been a while since you came across to see us, hasn't it? Anyway, I'm glad that you didn't completely forget your Mum and Dad. It isn't Jack that's been keeping you away, I know that. His Mum and I talk quite a bit and you haven't been to see them either, have you? I don't know what you two get up to that you can't keep a bit more in touch more often. Miguel told us that he's seen you but that's only because he's been over to your house, wasn't it? Anyway, let me get you a nice cup of coffee. You see, I know that you two just drink that, don't I? Your Dad and I still prefer our tea though. Your Dad should be home from work soon so, if you take your time over your coffee, he'll be here."

"Oh, we we're going to go and see Jack's Mum and Dad as well only we thought after we had been to have a cuppa with you two would be soon enough," Jennifer said. "We're sorry that we haven't been over a bit more but somehow, the time just seems to have been flowing past so quickly Mum. I promise that we'll try a bit harder in future."

"Hello, you two," Miguel said as he appeared from the rear of the house. "How come you two are here now? I haven't had any word from our lads at your house. Manuel and Javier were supposed to be with you, weren't they? You haven't just disappeared without mentioning to them that you were going out, have you? Hugo will go mad when he hears about this."

"Look, don't go and get them into trouble Miguel," Jack said. "We just fancied going out for a bit of a walk and we thought that neither of us had seen anything of our parents for a little while so, we thought that we could do that now. It hasn't hurt anyone, has it? No one seemed to even notice us as we walked down the street, did they, Jennifer?"

"Look," Miguel said, "I'll give Manuel a call and ask him to drive over here to pick you two up. If you want to go places, you will need to work with us if you want to have the security that you have asked for and are paying us to provide. When he gets here he can take you on to wherever else you want to go. If you want to go for a walk, just let us know and some of us can be with you to make sure that you are safe. Once you get moved into the new house, things should be a lot easier for you (and for us, I think). Then, if you want to go for a walk, well, there are all of the grounds to walk in aren't there?"

"Miguel," Jack replied. "Having a walk in the grounds isn't quite the same as having a walk to see our parents, is it? We do like to call on our parents now and then. I expect that you do that as well, at least you will do that, no doubt when you are in Spain you will, won't you? Yes, we did do a bit wrong in popping out like that but you must remember as well that a lot of this is all new to us as well, isn't it, but we do still want to live some kind of life as well, don't we?"

"Jack, I'm sorry if I appear to be having a go at you but just look at your Dad and Jennifer's Dad. They were told to stop working and that was going to remove a lot of pleasure from their lives, wasn't it? I'm not good at explaining it. It'll be better if we get Hugo to have a bit of a talk with you, won't it? I'll talk to him later and I'll try to explain a bit about what is getting at you."

"Jack, Jennifer, don't you two start having a go at Miguel here," Jennifer's Mum said. You know that he's right, don't you? As he's said, your two Dads' have both had a lot of limits put on them but they do manage to toe the line a bit even with the restrictions, don't they? As it's all down to you Jack, you should try and work with these poor lads."

"Jack," Jennifer said with a little laugh at his embarrassment. "You've walked yourself into a real battle here, haven't you? After all, Mum is right and we were wrong. We agreed that the security was necessary and so we should abide by their rules to keep us safe, shouldn't we?"

Jack put both hands in the air and said, "Alright, I surrender. I did do wrong and there can be no doubt about that so Miguel, I'm sorry and please don't tell Manuel off. There wasn't anything that he could have done. We'd been upstairs and then, we came downstairs and went straight out of the door. That's something that we often used to do and you do get used to doing that, don't you?"

Just as Jack finished talking, Robert Wood, Jennifer's Dad walked into the doorway. "Hello then strangers," he said as he entered. "We had begun to think that we'd lost all sight of you two. I'm surprised that you managed it today 'cos I can't see your car out there Jack. What have you done then, walked? That must be a strange experience for you lad, mustn't it? I thought that you and that new car were more or less stuck together, didn't you missus," he said to his wife.

"Don't you start as well," Jack said to Robert. "I've already had it in the ear from Miguel and Jennifer and her Mum. No, we just felt like having a walk and so we just popped out of the door and walked over here. Miguel has already told me that Hugo will go mad when he hears about it. He's called for Manuel to get over here with my car so you see, just because we wanted to come and pay a visit I'm getting roasted alive by everyone, aren't I?"

"No, not by me dear," Jennifer said, smiling ever so sweetly at her husband. "But I do agree with Miguel that we were daft to do it all the same. Oh, by the way, Hello Dad, it's nice to see you. Mum was just putting the kettle on, weren't you Mum? Would you like a cup of coffee as well Dad?"

"And if you carry on talking like that to me young miss, you're not too old to get a smacked bottom for being cheeky to your Dad. You know damned well that I never drink that horrid stuff. Tea, lass, that's the beverage for real people, you know. Don't you agree Miguel?"

"Mr Wood," Miguel said from where he was standing, "I'm surprised at you, trying to get me to disagree with both your wonderful daughter and of course her very, very wealthy husband. Without them I'd still probably be doing some tour guides work out in Spain, wouldn't I? However, I do know that you are supposed to be good to your parents so I'll agree with your Dad as well."

Jennifer's Mum, accompanied by Jennifer made their way towards the kitchen so that they could get the kettle filled and switched on. They had just about finished doing that and the sound of the doorbell made them all look around to see what or who it was that was at the door. Hugo had arranged for some very sophisticated doorbell alarms that showed on a screen who it was at the door. It was Manuel, obviously having brought Jack's car over as Miguel had asked him to do. Miguel pressed the door open button and Manuel walked in.

"I'm sorry Miguel," Manuel said. "I had no idea that they had gone out. Javier said that he hadn't seen anything of them either so somehow, we missed them. My apologies to you sir for not watching things more closely."

"That's O.K. Manuel," Miguel said. "Jack's already admitted that they should have let you know. It's just going to be a case of what Hugo has to say when he hears about it all. I'll have to tell him, of course. It was a lapse on our part, even if it was Jack who was just trying to nip out to see his parents and parents-in-law."

"Do you honestly have to tell Hugo," Jack asked. "I mean, it was my fault more than theirs, wasn't it? I'll promise that we won't do it again if we can just forget this one incident. Will that do, please? I agree that we made a mistake, yes, us, not you or any of your men and I wouldn't want Hugo to think that any of you had done anything wrong."

"If Jack says that," Robert said, "I do think that to get Hugo involved is going a bit over the top isn't it? You have to remember that before we went on that damned holiday, none of us had any idea that we'd be needing security, had we?"

"I just wish that you all realised that we are all ex-army and in the army, you do have to follow rules," Miguel said. "Hugo was our Major and he was one of the best and if he says that we must follow the rules, we follow the rules. Quite probably there won't be any major punishment handed down for what has happened but he does need to know. If a similar thing happened in the future, where would we be then? We could then just say, well, it happened before and it was all OK, couldn't we? No, it just has to happen the way that Hugo says that it happens or I'm pretty certain that he'll pull out of any contract with you Jack. We are offering service, a damned good service and we want to keep it to be a damned good service so we shall follow the rules. If you disagree with what I've said Jack, that is up to you to have it out with Hugo later."

"Do you know, I think that I've just been told off again, haven't I Robert?" Jack said to his father-in-law. The thing is, with it all explained how Miguel just did, I accepted it and we will follow the rules. Will that do Miguel?"

"Thank you, Jack," Miguel replied with a small smile. "I thought that you would see how it has to be. It's because of that that we can hopefully keep you and yours safe from any nasty incidents."

"Yes, that'll do for me," Miguel replied. "And Hugo will be pleased as well when he gets to know that you are starting to understand how we have to work."

They all settled down, Jack, Jennifer, Miguel and Manuel with coffee and Jennifer's Mum and Dad drinking tea. They had quite a chat and eventually, Jack and Jennifer asked Manuel if he could take them over to see Jack's Mum and Dad. After all, that was why they had gone out at all from home that morning. They knew in their inner minds that there could be a phone call coming in at any time (or so they hoped) from the Foreign Office to confirm that they did want to help to get Jack's proposed donation started to get some water to the interior of Ethiopia. That was going to be their first major donation and that was going to put their ghostly friends on their first big step towards getting a good few bonus points in their world. Manuel, being as helpful as he always was, did of course agree and the three of them left to make their way to Jack's Mum and Dad's house.

Chapter Two

Once at Jack's Mum and Dad's house they received a similar welcome from his parents who, like Jennifer's parents, asked why they left it so long between their visits. Of course, Jack quite quickly retorted that a similar question could be put to them. He just said that they hadn't been over to see them either and that in any case, they had been getting ready for the move that would be happening during the coming week when they would be moving everything over to the new estate that they had bought. Jack had, of course, asked his Mum and Dad if they wanted a flat in the major building that was being converted to provide, amongst other things, some rather nice luxury-type flats that would be used by the family as and when they wanted to use them. They stayed with his parents for a while and then Manuel once again, being their chauffeur as well as their security guard, drove them back to their home. Both Jack and Jennifer knew that they would have to see if there had been any telephone calls from the Foreign Office. They also wanted to pop away from the guards and see their friendly ghosts who were doing such an excellent job of looking after Jack's vast fortune that just seemed to keep on growing.

Once back in the house, Alvaro, the other security guard said how relieved he had been to hear that they were alright. Miguel had radioed through to him and told him what had happened. Alvaro said that he understood that Hugo was going to be back shortly from his latest visit to check on the completion of the work on their new estate house. Hugo had, of course, covered almost all points with respect to security to make the estate almost proof against entry by anyone unless they had been approved for entry. Jack had been consulted as things were happening and he was very appreciative of the way that Hugo and his men were looking after them all.

Jack went to the phone to check if any messages had been received he found that there had been one message and he played that back to check what it was. It was indeed the Foreign Office and they sounded to be almost as unhelpful as they had been the last time. Jack rang them back and eventually, someone answered and he told them who he was and they began to inform him that any offers of aid to the East African appeal must follow the protocol that had been laid down. Jack simply replied to that by telling the Ministry man that his wife had given them his offer and that since they didn't appear to understand English, he would now pass on the details of the offer to the National Press agencies and let them ask the public what they thought of the government ignoring the offer of an initial two Billion Pounds of aid. The official on the phone went quiet for a moment and then said that if he would wait, he would try and get the Minister to call him back. Jack put the telephone down with an air of disgust.

Jack happened to be on the telephone when Hugo walked into the house. He very carefully and quietly moved over towards the kitchen area (obviously he too wanted to get another coffee!). Jack saw Hugo and just gave a nod towards him. As Jack finished talking, Hugo came back through towards where Jack was and he said, "I take it from the little that I heard that that was once again the Foreign Ministry that you were talking to."

"Yes," Jack replied. "I think that they must breed that kind of people to work in the government departments, don't you?"

"Look, Jack," Hugo said, "You know that I and the other lads of our group all used to be in the army and doing political security work, well. That is more or less what we found and that was quite a major part of why we wanted out of that kind of work. Yes, I do agree that they must be bred to talk and behave how they do. I gather from what I heard that they still haven't moved on at all then?"

"No, you gathered right there, Hugo," Jack replied. "They just don't seem to want to listen when you tell them anything."

"By the way," Hugo said, "I am hearing that you and Jennifer gave my men the slip today and went out for a walk. You must remember Jack that as you upset powerful people in the government they all have enough power to send some other people out to sort you out as well. I know that it all happened to work out well today Jack, but please, do remember that we only want to safeguard you and your families. Miguel radioed me to keep me informed. I won't be taking any action against the men this time, but our rules are there to help you, to keep you safe. Do please try and help yourself as well Jack."

"I'm sorry Hugo," Jack said. "We never gave it a thought. We know that we often used to pop out for a bit of a walk to see our parents and well, old habits can die hard, but we will try and remember them in the future. There was nothing at all that your men could have done. We just came down from the office and walked straight out of the front door. You can't expect your men to anticipate what we are thinking, can you?"

Jennifer had by then walked back towards Jack with the cup of coffee that he had asked her to get for him. "At least this time, Hugo, it was Jack who answered the phone and had to reply to the government people. Maybe now that it is he who has spoken to them like that they will realise that they must start to take some action. If he (or we) do go to the press with the stories of their lack of reaction to his offer; that would surely cause them an awful lot of embarrassment wouldn't it?"

"Oh, there's no doubt that it would cause them embarrassment Jennifer," Hugo replied, "But as I was just saying to Jack, do remember that they do have an awful lot of power and if you upset them too much they can be quite nasty and underhand in the way that they would try to punish you for causing them any problems."

They had only just finished talking and the telephone rang once again. Jennifer picked it up and said hello. She had pressed the loudspeaker button as she picked it up so everyone could hear what was coming in.

"Good day to you. I am the Foreign Minister speaking on behalf of the government. Could I please speak to Mr Jack Dawkins? He has telephoned my office already today and he must understand that we do have certain systems that we do have to conform to. Is Mr Dawkins there please?"

"The calls made to your office today were made in the main by myself," Jennifer replied. "I am Mrs Dawkins and I was speaking on behalf of my husband. How may I help you sir?"

"Mrs Dawkins," The Minister replied, "I understand that Mr Dawkins has made a most generous offer of aid to the East African problem but no matter how much is offered, it must be made in a way that is acceptable to both this government and to the governments of the countries that are affected by the crisis. He, or you, appear to believe that you were only able to make the offer in a way that satisfied some criteria laid out by yourselves. Unfortunately offers like that are not acceptable. Those who are in charge of having to deal with the crisis are the ones best placed to decide just how any support should be handled. No doubt the offer was made with some good intentions but I am afraid that, no matter how much the donation may be, it must follow the prescribed way that any such aid must follow."

"Minister," Jennifer replied, "I do take it that you would be well aware that a crisis of the same nature as this one appeared only a few years ago, that was in itself a repeat of yet another crisis of the same kind again a few years before that. Since that appears to be the case, it would appear that nothing has been done to resolve the cause of the crisis. Is that correct? My husband's offer was a donation or donations to cover the cost of dealing with the cause of the crisis. He made an initial offer of two Billion pounds of aid to make a start on getting rid of the cause of the crisis. He was, and still is, quite prepared to increase that donation to the sum, or sums, that may be needed to get rid of the problems that cause the crisis. He has assured me that he does not wish to donate to any fund that may provide some form of income for any illegal persons who seek to gain from the money being donated, nor does he seek to enhance the income of any politicians who are trying to secure their own well being from any funds that are sent. Now, he has made the offer and the offer does still stand but it must be in the form that he has given already. If you, or their government, wish to refuse that aid then we can only presume that the press would not take very kindly to any such negative attitudes. If you can speak to your colleagues and discuss what has been offered and can come back to us we can then make a start on getting the project underway. I do take it that you can follow what I am suggesting sir?"

"Mrs Dawkins," The Minister replied. "I'm afraid that statements and accusations such as those that you have just made, unsubstantiated also if I may say, do not give any reason why Mr Dawkins offer should receive any consideration. I shall pass on the details of your remarks to others within our government and perhaps further action may become necessary and, good day to you madam." The minister ended the call.

"Wow," Jack and Hugo said, more or less together. "That certainly told them, didn't it Hugo," Jack said. "I suppose that they will now want some proof that at the past incidents, any money or food was taken by the baddies, won't they? Do you think that the press will want to do some digging for that kind of info for us?"

"Oh, I would imagine that the press would be there with you like a shot," Hugo said. "But don't forget what I said to you about the government. They can be quite nasty and I think that the sooner that we can get you moved into your new estate the better it will be. At least then we can surround you with some kind of protection. I would also imagine that all of the other major donors to good causes will also want to be with you. I think that you may start to get some offers of help from a lot of those quarters and quickly once the news gets out."

"I think that I could do with a little bit of quiet now. I'm going to have a lay down for a while. Are you coming as well, Jennifer?" Jack asked.

"Yes, maybe Jack," Jennifer said, "But I think that we still have one or two bits to get sorted in the office yet, don't we?"

"Yes, I hadn't forgotten that, Jack said. Maybe while we are doing that we may find some way of getting the government to toe the line, don't you think? I think that either Ray or Alec may have suggested something once, don't you?"

Chapter Three

Jack and Jennifer got up and started to make their way back up to their office. As they were going, Hugo called out, "Don't forget that you should be moving tomorrow so you will soon need to start getting things ready for moving, won't you?"

Jack and Jennifer both nodded their agreement and carried on walking to their office. They both had a good idea of what Jack had been suggesting earlier to Jennifer and said it in such a way that Hugo wouldn't be able to catch on to what they were going to be doing.

They got to the office and as they went in they could see Alec and Ray both hard at it with the computer and with some other papers by them that they had been using some of the times when they worked there.

"Alec, Ray," Jack said, "We appear to be having a problem with the government Foreign Secretary as far as the donation goes. We just wondered if there was any way that either you or one of your colleagues could kind of haunt some of them to make them toe the line. They are still saying that they will only accept money, you know, cash as an aid to the East African crisis and we, as you know, believe that that isn't getting to the source of the problem. Personally, I don't care how much the donation has to be to make it go our way but if they don't get water to irrigate the land, the problem will keep on coming back, won't it? Now, initially, Jennifer had suggested that I would be donating a couple of Billion pounds. We haven't had any costings at all and the final figure could easily be far more than that. Now, your bonus points depend on how much is spent on good work, don't they? Now I don't care if it costs one hundred Billion pounds to get it sorted, but I think that our way is right, and theirs is wrong. If you support me, then your bonus points would be skyrocketing, wouldn't they? I understand that the GDP (GDP meaning Gross Domestic Product, a figure that indicates more or less the total wealth of that country) for Ethiopia is between about ninety and one hundred Billion pounds per annum so if my donation matches (more or less to their GDP) I can't see how they can say no, can you? Now if you can somehow cause them to be haunted to make them toe the line, your bonus points would soar, wouldn't they? By the way, just how high is my cash fund standing at right now?"

"Hello Jack," Alec replied, "Your fund is currently at one trillion four hundred billion pounds. It should have started to go down with donations out, but up to now, there has only been an odd one or two that you have done from when you were getting money via Peter. What you are suggesting would certainly help to take that total down and it would get us some bonus points, wouldn't it Ray? As for haunting the Foreign Secretary, well, that's a new one for me, but I do like the idea of it. Damned government Ministers do need taking down a few pegs, don't they? We can make a start on doing something like that. I'm not sure who to ask but we do have a few people who wouldn't mind scaring some government people, I can tell you that. Give me a day to try and find the best ones for the job and then we can start to work on them."

As Alec was talking, Hugo walked up by the office door and Jennifer nudged Jack's shoulder to let him know.

Jack turned and saw Hugo near the door and said, "What is it, Hugo? Is there something that you need, or how can I help you? We do like to have our private time sometimes, you know, and Jennifer and I do like to get a few bits done in the office while we are alone."

"I'm, sorry Jack," Hugo replied, "It was just that I was down at the end of the corridor I heard another voice from down here and it was a voice that I didn't recognise. We have got some good security set up here Jack and we know that there's no one else in the house. What is happening? Who was it that was talking to you?"

Jennifer looked at Jack and Jack looked at Jennifer and then they both looked across at Alec, still sitting at the computer. "Hugo," Jack replied, "If I told you, I don't think for a moment that you'd believe what I told you, so I'll let you try and sort it out. The person sitting at the computer is Alec. He's an old and very highly valued friend of ours and he has been here all of the time since we returned from Spain. In fact, he was here before we went to Spain and he stayed here while we were away. Somehow, I don't think that your security system has managed to pick him up, or his friend Ray who is standing just beyond him. He has also been here all of that time. Well, what do you make of all that then Hugo?"

"Jack," Hugo said, frowning and with quite a concerned look on his face. "Our scanners would pick up anyone in here. We checked all of the rooms when you returned, including this office room and no one was here then. No, it doesn't matter what you tell me, I'll try and believe you, so you tell me whatever it is and then I'll deal with it."

"Alec and Ray are both ghosts Hugo. There's no other way of describing them. Have you put the other security lads elsewhere for a time, if you haven't, please do so now and then if you come back I will try and explain some of what has happened?"

Hugo left the office area and went to the other end of the corridor and called out some instructions to the other two security men downstairs and then he returned to the office.

"Hugo," Jack said, "Do please get yourself a chair and sit down because, believe me, you are going to need one when we have finished telling you what has been happening. The man sitting here at the computer is, as I said, called Alec. The other man behind me is Ray. They are both ghosts but they aren't the first of the ghosts that came to see me. Just to keep you in the picture, I can see them, Jennifer can see them and both of my parents can see them and now, apparently, you too can see them. I'll try and keep it as brief as I can but I do have to go back a few years to when it started for me. I had been doing a bit of writing, as I sometimes do, and suddenly a voice, quite close to me spoke and said something. When I turned to see who was there I saw my friend Peter. Now Peter had been in a car accident two or three years earlier and had been killed. He then was the first of the ghosts and he told me that he had come back because he had some work to complete. His work, it would appear, was to try and get me in some way to get enough funds behind me which no doubt you heard about, some horse race wins and then a lottery win. Once I had the funds available he brought his other two friends to see me, Alec and Ray. All of the ghosts that I'm telling you about didn't go up to the higher place, heaven if you like, nor down to the other place, Hell as it is more commonly known as. They all were living in an in-between world and they had to work to go up higher to aim at the higher place. Now before they died, Alec and Ray had both been high-flying stockbrokers and their purpose was to get someone still alive to work and get funds together to donate to good causes. None of the ghosts are allowed to take anything back from this world, but they can earn bonus points (for want of a better description) that can help to lift them and their colleagues to the higher levels. Alec and Ray have explained to me that they did think of what they are doing now when they were alive, but what they thought of doing was impossible since quite a bit of it requires advanced knowledge of how shares are doing. He said that it was called 'insider trading' or something. Anyway, they worked on my fund and they built it up and they believed that it would get to a point when it couldn't effectively be reduced. Whatever is donated from the fund is replaced by income from other shares and so on. So, that is why I now happen to be the richest man in the world. Does it explain things to you or do you now think that I need a ticket to the funny farm?"

"No," Hugo replied with quite a smile on his face. "I don't think that you need to go to the 'funny farm' as you call it, but it does answer a lot of questions that I had. I had accepted that you had the wealth but it had always seemed to me to be rather strange that you could have acquired so much wealth in such a comparatively short period of time. As I mentioned to you before, I do come from quite a wealthy family and I have had some dealings with the stock markets. Your growth just seemed to me to be far, far too rapid for it to be achieved without some help from somewhere. I also do happen to believe in ghosts and it has often been said that I can quite often detect the presence of ghosts when others can't. So, Alec and Ray, welcome to our world. I accept you and welcome you and all that you have been doing. It is an admirable target that you have got and we should all try, as much as we can, to help you along."

"Well, Hugo, Jack said, "After the reception that I had had from the Foreign Secretary I came in here to ask Alec and Ray if there was any way in which they may be able to haunt the Foreign Secretary to make him realise that what I was suggesting would be worthwhile and much more sensible than just giving cash to the criminals who are waiting to get hold of it. I had just told Alec that I thought that if it meant me donating a hundred Billion Pounds that should cover most things to get the system working. A hundred Billion does somehow just about equate to the GDP of Ethiopia as a country so that should impress as many people as is needed, don't you think? What do you think of my idea to haunt him to get him to agree?"

"Well, I think that I would agree with you there, my friend," Hugo replied. "If they can put some fear of God into those who supposedly run our countries, they could certainly help you to make your large donation. That in turn would help your friendly ghosts and everything should be near perfect, shouldn't it? I, by the way, am pleased that you have now confided in me and I assure you that your secret is quite safe with me. My colleagues and I will be only too pleased to continue to ensure you and your families some safety and no, I don't want a share of your good fortune in being aided by the ghosts. I still admire them though, and you two of course for what you are doing at making your aims now at helping these poor souls. Alec, Ray, I am also pleased to have met you again and I do most sincerely wish you well with your endeavours."

"And you, Hugo Moncado, I believe that that is your name is it not," Alec said. "You said that you and your family had done some dealings on the stock markets I believe. As it happens, in my other life, before this that I now have, I used to do quite a lot of work for your family on the stock market and yes, you and your family were quite successful weren't you?"

"My goodness", Hugo gasped. "Were you actually working at some time as our stockbroker then, in your early life, of course? I should have recognised you. I must say that I am quite honoured to meet you again sir as you are now and I do assure you that my team and I shall do all that we can to safeguard their interests."

Jack and Jennifer just stood there, almost in shock at what was happening. They were shocked that Hugo, as far as they were aware, a new face to the ghosts, was able to see and speak to them while they had been required to seek permission for Jack's Mum and Dad and of course, Jennifer to be able to see and speak to them. They were also quite shocked that in some strange way, one of their ghosts knew Hugo, their friendly security leader. "Alec," Jack said, "How is it that Hugo can see and speak to you just like this when we had to seek special permission for my parents and also Jennifer to see and speak to you?"

"Jack, as you were sought out by Peter who had known you before he joined us here in this life, so too did Hugo know me and my family when I was in my other life. I believe that it is in some way due to all of that for us to be able to see and converse as we can. It is strange, very unusual but in no way does it change our duty towards you and your families. It is quite probable that Peter also will get a shock like you have had when he discovers that we also know someone in your world who is connected with you. By the way, your choice of Hugo and his team for your security could hardly have been better if you had had any inkling of how to look for security people. The Moncado family are a very highly respected noble family in Spain and while I was living in your world I felt quite honoured that I was sought out in Spain so that they could use my services to get around on the stock market. By the way Hugo, as a matter of interest, Jack's fund is now standing at one Trillion four Hundred Billion pounds. That is quite a bit higher than we had aimed at but unfortunately, as Jack has explained a little, he has had some problems in being able to make some large donations. Currently, he is trying to make one of several Billions which would help and I believe that he is setting the maximum target of aid for that one job at a ceiling figure of one Hundred Billion Pounds. He hasn't mentioned anything like that to the Foreign Office yet, he only told them a couple of Billion Pounds, but he did say to me what his ceiling was possibly going to be. That would help them and it would help us as well, wouldn't it? That's why he has been asking if we may be able to haunt them a bit to get them to agree."

"I only hope that you can do a bit of haunting Alec, or some of your colleagues anyway," Hugo said, "But, I do hope that I may see you sometime later but I had better get back to my work and look after these lovely people. By the way, did Jack mention to you that they are hoping to move house tomorrow? I would imagine that for a day or so, while the move is on, you would be out of contact with the market. We will make the computer move as an urgent piece of work though. Cheerio for now then Alec, I'll have to go and see my men downstairs, and Cheerio of course, to you too Ray."

Hugo left the office and went downstairs to check up on how the security men were doing. He had a lot of faith in them though and he was fairly certain that they would have all been doing their jobs.

Jack looked across at Jennifer and said, "Well, that was a little bit of a shock, wasn't it? So we now know that we have a Spanish Nobleman leading our security team, don't we? I don't think it changes anything though, I still like the bloke, don't you?"

"You can both rest easy I would imagine when you have someone like Hugo looking after you," Alec said. "He and his family have all had some strong connections with the Spanish history for a long, long time, as far as I remember about two or three centuries I believe and I think that somewhere amongst his past there was also a connection with the Spanish Royal Family. Oh, he's good, and now that we know who you've got looking after your security it gives us in our world a lot of confidence that things will work out fine. At least for a time yet, your world won't be able to find out just how much your fund is worth. They'll know that it's a lot but they won't be able to trace quite a lot of it so they won't know a final sum."

Chapter Four

Jack and Jennifer left the office and went downstairs to join Hugo and his men who were at that moment all trying to help with some of the packing of items into the packing cases that Hugo had had delivered. Hugo wanted the house move the next day to be as smooth as it could be and he had arranged that some of his men would help to get some of the things packed up to be ready for the removal people. He had agreed with Jack though that the actual removal would be done by a removal company. The flat that Jack and Jennifer were having in the new estate building had been decorated (with quite a bit of input from Jennifer about colour and general layout) and was more or less ready for them as soon as they moved everything in.

After the short session upstairs in the office, Hugo had approached Jack and suggested that he make some special arrangements for the computer and office equipment to be moved first of all by his men so that it could all be installed and ready for use just as soon as Jack wanted to get in to use it all again. Jack had liked that idea, although he had generally been of the opinion that the security men should concentrate their efforts on just that, security. Hugo though had suggested to Jack that since a lot of what was happening was only being given to them by the ghosts who attended mainly where the computer was situated, Jack had agreed that that did make some sense.

Hugo was buying the house that Jack and Jennifer were leaving (despite Jack's offer for it to be a gift to Hugo) since Hugo had told Jack that he would like to own some property in England himself and that while he did consider Jack's offer to be very generous, he did have quite a bit of wealth himself. Miguel had also found a house that he wanted to buy and Jack had managed to get him to accept that house as a gift. Jack had also bought a small estate of houses close to the estate for some of the other members of the security team to live in and, (particularly the two married men) had been pleased to accept the offer of a rent-free accommodation. The other men (besides the two married men) had found this to be a wonderful bonus that they got with the job.

There were a further eleven luxury flats built into the upper two floors of the main building on the estate and up until now, Jack and Jennifer hadn't decided what they would do with them. There was always the option they thought that some of them could be made into staff quarters for when the men were at work doing their security duties, but until Hugo said that they didn't need anything like that, so the other eleven flats remaining empty. Hugo had increased the number of security men as the estate was being made ready since he knew that with so much area to cover, the number of men that he had to hand was quite a few short of being a sensible number. Jack had naturally given Hugo a free hand to hire as many men as he felt that he needed. Although neither Jack nor Jennifer were keen on the idea they thought that as a temporary measure, any new men could be housed in some of the flats until Jack had managed to get some other accommodation available for them near to the site. Hugo had said that he preferred it if they weren't housed in the flats since he didn't want them to believe that they could live such a life and that a 'barracks' was more to the standard that most of the men were used to.

Jack and Jennifer, as was quite usual for them, had made their way into the kitchen so that they could get some more coffee. They liked their coffee and they knew that most of the security men all liked their coffee so they made a start and thought that they could perhaps carry a tray of coffee through to the two men who were working packing some of the cases.

The men welcomed the coffee and said that they had made quite a good start on putting a lot of the items, well packed for both security and to minimise breakages, into the cases that they had there. Each case was marked with a paper that gave the details of the contents of that case.

Jack and Jennifer realised that they, remaining in the area where the security men were packing the cases were causing no assistance but more of a distraction so once again they decided that they should pop back to the office and see just how their stock broker ghosts were doing with their activities.

When they got to the office they saw that both Alec and Ray were still quite hard at work and, standing close to them was Peter. It had been some time since they had seen Peter in the office with them. He had generally found the work in the office to be, for him, quite boring. He was still interested though in how the fund was going on and how it would affect him, once some bonus points started to be issued.

"We don't see a lot of you now Peter, do we?" Jack said. "We had a bit of a shock earlier today and it surprised us. You see, the leader of the security team came to the office while we were here and he could see both Alec and Ray and he spoke to them. It appears that Alec, in particular, had been a stockbroker for Hugo's family in Spain some years ago. When we wanted my Mum and Dad to be able to see and talk to people it seemed to take an age to get permission for that. That was what surprised us today you see. Nobody had to get any permission at all for Hugo to talk to Alec and Ray. Maybe it was just that one they called the controller that was causing the problems. What do you think, eh, Peter? Anyway, if you want to help us now, we've asked Alec to try and arrange some haunting for us. Maybe you could do that sort of thing, Peter. What do you think? It would all help to get the bonus points moving, I do know that."

"Who do you want to be haunted, and why?" Peter asked. "I haven't done any of that before but it does sound like it could be good fun, doesn't it? Who were you going to get to do it, Alec? Had you got someone in mind?"

"Yes, Peter, I do have someone in mind, Peter," Alec replied "And I would imagine that he'll be damned good at it, especially when I tell him who it is that we want him to haunt. He was a friend of mine in the other world that we left and he was driven to some serious problems by one of the politicians who wanted to interfere with what he was doing. It's a politician that Jack wants us to haunt and he wants that done because this one is holding up us getting the donations going. Jack wants it to be, well; at most, a donation of a hundred Billion Pounds and that would get us an awful lot of bonus points, wouldn't it?"

"Crikey," Peter said, "Have you got the fund high enough now for it to be as much as that Alec? I thought that you'd only got it to about two or three hundred Billion pounds so far."

"Yes, Peter, the fund is now getting close to one and a half Trillion Pounds and that is causing us some concern," Alec said. "At the moment, we can keep the lid on some of it due to the way that we have spread things about but if it ever does get out then it could cause a lot of problems. If we can get this idiot to go along with what Jack is suggesting we can hopefully start to get some really good donations going out and that will hold the fund about where we want it to be. If my friend, who I want to do the haunting needs an assistant, I'll suggest you, shall I Peter? I'll bet that you'd like to make a start on doing something like that, wouldn't you?"

"Yes, Alec," Peter replied, quite excited. "I think that it would be something new and when it's going to help us to get those bonus points I'd say double yes to that. And did you say one and a half Trillion Pounds? Crikey, that's a lot of money, isn't it? I do wish again that I had been put in your position Jack. I'm not sure what I would have done with that sort of money but I'm damned sure that I'd have had a good try at getting Alec and Ray to work twice as hard to keep up with me spending it. So, when do I get to meet your friend, Alec, the one who you want to start doing the haunting of the politician? Can't you pop out now from those damned accounts and get him going now? By the way, do I know him?"

"He does get to be a bit excitable, doesn't he?" Jennifer said as she watched Peter almost jumping up and down with excitement at the thought of having a go at doing some haunting. "Maybe he'll only make the politician want to carry on wanting to be haunted if he doesn't calm down. I'd trust you to handle him anyway, Alec. Good luck when you do go to get that job started."

"I know that we do get in the way a bit when we're downstairs," Jack said," "But we can't just keep on hiding away up here, can we? I think that we'll have to go down and see them. Anyway, they can't keep on packing things all evening, can they?"

"OK," Jennifer said. "Let's go back down. If we don't go down soon they'll just get their minds working at thinking what else we may be doing up here near to the bedrooms," She said with a huge grin on her face.

"Madam," Jack replied, with an equally huge grin on his face. "What will our visitors think of us when you start to talk like that?"

"Don't worry about us you two," Ray said, laughing at the pair of them. "Do remember that once upon a time we were both your age and we too used to get urges but I don't think that your Spanish lads would think anything bad at all with you two. From the way that we've been reading it, and from the way that you've looked after them so well, they think that the sun shines out of the pair of you. Go on, get off with you. We can manage fine here and yes, we'll look after little Peter here."

Jack and Jennifer again wandered downstairs and again made it as far as the kitchen. Jack called out to the remaining two men working in the hallway by the packing cases. "Have you finished your coffee then? Do you want some more? Jennifer is just putting the kettle on again if you do want some more."

Hugo came out into the hallway from the lounge and said, "You do know Jack, don't you, that you spoil this lot something rotten. I think that they will start to resent the day that they ever had to look after the politicians for the army, won't you, you lot," he laughed at them.

He nodded at Jack and indicated to go to the lounge, which Jack noticed, and he then followed Hugo into the lounge.

"Have your ghosts said that they will try and do something with that damned politician for you Jack?" Hugo said. "I took it that you'd gone back up to your office to talk to them again to see what they were doing."

"Yes, they, or at least Alec, have decided on who he wants to get to do the job and it's one who had a lot of damage done to him in his life by some politicians and Alec believes that he will want to make this one suffer, just to make up for what they did to him. They are probably going to take along Peter as well, more or less as a trainee. It was Peter whom I met first. He used to be my mate but he got killed in a car accident a few years ago now and he just likes to have a lot of fun and he thinks that doing some haunting could be good fun."

Jennifer appeared in the lounge with a tray with coffee on for all of them. She told Jack that she had just presumed that the other two lads would want some more coffee so she had taken them a tray through to them first. "Has Jack told you what they reckon the fund has got to now," she said. "Alec has said that it is now at about one and a half Trillion Pounds and he is getting a bit concerned about the size of it. It seems that like you, he is starting to think that some people would start to wonder how Jack could have got so much so quickly. He says that he has hidden quite a lot of it though, different names, different banks, and different countries and I understand that he is hoping that due to the way that he has done it, it would take some serious digging to find what the total is."

"Yes, Hugo said. "That is more or less what I said earlier, isn't it? Mind you, if anyone can manage to hide things I think that it would probably be Alec that would do that. He was good when he was doing our money, and at that time he wasn't even doing just one account, like he is now with just yours, Jack. Oh, he's good and he'll hide things until he's ready to get you to donate. If you ask him, I'll bet you anything that he has some companies hidden in your fund that look as though they are going to go bust at any time but somewhere, inside them, they probably have a few Billion Pounds each stored away. He just seems to know how to use them like that to get the opposition to start to get overconfident. When he only has one account to deal with he will be able to put his entire thoughts onto that account, don't you see? Can't you for a start try and help say a small country that is in trouble somewhere? Say one of these places that have had an earthquake or a Tsunami or something? To give them a few Billion would help to start things off by getting some donations going outwards, wouldn't it? That at least would make a start on reducing some of the size of the fund for a time for you, wouldn't it?"

"Yes, I suppose that we could have another look for disasters somewhere in the World, couldn't we Jennifer?" Jack asked. "Let's get that little old laptop and make a start now. We can hold the computers being moved for a while, can't we, Hugo? After all, there are all those cases packed down in the hallway aren't there? They could be moved first to give Alec and Ray a bit more time on the computer, couldn't they?"

"Jack," Hugo said, "I'm buying this house, aren't I? You just get your laptop and make a start at finding any other disasters and then you can leave the computers and all of the office stuff here until it's more convenient for you to move it. As I am the buyer of this house, I'll give you free access to come and get everything when it suits you more. That does help, doesn't it?"

"Let's stop talking and let's start doing something," Jennifer said. "I'll go and get the laptop. Where do you think we should use it? We could take it to the office area anyway, couldn't we? I'm not saying anything against your men, Hugo, but we should be doing this when we are away from other people, shouldn't we?"

"You're right about that," Hugo replied. "Do you mind though if I come with you? I almost feel that I am a part of all of this now. I know that that is daft, but it just gets to be so infectious, doesn't it?"

"Somehow, Hugo," Jack laughed back at his head of security, "I think that both Jennifer and I do think that you are now a part of it all. All that we have to do now is find some way of spending a lot of money, and fast, isn't it?"

Jennifer had got the laptop and they took it back to the office area. Ray and Alec looked at them as they went in, but neither of them said anything, although Alec did seem to have a bit of a smile on his face as he got back down to work on the main computer.

"We've decided that we're going to look for any more Global disasters, Alec," Jack said. "Hugo said that he'd like to be a part of what we're doing as well so we're going to try and find somewhere else where we can send donations to."

"And who is this one then," Peter said from where he was standing against the wall of the office. "Is this what you meant when you said that someone else knows that we're here?"

"Yes, Peter," That's about it," Jennifer said and we believe that he could be a big help to us in finding ways of donating so that you can get a lot of bonus points."

"Oh, well that'll be alright then, won't it?" Peter replied, laughing at the industry that was going on in that small office. After all, they were now all working to get some bonus points and he did like the idea of them, didn't he?

Jennifer began looking on the laptop computer to try and search for 'world disasters', as she had done before. Finding which one would be most appropriate they could all decide upon together but first of all, she wanted to get a list of different ones, if she could get such a list! The search engine was revealing very little for them to look at. It was showing quite a number of very minor incidents, but nothing that could be classed as a major disaster. They knew that there must be a way of finding out some kind of list but they hadn't got a clue, between them, of how to word the request so that they could get some kind of list. Jennifer tried putting different ways of wording the request but none of them appeared to be working.

Chapter Five

As they were trying to find anything on the little laptop, the telephone rang and Jack answered it. He had put it onto loudspeaker and it was the Foreign Minister again. That did surprise them a little as they had been hoping that if it had waited until the next day he may have been haunted a bit by their ghosts. "Mr Dawkins," The Minister began. "We have looked at your proposal and apparently the use of desalinated water for irrigation isn't something that can work in practice. It seems that it is just something that sounds good in theory but it doesn't work. That being the case, if you do wish to donate some money we can accept your donation."

Minister," Jack replied, "I do believe that if your advisers have discovered that the use of desalinated water won't work for land irrigational purposes, or for providing water for livestock, as well as some that is safe to drink by humans they are wrong. I do believe that your advisers need to go and look at their sources of information. Minister, it has already been tried and tested in the United States, Saudi Arabia, Kuwait, Australia, Spain and Israel to name just a few countries that have tried it and found that desalinated water can do all that I have just said that it can. Yes, it will irrigate the land and it can provide water for livestock and humans, but the only problem that they seem to have found with it was that it was rather costly to set it all up. Now, since it is I who will be providing the cost to supply, erect, and make a start on the project that my wife described to your office, where exactly is the problem? I do believe that if you get your advisers to look again they will find both that I am correct and that they are equally wrong and if you would only check your historical records for that area you will find that it seems to be that every two or three years almost, there is another disaster caused by the lack of water. My answer is to deal with the cause of the disasters, not to fund some gangsters either in that country or somewhere in-between us and them (and it is rather pointless to deny that such things do happen, they do); I cannot quite see why anyone is objecting. Yes, my wife said that I would provide a donation of two Billion Pounds for the project. As it happens, I haven't had any firm costings yet, but if you wish, I will get some costings fairly soon and if it costs more than the sum mentioned, I shall foot the entire bill to get the project completed. At this point, I would say that I must put a maximum limit on my donation for now, and for that, I would suggest at this point a sum of one hundred Billion Pounds, if it does indeed require so much, which it may not. That I believe would just about match the entire GDP of Ethiopia itself, wouldn't it? The only other things that I believe would be useful would be for either you or the responsible Minister in Ethiopia, to provide some armed support to protect the workers, the equipment and the entire installation, especially while it is being installed. It is my understanding that once an adequate quantity of water has been pumped to the interior, a lake, or perhaps several internal lakes (and perhaps even some rivers) could be created and then what is regarded at present as a waste, desert type land could become useful land to grow crops and to feed the people. Once that is done, shouldn't the country become a much more prosperous nation in itself? Now Minister, I have explained some of my thoughts, would you care to go away and see how incorrect your advisers have been and perhaps if you come back to me we may be able to get the project underway."

"Mr Dawkins," The Minister replied. "You do appear to have done some serious investigation and I shall most certainly see my advisers and, if you are indeed correct and they are wrong then perhaps I may get back to you very soon to try and get this project started. I will say good day to you for now Mr Dawkins but I shall get back to you." The phone line then went dead.

"Crikey, Jack," Alec called from where he was sitting at the computer. "That certainly told him how to do it, didn't it? Your estimate of two Billion may be a little short of what will be needed but your maximum target I believe would be quite a bit more than what would be needed. Oh, this is certainly going to get us some bonus points, isn't it everyone?"

Peter was standing with his mouth wide open, shocked at what his old pal had said, and to a government Minister as well. "Can I just say that I'm pleased to say that you were once a good pal of mine," He said.

"I think that you did that well," Hugo said. "That Minister will certainly be going to tear some strips off of his advisers. Will you still please arrange the haunting though Alec? I think that that would finally convince him that he must support Jack in what he is doing. I think that I'll nip out now and make sure that that downstairs office is prepared and tidied enough to be somewhere worthy of meeting world leaders, don't you think, Jack? When he does come back, try and make the meeting a couple of days from now, it will just give us the chance to make things shine at the estate for when they get here."

"Do you know, Jack," Jennifer said, "You told us all that you didn't think that you could handle the talking to people about the donations and things. Well, I can tell you now that you did a damned good job of proving that to be a fallacy, didn't he everyone?" She asked everyone around them.

"Personally," Hugo said, "I think that he could be back to you before the day is out and he'll be asking to meet you to discuss things further. If he does do that, make sure that the blown-up little jerk that he is now going to be dealing with a very powerful man who probably has more money than many entire countries have. I would imagine that your Prime Minister will probably want to come with him, just to meet up with you. Don't underrate yourself now Jack. You are wealthy beyond the belief of most of these people and you therefore have so much power that with a few words from you, it may be that you could possibly bring down a government. Please don't make that another aim though Jack."

"From what you and we have heard just now," Alec said, "I believe that you could hold back on looking for any other disasters for a short time Jack. I think that he will be back to you soon and that it will be a starter. I will carry on though making the arrangements so that we can probably get the haunting in place for tonight."

Jennifer heard some steps from the staircase nudged Hugo and pointed at the stair head. Hugo gathered what she meant and he jumped up and went towards the stairs to see why his men had come upstairs.

"Hello, Hugo, we've finished packing those cases sir and we just wondered what else you would like us to do," One of the men said. "We have two men doing a circuit outside on the grounds and we have done the downstairs ourselves."

"If you've done all that I believe that Mrs Dawkins wouldn't object if you went to the kitchen and made all of you another coffee each. I've just been measuring up a bit how much we will have to move from the office later. I'll be down with you shortly and then maybe a couple of you could take some of those cases in the minibus over to the new site. I'll bet that you'd enjoy doing that, wouldn't you?"

The security man went back down the stairs and Hugo returned to the little group close to the office. "That was good thinking, Jennifer," He said. "I didn't hear them on the steps. I must be getting old, mustn't I?"

"If you're anything like your father and your grandfather you'll have to have quite a few years on your back before you get to be like that Hugo," Alec said. "You must remember that I've known most of your family, in one way or another for an awful long time. In fact, it surprised you when I remembered you when you walked into the office earlier, didn't it?"

"Alright then Alec," Hugo called back with a light laugh, "Remember that I did know one or two of your little secrets, didn't I? Like the time that you came to update some accounts and took some time off to deal with that little chambermaid that we had at that time."

"I didn't think that young lads like you were about then, Hugo, or would have dared to remember such things. Yes, it always does work two ways but your hearing isn't slipping. Your men have some very soft shoes on I believe nowadays, don't they? That must be why Jennifer heard them and you didn't."

"You know Jack," Hugo said, "If you are going to be getting some Ministers doing a visit I suppose that does put some urgency on getting your office moved and set up in your upstairs office at the new site, doesn't it? You will need to be able to keep abreast of how things are going and I know that Alec and Ray would prefer it if we did get this stuff done as a special move. I'll get those removal people to put a special team on to dismantle, load, move and re-install it at the new office. I'll bet that they'll do that in less than half a day if I give them a bonus, don't you?"

"Hugo," Jack replied, "You know damned well that if they'll do that job as a quick and secure one for us, of course, there'll be a good bonus for them. The computers and the rest of the stuff out of the office, that's all very, very important to us. I've already asked Alec, Ray and Peter if they will be able to find us at the new place but, of course, they, being ghosts said that I ought to know better. Peter said that he could find me no matter where I went. That did get me a bit worried at one point. I thought that he meant that he may be thinking of doing some haunting. He says that he has never tried doing that yet. Silly old me thought that all ghosts knew how to haunt people, didn't you?"

Chapter Six

Jack had increasingly been getting impatient and was, at times, causing Hugo some concern that he may start to do some silly things. "Look, Jack," Hugo said, "I know that it isn't anything to do with me really but while other people are getting on with the bits and pieces that they have to do, you seem to be getting more and more frustrated. You should try and find something to occupy your mind. I know that you have your travel book but that is getting to be 'old hat' to you, isn't it? You said once before about getting a pilot's licence. Why don't you try and do that and see if that gives you another interest? If you wanted to do something then, you have enough money you could probably buy yourself a little jet to take you about, couldn't you? Think of the estate as well Jack, the size, the space. You could even go and try for a helicopter licence as well. There's plenty of space in the estate for you to land there and we could soon get a hangar built for something like that. Things like that would give you another interest, wouldn't they? For a start, I could get one of the lads to drive you over to the local aerodrome and they would no doubt give lessons from there. If you went for a helicopter licence first, you wouldn't even need anyone to drive you there, would you?"

"Do you know, Hugo," Jack replied. "That's a damned good idea. I think that I will have a go at that. Yes, if I get a helicopter licence first that would straight away get us some more freedom, wouldn't it? I'll go right away and see where I would have to go to."

Hugo had indeed contacted the removal people and they had told him that they would make some arrangements to move the computers and all of the office equipment later that afternoon and it would be completely installed and operational by early to mid-evening time. Jack was delighted at this and he went to the office to let Alec and Ray know that the move was happening so quickly. They too were pleased but Alec said that it was probably just as well that it was going to happen then. He told Jack that he had been in contact with the ghost friend who had had some problems with the politicians and he was going out to make a start on the haunting this evening and that the ghost had asked Alec if he would care to go with him. In addition, they were also going to be taking Peter along with them, so it was quite a strange but well-intentioned set of ghosts that were going to haunt the Foreign Minister tonight!

Jack was delighted but also quite naturally he was curious about just how they would haunt the Foreign Minister and, naturally how it would make him react to the idea of supporting the project for Ethiopia. He did have a lot of faith and confidence though in Alec that he would know just what had to be done to get the result that they wanted. No matter though about the haunting, he was looking forward to the next call that he got from that Minister about the project in Ethiopia.

Morning arrived and with it came the removal people. Hugo had suggested that it may be better if Jack was absent from the house while the furniture and goods were being removed. He suggested, trying to be quite kind to everyone, that Jack and Jennifer pay a visit to their parents, just to find somewhere to stay while the removals were completed. He promised that he would contact them as soon as their flat had had the furniture and everything moved into it. The office, and all of the equipment for the office, including the computers, had been moved the night before, but Hugo thought that it may be easier on Jack if he didn't have to meet too many people who were aware that he was the Richest Man in the World. As they couldn't easily get to the computer, Jack and Jennifer were unable to find out how Alec had gone on and, despite having had the house phone diverted to his mobile phone, he still hadn't had the call from the Foreign Ministry yet.

Their first port of call during their forced (and temporary) 'eviction' (as Jack called it) from their house, was to pay a visit for a part of the day with Jennifer's parents. The parents, of course, had been delighted at this turn of events and thought that Hugo had made some rather good decisions in suggesting that. Jack did get on very well with his parents-in-law though, as did Jennifer with Jack's parents. That being the case, the day wasn't going to be too much of an ordeal for them both. Because they were going to be spending half a day with each set of parents, Jennifer's Dad and Jack's Dad had both made arrangements to have some time off of work. That, in itself, was quite an achievement as both of the Fathers so enjoyed their work that they had told Hugo outright that they didn't want to stop working when he had suggested that they do so. That had been at the time that they had discovered that Jack was the richest man in the World and had employed Hugo and his team to handle their security for them. Jack's Dad and Jennifer's Dad did get on well together but the strange thing was that they hadn't got a single common interest that they could share with one another. That didn't matter, they were quite friendly and they both appreciated that their child had married someone who just seemed to fit so well with all that they liked. Both of the Mothers did have one common interest and that was that they were both avid devotees of their kitchens. This had, in some way, carried on to Jennifer so, while Jack and Jennifer were at her parents' house, Jennifer was in the kitchen with her Mother while Jack was chatting quite amicably with her Dad. Jennifer's Dad knew that Jack's main interest was in travel. All of the family knew of Jack's now well-known tales in his travel book. He had started that many, many years ago and he had recorded everywhere that he had been to. Initially, it had started as a single book but now it has extended and it has become, so far, three volumes. It was anyone's guess how many volumes it would end up being. Now that he had started on his training for his helicopter licence though he knew (and kept telling everyone who would listen) that he could soon fill a few more volumes anyway. He had told them that if he extended that by getting a licence for a small jet, (and then if he bought a small jet as well) that would make it even more, wouldn't it? He didn't think that the estate was large enough for landing a jet, but it could certainly find space many times over to land a helicopter, couldn't it?

The morning had passed and Jack and Jennifer had moved over to his Mum and Dad's house and they had settled quite well (for these two who were now feeling quite desperate to find out how their house was going on, especially in their favourite office). It was about mid-afternoon and Jack's phone rang. He had hoped that it would be the Foreign Minister but no, it was Hugo who told him that he was pleased to be able to inform him that they could now move back into their new flat. Jack insisted that his Mum and Dad should go with them as well, just to have a look at it, but they declined. They said that they would pop over later but that for the first look, it should just be the two of them.

Manuel was once again their driver and he took the pair of them over to their new home. As they approached the gateway to the estate, the gates were closed but Hugo had made arrangements that each of their vehicles were fitted with sensors that activated the gate opening mechanism for them. Jennifer said it felt as though they were rather special people when the gates opened as they approached. Jack just said that it wouldn't matter anyway because there were security men at the gatehouse who would have activated the gate-opening mechanism for them anyway. They went and when they got to the main building, Manuel pulled the car up close to the main entry and they saw Hugo standing there waiting to welcome them into their new home.

They went into the main entry door and then took the elevator that carried them up to the floor where their new flat was. They had invited Hugo to go with them so that when they got to their office they could all discover from Alec just how the haunting had gone along. Jack had told Hugo that he hadn't heard from the Foreign Minister and Hugo said that he was very, very surprised at that and he just said that perhaps the haunting may have caused some upset in the man to make him leave his work for a day or two. He suggested to Jack that many politicians, despite their many claims of the hard work that they did, were quite often only too ready to take time away from work for some of the flimsiest of reasons.

They got to their flat went in, and made straight away for their office. They opened the door and went in and there, sitting at the computer was Ray with Alec writing some more notes onto his ever-present notepad.

"Well, how did it go with the haunting then, Alec," Jack asked. "We haven't heard a Dicky bird from the Minister yet. That did surprise us a bit but Hugo said that maybe the haunting could have upset them so much that he hasn't gone to work today."

"I don't quite know what has happened to him since we left but I'm pretty certain that he may have missed out on going to work today. By the time that we left him I think that he was on the point of calling for the 'funny farm', as you call them. Oh, he was upset, and I did ask my friend to ease off a bit on the haunting to let the man recover a bit. Peter though thought that the whole episode was hilarious. I think that he'll probably want to be doing some more haunting in the future. Don't worry, he wouldn't even think of trying to haunt you two. I believe that he said that he was thinking of doing it to some of his own family though. That, to us, did appear to be a bit mean, don't you think? Anyway, I would imagine that the Minister has gone to see one or two doctors to confirm that he isn't going mad completely. I did gather though that since a lot of the haunting did centre on the problem of severe thirst and death from a famine, it is possible that he may well have blamed a lot of the haunting on him having started to understand how your project could ease a lot of problems. Oh, I think that he'll come back onto you again and soon, once he's got his mind back into some kind of order. With hindsight, I have thought that we may have done perhaps just a little too much on him, at least for the first time. I'm no expert on haunting though so we'll just have to wait and see, won't we?"

"The office does seem to be a bit bigger than the last one, doesn't it?" Jennifer said. The main question as well is, where the heck is the kitchen in relation to the office? I mean, I know what you're like for your coffee, Jack. You're almost as bad as well, aren't you Hugo? Oh, we'll have to find the kitchen. Maybe when it was done we should have planned it with the office and the kitchen next to one another. If we'd done that Jack, you could have played in here with your computer and I could have played in the kitchen with my cookery, couldn't I?"

Jennifer just finished talking and Jack heard his mobile phone going off. He took it out of his pocket and turned it on (with the loudspeaker setting on). "Hello," he said, "Jack Dawkins here, can I help you?"

"Oh, Mr Dawkins," came the voice of the Minister. "We have done some more checking about desalinated water and apparently you were correct and my advisers had got their story completely wrong. From there, it would appear that perhaps we should have a meeting to see how we can move things forward. Did you manage to get any kinds of costings for anything Mr Dawkins? I realise that you haven't had an awful lot of time, have you? Maybe we could get together to see if we can perhaps help as well in getting some firm commitments for the project. Is it easier for you to come to London or would you prefer me to come and visit you?"

"Well, Minister," Jack replied. "I haven't had any time to get any costings out yet. You see, since we spoke my wife and I have just been moving house and today we have now moved into our new estate. Perhaps it would be easier for you to visit here. As you are no doubt aware since some notice has been put about regarding something to do with my current wealth, I am having to be very, very careful with respect to security, and that was one of the reasons for me buying this estate. If you could visit here I feel sure that we could start to get some things sorted out to get the project moving. Do you have a particular day or time when we could meet? Obviously, I do spend quite a lot of my time here where I know that I am much more secure."

"Oh, that would be no problem whatsoever, Mr Dawkins. I feel sure that we could make it tomorrow if that is convenient for you. If I may, I would like to bring the Prime Minister with me since this project can have a profound impact on our Country's relationship with so many other Countries. Could we perhaps suggest a time of eleven o'clock tomorrow morning? Would that be convenient for you? Oh, by the way, do we have the address for your new estate Mr Dawkins? Perhaps you could get that passed on to my secretary. I will get him to call you back as soon as I see him."

"That sounds to me to be ideal Mr Minister," Jack replied, with a huge smile on his face as he looked at Jennifer and Hugo. Jack then ended that call.

"I told you," Alec said. He was keen beyond belief, wasn't he? And he wants to bring the Prime Minister to meet you as well. Oh, things are now starting to look up a bit, at least I think so, don't you as well, Ray?"

"The other thing, as well," Jennifer said, "Is that you have started to do the talking Jack and I think that you've done a damned good job of making a good start on that as well. Oh, I suppose that I'd better see about getting some kinds of food ready for when they come tomorrow, as well shouldn't I? With them coming at that time it looks as though they could be here for lunch as well, couldn't they?"

"Yes," Hugo said, "I told you that you'd get a response and you can bet your life that the Prime Minister wants to meet you, particularly to see if you are going to top up their party funds for them. Personally, I wouldn't get myself involved with any of them if I were you, but there again, I went and joined the army in Spain, didn't I? I only did that though because it was a family tradition I think. With hindsight, I have often thought that that was a mistake on my part."

Leaving Alec and Ray still working in the office, Jack, Jennifer and Hugo went to have a look around the flat. They all agreed that now that it was finished, it was a beautiful flat and they liked everything about it. It was obviously quite a lot larger than what they needed, but it pleased them anyway. Yes, they had been there before, but now it had their own furniture in place and this was now their home. It didn't take them too long though for them to find the kitchen where Jennifer grabbed for the kettle and, having filled it again, put it on so that she could make them all some more coffee.

Jennifer made coffee for the three of them and carried it into the lounge on a tray. "Now, once you have had this Jack," she said, "You do need to go downstairs and start to sort out the rooms down there. You have a meeting tomorrow with two rather important political people and it would be better if you could impress them a little with what they see. In my opinion, they shouldn't see any of the two upper floors. Yes, there are some beautiful flats up here but that is for your information, not for theirs. On the ground floor, you do have a major office that will (or at least should) look after a lot of your day-to-day working documents. You should have a rather nice reception area where you can meet and greet your visitors and you obviously will have your own private office down there. That can be just as grand as you want it to be. It doesn't have to be if you don't want it to be, but you are at the moment trying to impress these people, aren't you? There is a large room that you could designate as a boardroom for when you have some larger gatherings of people. It doesn't matter what it really is, as long as it impresses them. You have the security block with all of the CCTV screens in one part showing how much of the estate you have covered. Hugo will naturally be able to impress them with what he is doing there, won't you, Hugo? Then, of course, there are the staff areas where the staff, including the security team, can relax with a little bit of comfort now and then."

"My goodness, Jennifer," Hugo said, "I couldn't agree more with all that you have now got planned and of course you are right. We have got the rooms laid out to look more or less as though they are what you have described Jennifer, and I agree that your visitors should not be brought up to see the floors with the flats on them," To Jack, Hugo said, "Have you made a start on trying to get any costings for any of the work that you told the Minister about? Even if it isn't a final costing, it may be worthwhile to try and get some costs for some of the parts, just so that you can say that you have these costs, but you do want to secure the best possible before you make a start on the project. I also think that it is a good idea to refer to it as the Project. I know that it doesn't make any difference really, but it does make it sound as though you have put a lot of thought into all that you are doing."

"Do you know Hugo," Jack said, "Just on the off chance that I could get some good information I think that I'll call my old boss, Stewart Robinson. After all, I am a director of that company, aren't I Jennifer? He, Hugo, has a business that does a lot of carrying and sometimes supplying things as well as the deliveries and everything. I suppose that there just may be an odd chance that he may know how I could get some costings for some weird and wonderful things like pipes, water pumps and the like. He may not know about things like any desalination units or about solar panels or ocean-going windmills or turbines to get the power, but he may be able to give me a lead on some bits of things. What do you think, Jennifer?"

"He may not be the definitive answer but I should think that he may be able to get you some kinds of costs for some things," Jennifer replied. "But why don't you just ask Alec and Ray to get you some costs for these kinds of things? They'll probably be more up to it than we are, don't you think? After all, these kinds of things are sometimes quoted for on the stock markets, aren't they?"

"Jennifer," Hugo said, "That is an excellent idea. Of course, they would probably know about them or, if they didn't they would have some idea of how to find out about such things as well, wouldn't they?"

Having all agreed that their friendly ghosts may be more capable of getting them some idea of prices for some of the things needed for the project, they all made their way back to the office. Ray was still on the computer and Alec was still making notes in his notebook (or so it seemed to the three watchers).

"Alec," Jack asked, "We've had a call from the Foreign Minister and he is going to come out to see us tomorrow and he's bringing the Prime Minister with him. I've already told him that I have been rather busy moving house and that I haven't managed to get a lot of costings yet for what will be needed for the Ethiopian

Project and we just wondered if somehow, using your wonderful skills, you could perhaps get us some rough ideas of the costs of solar panels, desalination machines, large scale water pumps and I would imagine something like a nine inch or so diameter pipe to get the water to the inland of Ethiopia. I suggested about three hundred miles of it. I know, we've got a cheek to come and ask you but we all accept that as far as anything to do with money is concerned, you're the best ones to ask. Is it possible that you could get us some idea of the prices? It needn't be exact, I wouldn't think, not at this stage, but it would make us look a bit better when they get here if we have some idea of the value of these kinds of things."

"I must say, Jack," Alec replied, "That is something that I don't think that I've ever done before, but I suppose that we could get some kind of ballpark figure for some of those things. Of course, if the government have decided to help, that may be the answer that they could then put some pressure on some people to get you some improved prices. Anyway, we'll do our best to find something to give you a starting point. So, the Foreign Minister is bringing the Prime Minister as well. You must have got them worried. That can't be down to us. We didn't haunt the Prime Minister, did we? Anyway, he has agreed that his advisors were wrong, hasn't he so at least the project is going to go ahead now. Now we'll have to start trying to find some other crises for you to donate towards, won't we? I'll get a few of our people to start looking. You see we are quite a bit better than an old laptop like yours, aren't we Jack?"

Chapter Seven

"Right then," Hugo said, "Now that you've got something going on with all of that, I'll get downstairs and make sure that everything is getting tidied up and ready for our visitors for tomorrow. As I'm Spanish, it may be more politically correct not to introduce me as your security team in England do you think? I'll just stay in the background and try and get everything else to run as smoothly as I can while you talk to them and get them to agree to whatever you want. Remember, it's you who is footing the bill so you can ask them to do a lot of the work, can't you?"

"Thanks' Hugo," Jack said as Hugo went off to go downstairs to try and chase everything up for them for tomorrow's visit. "I'll keep seeing you around though, I hope. I do seem to be relying on you quite a lot my old friend."

"Jennifer," Jack called out, "As we are going to have the Prime Minister here tomorrow do you think that we should let your Mum and Dad and my Mum and Dad know so that if they want to meet them they could pop over while they are here? I don't think that my parents are all that keen on politics anyway but I wondered if we should at least ask them. What do you think?"

"No, my parents aren't into politics at all," Jennifer replied. "No matter what colour politics the people are, so no, I don't think that we'd have to invite them. It wouldn't hurt to let them know that they are coming here to see you though, would it? I'm just going to go downstairs to see how Hugo is going on. He may need some help and I think that we've done almost everything that we can up here for now, haven't we? Oh, the Foreign Secretary did say that he would get his secretary to contact you for an address to find us. Make sure that you are about and then you can give them a clear address and a postcode. When you've done that, come down and see how things are looking downstairs, will you?"

Jennifer went downstairs, leaving Jack in their flat on the second floor. He hadn't got a telephone number for the Foreign Ministers secretary but he then realised that he had rang them before so he picked up the telephone (that recalled previous numbers used) and clicked the buttons to try and find the number. He found one that looked familiar so he rang it and the voice on the other end of the line said that it was the Foreign Office. Jack explained that the Minister had rung him and had said that his secretary would be contacting them to get the address for tomorrow's visit. This person on the line did seem to know all about it and so Jack gave them the address and postcode and suggested that they keep the phone number, just in case someone wanted to get hold of him. With that done, he decided that he too would go downstairs and see how things were taking shape.

Once on the ground floor, he found it to be quite a hive of activity. Jack found Jennifer and asked if there was anything that he could do to help.

"Jack, you are the person that they are coming to see. You are the important person," Jennifer said to him. "You just stand back, wander around and if you see anything, anything at all that looks as though it seems to be *'out of place'*, then get someone to deal with it. It is at this point that you must also *'appear'* to be the one in control, as well as being the one who is in control. If you can't find anything, then the chances are that it is all OK. I believe that Hugo is quite good at this sort of thing and he is generally dealing with it all. I think though that, despite what he said about him being Spanish, he should be introduced to them. He is after all in charge of security for you and it doesn't matter where he comes from. He too is important so, it's down to you but I think, and this is just my opinion, that tomorrow you should introduce Hugo to your visitors.

Jack did look around and he tried, as best he could, to try and consider anything that would be a part that could impress their visitors the following day. To his mind, Hugo and Jennifer had, between them, got everything sorted and yes, it did look impressive to Jack. Well, he thought, at least it impresses me, and I know that Jennifer and Hugo are still looking to try and find anything else that needs attention. To try and get his mind back onto a level that he knew anything about he went to his 'new' downstairs office and telephoned Stewart Robinson, his old boss. Stewart was pleased to hear from Jack, the benefactor to their company and Jack explained to Stewart what he wanted to know. He said that he wanted to find what diameter pipe would be needed for a major water supply and, that could be done using moling techniques (A process that he could remember reading of somewhere that could force a pipe underground to save the need to dig trenches), and could be processed, using that for several hundred miles. He did, being sensible explain a little to Stewart why he wanted to know and Stewart said that off-hand, he didn't know, but he said that he did have some other contacts that may be able to find out something about that process for him within the next day or so. Jack thanked Stewart for his help and said that he looked forward to seeing him again in the near future, promising that he would call to see him soon but, suggesting that perhaps Stewart would like to pop out to see his new place sometime, although he did tell Stewart that he would probably be a bit busy tomorrow!

Jack played about with some imaginary costings on a piece of paper, exaggerating where he thought of a figure and totalled it up as a guesstimate. He arrived at a figure of about twenty-six million pounds. Even allowing for double that sum, he knew that his maximum target of one hundred billion pounds would cover things so very, very easily that he could double all of the things that he was planning, and still not get anywhere near that sum. He knew that what he had done was more or less simply guesswork but he did at least have some figures perhaps for people to look at and try to criticise.

His calculations looked more or less like this;

1,   Two Desalination units, allow say three million pounds each, possibly a bit more

2.   Sea-based Wind turbine to get electricity, say four million pounds each

3.   Four Storage twenty thousand litre storage tanks (with compressors) to hold water for

*   pumping, say three million pounds in total*

4.   Four Pumps to send water across three hundred miles, say five million pounds.

5.   Take off units at seventy-five-mile intervals (inc pumps) say two million pounds

6.   Diggers to assist in trench laying, say two million pounds

7.   Labour for various tasks, say four million pounds

Gross total expected from the above guesstimates: twenty-six million pounds.

The maximum donation proposed so far to be one hundred billion pounds!

He waited in his office for either Jennifer or Hugo to come back so that he could show them his 'figures' and see what they thought. He was becoming more confident that once they had checked it through, along with any more information that he could get from Stewart Robinson and Alec and Ray, he must be well within his maximum targeted budget, probably laughably below that sum. Of course, he rationalised, if it needed more, there was nothing at all to stop him from increasing his maximum target!

Hugo did look into the office, he was just checking that it had been properly laid out and cleaned to make it look good. He saw Jack sitting there and apologised for entering without knocking, but said that he had just been trying to check everywhere to try and make sure that things were all going the be OK for tomorrow.

"Hugo, you know that you don't have to knock to come into this office, don't you? Jack said. "I have been sitting here waiting for either you or Jennifer to come in so that I could just show you some silly figures that I have been knocking together for tomorrow. I know that I haven't had any real information but, just using some reasonably safe guesstimates, can you just have a look at this and tell me what you think? I have spoken to Stewart Robinson, I mentioned him to you earlier, and he is going to try and get me some information and then we have Alec and Ray who are going to try and get some information. For now, just look at these figures please, Hugo." He pushed his piece of paper across the desk and Hugo picked it up and looked at it.

"Jack, these figures do seem to be quite generous and you seem to have allowed for more than one line being installed so perhaps they may be a good starting point. It will be interesting what they may think of them when they get here. Even if you have got some a little bit wrong, surely you may equally have overestimated some of the others. Yes, let Jennifer see it. I think that she'll be quite impressed, especially since you have also included your maximum targeted donation to do the job."

Just then Jennifer did walk into the office and Jack explained to her what he had been doing. She looked at the paper with the figures on it and said, "Some of these seem to be very large sums, Jack. Are you sure that things will cost as much as this?"

"No, Jennifer," Jack replied. I was just trying to get some kind of figures to play with and I do realise that some of these things will be quite costly so I may have gone high on some but equally, I may have gone a bit low on some of the other bits. It will be interesting to see what they think. I'm not sure that I will show them all of this though. I can say that I'm still awaiting some costs to be produced for me, can't I?"

"That's quite true," Jennifer said, but why don't we just go up to our office and see if Alec and Ray have indeed got anything through on the costs of these kinds of things? You never know, they may say that you are perfectly correct in what you have suggested."

The three of them went out of the office and then made their way to the elevators to get them back up to the floor for their flat. Hugo had by now included himself in all that they were doing and was equally, if not even more excited about it all than Jack and Jennifer.

They got to the office and there was Alec, working on the computer and this time with Ray appearing to be making notes in his pad. "Alec," Jack called out, "Have you managed to find any kinds of costings for some of those things that I asked you about? I've been doing some silly guesstimates to try and get a figure and well, they are always a bit disappointing, aren't they? We just wondered if you had had any more luck than we have had."

"Yes Jack," Alec replied. "Some may be a little bit out of date but we don't think that they'll be too far out. Where's your piece of paper with your figures on it and then we can compare them. Here are the figures that I got. Just you compare and see how they come out."

They all started to look at Alec's figures and Alec said as they were doing so, "Well, I don't think that you are a long way out with the desalination units, do you? I've got a figure of two and a half million, you've got three million. That can just be down to inflation, can't it? The wind turbine is a little bit harder to evaluate. Again I had got two and a half million, you have got four million. Of course that can also depend on the amount of electricity that you are going to be pulling in, can't it? Storage tanks, oh, you hadn't mentioned that to me but at your price I don't think that it would be too bad at the price that you have put. For the pumps, you have put five million for four pumps. I think that to be safe with that I would change it to eight pumps so that once they get going they can have a spare for each line in case one does start to play up. That then would become ten million pounds. They do that sometimes play up, you know. For the take-off points, you have only allowed for two million pounds. You say that for every seventy-five miles, that would be four points per line. You're suggesting four pumps which I would take to mean four lines, so that would be sixteen take-off points, wouldn't it? Why not double your figure twice for that Jack? That should cover that point. Oh, if you are going to have some pumps as well at the take-off points, (which would be logical) why not double it again to cover the extra cost of these pumps? For the diggers to assist in trench laying, you have four lines so multiply that by four to make it eight million pounds. Now, the costs of labour for various tasks; that can be so easily become a lot more money. Why not just put that at a nominal ten million pounds? Then, just see how it all comes out for your total. You will still obviously be well inside your maximum target figure, won't you? Well, doing it like that gives you a target budget of fifty-nine million pounds, doesn't it? Now, being generous, you could say that you would be putting another forty-one million pounds into feeding the people free of charge for working on the project (and perhaps to help feed some of the other people as well). How does that sound? At least it gets you to one hundred million, doesn't it?"

1,   Two Desalination units, allow say three million pounds each, possibly a little bit more, That's
       Six million pounds total there.
2.   Sea-based Wind turbines to get electricity, say four million pounds each. This is of course
       dependent on the amount of electricity needed for the project. (I have presumed one so far)
3.   Four Storage tanks to hold water for pumping, say three million pounds in total. (One tank
       for each line)tank size to be guessed at enough for a one-day pumping load per line.
4.   Eight Pumps to send water across four lines at three hundred miles each, say ten million
       Pounds (that leaves some spare pumps on each line).
5.   Take off units at seventy-five miles intervals on each line (inc pumps) sixteen take-off points in total, say eight million pounds (for the four lines)
6.   Diggers to assist in trench laying (where required) on the four lines, say eight million pounds
7.   Labour for various tasks, say ten million pounds
8.   Piping to provide a total of say, twelve hundred miles of pipes, probably about a 300mm pipe
       Say a figure of three million pounds.
              Gross total expected from the above guesstimates: sixty-two million pounds.

Feeding people for the work done on the project, thirty-eight million pounds'
TOTAL NOW OF ONE HUNDRED MILLION POUNDS!
Maximum donation proposed so far to be one hundred BILLION pounds!

"Do you know Alec, I think that you are marvellous," Jack said. "Even if we have got it wrong, it can't be that far wrong, and now it is showing that it is for four separate lines and it even gives them some food for the workers as well, doesn't it? I can't see how they would object to that. They may even come up with some other crises for us as well since they have seen the target donation of one hundred billion pounds. That helps us, helps some other people and of course, it helps all of you in the 'in-between world', doesn't it?

"I'm only too pleased that we have been of help to you Jack," Alec replied, "And maybe we will be able to help with some of the other crises as well if they get a move on. By the way, I have quite deliberately made some poor investments to lose some money from the fund. They won't be replaced later but I have now managed to get the total fund value down to one trillion three hundred million pounds. That's knocked off a couple of hundred billion and with what you are donating, that gets it down much nearer to the total ongoing constant one trillion pounds value that I wanted to get it to stay at, more or less, doesn't it?"

"Unless we can make sure that we can get some more good donations to go out soon though, Alec, It could start to rise again, couldn't it? Jack asked. "This was always a big concern of mine that having the constant factor in it always leaves it so that some companies doing better than you have expected, or hoped that they would or could perform, double it again, couldn't it?"

"Yes, in theory, that could happen, Jack," Alec explained. "But I do believe that I have now built in some safeguards to try and stop that. At the same time, I have hidden so much of your fund now in so many different places, intertwined quite a bit so it is always there, but if anyone really tries to find out your fund value, I believe that they would find that it is just a little under one trillion pounds, not over the trillion. That's taken a bit of doing, but I'm now quite happy that people won't start looking quite as much at your sudden rise to high wealth. I know that Hugo thought that it was unusual, the speed that you got there but a lot of that was caused by that damned controller who at one time was pushing for me to get it moving faster. Anyway, thanks to you, Jack, he has now gone so I can look after my friends, can't I?"

"Should I let the politicians see these figures that we have 'knocked together' when they come tomorrow? I could try and get them to come up with figures as well, couldn't I? And did you want me to introduce you to the Prime Minister, Alec? After all, it was the Foreign Secretary that you haunted, not the Prime Minister, wasn't it?"

"No, thank you, Jack, I think that it would be better if I missed out on that tomorrow but I can wish you well with it all, can't I?"

Having updated his list they didn't think that there was a great deal more that they could do and they all decided that they would call it a day and see what tomorrow would bring them. Hugo went back to just try and sort out what was now his new house, the one that he had bought from Jack and Jennifer and that he had admired so much before. Of course, the upstairs office in that house no longer had nay ghosts living there. He had considered having a little 'housewarming' party for his new house but he now realised that to do that he would have to invite his new friends, Jack and Jennifer and they, at the moment, had some rather big things on their minds with that visit tomorrow by the politicians.

Chapter Eight

The morning of the visit of the Foreign Secretary and the Prime Minister had arrived and both Jack and Jennifer were quite nervous. That, we can only expect, wasn't surprising. After all, they were too quite ordinary people who through no particular fault of their own had been thrown into almost an alien world of excessive wealth and also (which it is presumed doesn't happen to very many people) some financial wizards who just happened to be ghosts and were also their good friends (and sometimes advisers).

Their day started fairly normally with quite simple breakfasts, although it would be noted that neither of them particularly wanted to eat. Yes, they were both concerned about this visit. They may be concerned, but they both knew that it was going to be necessary for them to meet these people and that they must create enough anticipation in their visitors at what they were doing, (and that their ghostly friends would start to collect some bonus points for use in their world), due in the main, to the donations that Jack had begun to start making so that they could, in some small way, help those who were unfortunate enough to be on the point of having to beg for even the simplest of foods and water.

Jack was beginning to rely on Hugo much, much more and Hugo had only been employed to provide a security service to Jack,

Jennifer and both of their parents. Jack knew that it was probably quite wrong to put Hugo into such a position but, a lot of the reason for that was that Hugo had discovered the secret of their strange friends that occupied their small upstairs office, that they were the ghosts. Jack wanted them (the ghosts) to be their friends as well but he knew that each step he took was in some ways a step that he should consider far more carefully. Yes, he did want Hugo as a friend (and as an ally to some extent in the strange happenings that he was being subjected to) and, to some extent, that was possible. The ghosts though, he knew were merely the spirits of some people who no longer lived and, although he may regard them with some kind of benevolence, they could never be true friends.

With breakfasts done with, both Jack and Jennifer went down to the main rooms on the ground floor of their new main estate office. They wanted to be there so that when the visitors did arrive, they would be on hand to welcome them. They knew that the visitors weren't due until eleven o'clock so they busied themselves around, trying to find anything that would occupy their minds in some way until the visitors did arrive. Jack had been into his quite large, downstairs office (that was there in the main, for show, more than anything else since his upstairs office was where he did spend rather more of his time). He had spread one or two pads across his desk and, just for his own interest; he had laid out three of the books that recorded his travel records. At least when anyone entered the office the desk did have a look of being used a little bit.

The main reception area close to the main entry was comfortably laid out and Jennifer had arranged that there were an adequate number of comfortable chairs and small tables about so that they could offer their visitors some light refreshments if they wanted any.

Hugo did appear in the main building but he went straight to the 'security' block that held all of the monitoring screens for the many and varied CCTVs that covered the inside of the building and the security fence cameras view of the outside of the building. Jack saw him walk through and waited until he came back out again and then he called him over to where he and Jennifer were sitting, making themselves comfortable (as much as they could with their rather agitated states) while they waited for the arrival of the visitors.

"Hugo, Jennifer and I talked after you left yesterday evening and we have decided that you should be introduced to the visitors. Yes, you are indeed Spanish, but England is no longer at war with Spain so, as you are regarded by both of us as a very good friend and a major controller in a lot of the things that we do, it is only right that you should be recognised by them. I know that you said that in your opinion we shouldn't introduce you, but we now both regard you so highly that it is our opinion that you most definitely should be introduced to them. Please do make yourself available when they arrive. It wouldn't look good if I had to go and start searching for you, would it?"

"Jack, it is your decision," Hugo replied. "It is my opinion that they may feel somewhat aggrieved that you have not chosen an

English person to be in this position. As it is your decision, then I shall make sure that I am somewhere around. At the moment though, I think that I need to be checking to make sure that the security is indeed as good as you expect from me. I will see you later Jack, and you Jennifer." With that, Hugo went back out of the main door and left the two of them sitting waiting for their visitors. Jack called across to one of the waiters that they had employed for this part of the reception area and asked them if they could get some coffee for the pair of them.

Within a few minutes, they had been served, each of them with their cups of coffee. The time was then ten-twenty so they knew that they had enough time to have their coffee and then they had decided that they would have one more quick walk around in the entranceway to their new estate offices (and luxury flats) to check that there was nothing that was noticeably 'out of place'. They had wondered about going up to see Alec and Ray one more time to see just how their fund was going on. Jack was pleased that Alec had, somehow, managed to hide quite a lot of the assets so that if anyone did do a search they would never find that he had over one trillion pounds in his fund.

It was a few minutes before eleven o'clock and one of their security men came to them to let them know that their visitors had reached the main gate and were being escorted down to the main building. Jack had a quick glance around to see if he could spot Hugo anywhere but he couldn't see him anywhere. Jennifer knew what he was doing and she just nudged him and whispered that Hugo would turn up at a more appropriate time and that he needn't worry, Hugo, she said was quite on the ball and that he had listened to Jack's instructions.

The car containing the government Ministers arrived at the main entrance and as it arrived, so did Hugo, who was there with another security man who very dutifully opened the door for the Ministers to get out. Hugo then took over and led the two Ministers into the main doors where Jack and Jennifer were waiting to greet them. Hugo spoke first introducing the two men to Mr Jack Dawkins and his wife Jennifer. The Foreign Minister took over then, introducing the Prime Minister to Jack and Jennifer and then he gave his own name. Jack took over from there and said "I would like them to meet the head of security for his estate and our UK business, Mr Hugo Moncado, a former Spanish army Major who had at that time been responsible for diplomatic security in Spain".

The two Ministers did appear to be taken aback a little at this information but then Jack invited them to go into the reception area and he asked them if they would like any refreshments while they were talking. They gave their orders and the waiter disappeared to get their drinks for them The Foreign Minister then asked if Jack had managed to get any costings for the project.

"I'm afraid that I haven't got any hard costings that I would want to stand by, not yet," Jack replied. "As you can see though, we have only just moved into our new premises today, so we are still trying to find some time for some of the things that we had got planned. From the figures that we did have, we had got to around fifty Million Pounds, but of course that was allowing for four different pipelines going into the interior and of course, before anything could be done, there would need to be some surveys carried out to assess any terrestrial problems that there may be. I had anticipated that where possible we would try to use moling techniques to put the pipelines in, but that would depend on what the soil structure was like, wouldn't it? Anyway, some people think that I have been rather generous with some of the costings that I had so, even at fifty Million pounds it still leaves plenty of room before it gets to what I gave you as a maximum target for my donation."

"Oh," The Prime Minister interrupted, "You didn't mention what the maximum target of the donation was to me, did you," he said to the Foreign Secretary, with a very severe scowl. "I take it then that there may be some scope to try and do some other things as well from the way that you were speaking Mr Dawkins?"

"Yes," Jack replied, "I did suggest that I would limit my donation on this occasion to a maximum of one hundred Billion pounds if I had to. Of course, I didn't think that it would necessarily get to quite as much as that for this project, but I'm sure that there may well be some other useful projects that can be considered. As you may have gathered, my trip to becoming wealthy was something of an accident; I suppose that you could call it. Yes, I did have a lottery win but then I began to try out some investments that an old friend of mine, who died a few years before my win, anyway, he and I had talked about things that we would do, I'm sure that you know how it is. Anyway, they did just seem to work and I must admit that

I know little or nothing about the stock markets as such, but somehow it just seems to have multiplied as it went along and now, well, it appears to me that I should try and help out others who haven't been quite as fortunate as we have." He reached out and gave Jennifer a quick hug.

"My goodness," The Prime Minister said, "That is certainly some target donation that you have got planned, isn't it? Yes, I am sure that there may well be some other deserving causes that could benefit from some aid. Your idea for Ethiopia though, did appear to us to be quite a novel answer to what appears to be an ongoing problem in that country, didn't it? I didn't realise that you intended to put in four different pipelines. Of course, that would be a superb idea so that the irrigation of land could be quite tremendous, couldn't it? The Foreign Secretary also told me that you felt that if both we and the Ethiopian government could help with some army support to give some security for the equipment and the installation. From the amount that you are donating to make the project work, I'm sure that both of our countries could cooperate to provide some support. Did you have any idea of when you would want the project to get underway?"

"As I have already said, my efforts at getting some costings are not quite as good as I would like them to be so if I was given any support in arriving at some more realistic costs I would appreciate that. Once we have those costs, well, the sooner the better for a start to be made, wouldn't you think? At least then it should possibly prevent any further incidents of drought causing all of these famine problems. Once this is underway as well, I would welcome any suggestions of how the provision of some cash aid could help to prevent some disasters. I'm sure that you are far better placed than I am at finding such things sir."

"Oh, I don't for a moment believe that there would be any problems both with helping with the costings or in finding other worthwhile projects for some aid, do you Foreign Minister?"

"No, Prime Minister," The Foreign Minister replied. "It would be interesting perhaps if we could see the suggestions for costings that you have done, Mr Dawkins. Although no one would be holding you to them, they could provide a good assessment of how far away you are."

"Yes," Jack replied, "As a matter of interest, I did bring along my little list for you to see. As you can imagine, I am no expert at a lot of these things but, where I could, I did seek some outside help in arriving at some of the figures. As I mentioned before though, nothing in these is in any way concrete. Here you are, sir." Jack said as he passed across his typed-out list of his guesstimate costings.

1,   Two Desalination units, allow say three million pounds each, possibly a little bit more, That's
        Six million pounds total there.
2.   Sea-based Wind turbines to get electricity, say four million pounds each. This is of course
        dependent on the amount of electricity needed for the project. (I have presumed one so far)
3.   Four Storage tanks to hold water for pumping, say three million pounds in total. (One tank

for each line)tank size to be guessed at enough for a one-day pumping load per line.

4.   Eight Pumps to send water across four lines at three hundred miles each, say ten million

Pounds (that leaves some spare pumps on each line).

5.   Take off units at seventy-five miles intervals on each line (inc pumps) sixteen take-off points in total, say eight million pounds (for the four lines)

6.   Diggers to assist in trench laying (where required) on the four lines, say eight million pounds

7.   Labour for various tasks, say ten million pounds

8.   Piping to provide a total of say, twelve hundred miles of pipes, probably about a 300mm pipe

Say a figure of three million pounds.

Gross total expected from the above guesstimates: sixty-two million pounds.

Feeding people for the work done on the project, thirty-eight million pounds'

"It was my estimate that the people working on the project would need feeding but of course; some of the thirty-eight million pounds could also be used for some of the other members of the population, couldn't it? I do still object though to food being sent in to be handed out 'willy-nilly' to the public. That does tend to encourage the criminals to see an easy option to make themselves wealthy, doesn't it? Oh, by the way, the total there makes it one hundred **Million** Pounds. My target donation that I had in mind was to be One Hundred **Billion** pounds, so it still leaves plenty of leeway, doesn't it? By the way, although I have given you my target donation figure, I would prefer it if at the moment that figure could be kept away from a lot of publicity. I do want to donate but, like some other people; I don't like publicity when I can possibly avoid it."

"Oh, of course, Mr Dawkins," The Prime Minister agreed. "As you have said, from past experiences of aid being provided, far too much is lost to places where there are such weaknesses, isn't it? From a quick glance at your figures though, they do seem to have covered quite a few eventualities, don't they? As soon as we can get some surveys done we could get some of our experts to look at these costings and see if we could improve on any of them. I must say that our trip out today has been most revealing and pleasant. And on behalf of our government and that of the Ethiopians as well, I would like to offer you our most sincere gratitude."

"I'm glad that we have been able to help and that we will be able to carry on helping," Jack said. "We never asked, but my wife said that you may require some further food or refreshment before you leave. As I said before, we are both rather new at these things. I must say that I do rely quite a lot on Hugo Moncado. I know that he is our head of security but he has proved to be so much more in the advice that he has given to us."

Hugo, standing near the wall glowered a little at Jack when he heard this being said, although inside, he was quite proud of the fact that this man had just almost elevated him from being the head of security to being a part of the project overall. He was impressed as well with the way that Jack had handled the meeting.

"Thank you for such a kind offer Mr and Mrs Dawkins," The Prime Minister said, "But we should make a move. We do get quite pushed for time sometimes with our work, you know. Perhaps we may call again at some time once we get the project underway."

"Oh, we'd look forward to that sir," Jack replied. "As you can see no doubt, as I have gathered this wealth it has somewhat limited how much we can get about from here. I'm sure that you must also get a similar problem at times, sir,"

They all stood up and began to move towards the door. Hugo had taken out his small radio and had called for the Minister's car to be brought back to the main doors where they all shook hands and then they got into their car to make their drive back to London.

"Jack, if I may say so," Hugo said after the car had departed, "That was quite some presentation that you did there. I don't think that you put a footstep out of place in all that you did. They were impressed and that Foreign Secretary hadn't told the Prime Minister the entire story, had he? I'll just bet that now they are away from here he's really getting it in the neck. I don't think that he'd said anything about your target donation figure at all, do you?"

"No, I don't think that he had passed on much information but never mind, we did, didn't we? It looks as though as well that they will be providing some good surveys and some good people at costings to get the figures to come out how we want them to, doesn't it? I think though that the three of us could all do with another cup of coffee each, don't you?"

They made their way back out to near the main doors and then they got into the elevators to take them up to their flat on the second floor. Jennifer knew that she had a good supply of coffee in her kitchen there and anyway, they wanted to go and see Alec and Ray to put them in the picture about all that had happened.

Chapter Nine

They all had their coffee and then they all walked together to the upstairs office to see Alec and Ray. As was usual, one of the two of them was on the computer, Alec this time, and the other one, Ray appeared once again to be making some notes on his pad.

"And how did the meeting go then Jack," Ray asked, breaking off from writing on his pad. "Did they more or less fall in with what you had planned for them? More to the point, were they impressed with what you suggested? Alec has been having some more luck at hiding some more of your money. I must say that he's damned good at doing that as well. If anyone investigating was clever enough, I suppose that they could find it, but they would have to be a damned sight cleverer than anyone that I've ever seen doing checks on these kinds of things. Anyway, I think that he's now got it down so that it looks like you have a fund with a value of Nine Hundred Billion Pounds. You still have One Trillion three Hundred Billion in reality and that should stay fairly constant now, except when you start to donate some money out. So, you think that they will go ahead with all that you have suggested, do you?"

"Yes," Jack replied. "The Prime Minister agreed that they would get some surveyors in fairly quickly to assess what the ground conditions are where we want to put the lines in and they are going to get some people to assist in getting some good costings for us. The Foreign Secretary hadn't mentioned what the target donation was and the Prime Minister wasn't pleased at not knowing that. Anyway, he has also said that they would also make a start on trying to find any other projects that we may be able to fund some work on. All in all, I think that you could soon start to see some bonus points coming your way."

As they were standing there talking, Peter suddenly appeared and glanced at who was in the office. "Have you had your meeting then, Jack? Has it gone well? Come on, we do want to know what is going to happen. What did your Foreign Minister look like? We had quite a good time the other night with him. I really enjoyed doing that. I wouldn't mind having a go at some of my family now that I've tried doing it."

"Calm down Peter," Alec said from where he was at the computer. I'm afraid that our Peter here does get a little bit mad at times Jack. It's alright, he'll calm down soon. We are dealing with that but he did really take to doing some haunting. Never mind, he'll grow up eventually, won't he?"

"Peter," Jack said, in quite a firm voice, from near the office doorway, "Don't you think that it's going to be a big waste if all that you, I, and yes, Alec and Ray also have gone through to get bonus points for you and your people since you came back to find me. If now, because you are acting a bit stupid, you were to be sent by me to join that one who said he was a controller, and that one who called himself the allocator down at the lowest level, you wouldn't like that, would you? You must remember that it was I who made the decision that they had to go there, wasn't it? Now, if you want to join them down at the lowest level, you carry on behaving just as you are doing now and I will with some pleasure condemn you to that. Now, the decision is up to you Peter. Which do you want? Do you want to carry on and possibly get a lot of bonus points, or do you want to stay down at the lowest level forever? The decision is yours now Peter. I do want an answer, and if I don't get one then I shall presume that you want to go to the lowest level. What is it to be, Peter, NOW."

"I'm sorry everyone," Peter called out. "I wasn't trying to be a nuisance, honestly. I do want to get the bonus points and move upwards. Please, Jack, we used to be old friends, didn't we? Please, don't send me down there."

"Very well then Peter," Jack replied. "You can remain and enjoy the benefits of the bonus points, but if I hear of anything that you are doing wrong from either Alec or Ray then I will condemn you to that place. Now, as you do appear to be recognising what behaviour you are supposed to be having, you may now go and join your friends in your 'in-between-world'."

Peter just disappeared from sight. "Wow," Alec said. "That was something. That's a new one on me, isn't it on you, Ray? I mean, getting Peter to behave like that is quite an achievement and well done to you, Jack. How is it that you can do that? Yes, you did it with the controller and you did it with the allocator, didn't you? How is it that you have any power over our world?"

"Do you know Alec," Jack replied, "I haven't got a clue but somehow it did work with the other two so I just thought that I could maybe get Peter to behave in a similar way. I don't know how, because I can't have any power in your world, can I?"

"Sorry Jack," Ray added. "I think that you are wrong there, for some reason. You did send the first two and you did it as though you had some inner power to do it. That same sound came out when you told Peter to behave. I don't know what it is but I believe that in some way you do have a connection with our World. I know that you aren't a spirit from our world, but somehow, you do have some connection. Maybe when your time comes, you will be in charge here, Jack. With luck, I may have moved onto the next level but I do honestly believe that you do have some power in our world."

"Crikey," Jennifer said from where she was sitting in the office. "Jack and I have been around together and fairly close for a long time and I don't think that I've ever picked up anything of him along those lines Ray. I think that you may have got it a bit wrong this time, but anyway, Peter did seem to take heed, didn't he? That was the main thing, wasn't it?"

"Jack, you did speak with some authority when you spoke to Peter," Hugo added. "When you spoke to those government officials, they were almost hanging onto your words. I do think that somehow you have got some power. I don't know what it is or where it came from but I have seen in the army some senior Generals, just an odd one now and then mind you, they speak to some other ones and, because they had the power in their voices, the orders that they gave were obeyed. No Ray, I don't think that it has anything to do with your World or our World, it's just that some people do have some power, whatever it is and wherever it comes from, and I think that Jack does happen to have it."

"Well, no matter what you lot think, Peter does seem to have taken heed this time, doesn't he? Jack said. "You have to remember he was always a bit mad. I mean, his family were a bit like that anyway. They didn't have the best of reputations around the area. I never knew what any of them had done exactly, but they just weren't classed as one of the best. It was just that me and him always seemed to get on so well. He has said since that it was because he always wanted to have a family like mine. I suppose that that must be a compliment anyway so, as long as he's OK, I don't mind."

"I suppose that you could have something there," Hugo said. "I have known some people who have longed to have a close-knit family and when they haven't had one well, they more or less take it for granted that they will have to try and take a bit of someone else's to make up for it. Now, I'm no psychiatrist or anything, but that does then make it sound about right with Peter, doesn't it?"

"It doesn't matter what you all say," Jenny said, "When Jack was younger, he had Peter as a good friend and that must always count for something. You don't just discount your old friends on a whim because of one silly mistake. Give the lad a chance. I'll bet that you all wanted another chance, didn't you?"

"Oh, my lady," Ray retorted with a little bit of a laugh. "The lady has got a point there and OK, he has acted a bit daft at times, but let us all give him a chance, no matter if Jack has got some strange power or not. Well-spoken, Jennifer."

"Whatever has happened has happened," Jack said. I think that we should all let it go now and anyway, I could do with another coffee, couldn't you? Oh, sorry Ray and Alec, you don't drink coffee any more in our world, do you? We'll see you later anyway and thanks for all your help as well."

"That's OK," Ray called after them, "And do keep us updated when you do hear from the politicians. You never know, we may be able to help a bit more with some useful bits now and then."

Jack, Jennifer and Hugo left the office and made their way to the kitchen so that they could all once again top up with some more coffee.

"When do you think that you'll hear anything then?" Jennifer said. "From what I gathered when they were here today, they don't seem to really rush when they do anything, do they? The only thing was that the Prime Minister did seem to be a bit more awake than the Foreign Minister, didn't he? Maybe he will get pushed to keep it going now that the Prime Minister has taken an interest, don't you think?"

"Oh, most definitely," Hugo said, "I think that the Prime Minister wasn't at all pleased with the way that the Foreign Minister had handled things and, of course, for not having provided him with all of the information that you gave him Jack. The amount of your maximum target donation did, I believe, quite astound the Prime Minister. That amount was though, as you had said, a sum equal to the entire GDP of the country of Ethiopia and that, to a Prime minister, can mean a potential donor to their party. As I've said before though, I'd personally stay well clear of any of the damned political parties. Of course, you may be different to me of course, and you may like some political parties. My experience of working with politicians in Spain did really put me off bothering with any of them. If I had been given any other jobs in the army other than that of political and diplomatic security, I would probably have stayed in the army, and yes, I would have accepted the promotion to colonel. The job that I've got now though is many, many times better."

"I'm damned pleased to hear that," Jack said. "From the way that we do get on nowadays, you and I, it would cause me some severe headaches if I didn't think that I had you somewhere around to give me some support, moral as well as psychological I think. Thank you just for being there, Hugo."

Chapter Nine

It was three days before Jack did hear anything at all about some results of his potential donation. He received a message in the form of a telephone call from the Foreign Minister (sent to him only by the Foreign Secretary's secretary, not from the man himself), and that simply informed him that some surveyors had been sent out to Ethiopia to carry out some tests on the ground out there to discover how it would take either the moling technique or how much work would be required to start to dig trenches for the pipelines. The message also mentioned that some details of the potential donation had been passed to the Ethiopian government requesting their cooperation on the project overall. In total, Jack wasn't very impressed with the message and he had replied to the Foreign Secretary secretary that he would like to have a message passed to the Prime Minister that he would appreciate a callback, at the Minister's convenience, of course! The fact that he was asking a Prime Minister to call him didn't seem to sit well at all with the Foreign Secretaries secretary who did at last reluctantly agree to forward that request for him.

Hugo had been correct (once again), and the Prime Minister did in fact call Jack within less than a couple of hours of Jack's previous calls to and from the parliamentary offices. The Minister did quite openly suggest that at some time in the future Jack may consider offering support to their party. Jack sidestepped that one nicely by saying that while he *may* be able to offer some support to any party, his problems at the moment were in getting adequate information about how the project was progressing. He mentioned that the Foreign Secretary had left him a message that surveyors were going to go to Ethiopia to assess what the ground was like there and that also that some requests had been made to the Ethiopian government for their support. He told the Prime Minister that he had expected a somewhat more detailed report of what the thoughts of the Ethiopian government had been on the suggested project, and the amount of funding being donated. He also said that he believed that the Foreign Secretary could have provided him with some more detailed assessments of some of the costs. He made the point that, as they were in the process of dealing with many similar subjects, the government logistical departments must have some more detailed ideas of some of the costs of the various points that he had given them. Jack also said that he had been rather surprised that no one had been able to make any suggestions to him about anywhere else that was requiring some similar kinds of aid that he would be only too willing to support. The Prime Minister agreed entirely with all of the points that Jack had been making and he promised that he would have words with the Foreign Secretary and get back to him. In the meantime, he gave Jack his private telephone number so that if needed he would be able to call on him at any time to get some reports.

Jack had done all of this while he was sitting in the lounge of their new flat with Jennifer sitting by his side. As he finished speaking to the Prime Minister, Jennifer began clapping her hands. She said, "Is this the same person who was afraid of making public address statements? After the way that you handled that meeting with the pair of politicians and now this, I would imagine that you are as good as many of the Public Relations companies that try to sell their services. Oh, Hugo will be oh, so pleased to hear just how you have handled things so far. From now on, you are acknowledging that you are the master and they are to be your servants and I'll just bet that you can get them running after you now. So, you didn't need the allocator to do that job for you, did you?"

Following the interesting, if not at the moment, the productive phone call with the politicians, they had both decided that they would have a coffee each. They made it just about as far as the kitchen and the entry doorbell rang. Jack, who was the nearest, answered the device and it was one of the security men (it just happened that was one of the newer ones that Jack didn't recognise). "Yes, how can I help you? Jack asked.

"Mr Dawkins, sir, we have two people here who say that they want to see you, sir. They say that they are your Mother and Father, sir, can I allow them to come up, sir?"

"Simply get them to stand in view of the camera, please. Once they have been recognised I will release the door and I would appreciate it if you would note them and in future, accept them whenever they arrive. Thank you."

The camera moved to show his Mum and Dad standing there. Jack pressed the 'allow' button and the security man operated the access button for the elevator so that they could come up to see Jack and Jennifer.

Jennifer had gone quickly to the elevator door to welcome them in, quickly followed by Jack. As the door opened, they saw his Mum and Dad standing there.

"Jennifer, we must get Hugo to ensure that all of the guards know who our parents are so that we don't get something like this happening again, mustn't we? I mean, this is daft, isn't it? Maybe if some of the security guards are rotated more so that they get to know who we know and who we want to come and see us it would help. We'll have to do something though, won't we? Anyway, hello Mum and Dad," Jack said as the elevator doors opened. "Come on in. We can soon get the kettle going, can't we Jennifer?"

"Yes, lad," his Dad said, "I do think that it's a bit much when your Mum and Dad can't get in to see you. I know that there has to be some security, but do you think that it's going a bit 'over the top' like? You tell Hugo and see what he thinks. Maybe he'll agree with what you said, you know, for them to rotate their duties a bit so that the ones at the door have some idea of who your friends and relatives are. Anyway, let's get that cup of tea, shall we?"

"You know, for a few minutes there I thought that we were going to be sent away without seeing the pair of you," Jack's Mum said. "Oh, it is a nice flat, isn't it? If we'd have said yes to having a flat here, would ours have been something like this as well then?"

"Look Mum, we can take you into some of the other flats and if you want one, you can have one. Yes they are, more or less, all the same as this one is, aren't they Jennifer? The big shame is that there are still eleven empty flats on these two top floors. That wasn't what we were planning, was it? Anyway, have a good look around this one and then we can take you into some of the other ones as well, can't we Jennifer? I presume that we can get into them, can't we? Will we need to get Hugo to come and open some of them up for us do you think? I'll give him a call anyway and then he can sort out getting people recognised, can't he?"

Jack took out his mobile phone and called Hugo to ask if he could pop in to see them. He knew that his Mum and Dad thought almost as highly of Hugo as he did himself so he thought that it may be a good way of getting him over anyway to meet them again.

While they were waiting for Hugo, Jennifer began telling Jack's Mum and Dad about the visit by the Foreign Secretary and the Prime Minister. They had already been told that they were coming but they had told Jack that as they had no particular interest in politics, they weren't bothered about being there to meet them. Jennifer continued to tell them some things about the Prime Minister's attitude towards the Foreign Secretary who had, it appeared, failed to tell the Prime Minister about Jack's maximum target donation (this time) for the Ethiopian crisis. She said that the Foreign Secretary had then got his secretary to contact Jack today to tell Jack very little about what was happening so Jack had told that one to get the Prime Minister to contact him urgently. She said that the Prime Minister had rung back within less than half an hour and had agreed that Jack should have been given far more information and he had even given Jack his personal phone number in case he needed to get any more information about what was happening.

By this time, Hugo had arrived and he did hear the end of what Jennifer was telling Jack's parents. He smiled at hearing this since he now regarded Jack as something of a statesman himself in the way that Jack appeared to be able to handle people.

Jack's parents were delighted to hear all of this, but of course, as he was their son, they expected nothing less than that from him, but even so, they were very, very proud of what he was making start to happen.

"I was pleased to hear that the politicians did get back to you then Jack," Hugo said. I'm not very surprised though that the Foreign Secretary has failed to give you some proper support. After all, he was the one that caused the delays in the first place, wasn't he? I think that you may have to keep the Prime Minister with you though. He's given you his private number, use it and build something with him. He is the one who can make things happen much more than the others, isn't he? I don't suppose that it was just that that made you call for me though, was it Jack? Have you got a problem?"

"Well, yes, we did have a slight problem when my Mum and Dad came to see me. The security man down at the main entrance held them there until he had contacted me to see if I wanted to see them. Do you think that it may be an idea to rotate some of the security men so that they can all get some idea of who our friends and relatives are? All of the regular men do know my Mum and Dad I believe. It just seemed to be a bit 'off' when he seemed to be acting so strangely."

"You do have a genuine point there Jack and I will get it dealt with as soon as I can. For a start, if I could have some photos of your family members (and anyone else who you know and who may want to call on you) I will get them circulated to all of the men. I will also try and do some more rotation of some of the men so that they do all get to know people a bit more. The problem has been that since we have had to increase the staff it has been a bit awkward to keep the ones that you know at each critical point. Obviously, the ones at the main gate knew your Mum and Dad (or the car anyway with Miguel driving as well, I suppose), so they let them through that gate. The point is that they have been instructed to make sure that only people who you do know, and want to see, are able to get to you. It may seem a bit hard at the moment, but if they do stop one wrong person, that may be the one that was trying to get in to get at you. You can appreciate that, can't you? Security does require people to be identified, after all."

"Yes, I suppose that you are correct," Jack replied. "I think that the idea of the photos is a good one and I'll get you some, and then maybe that will ease things a bit. I think that Stewart Robinson may be visiting as well soon so I'd better get a photo of him hadn't I?"

"Yes, I believe that you said that you had asked him to try and help you with some of your costs, hadn't you? It will be interesting to see if a comparatively small company can get you some information faster than the Foreign Secretary can, won't it?"

"Now, Jack, and you Jennifer," Jack's Mum said. "Oh, and hello to you Hugo as well. Now, Jack, your Dad and I have been talking and we think that since Robert and Elaine are Jennifer's parents, they should have just a little bit more information about your friendly little ghosts. We think that to have a secret like that is wrong, so very, very wrong. You had a word with their people and you were given permission for your Dad and I to be able to see them, hear them and talk to the ghosts so we believe that it is only right that Robert and Elaine should be put in the picture properly. Hugo knows about them, doesn't he? Anyway, that's what we believe and we would like your opinion on it as well. Oh, by the way, Hugo. The main reason that Jack called you was to see if we could have a look at some of the other flats. We do like this one and we just wondered if they were the same as this. Jack says that they are but we just wanted to have a look if we could."

"Certainly they are similar, if not exactly the same," Hugo replied and I thought that I had shown Jack how to open them all up but, never mind, I'll take you to them myself now, if you like?"

"Thanks a lot, Hugo," Jack replied. I'd appreciate that and as for Jennifer's parents, Mum; Jennifer and I have both been thinking about that as well and, well, we agree with what you are saying, so we'll get them over here and then we can see what they think, can't we?"

"If both of your sets of parents did move into the flats," Hugo said, "That would certainly make security a bit more secure, I can tell you that. Were you thinking of moving into one then," he asked Jack's Mum.

"We don't know yet, Hugo," Jack's Mum said. We haven't seen what they're like yet, have we? You just said that you'd show us some of them and then we could decide, couldn't we?"

"Oh, of course, of course, Mrs Dawkins," Hugo said, "Come on now and I can show you some of them. Did you want the same floor that Jack and Jennifer are on or did you want the floor below? That is all up to you. Right, do you want to come as well Jack, Jennifer?" Hugo asked.

Hugo stood up and began walking to the door, quickly followed by Jack's Mum and Dad. Jack and Jennifer glanced at one another and then they both stood up and began to follow to go out of their flat.

Hugo stopped at the door to the next flat and tapped in a code at the doorway and then he went in, followed by the others who were following him. Once inside, he stood aside so that they could all take a look at what that flat had to offer. Jack's Mum went through the different rooms and then came back to where Hugo was standing in the hallway.

"Yes, I do like it Hugo, don't you Jim? She said to her husband. "I even like the furnishings that you've got in the place Jack. I'm surprised if this is what you chose for the flat. No, I'll bet that it was you, who decided on all of that, wasn't it Jennifer? I think that it may be an idea that we do think of moving into it Jim. Come on; let's have your opinion as well."

"Aye, well it does seem to have a lot of space, I must admit and generally I suppose that I'd have to agree with Hugo that it'd make all of the security that much easier, wouldn't it if we were all together, more or less. Yes, I think that I could live here."

"Do you want me to arrange for some furniture movers, as I did for Jack and Jennifer?" Hugo asked. "I think that I could get the same people to do it and they did do a good job, didn't they Jack? They'll even do all of the packing for you as well, if you want. Do you want any of your own furniture to come with you or do you want to leave it where it is? You have a think anyway and if you let me know, I'll get it all sorted for you."

They wandered back, out of that flat and back into Jack and Jennifer's flat. "As soon as you're ready to move I'll get the locking sorted for you," Hugo said. "At the moment, all of the spare flats are on one single lock code but when you move in I would get a new and different lock for each of the flats so you would know that your space is locked and is secure as your space. Will that do?"

"I'll tell you one thing Jack," Jack's Dad said. "It gets to look as though that do in Spain when you had to ask Miguel to try and find us some security firm or something was a damned good job when he found you Hugo and his team, wasn't it? There doesn't seem to be much that he doesn't miss out on, I'll say that for him. And, how do you like living in that house that was Jack and Jennifer's, Hugo? Are you settling in there now then? You know, even if you do own that house, there'd be nothing to stop you from having one of these flats, would there?"

"No, and I'm quite sure that Jack wouldn't mind too much if I said that I wouldn't mind *renting* one from him," Hugo laughed at the way that they had driven the topic of conversation. "The only thing is though would be that I would want to PAY rent for my flat. Jack just has a problem understanding that I too have some money. You see, my family and I used to use the same stockbrokers that Jack has working here. The only difference is that when they worked for us it was when they were in this World, our living World. Alec has done work for our family for a lot of years and he is damned good at his work. I think that even Alec's father used to do some work for our family. Now though, as Alec can now take one or two 'shortcuts', he can make some real magic with the way that he makes money work."

"Oh, so you knew Alec and Ray from before you did any work for Jack, did you?" Jack's Mum asked. "They do seem to be a nice couple of people, don't they?"

"It was Alec that I knew," Hugo replied, "I didn't meet Ray until I met him here, but apparently they knew one another anyway when they lived in this World of ours some time ago, so we may I suppose have met in passing at some time or another."

"I suppose that we should perhaps give Jennifer's Mum and Dad a ring and see if they would come over then," Jack said, "If we are going to be introducing them to our strange world of ghosts, spirits and spectres we may as well get on with it. Do you want me to ring them, or will you ring them, Jennifer? They are, after all, your parents, aren't they? Maybe we could get Miguel to stay near the main door as well as Hugo for when they get here? You know, so that they may at least be recognised?"

"Alright," Hugo said, "I'll make sure that there is someone on the main doors who will recognise them when they get here. Perhaps I'd better wait here though for a minute or two. No one has bothered to ring them yet. They may be out and visiting someone else."

"I'll ring them then," Jennifer said, and she reached for the phone and started to dial. The phone was answered very quickly and Jennifer said, "Mum, Jack's Mum and Dad are here with us. Would you and Dad like to come over, we wanted to talk some things over with you and we thought that it may be best when we are all here together. Is it Manuel or Javier that you have there today? They all know the way anyway, I think, don't they?"

Chapter Ten

Jennifer's parents agreed that they would come over to see them, but they were a little bit curious about what they wanted to talk about. Jack and Jennifer had already asked them if they wanted a flat but they had said that they preferred living in their house and that they felt that to 'downsize to a flat wouldn't suit them too much. Jennifer had tried to explain that they weren't tiny flats but rather large, generous sorts of flats that had all amenities in them; that being the case they would hardly be 'downsizing'. Anyway, they had agreed to come over and see what people wanted them to talk about.

Hugo made sure that there was at least one of the security guards who knew Jennifer's parents about who knew them for when they got there. In the main, the security men who had joined with them during that holiday in Spain when Jack realised that he would have to have some security, were the security men that they had at their houses. In general, they all got on quite well with one another, which was once again, a big help in ensuring that some security was maintained.

It was less than an hour later and the security man at the front door called through to say that Jennifer's Mum and dad were just arriving. He had, of course, been forewarned by the security men at the main gate and it just happened that the guard at the front door was Miguel, the person who Jack had first of all approached to see if he knew where there were any security people that he could hire. Miguel was known and was well-liked by most of the other guards and indeed by all of the people whom he was trying to guard. The car arrived at the main door and Miguel welcomed the visitors and guided them to the elevator doors, pressed the button and made sure that they were in before pressing the button to take them to the second floor, where he was fairly certain that Jack, Jennifer and Jack's parents would be all waiting to greet them (along with Hugo).

Indeed, they were all waiting there, including Hugo (who had suggested that perhaps he should leave them for this session, which may make it a rather difficult one for Jennifer's parents to understand) but Jack had insisted that Hugo should remain with them. Somehow, Jack just thought that now Jennifer's parents trusted Hugo; his words, he thought, may just help them when they began to explain some of the stories about the ghosts, and how they had been the ones to make him become the richest man in the world!

Jack's Mum and Jennifer's Mum always got on well together so they, along with Jennifer went to the kitchen area to start making some tea (and coffee) before they began to discuss anything. Jack's Dad and Jennifer's Dad also got on well together but both of the Fathers were perhaps a little more direct than the Mothers were.

"Now then lad," Jennifer's Dad said to Jack, "What is it that's so damned important that we had to rush over here today, more or less at the drop of a hat?"

"I do think that we should just hold back until you've got some tea to calm you down a bit for what we have to tell you. We can wait until the ladies return with your tea, can't we? Hugo does know what we are going to be talking about, that is why I asked him to remain with us. No, it isn't anything to do with security, but just you hold your horses until you've got your tea. My Mum and Dad also know what we are going to be talking about and both they and Jennifer and I have felt for some time that it was wrong that we hadn't been more open with you for a long time now. Ah, here's the tea and coffee. Once everyone has got themselves comfortable we can make a start."

The teas and the coffee were all served out and they all sat back in the chairs so that Jack could start to tell them what he had to. Jack began, "It started nicely after I had met Jennifer and at that time, no, she didn't know anything about what I'm going to tell you now. I was sitting at my desk just putting a few bits into my travel book (you know all about that anyway, don't you?) and all of a sudden I heard a voice behind me and when I turned, it was Peter Webster that I saw. Now, as you know, or I believe that you do know, Peter had had a car accident a couple of years or so earlier and he had been killed outright. The medics looked at everything and they said that it had probably been an instantaneous death. Now, Peter (or what I then presumed, was the ghost of Peter) said to me that he had had to come back to try and finish off some work that he knew about. As you may gather I was a bit flummoxed and I didn't say much but he continued that he wasn't either up above (in heaven, we presumed), or down below, (in Hell we once again presumed) but that he was in, for want of a better way of describing it, an 'in-between world' where they had to wait. He said that he had now been informed that if some of them could go back to people that they had known before (when they were alive) they could perhaps get that person to get some money so that they could donate for good causes. Now, they (the ghosts) cannot take any money with them but if the person that they have contacted donates to good causes, they (the ghosts), and others from their world, can get, for want of a better way of calling bit, bonus points that can help to raise them up a bit in their world." Jack stopped for a moment to have another drink of coffee.

"This sounds like it's a load of rubbish Jack," Jennifer's Dad said. "Have you called us over here just to listen to you telling us a few fairy stories? You should wait for Halloween before starting with ghost stories, lad."

"No Robert, Dad," Jack continued. "If you wait you will begin to get a lot more of the story. Now Peter (or his ghost) told me that he would help me to get some money and his first effort was to get me to put some money on some horses. I had never been into horse racing or gambling before then though. At first, I think now, looking back, that it was three horses on an accumulator, and I hadn't got a clue what an accumulator was at that time. Then with the winnings from that, he got me to put some money on four horses that were 'no-hopers' that had very good odds for me and they did get me a good bit of money. Then he said that it wasn't enough and he gave me the numbers for the Lottery and told me to put that on, which I did and that, as you know, did come up with quite a sum. Now that I had some funds, he told me that he was going to have to bring two of his friends from the 'in-between world' and they had been stockbrokers (in their living world) and that they would then turn the money that I had got into some real money that I could start to donate so that they could then get some bonus points. I know that it is hard for you to believe, but it did happen and it is still happening. First of all, I got permission for my Mum and then my Dad to see them, hear them and talk to them and then later, I got permission for Jennifer to see, hear and speak to them. Well, these two stockbrokers had had the idea (before they died) of how to make big money and yes, if they had done it then it would have been illegal as it is classed as something called insider dealing. The reason for that is because they needed to know what was going to happen in the future (as well as the past) and now that they are spirits, they can do that. One of them, Alec, (Mum and Dad don't know this yet) was the stockbroker in his real life for Hugo's family and he did help that family to become quite wealthy. I did get one or two problems and I have had to 'deal' with some of the 'characters' from the 'in-between world' and I am now rated quite highly by a lot of the people in that world for how I have improved their existences in that world. Now, I want you to come with us and meet Alec and Ray, the two stockbroker ghosts. They won't hurt you at all and I wouldn't want you to be scared of them at all. If they come or go, they do so instantaneously so don't be worried when they just disappear. I wanted you two to know, as do my Mum and Dad and Jennifer and

Hugo, about how I came to have all of this wealth. I am, at the moment trying to give away One Hundred Billion Pounds to some good causes. I know that's a heck of a lot of money. The first part of that is the drought and famine that is happening in Ethiopia and that is why the Foreign Secretary and the Prime Minister came to see me this week. I will get there, I will make donations to other places as well but Alec and Ray have told me that if I don't donate quite a lot and soon, there is a chance that the funds that I have could double and become over Two Trillion Pounds. That, I'll tell you now, scares me silly. Right, we can now go and meet them. Did you want another cuppa apiece first? If not, let's go now."

Jennifer's Mum grabbed hold of her husband and she was visibly shaking like a leaf. Her Dad held her hand and Jennifer said to them, "Don't worry, they won't hurt you and they will maybe be able to explain a little more about what Jack has done and what he is doing. I'll hold onto your hand, Mum, come on."

They did stand and they began to walk towards Jack's office. They got to the door and it was, as usual, standing open. They looked in and there, sitting at the computer was Ray. They could all see his hands moving about above the keyboard, not touching it at all, but just moving. As they moved, the screen was showing some kind of input. Alec had once again got his notebook out but they both looked across as Jack and the visitors looked in.

"Jack," Alec said, "You should have warned us a bit about this. It even bothers us when we have to meet people. Although we are, after all, mere spirits and we can be shocked. I understand somewhat why you have done this and we will bear with you for doing it for a while. Can you please get some seats for these people, Hugo? I feel that if you don't, some of them may fall down, and we wouldn't want that, would we?"

"I'm sorry Alec but Jennifer and I both felt that it was such a lie that we were leading a life and my Mum and Dad agreed that we should do it. I do apologise for not mentioning it first to you though, that was my personal stupidity and I am sorry. I have warned them both though that if you do go you will just disappear so I don't think that they will be too worried. Just to put some confidence back into Jennifer's Dad, can you give him some idea of the total of my fund at the moment, it may just get them to realise what I have to do."

"Yes," Alec said, "I suppose that that is as good an idea as I could have thought of myself. Mr Wood, Robert, if I may call you that? The total of your son-in-law's fund at the moment stands at One Trillion three hundred and Fifty Billion Pounds. I have explained to Jack that I have tried to do some 'bad dealing' now and then to lose some money but because of the way that it is set up, the fund grows by itself at a tremendous rate that offsets what is being donated outwards. I have 'hidden' quite a lot of the fund so that if anyone traced to find out about his wealth it would only show a total at some Nine hundred and Fifty Billion Pounds, which is still a lot, but not quite as bad as it is once it gets into the Trillions, is it? I suppose that Jack has told you that unless he can start to make some large donations very soon, it is possible that the fund could double itself. We are trying our very best to try and prevent that from happening. We had wanted to get it to a figure that would sustain itself more or less to eternity, whenever that is. What has caused the problems is that we had always planned it with the thought that some large donations would always be going out. At the moment, there have only been tiny ones going out. This latest one of Jack's is more how they will need to be in the future. If you should have any questions, do please ask and either Ray or I will try our best to answer."

"This is madness," Jennifer's Dad said. "Anybody can lose money and when you say donate it, that only means give it away, doesn't it? Anybody can give money away so what is stopping that?"

"The donations have to be of a kind that will be of some kind of benefit to some community or groups of communities. It can't just be a gift or passing some money to some gangster (or even just to some government), but it has to have some goodness somewhere wherever it is going to be. It may be a bit hard for you to understand at first, but I'm sure that inside you, you do know what we mean. At the moment you are totally confused and concerned at hearing that you are, in effect, talking to ghosts, aren't you? That will pass as you get more used to the idea and perhaps then we will be able to explain more later, once you can acknowledge that what is happening isn't a bad thing, not really, is it?"

"Do your parents know that you are here now and doing all this kind of thing then?" Jennifer's Mum said. "It does sound like you are trying to be kind to a lot of people, but because you do, in some way, cheat to get the money for Jack; doesn't that counter the requirement that is supposed to be for goodness that you do it?"

"That is a very good question," Alec replied. "No, it doesn't counter the requirement since many of the efforts in trading on stock markets are done, more or less, as a search for wealth and in many cases that search can result in a lot of harm to some people, sometimes to a lot of people. The stock market is equated by some to be little more than gambling. Take gambling as an example, in the world that you live in, it is of course quite legal and is supported by many, many people who may be reportedly good people who are trying to do good. That may be the case with some of them but, I'm afraid to say, in many, many cases it is due to greed, and greed of a kind that surmounts all other things. Such people cease to think of 'doing good'; they merely think that it is something that they are entitled to. It is believed that it gives them a feeling of Power. Now Power in itself shouldn't be harmful but just think of some of the leaders of some countries who desire, using Power, to take land and property from some other community or country. Look at examples such as Hitler in Germany, Idi Amin in Uganda, and some of the Russian so-called leaders. They have exhibited a similar greed, and I believe that you would admit that there is little that can be said to be good about any greed like that, is there? Goodness in itself can quite often result in causing poverty to the donor. In such cases should it not be the duty of those around the donor to aid and assist in getting them a better and more secure future for all of their good deeds? How many poverty-stricken donors like that do get any support from those around them? I believe that you would agree that there are few that do receive the support. Now the good deeds that these donations have to deal with are similar to that which Jack is trying to do at the moment. You have obviously heard of the drought and the famine in East Africa, mainly in Ethiopia where many, many innocent people are suffering and dying. Now the idea that Jack and Jennifer have suggested of taking water from the sea, passing it through a desalination system and then pumping that water hundreds of miles across deserts to create inland lakes can help to alleviate some future suffering. We do believe that Jack and Jennifer will achieve their aims. No one can be certain, but he is trying to do that. He has asked for details of any other crises that require money to aid the disaster and it is hoped that such information will be coming to him soon. Does that in some way then satisfy the need to employ some subterfuge to get the cash to provide the aid?"

"I do think that you have certainly explained that well, sir," Jennifer's Mum replied. "And I do hope that your parents are aware of just how much you are both trying now to do some good things. Maybe they will hear of what you have done, wherever they may be, and then that may get you some of what Jack described as bonus points. I do believe that the two of you do deserve the points that you need to elevate yourselves to a better world."

"Madam, I do most sincerely thank you for your kind words and I hope too that my parents may in some way know that we have at least tried to alleviate some suffering," Alec said.

"I would say thank you to both of you who are working so hard to try and generate the cash that is needed," Jennifer's Mum said. "Yes, Jack and Jennifer do seem to be doing what they can to try and help and I'll say thank you to them both right now but, that does not excuse them for not being honest with my husband and me about all of this. Yes, they are doing well now, but they do have a lot of ground to make up to counter the deceit that they have practised on us for this length of time. Yes, they will eventually be forgiven for that deceit. I suppose that it is possible for them to have believed that we would have scorned them for telling us that they had been aided by spirits or ghosts as we know them. They too both have minds and those two minds should have realised that we were equally entitled to know things."

"If I may say on their behalf," Alec said, "From when they first encountered Peter and then Ray and myself they were told that they must not let anyone know that they were communicating with spirits. Jack had to seek permission to let his Mother, His Father and then his Wife know about the spirit world that he was involved with. At that time there was a creature controlling our world that was known as the Controller. It was some time after they had been in contact with us that Jack faced that Controller and effectively removed that power from the creature, removing that creature to the lowest levels of our world. Similarly, he had been told that the donations would be dealt with by another creature known in our world as the allocator. That creature was also faced by Jack who removed that power from that creature and sent it also to the lowest levels of our world. Jack has been facing many, many problems and it is our opinion that he may be excused for some minor errors that he may have committed. We do hope that you will now perhaps see fit to excuse both Jack and Jennifer of their shortcomings and instead credit them with the much good that they have done on behalf of our world."

"My goodness," Jennifer's Mum again said, "We had not been told that they had in fact been dealing with any such forces and they will be forgiven for their lack of thought when dealing with us over such a minor point. We have now taken quite a lot of your time today and we thank you for permitting us an audience today. We, or particularly I, hope that we may meet again at some time in the future as it has been an extremely enlightening experience for me, and I believe for Jennifer's Father. Thank you so much for all that you have done, and may yet achieve."

The rest of the group were aghast at the way that the meeting had been dominated by Jennifer's Mum. Not just that she had been the only one who had said anything but about the way that the conversation between her and Alec had gone. Jennifer herself was quite proud that her Mum had taken to the idea of the ghosts so well anyway. At last, Jack said, "I believe that we should all leave Alec and Ray to their work and we could all get another cuppa apiece, what do you all say?"

They all stood up again and began to make their way back to the kitchen, the ladies again making a beeline for the Kettle.

Chapter Eleven

They all got their cups of tea or coffee and moved with them into the lounge area. They took some seats and Hugo said, "The more that I see of you people, the more that I become amazed at you all. I would never have believed that it would have been you, Mrs Wood, who would have taken to the ghosts just as you did. Before you went into the office to see them and meet with them I had presumed, quite rashly and incorrectly, that you were extremely nervous at the thought of meeting any spirits or ghosts, whatever you are supposed to call them. But no, you took to them and you could manage to find some very probing questions to put to them, couldn't you? Yes, quite amazing. I mean, I had known Alec for some time, but mainly from when I was a bit younger (and when he was living, in our world I mean). He did a lot of work with our family to get our wealth up to quite a sensible level. Of course, at that time he was alive and he couldn't just pop forward in time to find out what some shares or others were doing, could he? Now he can, and just look at how he's done it with Jack."

"Aye, I was quite surprised by the way that you took to it," Jennifer's Dad said. "I thought that you were a bit scared as well, but no, you did put some good questions to him, didn't you? And you, Jack, from what he was saying you've had quite a tussle with some spirits in their world, haven't you? He said that you had dealt with two of their people and demoted them to somewhere, I don't know where, but he was impressed with you lad."

"Never mind about the ghosts," Jack's Mum said to the other two parents, "What do you think of these flats then now that you've seen them? We've said that we think that we could move in and use one of them. Hugo said that he'll get us some moving people to get our stuff over as well. He is useful is our Hugo, isn't he? A grand lad, even though he isn't English."

"It's alright you saying about the flats," Jennifer's Mum said. "But this one is the special one that they've had done just for them, isn't it? I mean, the other's well, they'll not be quite like this one, will they?"

"Oh, we've been into another one," Jack's Mum said "They are like this, just like this and we've said that we'd like that one. Jack and Hugo have said that they are all very, very similar to one another. He said that they were built as luxury flats so they all had to be to a similar standard. Why don't you just go and have a look at one of them? Hugo knows how to get them open and then, if you want one he says that he'll get a special code done for you so that it'll be your own special flat. Come on, let's go and look at one then. Do you want this floor or the floor below? Jack says that there are twelve flats altogether and well, Jack and Jennifer have got his one and we've got another one on this floor so there are still another ten flats that are empty at the moment. Come on, let's go and look now, eh?"

They all stood up and Hugo asked if they wanted to look at one on the first floor or the second floor, like this one was. Jennifer's Mum said that she wasn't bothered which so they might as well look at one on this floor. Hugo led the way and went past the flat that Jack's Mum and Dad had said that they liked and he stopped at the next one, input the code at the door and opened the door, he then stood back while they all went in. Jennifer's Mum led the way then, followed by her husband and then Jennifer. The others just followed on with this little tour of the flat and then again they returned to the entrance hall and Jennifer's Mum said, "Yes, they are rather nice, aren't they? You never told us that they were as nice as this Jennifer, did you? I thought that you had just chosen the nicest and the largest one but they all seem to be quite nice flats, don't they? I do think that perhaps I wouldn't mind living here. We had lived in our old house for so long and we had become attached to it. When Jack won that lottery win and he got us our new house (that we live in now) well, it is a nice house I suppose but it has never quite felt like home, has it Robert? You've said so a few times if you remember, haven't you? We'll have a think about it and we can let you know later, can't we Jack?"

"You just say when and it can be yours," Jack replied. "I'm sure that if you want, Hugo would be able to arrange some removals for you as well. If you did move in here, it would get us both or two lots of parents handy for a visit, wouldn't it? You've often said that we should have got somewhere closer so that we could visit whenever we wanted, haven't you?"

"Well, I like it anyway," Jennifer's Dad, Robert said. "I've never much taken to that house that we have now. Our old house, yes, it may have been a bit smaller than our new house but that always felt like home. This one well, it does more or less give you that feeling of belonging, doesn't it? And, it saves you the trouble of having to go upstairs to get to bed, doesn't it? The kitchen seems to be a nice size and it seems to be a good layout. Of course, we'd have to get some furniture to match the place, wouldn't we? What do you do with the furniture that there is in here then Jack, you know, when someone moves in here, like? Do you sell it off, or do you have a store somewhere where you keep it?"

"Oh, the furniture goes with the house Dad," Jennifer said to her parents. "We tried to get some furniture that we liked and something that seemed to fit well with the place. It was mainly me that chose the furniture anyway, wasn't it Jack? If you want to, you could sell the other house with the furniture in it or you could rent it out as a furnished house, couldn't you? It would just be up to what you wanted. So, if you both like it and neither of you appears to have settled into that new house, do you want this one? The sooner that you decide, the sooner Hugo can get the door locks re-programmed for your own code, couldn't he?"

"Go on then lass, we'll move into this flat then," Jennifer's Mum said with her husband nodding away at the side of her. "Can you get some people to move some of our stuff then, Hugo? I think that we'd leave the furniture there but there are some things that I'd want in this new place. When are you moving in then Eileen? It's going to make us neighbours, isn't it? Yes, I think that I'll like it here once we get our own bits and pieces here with us."

"That's made it easier for you, hasn't it Hugo? Jack's Dad said. "It saves you having to have men spread around all over town just to protect the families, doesn't it? Yes, I think that we've all made a good decision today. Oh, of course, you that want to will all be on hand if you fancy having a chat with one of the ghosts, won't you?" he said with a laugh.

"Yes Jim," Hugo replied, "It certainly makes far more sense to have all the 'at risk' people in one place and we certainly have some good security on the estate now, don't we? By the way, being fair to the removal people I think that I'd better give them a week to get both of your families sorted and moved, don't you think? Hugo continued. "If you two ladies, I am presuming that it will be the ladies who decide, aren't I? If you can each give me the code that you want; numbers or letters, or a mixture of both if you want, I'll get the two door locks programmed for you so that then these two flats will be yours, even before you move your bits and pieces in. How's that then Jack, you've achieved it, you've got both sets of parents here as well, haven't you?"

"Yes, and it wasn't too painless, was it? Now all that we have to do is to get you to accept that you also should have one of the flats and then you would be 'on the job' more or less for whenever or whatever you are needed for. There's nothing, no reason whatsoever in you moving into one of the flats for why you need to sell your house. It is, after all, your house and you could live here and there, just as it suited you or you could rent it out to someone else, couldn't you? Go on; give us a good reason why you can't have a place to live in for when you are at work. You could get one on the first floor and then all of your men would know where to go to contact you if they should need you for anything, wouldn't they?"

"Yes, you do have a point there Jack," Hugo replied. "I suppose that I could call it an office, and class it as me having to have an office where I can sleep or eat at occasionally, just to make me much more readily available for the men if they should happen to need me. You do somehow seem to be getting stronger at this thing that we talked about the other day of Power, Jack. You can make your arguments just fit in with whatever it is that you want it to be, can't you? Why don't you try doing that with the Prime Minister and see what you can find out, eh?"

"Maybe later Hugo," Jack replied. "I think that it would be reasonable for me to give him a day or so to get things sorted and then maybe I will try him again. I could also start to push him a bit to get some other useful crises, couldn't I?"

They had been chatting away for a little while (with having several more cups of coffee as well) and the alarm sounded from the main gateway. Jack picked up the control pad and spoke to the security guard there.

"Good day Mr Dawkins, sir, there is a Mr Stewart Robinson at the main gate and seeks entry. Are you expecting him, sir? Shall I let him through?"

"Yes please," Jack replied, "And can you make a note of him while he is there and if possible take a quick snap with your camera to keep a photo of him for future occasions. I will be getting you a lot of photos soon of friends, relatives and people that I approve of for entry. Then you would know more or less who we were expecting, won't you? Thank you guard for calling me."

"This could be very interesting for you, couldn't it," Hugo said. "As I said before, if a comparatively small local business can come up with something that looks more feasible as a price for something, it puts even more pressure on the government people, doesn't it?"

"Yes, Jack replied. "I know that his business may be a bit smaller than some but they have got a good reputation for some of the things that they do. Anyway, it will be nice to see him again. He used to be my old boss but now I'm a director of the company now."

"Is that your old boss, Mr Robinson coming to see you then?" Jack's Dad asked. "You do sometimes keep in touch then? He has done quite a bit for the town as well, hasn't he Robert," he asked Jennifer's Dad.

"Oh, yes," He replied. "It's not just what he can buy, sell or get delivered but it's what he's done for the town itself. There are quite a few parts of the town that would have just closed up if it hadn't been for him."

"I'd better go down and see him then," Jack said, "Do you want to come and meet him, Hugo? I think that you and he will probably get on well together."

Chapter Twelve

They both went to the elevator and went down to the ground floor. They had timed it very near to perfectly as they got to the main door just about at the same time that Stewart Robinson's car pulled up by it. "Hello Stewart," Jack called out as his old boss and friend got out of his car. "Have you just come across to see what it's like in the slums then? This, by the way, is Hugo, he is in charge of my security. You never expect it to get to this but my goodness it has, and I'm glad that I have him and his team with us now. Anyway, Stewart, come on in and at least I can show you some of what we've got here. It's all still a bit new to me anyway, but I do know one or two bits of it. By the way, how are things going at the warehouse? Things are still all OK, aren't they? I know that I said that I'd pop in now and then but somehow, everything just seems to have snowballed somehow and I seem to get less and less time of my own. By the way, when you came to the main gate, I asked them to take your photo because I want people who are friends and relatives to be recognised by the security team and they can put your photo up with the others that I welcome here."

"Well Jack," Stewart replied. "I've been doing some digging around to see what I could find and it in general appears to me to be that your diameter of a three hundred millimetre pipe is somewhere near the top end that the system seems to like for moling. Generally, the suggestions that I got, and some of these were, to my mind, not completely accurate, that about twenty to fifty meters in length of pipe at a time can be dragged through. They were also suggesting that the diameter of the pipe can require a depth that can be up to ten times the diameter that it needs to be under the ground to minimise the risk of the pipe collapsing. To my mind, although for some smaller diameter pipes moling may be preferable, actual trenching sounds to be more practical for what you are talking about. I think that you said about three hundred miles, didn't you? That's quite a distance but if you considered it with moling it would probably mean having to dig pits at the start and the end of each run and the pits would need to be quite deep. No, trenching would appear to be a more feasible option for you for what you are planning. As I've said though, I'm no expert and the people that I have been quizzing aren't necessarily experts either. I'm sorry that I haven't been able to get a lot more useful information but I have tried."

"Stewart," Jack replied, "You have at least given me some info and that may be useful to me. Oh, by the way, yes, I did say three hundred miles but I wanted to put four lines in so it would get it to twelve hundred miles in total. Come on, I'll try and show you around what we have got here. Hugo will tell you when I get it wrong, he has been massively supportive of all that I've been doing here. If ever you need some security for your business, just give Hugo a call. I'm sure that he'd help whenever he could."

"Well, thanks a lot for that but I don't think that we are quite in the business that needs a lot of that kind of security," Stewart replied. "We may occasionally have a few bits and pieces getting pinched, but I suppose that we'll live with that. You've known what kinds of stuff we usually have, haven't you? We have in the past sometimes needed some space to store some stuff when it didn't matter too much about the weather. If that comes about again I may ask you then. There's a lot of open ground here that would suit us for those times of things. That may not quite suit your image though, I would think."

Jack took Stewart around the various parts of the main building, including the security block with the masses of screens showing the images of the various points being under the area covered by the CCTV cameras. Stewart was quite impressed with it all. Jack then asked if he would like a cup of tea and suggested that they could pop up to his flat and he said that both his parents and Jennifer's parents were up there and that they were huge fans of Stewart and the good things that he had done for the town. They went back to the elevator and back up to their flat where Jennifer had just boiled the kettle (because Hugo had phoned as they were walking back to the elevator and had warned her of this visit). They took him into the lounge area and introduced him to both sets of parents who were indeed serious fans of this man who had done so much for the town. They were quite impressed that this man had taken the time to visit their son (and son-in-law) and they assured him that their son still regarded the warehouse company in high regard.

They all had their drinks and then Jack accompanied Stewart back to the ground floor so that he could get back to this car. Jack promised that he would be getting out to the warehouse again but said that he couldn't say exactly when that would be. Stewart left and Hugo and Jack went back up to the flat.

The rest of the day passed quite calmly with the family gathering in the flat, two Mothers (and they were of course also Mothers-in-Law) considering all of the things that they would be able to do together once they had moved into their new flats. Their husbands, however, although they could get on OK with one another didn't appear to have any common interests, other than their families. They were both quite proud of their offspring and had been amazed at the way that the day had turned out for them both. Yes, just a family visit they had believed when they had all got into the flat but then they discovered that they were now going to be living in the flats themselves. Yes, they were quite pleased with the way that their lives were running, especially that now they could continue to keep their jobs (as long as Hugo was permitted to give them a security guard to chauffeur them to their work and back home after work!)

Apart from getting his parents and Jennifer's parents to agree to move into one of the flats, it had been quite a quiet and uneventful day for Jack. Yes, he had met Stewart Robinson and he had discovered that his idea of using the 'moling technique' to lay the pipes wasn't going to be quite the success that he had hoped that it would be. No matter, he thought, he had allowed for some digging machines in his costings to allow for some trenching work to be done in the place of the moling. The problem now though was that he knew that he would probably have to possibly double or even more the cost of that part of the job, along with an increase in the allowance for labour. No matter what he did though, it was still going to be a long way inside his target maximum budget.

Jack had at one point considered trying once again contacting the Prime Minister to see if they had found any other worthwhile crises that would enable some other major donations, providing of course that they did fit with his criteria that they must always be to aid some people. He had made it clear early on in his discussions that he would never consider giving donations to aid the 'beautifying effects' of buildings or such things when it did nothing to give aid and/or comfort to some of those who for no reason of their own were either starving, cold and hungry or suffering in some similar way. He left that and thought that perhaps it would be better to wait another day to see if he did get any response from those people.

It was the following morning, late morning for Jack; it wasn't until about eleven o'clock in the morning before he received a telephone call from the office of the Foreign Secretary. Once again, it wasn't the Foreign Secretary himself who called, but at least he had received a call. The caller introduced himself and said that he had been asked by the Foreign Secretary to set up some communication panels with Jack and he said that he had some information that had been requested.

Jack told the man that he had been waiting for some information regarding the Famine in Ethiopia and details that he needed for his donation to be made.

Hearing this, the man on the other end of the phone said, "My name is Peter Watson and, yes Mr Dawkins, the Foreign Secretary did say that you didn't wish to contribute in the more accepted manner and he has now obtained some more information for you. He has made several enquiries and in some adjustments to the figures that you provided he has asked me to advise you that in his opinion some of your figures would not be accurate enough for his department to put forward for approval."

"Yes," Jack replied, "At the meeting, the Minister was told that the figures that I gave him were only preliminary figures and that I had presumed that he may have some figures which could be more accurate. Just what are the figures that he is now suggesting?"

"Starting on the list that you gave to the Minister, it shows that you had allowed a sum of three million pounds each for two desalination units. The Minister has now found that the sum required for this would need to be three million five hundred thousand pounds each, making a total of seven million pounds."

"If I may interrupt you now," Jack said. "My further enquiries have indicated that for the quantity of water that is to be pumped through the four lines, two desalination units would not be adequate and I have been advised that that should be increased to four desalination units (one unit for each line) so that would make the total for those, using the Minister's figures, to now be fourteen million pounds."

"Thank you, Mr Dawkins," Peter Watson said. "That is quite an increase, isn't it? I do hope that it doesn't become too large a sum to make the project work. Now, the Sea-based wind turbines do appear to have a figure that could be approximately correct so shall we, for the time being, leave that sum as it is? In the case of the four storage tanks, for that point, I have been advised that would depend somewhat on what volume they were intended to hold. In view of that, perhaps that figure could be left as you put it. For the eight pumps, you quoted a price of ten million pounds. Our advisers suggest that that is a very generous figure but again, depending on the volume to be pumped it was felt to be advisable to use your figure. Your figures for the sixteen take-off units at seventy-five-mile intervals were again judged to be reasonably accurate at eight million pounds. For the digging machines you suggested eight million pounds and again this was judged to be quite a good estimate. Regarding the labour costs for the project, our advisers suggest that this may perhaps be a little low and they have suggested a figure of twelve million pounds. For the three hundred millimetre diameter pipes themselves worked out at two thousand five hundred pounds per mile and for that, it has been suggested that it should be increased to three thousand pounds per mile which would give a figure of three million six hundred thousand pounds. Do these figures cause you any real concern Mr Dawkins?"

"No Mr Watson, your numbers at the moment seem to be OK to me except that using the sums that you have given me, along with other information that I have obtained, I too have had to do some revising and have been advised that the ten million pounds for the eight pumps should now be increased to twelve million pounds. I have been advised that using the moling technique for a three-hundred-millimetre diameter pipe could possibly have some serious problems and it would be more practical to lay the pipes using trenches. Because of that, I have increased the initial cost of diggers to twelve million pounds and also because of that item, I have increased the cost of labour from ten million pounds to eighteen million pounds. If you could perhaps give me an email address I would get my figures (and your adjustments onto paper) and email you with what I believe to be a more accurate figure for now. Of course, as I explained to the Minister, I would like this project to be completed and, no matter the final cost, I would like to see it completed quickly. As a matter of interest, the Minister (and also the Prime Minister) was also going to find any other rather urgent crises that I could perhaps consider looking at helping with while this is going on. If he hasn't given you that yet, could you please ask him to make this an urgent request?"

"Yes Mr Dawkins," Peter Watson replied. "He didn't mention anything else about other crises, but I shall of course ask him as soon as I can. I am also sending you an e-mail with these figures on and from there you will be able to get my email address, won't you?"

Jack immediately began to make the amended list, typing it out again so that he could send it to the Foreign Office with a new suggested (somewhat initial) total for them to look at.

1.   *Four Desalination units, at three million five hundred pounds each, fourteen million pounds.*

2.   *One Sea-based Wind turbine to get electricity, four million pounds. This of course could*
        depend on the amount of electricity needed for the project.

3.   *Four Storage tanks to hold water for pumping, say four million pounds in total. (One tank*
        for each line) tank size to be about twenty thousand litres, about enough for a start of one-day
        pumping load per line.

4.   *Eight Pumps to send water across four lines at three hundred miles each, say twelve million*
        Pounds.

5.   *Take-off units at seventy-five-mile intervals on each line (inc. booster pumps) equals*
        sixteen take-off points in total, say eight million pounds (for the four lines)

6.   *Diggers to aid in trench laying on the four lines, say twelve million pounds*

7.   *Labour for various tasks, say eighteen million pounds*

8.   *Piping to provide a total of say, twelve hundred miles of pipes, 300mm diameter pipe*
        Say a figure of four million pounds.

> *Gross total expected from the above: seventy-six million pounds. Feeding people for the work done over the building of the project, initially, seventy million pounds'*
> **Total one hundred and forty-six million pounds**

Jack had printed out a copy of this new amended list and then he gave a call for Jennifer to come and look at his new 'amended' costs that he was thinking of sending to the Foreign Office. Jennifer looked at it and compared it with the figures that he had shown to the

Foreign Secretary and the Prime Minister. "They have gone up a little bit Jack, but not as much as either of us had expected them to, have they?" Jennifer said.

"No, and that does worry me a little. When I did those figures in the first place, a lot of it was pure guesswork (with maybe an odd glance at some web pages to get some guidance). I'm no expert or qualified estimator so how could I get some figures that to their experts seem to be about right? I know that he isn't a mathematician, but I wonder what Hugo would make of it all. I suppose that I could ask him, and I could also ask Alec and Ray to take a look, couldn't I? I mean, they are far more expert at these things than any of us, aren't they?

Jack took out his phone and gave Hugo a call. Jack still regarded Hugo very much as his friend and co-conspirator on what he was doing (despite Jennifer telling him quite often that Hugo was just supposed to be looking after their security). Hugo listened to what Jack had to say and then he said that he would come up and see him, and the list. He arrived in only a few minutes and Jack showed him the printed-out list of costs and asked him for his thoughts. Hugo had, of course, seen a copy of the original costing sheet that the politicians had taken with them.

Hugo scanned carefully down the list and then said to Jack, "They haven't changed much, have they, Jack? I think that what you said about getting Alec and Ray to look at these would be a good idea. They do have far more idea of some costings than we do, don't they?"

All three of them made their way to the office, with Jack carrying the paper that gave the details of the amended costings for the Ethiopian Project. As they went into the office, Alec and Ray were both in there and, it was strange and unusual that neither of them was on the computer.

"Hello, you two, has the computer broken down then," Jack said, with a little laugh. "I don't think that I've ever come in here without one of you two being at work on the computer. Is there anything wrong?"

"No, Jack," Ray said. "Things had been getting quite hectic and we decided to leave it all alone for a few minutes so that we could chat between the two of us and discuss what may be the best move for us now. I do include all of you as well when I say 'the best move for us'. Alec has been saying that he may try and lose some more money on some of your investments, we have both been very concerned at the rate of growth and also the market has been so very, very active for a couple of days. Quite a lot of your shares suddenly started to go up a lot and until we can get some of them to go the other way it may push your total fund a good bit higher than we want it to go. We have deliberately made some bad investments before, and we have got rid of some money, but the good ones are just getting out of hand in some way. We just were wondering about what to do when you came in."

"Well, we have had some communication from the Foreign Office," Jack said. "They have made some very minor suggestions on the costings that I gave them and well, Jennifer, Hugo and I all think that they haven't made enough changes, made enough criticism. None of us three are in any way experts at costings on things like this, and well, we don't quite trust them. We brought the 'amended' new list for you to look at so that you could tell us if they are being as honest and fair with us as we had expected. Here you are, you have a look at it all."

Jack passed the list to Ray, who was sitting closer to the door than Alec. He took it and had a quick scan and then he passed it on to Alec. "To my mind, Jack," Ray said, "They haven't bothered much with what you gave them. They have accepted some and made no changes to others. They should have had quite a lot more detail to hand for them to give you some far better support. I think from what I can see of this it's going to be a case of another lot of haunting for the Foreign Minister from Alec and his friends. What do you think, Alec?"

"From the quick glance that I've had at it so far," Alec replied, "I believe that you are correct Ray. I presume, from what I can see here that you have also changed a few bits yourself, haven't you? You have taken out the moling technique part, haven't you? I suppose that was in part due to Stewart Robinson getting you some info on that subject, wasn't it? You were right to remove that, and also to increase the amount for the diggers and also the labour. I believe that you were right to go for one desalination unit for each line as well. A lot of this was mere common sense and they, at the government offices should have done a lot better. I think that if I can get another session of haunting going and if you, Jack, can make a call to the Prime Minister it may stir things up a good bit. I noted that you had increased the food for the labour force. That was a good idea. If they became unsettled then that could hold up the project, especially if they decided to mutiny for food. That wouldn't look good, would it? Have you heard yet about whether the Ethiopian government are prepared to help at all with some guard duties? There does seem to be a blank spot as far as the government response is going, Jack. Let's see how another dose of haunting works on the Foreign Secretary. At least it would get Peter interested again in doing something, wouldn't it? Since you told him off, he has been very quiet and withdrawn. It just isn't like Peter to be quiet like that. I know that he enjoyed the haunting though, maybe it will help him as well as us. As far as the fund goes though Jack, I will keep watching it and, if necessary I will arrange to lose a few more billion. Petty sums like that won't affect the overall result, but it's just not in the way for stockbrokers to be *trying* to lose some money, well, normally it isn't but, there again, we aren't normal stockbrokers, are we?"

"Thank you, both of you Alec and Ray," Jack said. "Somehow, coming here to see you two does always kind of raise my spirits a lot, and I'm not meaning that in any funny sort of way so, no pun was intended!

"If it hadn't been you I could have almost taken that as a very serious effect on my sense of seriousness," Alec replied, laughing at Jack as he said it. "Go on, we'll just see if we can get that Foreign

Secretary moving after tonight. You have a good night off, the three of you."

Jack, Jennifer and Hugo then made their way back to the kitchen area. That was always their safe harbour when they wanted to try and think of something. "I do believe that Alec and Ray are trying to seriously reduce some of the funds for me," Jack said, "I mean, with it at the level that it is at now (if anyone knew how to find out how much there really was there) it could mean some funny questions for me, couldn't it Hugo?"

"Yes, Jack," Hugo replied, "That was what I was saying to you before. I know that I'm no fantastic money wizard myself, but it just seemed to be an impossibility for you to have made so much money in such a short period of time. To get to the big money position it can take at least ten or twelve years, and that's for people who know what they are doing with it. People know that you haven't had a history of money dealing so yes; it does get to look strange. The only thing is, absolutely no one can prove anything. It shouldn't be able to happen, but it has happened for you Jack, and thank goodness that there is Alec and Ray there, working their socks off to make sure that you can't be investigated for anything, aren't they? If only we could do something for them as well as just get them some blasted bonus points to lift them up a bit in their world."

"Let's just have some more coffee and then things may look a little bit better," Jennifer said. "At least Alec and Ray are on Jack's side, aren't they? Just imagine what it would have been like if it had been the other way around and they were trying to get at you, Jack?"

"Alec and Ray are too straight to have been trying to hide things and then get me into trouble," Jack said. "Like Hugo, I just wish that there was something that we could do for them besides these damned bonus points."

Chapter Thirteen

Jack was increasingly becoming concerned at what Hugo had said about the speed at which his fund had risen. It had made a lot of sense and, although the money that he had got into the fund had been done by the legitimate stockbrokers that he (plus of course Alec and Ray) had used, shares that he had bought (and sold) just did happen to have been bought and sold at the right and proper time so it was a totally untraceable fact that his fund had reached the level that it had. Since he had started to get a fund that was of staggering proportions, Jack had started to read (on the web sites on his old laptop computer and wherever he could find any material) on just what this 'insider trading' was and what people had to do or know to be able to do it. No matter how hard he had looked, there was no possible way that he could have had any such information. Increasingly it was, to him, getting to look more and more as though it was a pure fluke that his investments had paid off as well as they had done. He had discussed it all with Jennifer and he had even broached the subject with Hugo. Despite all that he had heard and read, Alec and Ray were correct, no one, nobody at all could in any way find any true evidence that he could possibly have had any information to aid his investments. For it to all be a pure fluke was the only answer, but fortunes aren't usually acquired by simple chance, are they? Yes, he was concerned, but he could find absolutely no reason for his concerns about anyone being able to discover any untoward way that he could possibly have known what to invest in and when. He did, at last, seem to feel that to concern himself any more with pointless worrying would only give him a cause to have some serious either physical or mental breakdown from an unaccountable wealth appearing in his fund.

Jennifer was aware of how Jack was concerned at the way that things seemed to be happening for him and, no matter what she said, he just didn't seem to be able to get away from these pointless concerns. She considered them to be pointless since there was absolutely nothing that he could do to change anything. Alec and Ray, plus of course Hugo, who even Jennifer knew that Jack now considered to be his good friend and confidante had all tried to reassure him that, no matter who or how any searching was done, could any untoward accusations be made against Jack. Rumours, yes, but then again, they could only be rumours and speculation that he had in some way done something wrong. His Lottery win had given him a substantial sum of money and, from there, purely by chance; he had happened to invest in a number of companies and shares that simply by chance had turned out to be successful. That then meant to Jennifer that (without knowing about their friendly ghosts) all of the wealth that he now had all amassed in his fund was there purely by chance; it was nothing more than luck, was it?

It was a day after Jack had sent his 'amended' list of proposed costings to the Foreign Secretary that he again received a phone call from Peter Watson, (the Foreign Secretary's secretary).

By this time, Jack had got Hugo to have their phone system adapted to let all conversations be recorded. Jennifer had at first objected to this, saying that doing something like that was invading her personal privacy. That if she wished to speak to one of her friends on the telephone, what she and her friends may say to one another should only be for their ears alone. Jack countered that by simply reminding her that that system hadn't been extended to their mobile phones and that if she did have any 'private' conversations that she had just spoken of, she should be using her mobile phone and not the main landline phone from their estate. She had no answer to that and, as she knew why he had had Hugo do that, she accepted what he said.

Jack took the call from Peter Watson who began to thank Jack for the email that had given the amended costings. He said that he had passed that to the Foreign Secretary and due to some sudden illness, the Foreign Secretary hadn't been in his office for several days but he had been assured that the information was now being assessed by their technical and financial people. He said that he had tried to discover if there had been any other crises that he could give details about to Jack but that he had been told that such disclosures were only to be done by the Ministers themselves. Jack asked if he had had any communication or some comments from the Ethiopian government but once again he was told that any such information was only permitted to be given by the Ministers themselves. Jack then suggested that perhaps he (Peter Watson) could, in the absence from the office of the Foreign Secretary, pass on these enquiries to the Prime Minister. That achieved a great deal of silence from Peter

Watson but eventually, he did say that he would try and pas the enquiries on for him.

Jack decided that enough was enough and that if he was going to get anywhere at all with the project he would need to contact the Prime Minister himself to try and discover some answers. Just to get himself prepared, he wrote out two or three notes on a piece of paper so that he would be prepared. He waited for a few minutes, trying to convince himself that what he was doing was both a practical and sensible thing to do. He picked up the house phone and then made his call to the Prime minister's number. Since Hugo had introduced this new system he knew (or hoped) that all of the conversations would be recorded in case he wanted any of the others (Jennifer, Hugo, Alec or Ray) to hear any of it.

The phone was answered within just a few minutes and Jack immediately recognised the sound of the Prime Minister's voice.

"Good day to you Prime Minister," Jack said, "I have had some kind of response from your Foreign Secretary and I am just a little concerned about some parts of it. I am also rather concerned that he hasn't been able to answer some parts that we had agreed would be looked at. If I may, I will briefly run through some of the points and then maybe you could give me your opinion on the content".

1.   "Has anyone heard anything from the Ethiopian government? The Foreign Secretary just intimated that it could take some time. Since the crisis in their country is, I would have thought, quite critical, someone should surely have been available to make some comments."

2.　　"Has anyone else in your government heard of any other crises that could need some help? As I mentioned to you the other day, to leave things alone when there is a crisis is almost asking for things to get worse rather than to get better. The Foreign Secretary left a message that someone would contact me in *due course*. Would you consider *due course* an adequate response to being able to fund problems at a somewhat earlier stage?"

3.　　"How are the ground surveys going on in Ethiopia? This, I presumed was a reasonable question and one that does require some urgency but yet again I feel that I have been 'fobbed off' by the Foreign Secretary with once again, very little of any answers given to me."

4.　　"Has the Prime Minister seen the costs that the Foreign Secretary sent to me sir? If you have, do you not find them somewhat odd? Some appear to have been accepted without any serious checking of them being carried out. I have personally sent some updated costings to him and, since even I, who am by no means any kind of expert at any of these subjects, found some rather massive discrepancies in them. No mention was made in his report regarding the use of the moling technique but I have already discovered from my own enquiries that this technique while being a useful process may not be practical for what we are wanting in Ethiopia. In an attempt to counter this somewhat, I have therefore increased the sums allocated for digging equipment to channel the pipes out and I have also shown a rather large increase in the proposed cost of labour. With the additional cost of labour, I have also allowed again, a larger sum to be available to feed the people employed on the project. As you will see, the total costs are still only fractional compared to what I am prepared to donate in an effort to resolve the problems for those people"

"As you can no doubt gather from this, the response from the Foreign Secretary has been anything but impressive. I do most certainly want to donate to provide some support for those poor people and I do not feel that the Foreign Secretary does, in any way, support my aims and wishes, aims and wishes that I do believe that you did offer support, sir."

"No, Mr Dawkins," The Prime Minister responded. "I haven't seen anything of his report sent to you and indeed, at present, he is suffering from some rather complicated debilitating condition and has not been in his office. I shall most certainly contact his staff and have any information re-routed to myself and, if necessary I shall allocate a separate Minister to work with you to handle the problems that they are having in Ethiopia. Thank you very much for calling me and I shall make some very serious efforts to get to the bottom of these unusual and concerning events. If you do need me again, you do have my number and do, please feel free to contact me at any time. Thank you once again for all of your concerns and efforts to assist with these problems." The line then went dead and Jack went to find Hugo to see if they could possibly get a copy of the phone call so that he and Jennifer could hear it all again.

Hugo did spend some of his time in the security room where the CCTV cameras displayed the scenes from all around the estate and so Jack went into that room to try and find him. As expected, Hugo was in there and so Jack just told him that he had just had a telephone conversation with the Prime Minister and he wondered if they may be able to get a copy of the recording of that conversation. He said that he had done that due to a lack of response from the Foreign Secretary. He then told Hugo that the Prime Minister had told him that the Foreign Secretary had not been into his office and that he was temporarily absent due to some complicated debilitating condition, which he just presumed, was some after-effect of the haunting that Alec had been going to arrange for him. Hugo said that yes, he should be able to get a copy for them and if he would like to go and get some coffee ready in his flat, he would bring the recording up to him. Jack was delighted and he quickly made his way back to his flat and went to the kitchen, calling out for Jennifer as he did so.

Once in the kitchen, he filled the kettle and got out some cups for them all to have some coffee. By that time, Jennifer had also arrived in the kitchen and she wanted to know just what was getting him so excited. At about that time, Hugo appeared also at the kitchen door, holding a small tape player in his hand.

Jack carried on making coffee for the three of them and, as he was doing that he began to explain that he had been so disgruntled at the response that he had from the Foreign Secretary that he had decided to telephone the Prime Minister. He reminded Jennifer that Hugo had been telling them that they were now recording any phone calls made to or from the estate's entire landline telephone system so he had asked Hugo if he could get them a copy of what he and the Prime Minister had talked about.

Hugo put the tape player on the kitchen work surface and asked if they wanted to hear it there, or did they want to go into the lounge to sit more comfortably while they heard the recording. They agreed to this much more sensible solution and off they went. Once they were all settled, Hugo played the tape for them to hear.

"Yes," Jennifer said, "It does sound as though you've done the right thing there, Jack. The Prime Minister hasn't heard anything from the Foreign Secretary and he did sound to be far more impressed than the Foreign Secretary had been, in any of his messages or calls."

They were also fascinated that the Prime Minister had told Jack that the Foreign Secretary wasn't in his office and that he had been suffering from some rather complicated debilitating condition. They all laughed at this and they all presumed that it was Alec and some of his friends who had been out doing some haunting of the Foreign Secretary. They agreed that they would straight away take it to the office and let Alec and Ray here the tape. As they had, by then, all finished their coffees; they went off to the office to see Alec and Ray.

When they got to the office door they saw that this time, Alec was quite busy moving his hands above the keyboard and making some things happen on the screen. Ray had been writing in his notebook (they thought this, as it was close by him) and he looked across at them as they entered the office.

"Alec," Ray called out, "Look who's come to see us, at last. I'll bet that you have been a bit surprised with what the Prime Minister has told you, haven't you," he said. "Alec and his pals, along with young Peter, of course, went to haunt the Foreign Secretary and apparently they say that by the time that they had finished with him, he was nothing more than a bag of nerves laid on the floor and shivering."

"Yes," Alec said, breaking off from working on the computer for a short time, "I would imagine that if he gets back to work this month even, he'll be a changed man. I must admit that doing some haunting was a new one for me. I've never done it before but it certainly did change that man. We did get quite a few bits in about suffering and famine in East Africa. I don't think that any of us actually named the country Ethiopia, but I feel sure that he got the message. What did the Prime Minister have to say to you then?"

"Well," Jack said, "We thought that you'd like this and, since Hugo has fixed up this estate so all landline phone calls are recorded, we got a copy of that recording for you to hear. Can you play it for them, Hugo?"

Hugo took out the tape player and switched it on. The office went silent, except for the voices of Jack and the Prime Minister coming from the player. It ended and Hugo put the player back into his pocket.

"So, he's debilitated is he," Alec said. "I wouldn't have expected anything less you know. And, as for you young man," Alec said, pointing at Jack, "That was a fair old presentation, wasn't it? You are the same person who told us that you couldn't face doing things like that, aren't you? In my opinion, you did that just like an expert. Well done, Jack, well done indeed. Well, with that done, I can tell you now that we have lost another load of money so we have now got your fund down now to one trillion one hundred and twenty billion pounds. That is more or less about where I wanted it to get to in the first place so I'm quite happy as well. If you can get these things done with the government then it should put us well on the way to getting things going properly."

"Yes, I was also pleased that we had got it down to that, Jack," Ray said and I think that some congratulations from me wouldn't be out of place at how you did on that tape. Well done Jack. We have both now had a good look at the fund total and we are both quite confident that we can hold it so that it won't go up massive amounts unless we want it to go up again."

Thank goodness for that," Jack said. I was only talking to Jennifer earlier today and I was saying to her just how worried I was about it all. I think that after all this, you two; we need another cuppa apiece, don't we?"

They left the office and once again made it back to the kitchen so that they could 'top up' their caffeine levels!

Chapter Fourteen

The following morning came and Jack thought that as he had done most of his tasks that he knew that he had to do the day before, today was, he thought, a day when he could start to relax and try, in some way, to plan for a nice relaxing day both for him and Jennifer. He knew that Hugo may have one or two things to say to him if he heard that they wanted to go out for a day out again, but he believed that they weren't supposed to be prisoners, and anyway, not that many people knew what he looked like when he was away from the estate so, he thought that they could just go out and have a day of relaxation. He wasn't bothered particularly if it was going for a walk or going for a drive, but he just had the feeling that he needed to get out and away from the restrictions of the estate. He called out to Jennifer, who was only in the next room. She, he knew had intended to have a day working in her kitchen. Jennifer, like her Mum and also Jack's Mum, enjoyed their time in the kitchen, but Jack wanted to get out, and he wanted her to escape with him when he went!

"What is it that you want now, Jack," Jennifer asked. "You knew that I was hoping that I could have a day in the kitchen today. I've found some wonderful new recipes and I wanted to try them out today. It will be something different."

"That's just what I was thinking as well," Jack replied. "I'm just getting fed up at being held here as a prisoner. I think that we should both of us, try and get out and do something different. I don't particularly know where we would go, but being held in here each and every day is slowly driving me mad. What do you say? Shall we try and get out? We could get in the back of one of the vans that are delivering and no one would notice us, would they?"

"You, Jack Dawkins are mad," Jennifer said with a huge smile on her face. "Do you know, that's exactly what I want to do as well now? You have some loose cash on you, I've got some loose cash on me so we could just get out and then get on a bus. It won't matter where it's going, we can always catch another one back, can't we?"

With their madcap plan started, they both went down to see if there were any delivery vans anywhere outside. Yes, there was a furniture-type van just bringing in quite a lot of loose furniture for one of the 'rest rooms' for the people who worked at the centre. Together they strolled across to have a look. The van had, more or less, been emptied of things and yes, there were further inside the rear of the van, a number of cloth or carpet stuff things and it didn't look as though it was the kind of stuff that they used on the estate so the pair of them ran into the back of the van (it just happened that the rear of the van had a ramp for the ease of unloading). They ran up the ramp and got to the back, by the carpets or cloth and hid themselves behind it all. They both kept as quiet as they could and eventually, they heard some people closing up the rear door of the van.

Jack reached across to Jennifer and touched her arm, "We've done it, haven't we?" He said. "Now it's just going to be a case of wait and see and then we may find out where this van is going. It must be a local one though. I know that most of the stuff that is used is sourced as close as they can to the town. Maybe it'll be to the warehouse. It won't have changed a lot from when I worked there and then we can easily get out, can't we?"

"You know Jack," Jennifer said, "Hugo will go mad at you when he finds that we've gone, won't he? I do know that it's going to take a good bit of talking to get us out of trouble this time, isn't it?"

"I know," Jack replied, "But I think that Hugo knows how we feel about being locked onto the estate unless we go out with a load of security people with us. There's not much fun when it's like that, is it? I think that I can get around Hugo when we do get back. He'll probably put a few more restrictions on us for a little while and he'll definitely have to give us a good talking to, won't he?"

The van did soon come to a stop, far sooner than they had imagined that it would, but they weren't too concerned. It may just be that there is a lot of traffic or something as it wanted to get onto the main road. They just kept quiet and waited. Another few minutes passed and then the rear door started to be opened once again. Maybe it's another delivery that the van had to make, Jack thought. They heard quite a lot of footsteps on the ramp area at the tail of the van and then their cloth and carpet that had been covering them was pulled back and there, looking down at them was Hugo.

"Come on you two, you didn't think that you could just get out like that, did you? Let's get you back to your kitchen area to have some more coffee. You did, after all, employ me and my men to run a security system around the estate, didn't you Jack? And you can come out as well Jennifer? I had expected a bit more of you. I know that Jack is a bit mad at times, but

I thought that you were the sensible one. If you want to go out for a while Jack, you only have to ask and I can arrange for some transport that's a bit better than this old van you know. Seriously, I am rather annoyed at you trying to do things like this. If you don't want security then I can soon cancel our contract and take out all my men and go back to Spain. I don't think that you'd want that though, would you Jack? We both thought that we were friends of one another, didn't we? If we are friends then Jack, let's have some understanding. If you want to go out, mention it to me and we will arrange something just whatever you want. Come on now, let's get you some coffee. That usually calms you down a bit, doesn't it?"

They got out of the back of the van and there, waiting for them was Jack's car parked immediately behind the van, still inside the grounds of the estate. So, they hadn't got out as far as Jack had thought. They both went and got into the car and Hugo went and took the driver's place and he took them back to the main entry to the offices and flats.

Up they went to their flat once again and Hugo led the way to get them into the kitchen. "Just how did you know what we were doing though? Jack asked. There was no one about and we did try to look as unobtrusive as we could and I mean, we were in the van in the blink of an eye almost. How did you know?"

"Jack, Jack, you know that we have the CCTV everywhere. One of the operators saw you walking outside the main building towards where the van was parked and he thought that it seemed odd so he called me. Once I saw the screen, we both saw you nip into the van and then well, it was just a case of wait and see, wasn't it? It has given me another point to watch out for and I think that I may arrange that any vehicle leaving the estate has to have a quick search done before it leaves the estate. That can be done at the main gate, can't it? That then lets you know that there isn't a lot of point in you trying to do it again. Jack, we have the cars, the minibuses, the drivers, and enough security people. You can go out whenever you want, but please, do try to be a bit sensible and work with us. If you want to end the security, just say so. I'd be sorry to leave, but there must be trust between us Jack. Episodes like this don't show much of that, do they?"

"Hugo, I am sorry," Jack replied. "It wasn't Jennifer; honestly, she was going to have a day working in her blooming kitchen. I was just plain and simply bored and I wanted to go out. To go out on a planned trip as we do now, you know, with a few guards with us well, it's not the same as going and catching a bus and seeing a lot of different people, is it? Please accept my apologies and no, don't think of ending the contract. I do think of you as my friend and yes, we do both still want you to be around, but you must know what we mean when we say that we feel trapped almost when we can't go out, just by ourselves."

"Jack, of course, I know what you mean. I may not be quite the same as you, but I can imagine the frustration that you get at having to be looked after as you at present have to be. I honestly do not know the answer to it. Yes, you may get out and, as you say, go on a bus ride but what if it is that one time when someone does happen to know you and sees a way of making money by taking Jennifer away from you and starts to threaten you that either you give them money or they hurt Jennifer. In a case like that, there is no assurance that if you paid the money that Jennifer wouldn't be hurt, don't you see?"

"Yes, yes, Hugo," Jack replied, resignedly, "I know full well that what you are saying is right and I was a damned fool to try to get away like that. I'm sorry Jennifer, I shouldn't have put you at risk but it is maddening to just have to be a prisoner, more or less, just because I happen to have some money in the bank. I won't try again but somehow, we must find some way for us to go out somewhere, sometimes, without a troop of security people around us. We'll have a think and maybe you can also think for us Hugo."

Jennifer had by then boiled the kettle and she made each of them a cup of coffee. "Here you are," she said to them both. "It wasn't right to just blame Jack like though, Hugo. Jack had told me what he wanted to do and to me, it sounded as though someone had just opened the door of the cage and we could then fly out and be free. Yes, we were both of us wrong to do it but you must appreciate what we do feel like with all of the restrictions. Even our old-time friends aren't keen on coming to see us anymore. They have told me, well my friends have anyway, and they say that it's like paying a visit to someone in jail. I know, and I know that Jack realises, that it was wrong, and we won't do it again. We do value your friendship, Hugo but you can have some friends amongst your men, can't you? We can't even do that, can we? When we were in Spain, Miguel was almost a friend to us as well but it's been weeks since we even saw him. I know that we can't pick and choose who we have as guards but partly because of that, we don't know any of them either, do we?"

"Look, Jack," Hugo said, "Why don't you make some arrangements for the pair of you to go and see Stewart Robinson? I know that he used to be your old boss but you got on well with him. He thinks a lot of you, the pair of you and, let's face it, if it hadn't been for you; his company would have gone down, wouldn't it? It may only be a small thing but at least it would get you out somewhere, wouldn't it? You would be meeting someone else, wouldn't you? I'm sure that he would appreciate it and certainly, the people who work there would as well. They also know that you were the one that saved them all from losing their jobs, don't they? Well, what do you think? Is it worth a try? If you think so, I'll get it set up and we can soon get Miguel to drive you down there. If we do that you'll be seeing him as well, so that will be another old face that you are seeing, won't it?"

"That sounds like a marvellous idea," Jack said. "Don't you think so Jennifer? I know that you haven't seen the place before but you do know Stewart a bit, don't you? Yes, it will be nice to see Miguel again as well, won't it? I'll give Stewart a ring and then maybe we could get something set up for a visit. I know that you haven't met Stewart, Hugo, but he is a grand type and, according to both of our parents, he has done an awful lot for this town, he's almost a village hero when you hear them talking about him, wouldn't you agree, Jennifer?"

"Right then, the pair of you," Hugo said, "Let's all of us forget this morning's bit of silliness and we can all start again. Yes, once you've got it set up, I'll get Miguel to come over to see you and then he can drive you to the warehouse."

They were drinking their coffee and relaxing together when through the door (not the doorway, but the door) in walked Ray. They were all three of them amazed at this. They had never thought of their friendly ghosts being able to walk about outside of the office. "Good morning to you three. Alec was going to come and have a look around as well but he just wanted to finish off one or two more adjustments before he came. We did have a look around at your other house Jack and Jennifer, but so far we haven't had much of a chance to look around here. I must say, it is a rather nice little apartment, isn't it, and not so little either. Oh, Alec and I would both have liked to have a place like this when we were in your world. Yes, we had decent enough places I suppose but this, well, it does you proud that you have chosen so well in all that you have been doing."

As Ray was finishing talking, Alec also followed him into the lounge area. "It's a bit grand, is this, isn't it Ray? Yes, Jack, you've done well with this and I don't blame you one little bit. It does seem to be a rather nice apartment. How are your neighbours? Have you met any of them yet? I would imagine that they'll soon get to know you well and you'll get on well with them then."

"Oh, Alec," Jack said, "We didn't know that you could walk about outside of the office, did we? Oh, there are twelve apartments like this in the new estate main block and the only other people on this floor are my parents and Jennifer's parents. Hugo has taken one of the apartments on the next floor down and he is using that as an office as well so that if any of the security men need to get hold of him they can find him there easily enough. Of course, he is still keeping our old house that he bought from me. He wouldn't accept it as a gift but insisted on paying me for it. I don't know what he'll do with that one. He may just keep it so that he has an escape place when he gets a bit tired of us lot, or he may rent it out we suppose, that's up to him of course."

"Oh, we hadn't realised that you had bought their old house, Hugo," Alec said. "Yes, that was a nice house as well and well, you could have accepted it a a gift. There were no strings attached and you should have known that. By the way, Jack, the fund, your fund has now stabilised, as I had hoped that it would and as soon as you get that Ethiopian project underway it may just dip a fraction but then it will recover again. Well, Ray, we do need to do some work, don't we? Come on, we can get back to work now, can't we?" With that, both Alec and Ray disappeared.

"My goodness," Hugo said. "That was a bit of a shock, wasn't it? I know that it wasn't haunting but just seeing ghosts wandering around in your house does make you wonder a bit, doesn't it? So, they've had a wander in your old house as well then Jack. I know that it is more or less some understood belief that ghosts can walk and do that sort of thing but well, you just don't kind of expect it, do you?"

"No, I didn't expect it," Jack said, "But as they have done so much for me and mine I don't mind and I'd say welcome to them if they fancy having a wander around now and then."

"That's alright Jack," Jennifer added, "But I'm not all that keen on them wandering into our bedroom just when it suits them, do you? And what about the way that they came through the doors? They didn't bother to open them, did they? They simply walked straight through the door itself, didn't they?

"Well, now we know that they can, don't we?" Hugo said. Of course, they are the ghosts so it has to be up to them what they do and when they do it hasn't it? With that out of the way, Jack, why don't you give Stewart Robinson a call and arrange a visit for the pair of you? If you both go, you'll be able to show Jennifer just what you did at that place, won't you Jack?"

"I'll get his number right away and give him a call," Jack said. "Then I can thank him again for his help the other day when I was able to ask him for some advice, can't I?" He took his mobile phone out of his pocket, looked at the contacts file and picked out the one for Stewart Robinson and pressed the start the call button. He also put the phone on 'open' or loudspeaker mode and waited. The phone rang and in minutes Jack was speaking to Stewart. He told him that he and Jennifer had been stuck in the estate offices for some time and he just wondered if they could perhaps pay a visit and he could show Jennifer where he used to work. Stewart told Jack not to be daft; now that he was a director of the company and that they would be welcome at any time, so Jack said that they would be there within the hour.

"Can you get Miguel to take us in please, Hugo?" Jack asked, remembering that it was only a short time since Hugo had had to tell him off for his silly escapade plan that failed.

"Get yourselves ready, the pair of you," Hugo said. "I know where Miguel is supposed to be at the moment so I'll get him to get a car to the main entrance doors to pick you up. Just enjoy yourselves."

Jack and Jennifer got themselves ready and went down the elevator to get them to the main doors. As they arrived there, the car, being driven by Miguel also arrived and stopped for them to get in. Once they had got in, Miguel asked Jack if he could give him some directions since he knew approximately where the warehouse was, but he hadn't got the full address. Jack was delighted to be able to guide Miguel and they arrived at the offices of the warehouse company where Jack had spent so much of his time when he was younger, working there. As they stopped, Jack and Jennifer got out but Miguel remained sitting where he was behind the steering wheel of the car.

"Come on Miguel," Jack called, "You can come and see where I used to work and at some of the work that I used to do."

"Jack, I am supposed to remain with your vehicle to ensure that it is safe," Miguel answered, "I shall be here when you are ready to return."

"Miguel, the car will be safe," Jack called back. "No one is going to bother with the car, I assure you of that."

As Jack was talking to Miguel, Stewart came out of the offices (he had obviously seen them arrive on their CCTV). He saw what was happening and he called out one of the men from just inside the office doorway. "Jack," Stewart called out, "Alan here will stand by the car to make sure that no one goes near it while you are in the warehouse with me." Alan, the man that Stewart had called came and stood by the car and Miguel, seeing that they were trying to help, he did get out of the car, locked the doors and then walked around to join Jack and Jennifer with Stewart as they began to walk into the offices.

Inside the offices, the receptionist who hadn't recognised Jack before (when Jack had been helping to stop the company from going into receivership) saw him now and did recognise him this time and smiled as he walked past her with Stewart. The four of them, Jack, Jennifer, Miguel and Stewart went through and into the main boardroom offices where Jack had been before when he met the other directors. They were all there and they all welcomed the pair of them once again.

Stewart asked Jack what he wanted to see, and where he wanted to go and Jack simply replied that he wanted Jennifer and Miguel to see where he used to work (and some of the things that he used to do there). Stewart took them through another door and immediately, Jack knew where he was. Yes, this was one of the rooms where he used to collect the lists of things that had to be moved, and loaded (or sometimes where he would have to go to get some other goods unloaded). He chatted away to both Jennifer and Miguel, telling them what he used to do, and sometimes how hard the work had been and at other times how bored he had been with the work.

"Ah, but you did know what needed moving first sometimes Jack, didn't you?" Stewart said. I knew that you were a bit unsettled sometimes, but you knew what was needed where and you sometimes did it better than the lists that we were providing you with, didn't you?"

"Yes," Jack replied, "I don't know who produced those damned lists but I often thought that whoever did do them should sometimes have come into the warehouse to see what it was like, get to know some of the drivers, to have an idea which ones would be back first and be wanting another load onto their van. Yes, they were interesting times; I'll give you that, Stewart." Jack reminisced quite a bit about some of the things that he had done; memories that sometimes brought a smile to his face. They got to the end of the warehouse and Stewart asked if they would like a cup of coffee, so they made their way back to the offices.

They got their coffee and Jack asked Stewart how things were going (and were they all OK now for funds), to which Stewart smilingly admitted that things were fine now. Jack also thanked Stewart for the advice that he had been able to give him a couple of days ago and said that he would like to keep popping back now and then, just to get him back to some reality. Stewart took them back out to the front of the offices where the car was waiting (with the man called Alan that Stewart had asked to watch the car still standing by it) and they went to get in to drive back to their flat once again. It had been a bit different, Jack admitted and as they arrived at the front door of the main offices and flats, Miguel stopped the car for them to get out. Jack and Jennifer got out but Miguel, once again remained sitting in the car behind the steering wheel.

"Come on Miguel," Jack called, "There is some time for another coffee, you know. Now that the car is here, someone else can look after it, can't they?"

Miguel appeared to be looking around but he did get out of the car. One of the other security team wasn't far away and Miguel asked him if he could please put the car away for him. Jack and Jennifer moved into the main doors and the elevator door to get to their flats. Miguel followed somewhat reluctantly but eventually, he did get into the elevator with them.

"Look, Miguel," Jack said, "We asked Hugo why we didn't see more of you. You were, after all, the one person who got us a security team way back in Spain, weren't you? We regarded you then, and now, as a friend and we do like to see something of our friends from time to time. Come on, we can go to our flat and have a cup of coffee. You haven't been to this flat, have you? I know that you saw our other house and I believe that you liked that one as well, didn't you? I know that Hugo also wanted it and he said so first so he got it but you have now found a good house in the town, haven't you?"

"Yes, Jack," Miguel replied, "I've got a beautiful house and that has encouraged me to send for my lady friend to come and join us in England. No, we aren't married yet, but I think that we shall be shortly after she gets here. She is bringing her Mum and Dad with her since they were living in a rather remote village in Spain. I know that they do speak English so, hopefully, they will settle well and then perhaps they may want also to get a house near to us."

"Miguel," Jack said, "If they do want to stay and they want to get a house, do keep me in touch. I'm not just showing off or anything with the money, but you have been a good friend to us, so, if they do need a mortgage or anything, do please ask me and I will do something, as I did with you, if I may? Does that sound helpful at all to you Miguel?"

"Jack, yes, I was so grateful for what you did for me but you can't just carry on giving things away like that," Miguel said. "Hugo would be so angry if you did that, he would say that I had asked you to do it, I'm fairly certain of that. You won't know, but Hugo is a distant cousin of mine and my part of the family was not the wealthy ones, but even so, he does seem to like to point that out sometimes. Thank you though for such a very kind offer."

"Miguel," Jennifer said, "If you are our friend then we may help our friends whenever we wish and it has nothing whatsoever to do with

Hugo. If your wife (to-be) parents need a house, let Jack and I give them one. We want you to be settled as well in this area so it is our decision, not Hugo's and, if necessary I will tell him and I'll deal with anything that he has to say. Now, let's get some coffee."

They did indeed get their coffee and Miguel stayed with them chatting for a little while and when he went, they did tell him that they would like him to become a more regular visitor.

Chapter Fifteen

Hugo came to see Jack and Jennifer the next day to ask how they had enjoyed their 'day out' visiting Stewart Robinson and the warehouse. Jack told him that they had both enjoyed that day and that he had insisted that Miguel should accompany them for a look at the warehouse. At hearing this Hugo frowned a little but he did not comment.

"Look Hugo," Jack said, "Stewart got a man out of the office to stand by the car while we were inside and that man remained there until we left the place. To me and Jennifer, to leave our friend Miguel sitting in a car while we went in would have been so very wrong. The car was quite safe; surely they aren't going to bomb the car, are they? As we told you before, we met Miguel when we had the holiday in Spain and all of the lot of us on that trip got on well with him and we all regarded him then, and now, as a friend. It was down to him that we were able to get someone to provide a security service for us so, that when we go out with Miguel driving, he can visit with us as well. I saw you frown and I took it from that that you weren't pleased because he didn't just stay with the car. That just won't happen Hugo when he is out with us."

"Look, Jack," Hugo said, "Security includes you and Jennifer at all times and if the car is left unattended anyone could fix a booby trap to it. That can be dangerous Jack, face it."

"As I told you, Hugo," Jack replied quite hotly, "Stewart saw us there and when I asked Miguel to go in with us, Stewart immediately told a man to come and stand guard on the car. As that was the case, how the hell would anyone be able to fix a booby trap? You too, Hugo needs to have to look at reality. The car was guarded while we were inside. If anyone had approached, that man would either have dealt with them or told us when we came out."

"Jack I shall disagree with you on this and, if you feel so strongly that my idea of security and yours is not compatible then I will quite willingly agree to end the contract to give you security. That decision of course is yours to make."

"I suppose then that there would be nothing whatsoever to stop you broadcasting that I have had the assistance of ghosts, spirits, call them what you will, to create my fund? Is that what you are intending? That, my friend, is unlikely to work since how would you prove that there are any ghosts? No, it would possibly get you moved into an asylum for the mentally deranged, wouldn't it?"

"Well, no," Hugo replied, "I don't think that I would disclose how you got the money, but I most certainly would not wish to work with you if any aspect of security that I want to be in place is challenged so often and so easily by yourself."

"I do think now Hugo that you had better start changing your mind a little bit or you could also suffer quite a lot," Alec said as he was stood near the door with Ray standing by his side. "We have done a lot of work and you and your family, and you Hugo, are being quite self-centred with some kind of family squabble in your family from years and years ago. You have tried to do all of this because you feel a need to make Miguel understand that you are the wealthy one, haven't you? Yes, Jack, they are cousins and it just happened that Hugo is from the wealthy side of the family. If he should ever try to cause problems to you or your family Jack, it is we, from the other side that will deal with him. Hugo, Miguel's part of the family should have had some equal shares (and you now that) but it was your grandfather who fiddled things to cut them out. Yes, he fiddled things, and not very honestly. Now, if it should happen to come out, it could still be investigated and that wrong could quite possibly be corrected by the courts. I believe that this silly feud has to end and it has to end now or you will feel the full fury of the 'other world' on you and all that you think is yours. Now, do you understand?

"Alec," Hugo stammered, quite quietly, "You are now threatening me, aren't you? I did know what my grandfather did and I didn't agree with it, but my father knew and he did agree. That is why I have gone along with it but I can't go against my father's wishes, can I?"

"Yes, Hugo, I am threatening you." Alec continued, "Either you admit that your father was wrong and correct some of that by accepting Miguel or we, and I don't just mean Ray and myself, but many, many others who are aware of this distasteful incident. Now I wouldn't expect you to settle a load of your fortune on the lad, but do please accept him and realise that he too became friends with Jack and Jennifer. It won't cost you a lot, other than some pride, but it could keep you working with Jack and could perhaps build a much better relationship with Miguel. Now, the choice is yours, what is it to be?"

"I do know that my father was wrong, Alec and yes, it was very, very wrong so yes, I will try and make amends with Miguel, but I can't openly admit to what was done all those years ago, can I? You wouldn't expect me to do that, would you? Yes, he's my cousin and I could make his life a bit easier so alright, I will do that. Is that satisfactory for you?"

"Yes," Alec said. "When you admit, as you just have that your family did do some wrong and that you will now start to look after the lad a bit, we'll say that that is enough."

Alec and Ray simply disappeared from where they had been standing, leaving Jack and Jennifer with open mouths at the shock of what they had just seen and heard. Hugo was standing equally shocked and it was Jennifer who broke the silence. "Come on Jack, and you Hugo, let's get some more coffee into us, eh? That'll make us all feel a lot better, won't it?"

Jennifer moved to go to the kitchen and Hugo held up his hand and indicated that she should stop for a minute. "Look," Hugo said, "I haven't a clue quite how Alec could have known so much of my family history, but obviously, he does. Yes, Miguel and I are cousins and there has, for a good number of years been quite a family feud between the two parts of the family. I do know about what had been done and I have always believed that my grandfather was wrong to cause it all. My father tended to agree with his father, my grandfather, and so in some way, I too went along with it. I was wrong, I know that I was wrong and obviously Alec knows a heck of a lot that I didn't know that he knew. I cannot settle the amounts of money onto Miguel but I have never aided him when we were in the army, not as I should have done. He is quite an honourable person and in future, I shall make efforts to aid him if I can. It was perhaps unfortunate (or indeed maybe it was fortunate) that you heard all of this but you heard it, and I will promise, here and now that I will help the lad from now on. Yes, when I heard that he left the car to go with you, I was going to punish him. That is the kind of thing that I have done when we were in the army. That was wrong and I apologise to you two as well. Yes please, Jennifer, could we have some coffee please?"

They all got their coffee and went into the lounge. As they were sitting comfortably Jack said, "Hugo, when we got back yesterday, we brought Miguel up here to give him some coffee and while we were talking he said that now that he is settling into that house he got, he is going to get his girlfriend and her parents over from Spain and I told him that if they do settle here and want to stay that I would help them to get a house. He told us then that you wouldn't like that, but I said that as it was our money we would do whatever we wanted. He said that that wouldn't please you. Now, from what we have heard, I will tell you now that we, Jennifer and I have regarded the pair of you as friends and we didn't know of any animosity between the pair of you. I take it from what we just heard in there that you won't be too upset at me helping them then?"

"No, of course not Jack," Hugo said, smiling now a little. "And those silly words about me breaking the contract that I said to you earlier in there. I do hope that you will ignore them as well. I would like it if we could all remain as friends and I will have a talk with Miguel later and tell him that I'll be trying to make things easier for him as we go along. Just as a matter of interest though, if you do have to go anywhere I will arrange for there to be two drivers so that only one can leave the car. That part that I said was correct. Booby traps are so easily fitted. Anyway, thank you, the pair of you and thank Alec when you see him again. Tell him that I have now seen some sense."

After a rather different and in some ways a disconcerting day, Jack and Jennifer had a much quieter afternoon. Jennifer didn't manage to get to try out her new recipes but probably Jack will eventually be able to benefit from them the next time that she does get going in that kitchen.

His Mum and Dad had by this time moved into their new flat and they did occasionally pop in to see Jack and Jennifer. Her parents were due to be moving in the week later so for Jennifer (and them) it was a rather hectic time. It needn't have been too hectic for Jennifer since she was remaining in her flat, but her parents were continuously telephoning her for some more exact measurements for some area or other of their flat and Jennifer then had to get her tape and go and get those measurements for them. They were all six of them excited and Jack and Jennifer were even more so because each of them knew that their parents were going to 'be on hand', as it were, once the moves were completed.

It was while Jennifer was doing one of her measurement 'runs' for her parents that Jack was alone in their flat and the phone rang. It was someone called Norman Brooks that the Prime Minister had put in charge of answering the queries that he had had from Jack.

The surveys were all going on well, he said. Yes, here were some areas that were largely sandy but there were also some considerable areas that some hard rock and other hard minerals that would need to be dealt with. In quite a few places it was anticipated that the pipeline could go underground, but due to some of the terrain, in some places, it may need to be carried above ground so that could involve some other expenses in erecting some structures to support it as it would be necessary.

It had been decided that the best place for the work to be carried out would be close to a place called Tadjoura, a coastal area that is actually in Djibouti but close enough to get to the inner parts of Ethiopia. Jack was informed that Ethiopia had very limited (if any) coastline itself but that Djibouti and Somalia (the countries close to Ethiopia did have coastline that could be used). The authorities in Djibouti had already agreed that they would permit the development there but they had also asked if they could benefit from it as well. Apparently, the governments of Somalia, Eritrea and Sudan who had heard stories about what was going to be done had all been asking why something like this could not be done in their country to try and solve their drought problems and the Ministers had said that they would make some enquiries.

The off shore wind turbine had now been ordered, the four desalination units had all been put on order, as had the pumps that would be needed. Jack was delighted with the things that were at last beginning to take place. The Ethiopian government had expressed their delight at what was being planned for their country and had agreed without any further discussion to provide some army support once any equipment started to be delivered, or even before that if Jack required it.

Jack knew full well that completion of the project could certainly take some time, but at least things were now beginning to start moving. The caller, Norman Brooks had also told Jack that it had now got to the point that some money would now have to be put in place for these many orders to be started and before any work could progress. He told Jack that he was now enquiring if there were any other notable crises that could benefit from anything that he could do (besides the ones that he had already mentioned in Eritrea, Sudan and Somalia) and that he would keep in touch. In the meantime, he gave Jack his telephone number and email address. Jack told him that the payment was quite a minor thing and he said that if each of the suppliers could let him have a pro forma invoice for the item (or the work) that was being started he would then make arrangements for immediate payment. Jack had by this time also appointed some accountants to manage his business interests and they were instructed to ensure that rapid payments would be made for anything that was to be used for the project.

Jack thought that once again he should get Hugo to get him a copy of the recording of the telephone conversation. He called Hugo and explained what he wanted and, once again, Hugo said that he would a copy of the recording and he would bring it to him. Hugo was fairly certain about where Jack would be taking the recording to but he went and got it for him anyway.

It didn't take very long and Hugo arrived at Jack's flat and produced the tape player once more, this time they both had called out for Jennifer and, with each of them with a coffee in their hands they went to the lounge to hear the recording. They had only just finished it and Jack said, "You know what we have to do now, don't you? Alec and Ray will want to hear this and considering the almost pitiful sum that the present project is costing me I think that we should set about doing the same for each of these countries. To hell with the Foreign Secretary I can take this straight to the Prime Minister, can't I and suggest a donation of one hundred billion, as I had suggested before. That will probably be enough to do all of these countries, won't it and still leave some spare cash over, then we shall have stopped a lot of suffering and provided a lot of bonus points for our friends, won't we?"

"Yes, Hugo replied, "But there may be other crises that are going to need some kind of support. You can't support all of them, can you? I suppose from what it is costing for this first project, one hundred Billion pounds would probably cover all of these countries and leave some money over but I do think that you need to exercise some care in how you do it."

"Look," Jennifer said, "You could get this project going and, if it starts to work how you think that it should work, then you could start work on the others. That would mean that you had a proven test case if the first one works, wouldn't you? Let's see what Alec and Ray think about it all first, eh?"

They had all finished their coffee so, together they went to the office and found Ray on the computer and Alec appearing to be marking in his notebook. "We've had another response from the government," Jack said. "Can you play it please Hugo?"

Hugo played the recording and both Alec and Ray stopped what they were doing and looked across at the three of them after they had heard it. "Well, at least that was a positive response, wasn't it Jack? Alec said. "It looks as though, being realistic, it could be a couple of hundred or even three hundred million pounds for the one project when it is all added up, doesn't it? That may settle the one country, but what if that pipeline wasn't long enough? What if it needs another three hundred miles? If it does all work then that's a good start but, what do you do about the other countries that they mentioned to you, Somalia, Sudan and Eritrea? If you wanted to do it, Jack, you could possibly do all the lot of them comfortably for the hundred billion pounds that you originally said, couldn't you? If it works, that would help them and, my goodness, it would certainly help us, I can tell you that. What happens though if it isn't quite as effective as you hope that it will be? What happens if some other crises turn up that also need some funds to help combat the problems? How will you decide which one has priority? You certainly have enough in your fund to cover them all and still leave enough to handle some other less costly crisis, don't you? Now, Jack, it seems to me that the decision is one that it will be you who will have to make. Yes. You could ask someone for some advice but no matter who advises you, it will, in the end, have to be your decision."

Jack was flabbergasted. He said nothing to any of them and very slowly, he turned away from the office and began to walk back to the lounge area.

"Jack," Jennifer called after him, "Where are you going? What are you going to do? Don't just walk away and leave us. We are all as concerned as you are, aren't we, Hugo? Aren't we Alec, and you Ray? Jack, you must talk. It doesn't matter who you talk to but you must talk and then we can listen and we may together be able to provide some answer to help you."

"Yes," Alec said, "You certainly picked wisely when you chose Jennifer as your wife, Jack. She has only stated what is necessary and you MUST listen and then, when you have listened, seek advice from those that you trust so that you can then try and arrive at some kind of sensible answer and potential solution to the problem."

Jack had reached the lounge area and he simply fell down onto one of the large chairs there. "Alec has just said that whatever happens with those poor people it has to be my decision, hasn't he? I never asked Peter to come back to me and to make me wealthy beyond any normal person's dreams, did I? What have I done so wrong that it seems that it is all being left to me to sort out these problems, isn't it? If the people starve, that is my fault. If the crops all fail and all of the animals die, that will be my fault. If the desalinated water proposal doesn't work then they could so easily die, the crops could so easily fail and the animals could all so easily die. I simply had the idea of taking the salt out of the water to try and solve their problems. I'm no expert, am I? Who would want to talk to me and try to help to make some suggestions if I say that part of the responsibility if it fails, is down to them as well as being down to me? This just isn't fair, is it? I honestly don't have a clue what to do."

"Jack," Hugo said, "You told the Foreign Minister that it had already been tried and tested in the United States, Saudi Arabia, Kuwait, Australia, Spain and Israel to name just a few countries. They were your words, Jack. If it has been tested in those countries and has been proved to work, why shouldn't it work in Ethiopia, Eritrea, Somalia and Sudan? Yes, some of these extra ones are larger countries and it may take perhaps a few more hundred miles of pipes but it should still work, shouldn't it? You had suggested take-off points at seventy-five-mile intervals with, where necessary some booster pumps. Yes, it may need more booster pumps and they may need some solar panels to get the power to make the booster pumps run but that's only a drop more cash to do that, isn't it? Where's the Jack that wanted to get some freedom now? You would be giving freedom perhaps to a few million if you get this work all done. Come on, Jack, can we have the other Jack back, the confident one? The one who can call up the Prime Minister and say, look mate, I want some advice."

Ray and Alec appeared in the lounge area and Ray said, "Look, Jack, your estimate that you bandied about to the Prime Minister came to about one hundred and forty-six million pounds, didn't it? For basic figures, Jack, do remember that it takes one **thousand** million pounds to make one billion pounds and it takes one **thousand** billion pounds to make one trillion pounds. You at present have in your fund just a bit over one **trillion** pounds Jack. **THINK.** Now, for your Ethiopian project, you didn't include any workshops or offices at the site and you probably forgot a number of other things so to try and accommodate your errors, multiply your figure of one hundred and forty-six million by three and that will come to four hundred and thirty-eight million pounds. That may not be exact by any means but, let's say that it is OK as a working guess. So you now want to consider doing about the same for some other countries, such as Eritrea, Somalia, and Sudan so that is four countries so multiply the sum that you guessed for Ethiopia by four and that then becomes one thousand seven hundred and fifty-two million pounds. That is **one billion** seven hundred and fifty-two million pounds using the figures that I first of all explained to you. Now, your initial donation figure that you took straight out of thin air when you said that you would donate didn't you? That was one **HUNDRED** billion pounds. The sum that you have for doing all four countries is a mere pittance against that sum, isn't it? Now, where is that Jack who could talk to the controller and the allocator as though they were mere rubbish figures? I would like to see that person reappear and realise that he needs to be setting up a business and get it going to run all of these various projects. You can't expect any government to do that job. They could waste more than that with no trouble at all, but they probably wouldn't get the job done, would they? Yes, you may ask for their assistance, as you have done, but stop saying to Jennifer that you want to escape from the estate and grow up, and start running all of this like a business. What did you say to Stewart Robinson about the lists at the warehouse? You said that the person who did that should get on the floor and see what things are like. Have you visited any of these countries? No, you haven't, have you? Hugo, there has been putting his cousin down for years now. He and you believe that you are helping one another. If so, why hasn't he suggested to you that you visit these countries and talk to their leaders if necessary and then, if you are going to fund the operations, they will fete you almost as a God? Get up man and start to think as did the Jack of old that we knew."

"My goodness," Hugo said, "I think that we've been told off Jack. I know that you have but he also included me in it all as well and the thing is that he's probably quite right in what he has said. Jack, we must start to make some plans to visit each of these countries and it may be a good idea when you are doing that you need to be accompanied by your Prime Minister. If he thinks that he can get some glory by hanging onto your shirt tails, he will be there, I can tell you that. You can tell them what you intend to do and give them the sum of up to One hundred Billion Pounds to get their problems solved and they will all want to know you. Yes, Jennifer is your wife and she also must go with you. If I am permitted to, I would also like to go with you as well. To make you happier, I could leave Miguel in charge while I'm away, couldn't I? If necessary, you can charter an entire airliner and you have already done that before when you were on holiday with your family, haven't you? So, you know how to do some of these things, now start to do something. Think big Jack, not small like nipping out to go on a trip on a bus. You are intending to solve some major drought and famine problems for the world. You can afford to do that, can't you? Alec and Ray will no doubt be working overtime to make sure that they keep the fund total at just over one Trillion pounds, won't you Ray and Alec?"

"Thank goodness, at least one of them has got some sense, hasn't he" Alec said. "By the way, Ray, I liked the presentation that you did when you started on them this time. I think that this time we are going to get somewhere, don't you?"

Alec and Ray seemed to realise that they weren't needed there for the moment and they just disappeared. Jack appeared to have just woken up and Hugo and Jennifer also had started to realise that they were going to make a start on getting the entire job on its way for the four countries that they had mentioned. If there were similar problems with some other countries, then there would be other very wealthy people who would no doubt want to make a name for themselves.

Chapter Sixteen

Jack had picked up the telephone and he had input the number to contact the Prime Minister. The phone only rang for a few minutes and the Prime Minister answered.

"Good day to you Prime Minister," Jack said, "It's Jack Dawkins here and I've had a look at the report that your assistant Norman Brooks sent to me and, from that, I have decided that, with your support sir, I would like to try and deal with the droughts and famines of all of the countries that he mentioned, namely, Ethiopia, Eritrea, Somalia and Sudan. Now I and my staff realised that there were quite a few bits and pieces missing from all of our rough costings that we've been looking at so I have decided that if I do donate up to **one hundred Billion Pounds**, (as I originally said that I would,) that will probably be enough to provide a similar result to what we had been speaking of before for all four countries (and leave a fair sum of cash over for other projects). You and I believe and know that I can comfortably cover the cost of all four of the country's problems for just over two Billion pounds. To do this I do feel, however, that a visit by both me and your good self to these countries would enable a much firmer relationship and footing between those countries and our own to be achieved. What would you think about such a visit, sir?"

"Oh, most certainly Jack," The Prime Minister replied. "I do believe that the relief of so much suffering could only do some good for them and our own country. When were you thinking of making the visit then?"

"Oh, I can't see any great advantage in delaying it, do you sir?" Jack replied, quite grandly. "I would imagine either this week or, at the very latest, next week, wouldn't you, sir? I have now started a new office here at my estate to begin making some plans for such projects and I have placed the orders for quite a few of the things that we believed that we may need. Of course, with some of the other countries that we shall cover, the three hundred-mile pipelines may have to be extended somewhat and of course, none of us thought about the offices and maintenance buildings that would be needed at each of the start-off points for each project, had we? They are now being planned by me immediately. I had already said that I would fund up to **two hundred Billion pounds** sir but if our costings do sensibly indicate that it does need a little more than the simple two Billion pounds that my calculations have so far indicated, I feel sure that my upper limit of this donation will not be breached in any way, wouldn't you sir?"

"Oh, Jack, I can see the need for that urgency." The Prime Minister replied, now getting quite excited. "If you could just hold things until tomorrow I will see if any of my appointments can be postponed or changed in some way and then yes, perhaps an immediate visit would be advantageous. I shall of course also have to make arrangements to contact the government leaders of each of these countries. I am sure that they too will be impressed with the urgency that you are applying to the projects. Perhaps I could call you again tomorrow morning and then we could finalise some details."

Jennifer, Hugo along with Alec and Ray had been sitting near Jack when he had made that phone call and, as the call ended, they all collectively clapped him for the way that he had handled the Prime Minister. "It's like I once said to you before Jack," Hugo said, "By the time that the first one of the projects is finished I'll lay bets that you will be entitled Sir Jack Dawkins!"

"Don't you be daft Hugo," Jack said. "They don't do things like that to ordinary folks like us, do they, Jennifer?"

"Oh, I don't know," Jennifer said, laughing at Jack, squirming in his seat at the thoughts of having to be a personality again. "That would make me Lady Jennifer Dawkins, wouldn't it? Hmm, Yes, I think that I could manage that. I'm not quite sure though what our parents would have to say."

"Personally, I think that I'd agree with Hugo," Ray said. "It would be the politically correct thing to do and the Prime Minister wouldn't want to miss out on a bit more glory for doing the right thing, would he?"

"Well, I spent quite a bit of my working time in France and Spain, as you know, Ray," Alec said."But it does sound as though it could be a British sort of thing, doesn't it?"

"Look at it another way," Ray said, "If the Prime Minister comes up with a few more crises for Jack to attack as he has done with this one, they may even be giving him a seat in the house of Lords, don't you think? I mean, he will have done well with these four countries so they may even be offering to him the same sort of honours in those countries as well, don't you think?"

By this time, Jennifer, Hugo, Alec and Ray were rolling around laughing at Jack's face. He was going all shades of red at the thoughts of what they had been suggesting for him. He had admitted to them all several times before that he didn't like publicity and what they had been suggesting was to him now an almost unbearable amount of publicity.

"Mind you," Alec continued, "If they discovered that he'd made all of his money by dealing with ghosts to do some illegal insider trading over the past few years they may even be thinking of giving him a few years in Dartmoor prison. Oh, the poor lad if they did that to him. I believe that nowadays, Dartmoor prison is something of a tourist attraction so the politicians would be making some more money by charging the public to come and have a look at him. 'Jack the lad' they may call him, don't you think?" Alec continued, "We are all only having you on Jack. No one knows what the future will bring (except us ghosts who can nip forward a bit now and then). And if they did decide to honour you, I feel sure that you would have to accept it with good grace, wouldn't you? You've handled being the richest man in the world, haven't you? You've handled talking to the Prime Minister, so you will handle whatever they do throw at you, Jack. We believe in you, all of us. No matter what happens, we will all be here for you and you know that, don't you?"

"Look, Jack, I've known that you were a good person for a heck of a long time," Jennifer said, "And I feel quite sure that you will be able to handle whatever does happen so don't you worry. As Alec says, we will all be here for you, won't we?"

"You lot are all mad," Jack said. "Alright, so I've asked the Prime Minister to go to see the leaders of these countries. You watch, if anyone is going to get the kudos, you can bet that it will be the politicians, not ordinary people like me. Anyway, he may ring back and say that it isn't going to be convenient. You hadn't thought of that, had you?"

"Are you suggesting that a senior politician wouldn't want to dash in if there was a hint of a chance of some strong publicity?" Alec said. "Jack, that kind of politician hasn't been born yet. It's the publicity that gets them the votes, it's the votes that keep them in power and most of them are all seeking to get more and more power, aren't they?"

It was the following morning and Jack had only just finished his first cup of coffee and the phone rang. He hadn't a clue who it possibly might be ringing him so early in the morning, but he answered it and it was the Prime Minister. "Good morning Jack," said the Prime Minister. "I've had some replies from those countries that you have included now, following my messages to them. They were all so delighted that you are also considering offering some aid to their countries and yes, they would all welcome a visit just as soon as we can. I have told them that since you don't know their countries much yet you possibly may need some more detailed information about their coastlines, and the affected areas that could benefit from irrigation. They had all promised whatever aid they may be able to find to help you, and they say that by the time we arrive, they should indeed have managed to get some survey reports to help you with your decisions. Now, when exactly were you thinking of going there, Jack? I do have a few things for this week that I cannot put off, but I could certainly be free for next Monday if that is going to be alright for you. Who would you like to include in your party?"

"Oh, there would be myself and of course my wife Jennifer, plus I think that it would be useful for me if I could include my aide and head of security, Hugo Moncado, I have found him to be far more useful than just the leader of my security guards. His family connections with the Spanish Royal family have also on occasion proved to be quite useful for me. I can't see any need for any others. And how many people do you think that you would need Mr Prime Minister?" Jack asked.

"Oh, as you suggest, we could perhaps keep the numbers down to a more manageable level. Perhaps two or three of my aides and secretaries should be adequate. I will try and see if we can get allocated an RAF aircraft to take us there. I feel quite sure that for an event such as this that may prove to be, it would be far more than sensible, don't you? Perhaps if I should arrange for us to depart from

Northolt, with a departure at ten-thirty a.m. should be adequate. Would that all be satisfactory for you? I take it that you would manage the transport to Northolt alright, or would you prefer that I send out a car for you?"

"No, I'm sure that we can manage to get to Northolt quite easily and so I shall look forward to seeing you on Monday next sir, ten-thirty a.m. at Northolt." The line closed at that and Jack knew that he would get Hugo to get a copy of the recording for them and also make arrangements for a car and driver to be available to take them to Northolt air base.

Hugo responded just as Jack had known that he would and he told Jack that as he had already spoken to Miguel and told him that while Jack, Jennifer and himself were away going to the East African countries, he was to be in charge and responsible for the security at the estate. This had pleased Miguel and Hugo knew that he had made a start perhaps on righting some of the wrongs that had been done within his and Miguel's family all those years ago by his own Grandfather. Alec, Hugo thought, would be proud of him for having tried to make a start on correcting those wrongs of his family.

Hugo took the tape of the recording to Jack and together, along with Jennifer they took it so that Alec and Ray also could hear what had been arranged. Both Alec and Ray were delighted when they heard the recording and that the trips out to see the leaders of these countries were well underway. Jack also assured them that the company that he had started to oversee the completion of the project were all quite good, and well-selected people that he had chosen to minimise any delays in getting the four projects completed. He explained to them that although his fund could adequately cover all that was needed for the four projects, he was now making it clear to the leaders of these countries (when he met them on this next trip) that they too should play their part by, where it was needed, extending the pipelines to irrigate as much land as was needed beyond the pipe lines that he was going to get installed for their peoples. This, both Alec and Ray thought was a very sensible and useful idea because it did demonstrate that, if it can be done, they then should be quite prepared themselves to fund any further extensions that were needed in order to protect the well-being of their people.

Jennifer was also very pleased at the way that Jack had at last accepted that he could get some things going again and she was also very excited about this new trip that they were going to be making. She knew that for Jack (accepting that it was necessary for the work in completing the projects) it would be so much more for him to write about and include in his travel directory. That had, of course, always been a major project in his life, from well before any of this business with the ghosts had changed his life.

Jack, along with Hugo went to see the new department that he had made that was to oversee the build-up of materials, skills and transportation of all of the needed articles for the projects. Jack had also told Hugo that since he had now had to become involved in far more than just the security, he too should change his work description and that in future he should be known as the Project

Controller for the Dawkins Project Company Ltd. (He had, without telling Hugo, had a new company formally created and formed using that name). Hugo was surprised and, naturally quite grateful for the honour that Jack was placing on him. He suggested that in view of this new title and workload, he should perhaps go and have a few words with Miguel and explain that he was now promoted to being the head of security for the Dawkins Project Company Ltd. This, Jack knew may be difficult for Hugo but he had quite definitely seen a change in the way that Hugo was dealing with Miguel and he just hoped that he, their combined employer, would appreciate properly what he thought of the pair of them. After all, they were both now regarded as his friends, weren't they?

Chapter Seventeen

In fact, Hugo's attitude had most certainly changed and he was trying, in any way that he could, to correct some of the wrong things that his Grandfather and his father had done all those years ago. The opportunity to enhance the position of Miguel within the business, was, to Hugo a heaven-sent chance and he made sure that Miguel fully understood that he now believed that they should make their kinship become a thing for them both to enjoy and celebrate. However, now that Miguel had been promoted to become the head of security, Hugo didn't believe that it would be correct for Miguel to drive them to Northolt airport since as Miguel was now acknowledged as the head of security, it wouldn't be right and proper that he was going to be absent from the site while they were simply going to go and get on a 'plane to go to some other countries. Miguel though did appreciate the way that Hugo explained all of that to him and he said that he would ensure that there was a good and reliable driver to take them to the airport and if Hugo could give him an arrival time for their return, he would similarly arrange for a well tested and secure member of staff to be there to meet them and drive them back to the estate.

In the meantime, Jennifer had been phoning both her Mum and Dad and Jack's Mum and Dad to tell them that that she and Jack, along with Hugo and the Prime Minister (with some of his aides and secretaries) were all going to be going over on some state visits to some of the East African countries so that Jack could tie up this aid that he was planning for them all. She was excited and both sets of parents were excited, far more so than had Jack been when it had all been settled. He had eventually come around to the idea that perhaps it would be necessary after all. Initially, he had believed, for some foolish reason generated within his own mind, that the allocator, whoever that had been, would have been the one facing all of that publicity. At that time it hadn't really dawned on him that as the allocator would themselves be a ghost, it would have been totally impossible for that one to have met any mortals, Prime Minister or commoner!

The time for the arrival of the Monday departure was passing quickly and Jack was becoming more and more nervous at the thought that it would after all have to be he who would need to be doing the talking to the leaders of these nations. He knew what he had said to Alec and Ray about how he was going to insist that they must also start to contribute some effort to extend the areas of land that would be well irrigated beyond that which he was doing for them. Yes, he would, no doubt have some other experts to back him up, but in the first instance; it was going to have to be him; Jack Dawkins himself, who now, it appeared, would have to be the hard talker.

At last, Monday came around and Jack, Jennifer and Hugo were ready to depart. They had a small amount of luggage and

Miguel had chosen as their driver, Manuel (Another of the security team that Jack and Jennifer had known from their first connection in Spain with his security group). Jack was pleased that it was one of the men that he knew fairly well since the security team had grown, to meet the needs and demands of the protection needed; some of the new members were now quite unknown to Jack.).

They were due to be at Northolt in time for the flight to leave at ten-thirty am so Hugo, being Hugo had allowed enough time for the journey (plus a little more, just in case they ran into any hold-ups on their way there). His timing, as it happened was once again, quite accurate and they drove into the air base gates at ten o'clock am exactly. They were guided to where they were to meet the Prime Minister and his entourage and Manuel dealt with their luggage (such as there was) Hugo knew that at this point, as they were now within an RAF base, security should be more than adequate for Jack and Jennifer.

The Prime Minister, meeting Jack again (the first time since he had paid a visit to Jack and Jennifer's estate, along with the Foreign Secretary) and since he was now beginning to realise just how much kudos Jack's action was going to have, he was almost servile in his treatment of this honoured guest for these meetings. Eventually, the various pieces of luggage were loaded and all of the travellers boarded the plane and took their seats. It was going to be quite a lengthy journey so they all tried to get as comfortable as they could.

The Prime Minister told Jack that since Ethiopia had been the first country to have been mentioned when he was considering giving aid, they had made arrangements for their first stop to be there. The leader of the Ethiopian government would be meeting them there and, as the site where the desalination was going to start from was in Djibouti, the leader of that country also would be in attendance. To try and rationalise the visit, the Prime Minister continued, that the leaders of Sudan, Somalia and Eritrea would all be attending the meeting since all of these countries did suffer from the same (or somewhat similar) problems and were all hoping that Jack may favour them with some aid. Jack said that he believed that making the arrangements in such a way was admirable since once they had managed to get the basic points sorted out, there would obviously be quite a number of specifics which may require further visits to examine the sites being selected in the different countries. That being said though, Jack said that he felt that the leaders of these countries could each nominate a more suitable site for the project to start from and that he would anticipate that they then would be able to make the arrangements for some surveys of these critical areas. Jack said that although he expected the checks to be done, he would expect the countries themselves to do their part and provide some support. Jack also pointed out to the Prime Minister that his original intention was to provide aid for one country, but now it had grown enormously to include five countries. He said that he did hope that the British Government may be able to assist in some of the work, if only by arranging a 'smoothing' of any diplomatic issues that may appear while they were getting the projects underway. He also suggested that the Prime Minister could perhaps take advantage of what his aid to these countries was doing for the British Government itself to further develop relations with these governments. He said that although he was in no way a politician himself, there must be many ways in which Britain could benefit from a close relationship with each and every one of the countries. Each country, he continued, must, in some way have some produce, or some services that could be of benefit to Britain and then, his efforts to help these countries would also be providing some help to our own Great Britain.

The Prime Minister said how impressed he was that Jack should have thought of any of that since it would quite naturally be of benefit to Britain to develop stronger ties with some of these countries, both political and commercial. Jennifer and Hugo were quite astounded at the way that Jack had begun to make the spiel to someone like the Prime Minister about how he wanted some benefits to come back to Britain. Neither of them had ever heard him talk in such a way and they were both quite amazed at the way that he was getting the Prime Minister to believe that he was an ardent Nationalist of Britain.

From the time since they had met, Jennifer had never heard any kind of Nationalistic fervour from Jack and she just began to wonder where all of this was coming from and was equally amazed that their Prime Minister appeared to be accepting all that Jack had been saying. Hugo, being Spanish didn't know as much about Jack's former ideas about Nationalism, but he did find it strange since he had never, in all of the talks that he had had in the past with Jack heard anything at all that would indicate such a strong allegiance.

Jack, of course, was talking simply off of the top of his head and was saying the kinds of things that Alec and Ray had been getting him used to so that he would be well prepared for this first visit. Neither Jennifer nor Hugo had known that Alec and Ray had been doing this for some time in a few visits to the office so, to both of them, what Jack was saying were words coming straight out of his head and, to be perfectly honest, they were both impressed that the Jack that they both thought that they knew so well could be so very well versed in international diplomatic fervour.

The flight did indeed take some time and as they were flying a little lower over Ethiopia, the pilot came across the loudspeakers and said that if they looked out now, they would see some of the areas of Ethiopia that had been devastated by the drought. They all looked and were quite amazed at the dry parched looking land that they were passing over. They had been forewarned of the expected time of landing at Addis Ababa by the pilot and they were indeed on time when they made their arrival and they were all quite ready for it. As the 'plane taxied round to the main airport buildings, looking out of the windows of the aircraft they could see a mass of people approaching, along with what looked like a formal military band. Jack, poor Jack, who didn't like the idea of publicity at all, cringed in his seat. He knew that it would happen, but even so, it was something that he just did not like the thought of.

The 'plane came to a standstill and the boarding ladders were all put in place and then they began to move down the 'plane to be ready to get out and meet the crowd of people who were going to be representing the leaders of all five of the countries that were wanting to receive the money to start the aid work. Jack let the Prime Minister lead the way and then he followed, accompanied by Jennifer, his wife and then Hugo, as his main aide. The Prime minister's aides and secretaries followed at the rear. Jennifer, unlike Jack, was thoroughly enjoying all of the thrills of being welcomed in such a manner by some people that, at least Jack, Jennifer and Hugo had never before met. Jack, of course, was the celebratory that they were waiting for. He was the person who had decided to try and aid their people by turning the seawater from the coastal area into a much more useful and life-giving fluid far into the centres of these countries. The military band began to play some music that would welcome these visitors. They played the British National Anthem and several other tunes that Jack remembered hearing before, but he didn't know what any of them were called. The music ended and then it was a case of the introductions. Jack was just hoping that someone from their party would be able to remember the names because he was soon lost after having had to meet so many people, and all at once. Jennifer squeezed his arm and he remembered that at least he had got Jennifer with him. That was quite a relief and he also hoped that Hugo may perhaps be better than he at dealing with some of these people.

They were escorted to a group of waiting limousines that were to carry them, with an escort of both police and military, all of the way to their hotel for the night. Apparently, it had been decided (probably also by the Prime Minister agreeing), that because of the length of the flight that they had just had, they would be able to have a night of rest before the meetings started. The cavalcade of limousines carried them off, escorted by both a military and a police escort to a large hotel in what was obviously a premium site in Addis Ababa and, after getting out of the cars they were escorted into the hotel where the management was waiting in an almost servile attitude to their exalted guests. Jack and Jennifer were taken to the rooftop apartment at the hotel, an absolutely massive apartment and they were told that full room service would be available for them or, alternatively, the dining room may be accessed if they so desired. Neither of them was very hungry, but they were both quite tired. It had been a long day; and a long flight; so they simply turned in for the night. They just hoped that Hugo had also got a good room.

The following morning, Jack was up and about quite early and after making a quick call, breakfasts were brought up to their apartment and they had been told that cars would be arriving at 9:00 am to take them to the meeting place. Once again at 9 o'clock, a cavalcade of limousines appeared to take them to their meeting place. Once again they had both a military and a police escort and they were taken into the centre of Addis Ababa when the meetings were going to take place. In his car, he was relieved to find that he had both Jennifer and Hugo with him. He had with them in his car some leader from one of the countries, but thankfully for Jack, no one apparently was expected to be saying a lot at that time. The Prime Minister had been escorted to a different car and he was, Jack believed, with the Prime Minister (or president, if that was his title) of Ethiopia. It wasn't a particularly long drive and with the military escort clearing the way for them it didn't take very long at all to get to their destination. They did arrive and then, once again, they left their cars and joined what was, to Jack's mind, a procession of people into the large central building where the meetings were to take place.

Chapter Eighteen

Jennifer leaned a little closer to Jack and whispered to him, "You do know Jack, don't you? They will be expecting you to make quite a few speeches once we get into the main meeting hall for the shindig to begin. If you can speak there as you did with the Prime Minister on the 'plane that would be terrific. That was so impressive and I have every confidence in you. You must remember that it is your money that you are going to spend. You are the Celebratory, not they."

"I realise that Jennifer," Jack whispered back to her, "But I just wish that I had been prompted a bit more about this by Alec and Ray, as I was for how to talk to the Prime Minister. Somehow, we'll get through it all. I know that but it's just this thing of having to be looked at and to have to shake hands with so many people. I just can't remember their names, can you?"

"No, I can't remember all of their names," Jennifer replied, "But the Prime Minister's aides will have all the details to try and help you out. One way would be to not try and make your point to any single one of them. Make your point to them all as a group. After all, it is they who all want you to help them. You don't need them to help you, do you? You have the money, far more than they have. You now can be quite bossy if you want. Just be forceful about insisting that they play their part once you have got the main pipelines in and then that it is they who then have to extend the irrigation. I think that the Prime Minister understood you and agreed with you. He'll probably say something along those lines to help you as well, anyway, won't he? By the way, you never said that Alec and Ray had been prompting yu on how to speak to the Prime Minister, did you?"

"I only hope so," Jack replied, as they seemed to have reached the end point of the procession and were all starting to be guided to places around a massive table that seemed to fill the room. Jack was pleased to see that he had Jennifer seated next to him at one side and Hugo at the other side of him.

Hugo leaned across to Jack and in a very low voice said, "Give them hell, Jack. You're the donor, they're the recipients. Remember that they have to do as you tell them to do things, or that you may have to withdraw your support to any of the people here that disagree with you."

It wasn't a very long break before the meeting started. To Jack's relief, the Prime Minister had mentioned to Jack that he would open the meeting and quite briefly, he would say, more or less, what Jack was intending, and then he would introduce Jack to the meeting. To Jack, it was a relief anyway that it wasn't he who would have to start the meeting. The Prime Minister did start things and then he said that for them to all perhaps understand a little better, he introduced and welcomed Mr Jack Dawkins to the meeting.

Jack realised that he wouldn't just be able to speak from where he was sitting, he knew that he would have to stand up. Alec and Ray had previously told him that some of the people may have only a limited understanding of English and that he should speak, firmly as though he knew all about what he was going to tell them, but that he should speak perhaps just a little slower than he usually did. That, they had suggested, would enable those who were interpreting to be able to get the fullest impact of what he had to say.

Having composed himself a little Jack began, "Ladies and Gentlemen, my name is Jack Dawkins and as you are no doubt aware I am not from your country, but I can most certainly feel compassion and sorrow for the suffering that so many of your people have been subjected to; due to a severe drought and a subsequent famine. Now, I am not a farmer and therefore I am unable to speak with any detail about the problems that you and your people have suffered from. I have, during my life been fortunate enough to be able to drink clean water whenever I have wanted to and I have never known a time when I have been drastically short of food. For now, just nicely over a decade, I have been fortunate enough to see my fortunes grow to some rather unusual and some rather impressive levels and I do just happen to have some considerable wealth. From there, I now believe that I must try to assist some of your people to begin to have a fuller and much more settled life. With my wealth, I do intend, providing that the leaders of your countries agree with my aims, to fund the establishment of sea-based wind turbines and some land-based solar panels to generate electricity. Now you may say that it is not electricity that the people need, but water and food. With that electricity from the turbines and the solar panels though, it is my aim and intention to provide some large desalination units to make use of the plentiful water in the oceans that surround you. Now, you may again claim that the shortage of water is not near to the coasts, but far, far inland. It is my aim then that the desalinated water will be pumped, using some very large pumps (powered by electricity from the turbine and the solar panels) to pump that water several hundred miles into your countries; so that it might enable irrigation of the land to help to grow crops, water to help your livestock to prosper; to help your people who tend to the crops and to care for the animals to live and drink clean water when they need to. Now, I intend to take the pipelines of water some long distances of miles inland and hopefully, it will enable some internal lakes to be created, possibly some rivers and for the land to become good, wholesome and fertile once more. Now, one part that I do insist upon is that the leaders of your countries should also play their part in this plan by extending pipelines and installing more irrigation further beyond where the pipelines that I am going to lay will end. This is, I believe a reasonable request, nay, it is from me a demand and, if any of your leaders see a reason why they should not play their part, do let them speak now and then it can be arranged that no pipeline project need be given to those countries. I would also like, and expect each country to provide some support, military if you like, to protect the equipment, the work and the people who will be doing this work for you. Some of the items may take some time for the manufacture, erection and installation to complete the projects. Other items, such as the pipelines themselves should commence quite soon (indeed, as soon as we can get the pipes delivered to the sites that you choose as the starting point) and I expect your cooperation in getting the land prepared and the pipes installed. The pipes must be in place anyway, mustn't they, before any water may be desalinated or pumped. I have already made a start on my part at achieving my aim. In England, for my part I have already started a team of people to work and who are at this moment sourcing materials and the skills necessary to get these pipelines underway. For the laying of the pipes, some labour may be required (as well as the machinery that I will get sent to help with the work) and I do hope to be able to offer some of that work to some of your people, I do assure you that they shall be paid a fair payment for that work that they do and they shall be well fed while they are doing that work. In Britain, we do not support or tolerate slavery so I shall be paying and feeding the workers. I do not see any need for tardiness in getting the jobs started; worked on and completed; so that all of your people can benefit from having the basic necessity of clean and wholesome water available to them. Ladies and Gentlemen, please let me know your decisions on whether or not you would like a pipeline to be installed for your country. To carry out this work it is my aim, initially to donate two billion pounds sterling, and I assure you that if any costs do exceed that sum, I shall quite personally make every effort to ensure that these pipelines are completed. These plans, in my opinion, need not be thwarted simply due to some monetary tardiness. Thank you, everyone, as many people will tell you, I am not a speaker so I shall now sit down and I would like to hear any comments or remarks that you may have."

Jack did sit down and Jennifer patted his arm and said, "That was quite a marvellous speech there Jack, especially from someone who told me that he was never a public speaker."

"I would also compliment you on your speech, Jack," Hugo said. "It would surprise me if they don't start to pile the treasures of office on you right away."

There was a general hubbub of noise in the room and then, one after another, the five leaders of the five different countries stood and made their thanks and gave a commitment that they would most certainly both extend the pipelines and ensure that workers were made available after Jack's initial work was completed.

The Prime Minister again stood up and he began to close the meeting with the assurances that the British Government would assist wherever and whenever they could to get these projects started, worked on and completed. He thanked the people at the meeting for their support and said that he felt sure that Mr Dawkins may have to return a few times to get some of the minor details sorted out. He thanked everyone for their support and suggested that they close the meeting. The Prime Minister sent one of his aides across to speak to Jack and he said that arrangements had been made for them to have accommodation for the night at the same hotel and in the same rooftop apartment and that a banquet was being held in their honour in respect to the work that he had already put in place.

The Banquet will be held in the next room to the meeting room. He also said that the Prime Minister had said that he was very proud to have been enabled to be present at such a wonderful occasion and that he felt that Jack should accept the honours that these five countries now wished to bestow on him.

"As the aide left them to return to the Prime Minister, Hugo nudged Jack and said, "What did I tell you, Jack? They think here at least in this country that you are some marvel worth praising, don't they? I'll just bet you that when we do get back to Britain they'll start clamouring for the same for you there as well. You just wait and see."

"Oh, give up Hugo," Jack said, squirming at the thought of having to face a lot of publicity. "They just want me to spend my money and help to get their people's problems sorted, don't they, Jennifer?" he asked.

"No, Jack," Jennifer said, "With the kind of reception that you have been getting here, I do think that what Hugo is saying could well come true once we get home. Anyway, we have to go to this banquet first, don't we? I've never been to a banquet before. Have you been to one before, Hugo? Oh, I suppose that with your connections to the Spanish Royal Family, I suppose that you only had this kind of thing on one day of the week didn't you?"

"Yes, I have been to one or two banquets, Jennifer; and they can be quite a thing. I still don't know where you get this idea of me being connected to the Spanish Royal Family though. At the banquet, they may start to offer you food though that may be a delicacy in their country but it may be something abhorrent to your idea of food. I'm told that if you don't eat the speciality food of the banquet you may well have insulted them. Just think about that then, Jack." Hugo went on, laughing at his friend and boss.

"Oh, yes," Jennifer continued, picking up on Hugo's trend to get Jack going. "Don't they sometimes give you sheep's eyes boiled in something as the main treat of the evening? Oh, you'll soon get used to being a celebratory Jack," she continued.

"You lot, you are all being rotten to me, aren't you," Jack said, quite aggrieved that his wife and his friend who he felt sure were just trying to get him going. They were succeeding though, as well!

They thought that they were quite alone with their chatter but as they were talking, one man came up to Jack and said, "The President of Ethiopia has asked sir, if you would care to please sit with him at the banquet. Your wife and your aide as well sir will be most welcome. He feels that as this meeting is being held in his country he should make you as welcome as he can sir."

"Thank you, sir," Jack replied, "Yes, we would all be delighted to be the guest of the President, wouldn't we, Jennifer," he said, smiling at his wife as he said it. "Oh, he said to the President's aide, my aide is Hugo Moncado who is a somewhat more distant relative from the Spanish Royal Family. I feel sure that the President would welcome any ties that he can make with someone so well connected, wouldn't he?"

"Oh, yes sir," the aide replied, "I shall of course inform the President of Mr Moncado and his connection to the Spanish Royalty sir. Would all three of you care to accompany me and I will guide you to the seating area for the banquet.

They all stood up and they followed the aide as he led them through one doorway and into yet another massive room that was all laid out ready for the banquet. He took them along the rows and rows of seats until he reached the centre of the top table where the President was waiting to greet them. Jack noted that there did appear to be quite a few 'heads of state' quite close to where they were going to be seated, quite obviously they would be the main people from each of the countries that he was going to try and aid with his water pipelines. Jack, realising that everyone appeared to be watching him, he just smiled at those who he could see that were fairly close and then commented to the President that the event had brought them a lot of visitors to their country. "I do hope," Jack said, "That they and the entourages of all of these people are all only too willing to support the efforts that you have put into arranging this meeting. I can only say that I shall be even more pleased when all of the countries involved have finally managed to create some fertile lands with which to aid your people and your countries."

"Thank you, Mr Dawkins," The President replied, "And I do hope that you may wish to return to our countries once the work is completed so that you will be able to see the many, many benefits of your initiative. These constant droughts and famines that we have continued to have from time to time have most certainly hit the people of our countries. Yes, we are indeed blessed in that we do have a beautiful country to live in, but if the cost to that beauty is so often the destruction of so many people it can have so many negative effects on the total way of life of so many of our peoples."

Hugo, Jack noted was, or appeared to be in some deep and earnest conversation with the people sitting next to him while Jennifer was, it would appear, captivating some of those who were next to her, both with her looks and with her what appeared to be very witty conversations that she was having with them. Jack was so pleased that both Jennifer and Hugo had taken so well to this event. He still was concerned though about what Hugo had been saying about the possibility of him being honoured by the country. Yes, he did want to help them, but he didn't want what he regarded as the glitter of being a personality and having to face so much publicity. In general, the banquet did seem to be proving to be quite a success to those who had been invited, but Jack, being Jack had yet another thought and it was just in his nature that he had to say something.

Jack turned and said to the President, "This is a somewhat marvellous banquet that has been arranged Mr President, but what of the state of your country as a whole? It was the fact that so many of your people were starving due to a famine, yes, caused by the drought that initially caught my attention; that made me want to help to alleviate the suffering. But when there is a famine and some of your people are now dying from a lack of food, does it not appear to be somewhat ironic that such a banquet as this one being served here, can be so easily arranged, and at a time when so many more of your people may be now dying due to a lack of basic food? I know that I am a visitor here sir, but I would most certainly welcome any observations that you may wish to give."

"Mr Dawkins," The President replied, "I can only agree with all that you are saying and yes, it is quite deplorable that a banquet such as this is now being served while so many of our people are starving. Perhaps it is somewhat insensitive to arrange a celebratory banquet at such a time. However, a part of the reason for the banquet was as a thank you to your good self for offering a lifeline to perhaps try and eliminate future droughts and famines. The food that is being served here Mr Dawkins is, I do assure you, not a kind of food that so many of our people could easily accept and digest. Yes, I would agree that it does seem to be quite unfair when we are feeding so many people here while some of our people are starving. We do, I assure you, make every effort to feed these people but with a kind of food that they can more easily digest. I believe that in your country, many people can eat anything, some items appearing to others as almost inedible items while other people would welcome such items. It is, in a way, a similar thing with our country and if we did try and feed these foods to some of these people it may, just may, I say, make them quite ill."

"In that case Mr President," Jack said. "If you do have a kind of food that they can eat with no harm to their systems, may we ensure that they do get that kind of food within the next few days?

To try and help with this, I shall on my return to the UK make a further and quite separate donation of one million pounds to purchase plenty of the food that those people need. If that is not enough, please let me know and I shall increase the donation. Would you equally be able to ensure that there is a good and equitable distribution of the food? We do hear sometimes of there being a mad scramble for food, some people getting a lot of food and others getting almost nothing at all. We must, together try and address such problems, Mr President."

"Mr Dawkins, "The President said, "Your generosity appears to know no bounds. You are already now providing the much-needed aid to make our lands more fertile and useful and now, you are offering a vast sum of money in itself to help feed the starving. Mr Dawkins, I must offer you my most sincere thanks from the bottom of my heart. I shall most certainly make sure that there is some order put in place for the distribution of the food. Perhaps when you do return to see the completion of some of the work we may find some way of giving you the honours that you most certainly deserve."

Jennifer, sitting at the side of Jack heard some of this and she nudged Jack and said, "You are just trying to impress Alec and Ray, aren't you? No matter, I'll just bet that they will be pleased with a touch like that, don't you? Just remember as well what Hugo has told you, if you do carry on doing things like that they will only want to pile even more honours onto you, you know. If they do, I'll be quite happy to bask in your glory so now you know? I don't mind you being a celebratory, do I?"

The banquet continued for some time and then the Prime Minister made his way across to see Jack. "Jack," The Prime Minister said, "The events of the past few days have been an example of just how things should be done. Your speech to the leaders of these countries included all of the various points that you had made and I do feel that you will be very much a favoured son of all of these countries, not to say of your own country, once the words of how things have gone along here gets out. My goodness, it has outshone any of the good deeds of the very wealthy American people who do try to create some level playing fields. I must say, I do feel honoured to have met you. I understand also that the hotel they have put us into is a very special hotel in the centre of Addis Ababa and then we can, tomorrow, start our return flight back to Britain. I take it from what you said at the meeting (and some other comments that I heard) that you do intend to occasionally come back to oversee some of the work that is being done. I also heard that you quite amazed the President of Ethiopia when you told him that you are also going to donate a further one million pounds to provide food for the poor and starving wretches that have been hit hardest by the drought and the famine. Well done sir, I compliment you on your actions."

Eventually, the various sectors representing the other countries made their way to speak to Jack, all of them praising the way that he was aiding their countries. He informed them all that over the coming months he hoped to be able to visit each of their countries and that he hoped to see some noticeable work underway on the projects for the five countries.

The Prime minister's aide found Jack, Jennifer and Hugo and said that if they would care to follow him, he would guide them to the cars that had been made ready to take them to their accommodation for the night. Once again, seated in their limousines they left the meeting hall, once again with a full police and army escort they drove across Addis Ababa to get back to their hotel accommodation. They entered the foyer of the hotel again and were met by even more officials who assured everyone that their wishes would be dealt with by all of the people at the hotel. Jack and Jennifer were taken to their apartment again, Jennifer was delighted at all that they were being offered and told Jack that she could soon get used to living a life like this. Jack simply muttered something about it being far more than what they needed. They hadn't been in the apartment very long when their internal phone rang. Jack answered it and he then discovered that it was Hugo on the line. He wanted to know where they were and he told them that he too had been given an apartment, not perhaps the rooftop one, but a large apartment for all that. Jack invited him to come up and see their apartment, to which Hugo agreed that he would like to see 'how the other half lives'!

Chapter Nineteen

It was only a few minutes later and there was a knock at the door to the apartment. Jennifer happened to be the nearest and she answered the knock and there was Hugo. He came into their apartment and even he gave a little gasp when he saw what they had been given for a night's sleep. He told them that his apartment would have been quite large enough to hold a good company of his men when he had been in the army. He assured them that he was equally satisfied with the way that the government of Ethiopia had provided security for them all. He said that their flight on the following morning was due to leave at ten o'clock in the morning and that a similar cavalcade of vehicles would get them there with a minimum of disruption. He asked Jack how he had got on with the President of Ethiopia (whom he had seen him in deep conversation with at the banquet).

"Oh," Jack said, "I told him that to have provided a banquet like that when they have so many people starving is almost criminal. He told me though that some of the people in their country couldn't manage to digest the kinds of food that we were served. He said that it is a problem and they did try to find enough to alleviate some of the effects of the famine and they were already trying to import enough of the food that they needed. As that just meant to me that they just didn't seem to have the money I told him that once we get back to England I would donate a further one million pounds to feed those people. But I said that I wanted the distribution to be far better organised than some that we have seen on our television screens at past famines. He assured me that they would make sure that the distribution was fair and quite rapid so, I said that I would hope on my next visit to see the evidence of some better-fed people. He even had the cheek to suggest that they would have to honour me if I returned to their country once again. I don't want honours; not like that I wouldn't. Would you?"

"Jack," Hugo said, "I have kept telling you that they are all going to honour you in some way. Maybe getting you into the House of Lords was a bit over the top but I don't think that I'd rule out a knighthood. Alec and Ray, both of them agree that I'm not too far away with that as well, don't they?"

"I just think that you're all going over the top about this," Jack replied. "Let's face it; what I'm doing is not a lot different to what a lot more people are doing. Many, many people donate to a charity. It may just happen that I happen to have a lot more money than some people but I'll bet that if you assess the percentage of their wealth to the amount that they have donated, a lot of people could be doing just as much as I am."

"I suppose that when you consider it in percentage terms," Jennifer said, "It may be possible that you are correct. However, because of the amount that you, the very wealthy man, can donate; it can materially affect the entire lives of so many people. This latest incident is a classic example of that, isn't it?"

"By the way Jack," Hugo said, "Do you realise that this hotel is putting on yet another massive meal for you for tonight? The Prime Minister and his entourage will be there. You are expected to be there and no doubt some of them may just expect you to once again stand up and tell them how they should all be helping to put the World to rights. You did know about that, didn't you?"

"Hugo," Jack replied, "We've only just had a massive meal at that banquet. How can they expect us all to eat so much? I don't eat massive meals, do I, Jennifer? I don't suppose that there's any way that I can get out of it, is there?"

"No," Jennifer and Hugo both said together. "Jack, you are now the person who is going to save a lot of lives in this country (and in another four countries as well)," Jennifer said. "You will just have to bite the bullet, as the saying goes and get on with it. You'll soon think of something to say and, if you don't want to eat a lot of the food, they won't punish you for leaving some, will they? Now stop being daft and get yourself ready to go and meet your audience in the dining room. We'll both be with you there, won't we, Hugo?"

"Oh, yes," Hugo said, "We'll be there and by the way. You keep telling them that I am somehow a part of the Spanish Royal Family. That isn't true Jack. I'm not quite sure where you got the idea from, but my only connection goes back many, many decades, if not a couple of centuries or so. So all that of it was related to one of my ancestors having a fling with one of the Royal Family and in doing so creating an illegitimate baby. Now, as far as I'm concerned, that doesn't make me related to the Royal Family, does it?"

"Oh, I see," Jack said with a huge grin on his face. "So you had some naughty people in your family in days gone by then, did you? In fact, I believe that it was Miguel who told me, or at least hinted somehow, that you were connected with the Spanish Royal Family. I can suppose that if they did get that close that they got a Spanish Princess pregnant, somehow then your family were related in some way. Mind you, if that had been in England, no doubt they would have had their heads chopped off for that, wouldn't they Jennifer?"

"Look, Jack," Jennifer said, "Hugo is supposed to be your friend, isn't he? Don't just keep on going at him like that. After all, he is a man of principles and if he thinks that his family have done wrong, he tries to put it right. He has already shown you that he can do that with Miguel, hasn't he?"

"Thank you, Jennifer," Hugo replied, "But seriously, I do think that we need to be getting ready now for this dinner that they are getting set up for downstairs. No matter what you think Jack, you will have to go to it and you will no doubt have to make some kind of speech. From what we've seen and heard so far though, I wouldn't think that you will have any trouble at all with it."

"Oh, OK, I'll go but I don't want any more funny cracks about any damned honours, do I?" Jack said. "Come on, Jennifer, time to get ourselves ready. We'll meet you downstairs then, Hugo. Don't you be late either, cos, if you are then I'll tell them that it'll be you that's going to do all of the talking, how does that sound eh?"

They did all get ready for the dinner and Jack was quite resplendent in the new evening suit that Jennifer had insisted that he needed to wear sometimes (just to try and impress some of them). They arrived at the dining area almost at the same time as Hugo and, as they arrived, the Prime Minister's aide came across to them to get them to their places.

On this occasion, Jack was being seated by the President of Somalia, once again, having Jennifer by his side and Hugo at her other side. This kind of seating suited Jack's peace of mind somewhat, but he couldn't say why. He just had a feeling that in some way, Jennifer had to be protected. Jennifer knew this and found it to be so charming that he did want to protect her like that.

The President of Somalia said to Jack, "I am so pleased that we have at last met Mr Dawkins. The things that you are doing are, you know, so critical to our well-being as a country. I know that our country is large, but it does need to have a lot of controls in place if we are to keep the peace. I was pleased when you asked all of the countries where you are carrying out projects to provide protection. We all have to be realists and, if something is laid down, there are always some people who feel a need to steal it. We have told the people of Somalia that since you are in fact doing us the great favour of protecting our peoples and our lands, that all of your men and all of your properties will be forbidden to any of them. I have made it known that if anyone should in any way break that confidence that you must have, they will be subjected to the most severe punishment that we can give. I feel quite confident that those words have had some effect, and I have even been told that some of the brigands that inhabit our country have all verbally expressed their support for you and all that you are doing for our country."

"It is pleasing to hear that the brigands that you have heard of talking do appear to support our aims," Jack said. "It is also pleasing to hear that you are going to provide some protection. That is so very definite if we are to be able to get the project completed in the way that I do want it done. However, I do hope that the punishment will not be such that it could involve a loss of life. It is our perception in our country that all life is valid and if someone does wander away from what is expected of them, a period of training, or re-training is far more preferable. After the re-training, I understand that many people then become even better citizens than some who have never had such further instruction. But, Mr President, I am sure that you know only too well how to re-train any ill-doers in your country."

"Thank you, Mr Dawkins," The President replied, "Yes, we have had many years of finding the most appropriate way of punishing wrongdoers in my country. I am already in the process of obtaining some of our people to help with the pipe-laying work that you spoke of. I feel sure that, once a definite line for the pipeline is agreed upon I should be able to provide all of the workers that will be required. There are so many who will want to do the work to help our country that we may even have more than will be needed."

"That too, is an essential for the completion of the project," Jack replied, with a small smile. "As I said at the earlier meeting, there is no point in having desalination units or water pumps of any size or any kind if there is no pipeline for the water to be put into, is there? I do feel that the project in your country will progress well. Have you or your people given much thought to the extension of pipelines; to further irrigation systems and methods? Not necessarily as large as the initial pipeline maybe, but beyond the main pipeline there may well be several kinds of irrigation methods that could help the land."

"Yes," The President said, "There has been much talk of how this should be done and I am sure that by the time that your first and major pipeline is in place, we shall by then be making plans to extend the water supply much, much further."

The talk had, for Jack, been somewhat limited for him with this President, since he could see some problems in that country from the way that their President had been talking. He didn't like the idea of the punishment that had been intimated at, but he was equally well aware that there would have to be some deterrent to anyone trying to get hold of the materials that they were going to be putting into doing the job. He didn't like either the veiled intimation that if necessary they may be going to introduce slavery of some kind. It was then at about that time that Jennifer had spoken to him and he briefly turned to see what it was that she wanted.

"Jack," Jennifer said quite quietly, "I have heard some parts of what has been said to you from that man but do be careful. We don't know what any of these people are like really and it could be so easy to agree to something without knowing exactly what they are meaning."

"Yes, my dear," Jack replied, "I have thought along similar lines to what you are suggesting and it is my opinion that with some of the people like these, we shall all have to be careful. I must talk to the Prime Minister when this is all over with. I think that it may take some tact and diplomacy to get things smoothed out properly." At that point, Jack raised his arm for the Prime minister's aide and that man came across straight away.

"Yes, Mr Dawkins, is there anything that I can do for you?" the aide said.

"Yes," Jack replied, "There are two things that I wanted to ask you. First of all, are you Norman Brooks, the person who contacted me before all of this? I didn't ask your name before and I was just a little curious if it was indeed you. The other point is that when the dinner is over and done with, could you let the Prime Minister know that I would appreciate a few words with him? It isn't anything critical, but I would just feel a little more comfortable."

"Oh, of course, Mr Dawkins, I'll get him to make a point of getting to you after the dinner. And yes, I am Norman Brooks; I hadn't expected you to remember me from that brief conversation. I believe that the dinner should end very soon so I will get him to come to your apartment if that would be alright?"

"Oh, thanks, Norman," Jack replied, "That would be ideal. There are so many people here and I'm afraid that my memory for names just isn't what it should be. To be honest, I think that my memory is pretty rubbish at the moment, it must be due to all that flying about that has done some of it, and don't you think so?"

"Yes, sir," Norman Brooks replied, "I think that it can soon get to you and so easily. Never mind, we'll soon be back home again and then things will all return to normal for you, won't they?"

Norman Brooks went off to have a word with the Prime Minister and then the President sat next to Jack said, "Yes, I'm afraid that I too suffer from memory problems when I have had to do a lot of flying. It does seem to be a strange sensation, doesn't it? Fortunately for me and most of the people here, we don't have any great distances to go to get home, do we? I suppose that for you though, with the trips that you will be having to make out here to follow up on all five of your, 'projects', I believe that you call them, you will be getting a lot of jet lag, won't you?"

"Yes," Jack replied, "I suppose that I shall, but it has to be done so that is it, isn't it? I had always believed that it occurred more when you travelled from West to East but for me, this time it has happened when we have travelled from more or less North to South East, haven't we? I just hope that I do soon get more used to it or maybe I'll just have to stop all of this travelling about and let other people do it for me."

"One must presume that with your wealth, it will become much easier to delegate some of your work to others. However, I do hope that you will be able to return to see the many benefits of what your system, and your 'projects' are doing to aid our countries out here. That must give you a good feeling to see a successful result, mustn't it?"

The dinner did come to a close and Jack, Jennifer and Hugo began to make their way back to Jack and Jennifer's apartment at the roof area. Jack had mentioned to Hugo that he had asked the Prime Minister to come since he wanted to have a few words with him if he could. As they were walking back to the apartment, Hugo commented on how well the dinner had gone. He told Jack that he had heard so many very, very complimentary remarks about him, the projects and the way that he had been able to deliver his address at the meeting earlier. He said that no doubt there would be some problems but that it was his opinion that from what he had heard, any of the countries that tried to back away from their obligations that they had agreed to would be quite well nipped in the bud by the other countries.

They reached the apartment at almost the same time as the Prime Minister (who was accompanied by Norman Brooks) and together, they all went in. Once inside, the Prime Minister remarked that he too had been allocated a very nice apartment but that he thought that Jack and Jennifer's apartment certainly took the prize.

"What is it Jack that is troubling you," The Prime Minister asked. "I seemed to get the impression from Norman that you may have some kinds of misgivings about something. If we can help, do let us know and we'll see what we can do."

"I couldn't say that there is anything specific that was said that got me a bit worried," Jack said, "But the President of Somalia that was sat next to me at the dinner did seem to give off some rather strong and unpleasant vibes. I know that he is just one person but he did seem to be kind of inferring that they did have a number of bandits who are likely to be carrying out raids. He did say that some of them have agreed to try and help rather than hinder, but he was then saying that he knew how to give a punishment that would deter any wrongdoing. I may have misheard or got it wrong, but I did get the feeling that he was talking about just killing off some of the most notorious ones. He also suggested that, but not in so many words, I do agree, that he believed that he knew how to get the workers to help with the pipe laying. I thought that he was inferring that he could in effect be creating a slave labour force. All in all, I found the man to be a very unpleasant kind of person and it does give you a strange feeling when it gets like that. Now, I have met the President of Ethiopia and I found him to be quite a nice man and with some good intentions. The President of Somalia however didn't, to me appear to be anyone that I would like to say that he was a nice man. I know that there isn't a lot that we can do with someone in that position but it then made me a little nervous about the leaders of Djibouti, Sudan, and Eritrea. I don't know if you have met with them or know any more about them but it does make me a little nervous after meeting Somalia's leader and when he turns out to be like that.

Do you know anything about these other leaders and their governments?"

"I'm afraid that I don't personally know a great deal about any of these other governments but I would imagine that the ones for Eritrea and Djibouti would probably be much more amenable. I know that it doesn't answer your questions and perhaps with Somalia, your impression may not be too far off the line. In the past, Somalia has had something of a bad past reputation but I understood that this man was now trying to put things right again. Maybe I misheard something or was misinformed. I shall continue to make enquiries. I would hope that the President of the Sudan may be more like the President of Ethiopia. I will most certainly do some digging and find out what I can. Can you make a note of all of this for me Norman so that I can try and get some answers for Mr Dawkins?"

"Yes, sir," Norman Brooks replied, "Mr Dawkins has also mentioned that he does appear to be suffering quite badly from jet lag. I know that we may not be able to do a lot to remedy that sir, but perhaps it would be a good idea for everyone to get a good night's rest so that we can be ready for tomorrow's long flight again."

"Oh, yes, of course, Norman," The Prime Minister said, "You are of course quite right and perhaps it would be better if we did all turn in and got a good night's sleep. We'll see you in the morning then Jack, Mrs Dawkins and of course you Hugo. You must some time let me know a little about your life with the Spanish Royals. Good night everyone."

The Prime Minister and his aide disappeared and Jennifer said, "Perhaps that was a good idea that we all get a good night's sleep, what do you think, Jack?"

"Yes, I'd agree with that Jennifer," Hugo said, "But you see what your little indiscretion has done for me now Jack. He thinks that I'm connected with the Spanish Royal Family. Oh, my ancestors, what have they done for me? Good night to you two, see you in the morning."

They did all turn in with hopes that they would get a good night's sleep to prepare them for their long flight to get them back home to Britain. Neither Jack nor Hugo troubled to phone home to get plans ready for a car being at Northolt to collect them. Hugo said that he would prefer to wait until they were on the 'plane and then they would be able to get a much more accurate time of arrival.

Chapter Twenty

Once again, with a cavalcade of limousines escorted by both a police and a military escort, the party moved from their hotel and to the airport where their RAF aeroplane was stood waiting for them. They boarded and they were informed that the flight was going to leave exactly on time. The pilot had given them some indication of their arrival time at Northolt so Hugo took out his mobile phone and called through to the estate to speak to Miguel. He gave Miguel the anticipated arrival time and asked if he could once again get Manuel to get a car to Northolt to collect them. Just as a matter of course, Hugo asked Miguel how things were there. Had there been any problems at all at the estate while they had been away, especially any that Jack may want to know about? Miguel confirmed that there had been no problems of any kind; indeed, he said that things had been so much quieter. For a little bit of a laugh, he suggested that as the three of them, Jack, Jennifer and Hugo had all been away he could only deduce that they were the cause of any problems anyway. Hugo realised that Miguel was trying out his own sense of humour on him, but he told Miguel that he would relay that comment to Jack and Jennifer and he could see for himself what they had to say about his remarks when they got back.

Jack and Jennifer thought it was so funny and they both had quite a laugh at the way that Miguel had been playing Hugo on a bit with comments like that. It just seemed so good that the family differences did appear to have been bridged by Hugo, and they both thought that Hugo himself was quite pleased that it was going well between Miguel and himself.

The touchdown at Northolt was just about perfectly on time, as you would expect from the RAF, wouldn't you? Manuel was already waiting and they soon had their little bits and pieces of luggage stowed away in the boot of the car. The Prime Minister and his aide both said farewell to Jack, Jennifer and Hugo and the Prime Minister said that he would keep in close contact with Jack to see just how developments were proceeding. He had told Norman Brooks to give Jack his phone number so that Jack would always have some good numbers to use whenever he needed them.

They all parted at Northolt with Jack, Jennifer and Hugo being driven by Manuel back to the estate where they could once again update their friendly ghosts who were, they were sure, eagerly awaiting any news of how things had gone on with their trip to the Horn of Africa. Their first stop though was to get to their kitchen so that they could all get some more coffee. None of them had been very keen on the coffee that had been served to them on the aeroplane. Their own brand they all knew was something that they all liked. Each with a cup of coffee to keep them going, they made their way to the office to update their stockbroker ghosts on their progress.

In the office, it was Ray that was sitting at the computer this time with Alec appearing to be making notes on his pad. "So, our conquering heroes return, do they?" Alec said, looking up from his notepad. "And was it worth all of the trouble of you going there? Did you, after all, make a speech then, Jack? I know that you told us before that you wouldn't know how to go about that sort of thing, didn't you? Maybe it would be better if I asked Jennifer or Hugo. At least I would get a much fuller and detailed answer from them, wouldn't I? And were they some of the senior members of their governments that you met? Oh, do come on Jack, get going and fill us in on what has happened. Remember, we were stuck here, weren't we?"

"Oh, give the lad a chance," Ray chipped in. "He'll be far more used to hobnobbing with high-grade politicians rather than mere ghosts of old stockbrokers, won't he? I'll bet that Jennifer enjoyed all the pomp and stardom of it all, didn't you Jennifer?"

"Yes, I did enjoy it." Jennifer replied, "I think that I enjoyed it far more than Jack did, but there again, being fair, he was sat by the President of Ethiopia at the banquet they had set up for after the meeting and they did seem to get on well. Indeed, I do believe that I remember that President saying something about him having to be honoured when he goes there again. Mind you, Jack wasn't any too keen on the President of Somalia who sat next to him at the second dinner that we had to go to. In fact, he told our own Prime Minister that he would like it if they could get any useful information about the man, and the government there. Apparently, some of the things that he had been suggesting did sound a bit harsh and barbaric but, there again I suppose that that may just be a bit of how their life is out there. The rest of it though was super; convoys of cars to take us everywhere escorted by both army and police. That was marvellous, it made you feel as though you were almost like a pop star, didn't it, Jack?"

"Yes, I suppose that you have more or less told them everything, haven't you Jennifer? Jack said, quite resignedly. "Yes, in a lot of ways I did enjoy it and I do honestly believe that those five countries, perhaps Somalia apart for a short time, will all work to make it a success. I did also say that if it went over the two Billion pounds I wouldn't let the projects stop just for the sake of a bit of cash. At least that will help you all to get some more bonus points, won't it?"

"Neither Jack nor Jennifer have said anything anyway about the terrific talk that he gave at the first meeting," Hugo said. "He did seem to cover most points and he told them all; that he expected them, each and every one of them to extend beyond the pipeline that he put in to irrigate more land and also in other things that they had to play their parts in making all of the projects work out. He had them eating out of his hand by the time he finished his talk, oh, and yes, I heard the President of Ethiopia say something about Honours for him. I believe that his British Prime Minister did more or less hint about the need for some honours or something. He has also made sure that Jack has the phone number for his aide so that if he isn't personally about, at least Jack will have direct contact. Now, we just have to make sure that our people are getting things going at getting the desalination units, the large Pumps and the water tanks ordered. As soon as they can give us the sites that will be the base for the pipelines I believe that we shall need to get deliveries of pipes out to them since Jack also told them that he wanted them to provide some labour (that he would pay a reasonable pay for their work) to get started on laying the pipelines. I suppose that we could also get some digging machines out to them as well, couldn't we?"

"My goodness," Alec said, "Between you, you have been a busy little team, haven't you? Well, your fund is still keeping at about the one trillion pounds in total, Jack, sometimes going up a couple of hundred billion over and then dropping back to the straight one trillion. That's more or less how we had hoped that it would be. Of course, if you should happen to decide to make more donations then we could soon activate it a bit, just as soon as you need it."

"Oh, by the way," Hugo said, "The President of Ethiopia was criticised by Jack for the amount of food at the banquet when they had so many people who were starving. Then the President told Jack that some of the people who were starving could be made ill if they were served some of the kinds of food that were being served there. He told Jack that they were going to try and find money to buy more of the kinds of food that they needed so Jack said that if they could identify where that food was and if they could ensure a good and ordered distribution of that food, he would arrange another million pounds donation when he got back to Britain. So, he has already started to make some more donations, hasn't he?"

"Jack, Jack," Alec said, "That is a marvellous piece of news. I know that you said that you didn't like the way that the food had been distributed before, but if you have told the President that you want it to be an ordered distribution then that should ensure that it all goes out well, shouldn't it? Oh, well done, Jack."

"Now that we've updated you then Alec, and you Ray," Jack said, "I think that we need to be going down to chase up some of the stuff that we are going to need out there at the 'Horn of Africa'. You see, I'm even getting to know a bit more about some geography, and names of different parts of the continents aren't I? Come on Hugo, let's get a move on and see that they are doing things, eh?"

Jennifer said that she was going to see her Mum and Dad next door and Jack and Hugo left to go and see that the things needed for the pipeline work were all getting sorted. Hugo had put an office on the ground floor dedicated to looking after these things for them.

Jack and Hugo arrived at the office that was dealing with the acquisition of items and materials for the pipeline projects and Paul, the man who had been appointed as manager came over to see them.

"We have now sourced and have ordered the four desalination units, sir. They are now well in the process of being made and we have been told that delivery should be within the next five or six week's time. We have got the four pumps ordered and they should all be with us within two months. I have told them that I would like them to be delivered within one month and I think that we may get that down to six weeks if I keep pushing them. The storage tanks are being made now and they should hopefully be here within a couple of weeks. And the Sea-based wind turbine is taking just a little longer and that could be two months sir. Once we do have it, there is the problem of shipping as well, but I'll keep you informed as we go along. For the other smaller pumps for the 'take off points' I suppose that I could get some of them by the end of next week and, of course, you suggested some solar panels to power them up, didn't you? They don't take too long and I should have them as soon as we want them. The Pipes themselves, I'm expecting that delivery to be confirmed by tomorrow and as soon as we have a destination, they can get underway."

"Well done," Jack said. "The only problem is that it looks as though we shall now have to increase everything as I have agreed to furnish the materials and the work for another four countries. Generally, I suppose that that is just a case of multiplication for you, isn't it? Hugo will be able to fill you in later with most of the other details since one country, Djibouti, is much smaller and doesn't have to have quite the same need for more water so I believe in their case a couple of desalination units would be enough. We have reduced as we went along for what they need. Some of the countries are a little larger and they may require a good deal more pipes to make their long pipelines. As I say, Hugo will give you some details. I'm sorry about the short notice but when we notified one country we had requests for similar treatment for another four countries so I had no choice but to increase my donation to try and put an end to the droughts and famines in those countries. The pipes are still the major ones as they will all have to be laid before we can desalinate the water and then start to pump it out, won't they? It looks to me as though your work has just increased somewhat, hasn't it? It is of course possible that there may be quite a few other bits and pieces for us to get all of these pipelines operating but I have confidence in you and anyway, I can assure you that there will be a good bonus for you when we get it all done. Hugo here will be chasing things up a lot for me as I never know at the moment just what I'm going to be doing and where I'm going to be. Anyway, you can do it, can't you? By the way, we still haven't managed to get the actual sites for some of the deliveries. You have the first site address don't you; That's in Djibouti, so that lot of pipes can be shipped, can't they?"

"Yes sir, I can get those pipes directed to wherever you want them to go to. When do you think that you'll get the other destination addresses? This must be costing you an absolute fortune sir. That of course, is none of my business, and it does seem to be a grand piece of good for humanity that you are doing, doesn't it? I'll keep Hugo informed about the situation as well sir."

Having seen the supply department they both felt that they deserved another cup of coffee. That meant another trip to the flat to get to their kitchen. Hugo was becoming quite impressed with the way that his new boss was organising everything and he also realised that increasingly he was pushing a lot more work onto Hugo to follow things up for the projects to get anywhere near to completion.

On their way to the flat, they happened to meet Miguel who had just been checking on some of the security features. He, of course, was also invited to join them for a cup of coffee.

Once in the kitchen, Jack filled the kettle while Miguel ran through one or two points about the security for Hugo that he believed Hugo would need to know about. Hugo stopped him before he had gone very far and said, "Look, Miguel, I spoke to you before Jack and I had to go away. You are now in charge of the security company. The thing is, Jack has now asked me to take on other duties, as you well know. Since that is the case, I am no longer in charge of security. Yes, if you want some help at any time, do come and ask me. If I can help, I will help, but you are now the big man for the security, not I. I know that there used to be that big rift between the pair of us but I do honestly believe that a lot of that was wrong, very wrong and I now want to acknowledge that, no matter what I did in the past, that is in the past. I believed that you were quite capable of running the security, so you don't have to report to me anymore. Just report it to Jack, if you want to. He'll no doubt tell you to see me but we all know that you are the security man and so do all of the lads out there, don't they?"

"I know that you said that I was to be in charge of security, but Hugo, you're still the Major, aren't you? You have always been the senior officer. Alright, I'll take it that I have to look after security but no matter what, I, and I think a lot of the lads as well, will still consider you as the boss. Yes, Jack is your boss as well, but for us all, you have been the boss for so long so it will never change for some of us. That, by the way, is a compliment to you."

Jack, standing by the kitchen work surface and the kettle heard all of this and smiled at the very gentle way that Hugo had more or less undone all the ills of the long-lasting feud that had been entwined into both of their family histories. He knew that neither he, nor probably anyone else, would ever know what had caused that initial rift, but at least it now was over for good and all. Jack carried on and made coffee for each of them and called them over to come and get their cups.

Chapter Twenty-One

It was about a couple of days later and Jennifer had been to the other nearby flats to see her Mum and Dad and she ran back in and called out for Jack.

"Jack," she said, quite excitedly, "While I was at my Mum and Dad's flat they had the news on and it has been announced that the man who was the Foreign Secretary has had to resign from the government and he has had to be taken away to a hospital. They are suggesting that he has more or less lost his mind. Do you think that this may have been caused by these ghosts of ours doing some haunting? Jack, that kind of thing isn't nice and it isn't right, is it? Do you think that you need to be talking to Alec and Ray to discover just what they have done to the poor man? I mean, he may be married, he may have children and he will almost certainly still have some parents. What a terrible thing to have happened, isn't it?"

"Let's have a look at some news first," Jack said. "I do know that I said that he hadn't been much help to us but I, and I don't think that you either intended anything like this. Yes, once we've seen some news I think that we will need to talk to Alec and Ray. We can't be doing some good with one hand and then doing so much harm on the other hand can we?"

They got their television switched on and found a news channel. It took quite some time before anything came up that related to the Foreign Secretary and then they simply watched and listened. It appeared that it was all as Jennifer had said to Jack earlier. He had had to resign from the government and as an MP and yes, he had had to be taken away to a hospital for some treatment for his mental condition. Jack and Jennifer turned off the television and went to the office to see Alec and Ray.

They had simply blurted out the full story (as they had heard it on the television) to Alec and Ray and they just asked what they thought of that. "What has happened here, Alec?" Jack Said. "I thought that it was just going to be a case of making him start to see things more from the point of view of the starving people in these countries. We never thought that any of you would have gone as far as to drive him mad. Didn't you go with them once Alec, or was it you that went Ray? Can you get hold of Peter and that man who you thought would want to haunt someone because they were a politician? None of us meant it to be done in such a way. What about his family? We can't say that we are going to be doing good things on the one hand and then hear that we are responsible for such an evil action as this on the other hand, can we?"

"I haven't a clue what they can have done," Alec replied, quite shocked on hearing this news. "Yes, I did go with them once, but the man just seemed to be a bit upset when I saw him but he wasn't in any way being driven mad. We will have to find Peter and that other one who wanted to haunt a politician. I'd agree with you that something as bad as this could so easily undo anything that we are doing to earn bonus points for our people. Oh, dear, Ray, come on, we'll have to go now and see what we can find out, won't we?"

"Too true we will," Ray replied. "I wouldn't want to be associated in any way with anything like this. As you say, it may well undo all of the work that we've done to get bonus points for us if we can't get something sorted quickly."

Alec and Ray both disappeared from the office area, leaving Jack and Jennifer wondering just what they should do next, if they could, in fact, do anything at all. They did know that they would also have to let Hugo know about it, and he would be blazing mad when he heard. Yes, he had known that they were going to get some haunting done of someone, but this, oh dear, no, this was terrible news.

They got onto their phones and asked Hugo to join them in their flat as soon as he could. They knew that it would be Alec and Ray that would be able to help, far more than Hugo, but by this time, Hugo had become such a major part of what they were doing and they valued his opinion so much.

Hugo was with them both within half an hour and he smiled as he said, "That sounded like an urgent call just to come and get some coffee. There isn't anything else, is there?"

They explained as much as they could about the news programme that they had seen and how the Foreign Minister had had to resign from the government as an MP and that he had now been taken, more or less, into a mental hospital. Hugo was almost as shocked as they had been.

"Have you been to see Alec and Ray and told them about this," Hugo said, knowing that these two would of course done exactly that. "What can Alec and Ray do then? Can they 'un-haunt' someone?" Things such as this had never been dealt with any of Hugo's time in the army and he was equally as disgusted as were both Jack and Jennifer, but he couldn't think of a single thing that he knew of to try and remedy the problem.

They all went back to the office area to see if Ray or Alec had returned. They looked in the doorway and there was no one there. Jack said, "Hang on, when I first started to deal with the ghosts they told me that I could call them up whenever I wanted to so, here goes, 'Alec, Alec, Alec'," he called. Almost immediately, Alec appeared in the office and saw the three of them waiting for him.

"We did find Peter and Peter has told us that he and the other bloke did go back a few times to haunt him. Peter says that he got quite bored with it himself and he stopped going to haunt him, but he thinks that the other bloke just carried on, almost every night going to haunt the man. We haven't been able to find him yet. Ray is still looking around and I feel fairly sure that we will get him eventually. I'm not sure what we will be able to do but there must be something somewhere that can be used to reverse, to some extent at least, the effects of the haunting. I'm sorry that I haven't got anything more positive to tell you at the moment but, as I say, Ray is still looking.

Look, I'll probably be more help if I get back to help Ray. We will both come back and let you all know whatever we can, I promise you that." With that, Alec simply disappeared again.

"Well, yes, you did say that maybe the Foreign Secretary needed haunting but I don't think for a minute that you meant anything like this," Hugo said. "I do know that where I come from, religion is a major thing and, although I have never in the past been a strict devotee of the church or anything but, on this occasion, I think that I am now going to try to make few prayers that we can get a positive outcome from it all. I know it may sound feeble to you, but maybe if we all do it we could just get a bit of divine help to put things right. I'll see you later and maybe you will have heard something from somewhere that is better news than this."

Hugo left them and went out of their flat. Jack and Jennifer just looked at one another and then Jennifer said, "Hugo may have gone to try to pray but since neither of us is in any way religious (to my knowledge) it doesn't seem to be right to just pray when you have a problem, does it? I'll maybe say something in my head to some vague being sometimes, but I don't think that I could be so hypocritical as to go to a church only when I have a problem. What do you think? You're no churchman type either, are you?"

"No, I must agree with all that you are saying Jennifer," Jack replied, "But if Hugo does believe in what he is doing, then I do wish him all good fortune with it. I think that we could do with an awful lot of help at the moment and I'm not too proud to accept help from anywhere, anywhere at all. In so many ways, I hold myself responsible for this terrible incident since it was me, being foolish because the man didn't agree with me, I told, or at least suggested to, the ghosts that he needed to be haunted. I think that in the meantime I'll just pop over and see how the lads are doing at getting the materials and things ready for shipping them out. At least then I may feel I am doing something positive."

Jack wandered down into the office where the orders were being put together and Paul, the manager, seeing him wandering across, came up to him and said that most of the items were now moving along. He commented that it had raised quite a few raised eyebrows when he had placed the additional orders that Jack had said would be needed. He believed also that due in part to the total number of orders being placed by Jack they had managed to get some prices adjusted in Jack's favour.

Jack could see that the room was humming with activity and he was quite well aware that he was doing no material good to any of the work so he wandered out once again and he quite slowly began to walk around some of the parts of the estate. He had known that there were some other, older buildings at one part and he just wondered what they may have been used for in days gone by. As he was wondering and walking, one of the security men came up to him in his small van and asked if he wanted him to drive him closer to the old buildings. Jack took the opportunity and the man drove him right up to the closed doors of the first building. It wasn't quite 'massive', but yes, it was a decent size and in general it didn't seem to be in too bad a condition, but Jack knew that he was no surveyor himself. The security man then drove him close to the other unused buildings and Jack once again had a look to see just what they had got there. He knew that there was no initial purpose that he could think of right away but he asked the security man to drive him back to where Hugo was now stationing himself. Hugo had found one room in the main building on the ground floor, not a large one by any means, but he had classed it as 'his office' and most of the people on the site knew that they usually would find him working in there.

Jack knocked on the door of Hugo's 'office' and Hugo's voice from inside said to enter so Jack walked in. "You see, Hugo, you can't just hide like that, can you? I have at last found you and your little hideaway."

"I'm sorry, Jack, I should have mentioned that I had decided to use this office for myself. After all, it was spare and it does give me somewhere to disappear to at times. I didn't go out to find the church around here, but I thought that I could say one or two quiet prayers while I was here and alone. Was there something else that you were wanting, something wrong (as well as that business of the Foreign Secretary)?"

"It may be nothing at all, Hugo," Jack said. "I've just been having a wander around some of the other parts of the estate and I got down near to some of those old buildings. Have you seen them? Oh, of course, you would have seen them. Have you had a fair look at them though Hugo? It was just that I thought to myself that it wouldn't take much to get them so that we could start to use them to stockpile some of the bits and pieces that we needed for the projects. I know that I'm no expert, but they don't seem to be in too bad a condition. It was just a thought and I then decided that if anyone could say if I was right or not, it would be you. Go out some time and just have a quick look at some of them and see if you think that they could be of any use. I know that for some of the things that we are going to get for the projects, some come quickly and some come slow and if we could perhaps stockpile some bits and pieces there I just thought that they may be safer there than just laid on the coast in some of those countries."

"That does sound sensible, Jack," Hugo replied. "Yes, I will have to wander over and have a look at them. I'll let you know once I've been inside them. Storing stuff just at the coasts would, as you say, be a bit risky and if some of it goes missing it could slow down quite a few of the projects. Yes, I'll get down there today."

Jack took his leave and wandered once more, looking here and there at the vast spaces that they had in this huge building that was now the base for the luxury flats on the two upper floors and was fast becoming the hub for all of the work that he was now planning on doing. Having wandered around downstairs though, he soon found his way back up to the second floor and into his flat where, when he got to the kitchen, he found Jenifer very happily working away at trying out some new recipe for something for their meals.

Jenifer saw Jack come into the kitchen and she just said, "I suppose that you'll just be wanting more coffee, won't you? Well,

I'm a bit busy at the moment so if you just want some coffee, you'll have to get it yourself. If you can't manage that, you'll have to wait until I've finished off these things that I'm doing at the moment."

"No," Jack replied, quite resignedly, "At least, yes I do, but it can wait. I'm getting a bit bored and I don't know what I can do. I've been down to see if the stuff that we're ordering is still all going OK, and that seemed to be fine. I had a walk to look at some of those old buildings that we haven't used yet and well, I've been to see Hugo and asked if it would be any good for us to get stuff needed for the project stored up there so that then it can all go as a single load when we get enough stuff ready. It seemed to me to be a shame that they look as though they are reasonable buildings and we just don't use them for anything. I'm just bored and I knew that you'd just be stuck in here doing some more cooking. I've filled in my travel book, and I've re-done that quite a few times. I'm just stuck for something to do with my time."

"Look, Jack," Jennifer said. "I find some things to do to occupy my time. You will just have to start looking around and find something for you to do. Go and see Miguel and see if you can't just do a walk around with him on his security circuit, or whatever he does. I can't tell you what to do, there's going to be some time before a lot of the stuff is ready for shipping so you'll just have to wait, won't you?"

"OK then," Jack said, "I'll pop over to see Miguel. It may be interesting to see what they have to do with the security. I'll probably be back here within an hour at the outside, I suppose." Jack then just wandered out of the flat and began to make his way to where he thought that Miguel was usually based. He found Miguel but as with everything else, Jack found little of interest to him and he wandered back to their flat. Just to try and ease his mind, he wandered out to the office to see the ghosts there and to try and find out if they had discovered anything about the haunting. As he went in, he saw Alec standing near the computer while Ray was moving his hands above the keyboard.

"Have you found out anything about that problem of the haunting yet," Jack asked. "It's just that I do feel a lot of the responsibility for it and I feel bad."

"Yes," Alec replied, "We found the idiot that had overdone the haunting and he has been told that he will now move down rather than up in our world for quite some time and since Peter said that he had just stopped because he found it very boring what the man had been doing, he'll more or less be in the clear. They have told us as well that the effects of the haunting will probably pass off after two or three weeks, especially if he does get some decent sleep to make up for it all. I would presume that he will get that if they have moved him into a hospital, wouldn't you?"

"Oh good," Jack replied. "It was really getting at me when we had heard that on the news. I knew that it was me in the first place that said something about him needing haunting so I felt really responsible for it all. By the way, I understand that most of the parts are now getting well underway and we have sent quite a lot of the pipes out so that they could make a start on laying the four pipelines from the coast at Djibouti to get that and the Ethiopian section well underway. I have increased the amount of pipes for that one so that they could lay a fifth line out into Djibouti. The Ethiopian's I understand have made some decisions on the lengths of their pipelines. They have decided that they needed some to be a good bit longer and some shorter ones would well manage other areas. I told them to do whatever they thought most appropriate. I think that one line for Djibouti could possibly be enough. If they do need any more pipelines in the future, we can soon deal with that, can't we? Oh, that sounds like it's Jennifer calling for me. I'll see you all later, cheerio." Jack went back to the kitchen to see Jennifer who he saw when he got there had made him some more coffee.

"I've just been talking to Alec and Ray," Jack said, "They've just been telling me that the ghost that did the haunting had done too much and he has been demoted quite a bit in their world now. They said that because Peter had stopped doing any haunting he'll probably be in the clear now. Alec said that they understand that the foreign secretary will make a full recovery, possibly in two or three weeks if he gets some good sleep. As Alec suggested, if he is in hospital they will no doubt be making sure that he does get plenty of good quality sleep, won't they? It did relieve me to hear that. I had been starting to believe that it was I who had caused it all. I'm so glad that he is now probably going to make a good recovery."

Chapter Twenty-Two

It was about a couple of months later and Hugo gave Jack a call and said that he thought that they now had got quite a bit of stuff, more or less, ready for shipping. Jack was, quite naturally, elated at this and went down to meet Hugo in the office that had been dealing with the acquisition and ordering of the materials that they would need. As he got inside the door of the office, he saw Hugo in conversation with Paul, the manager of that department. He went over to them and they began to explain how things were progressing.

"The sea turbine is now ready for Ethiopia, as much as it can be here in the UK and it is ready to be shipped," the manager told Jack. That could take over a week, depending on how they go on at getting it through the Suez Canal. They should be OK, but you always have to be careful in what you say WILL happen. The eight major pumps are now already for shipping. The storage tanks are all done and ready to be shipped. The sixteen take-off points (and their smaller pumps, along with their solar panels) are all ready. We have quite a few more diggers and two or three more bulldozers ready to be shipped (we had already sent them four, so that should be OK) so we have almost got a full shipload of things ready to go. I have been told that the four desalination units will also be ready next week which means that they could go on the same ship. I have got all the rest of the stuff that you said that you needed to do the work in the other countries all ordered and pretty well tied up and in the process of being made or brought over here for storage. Those older buildings that you suggested to Hugo were ideal for holding a lot of those things and they have been an absolute godsend for getting the order into some kind of position for making the job go. All in all, most of this should be in place at Djibouti within two weeks on the outside. I just hope that we can do as well for the other three lots of stuff. You did say also that you may want some additional pipes for Sudan and Somalia I believe. You weren't sure how many miles inland you would need to go, were you? I have got all of that stuff on order and it shouldn't be long in coming. Once we get this first lot out, they can all start doing some work in laying the pipelines, can't they?" I know that you said that they have done a survey, but are you happy that their surveyors are up to the job? I mean, they do need to get the straight line but they won't want the pipeline to keep going into a depression and then cause the water to have to push uphill again, do they? And they do need to check all of the joints as they lay the pipes. If they don't it could end up like a colander and get little water to where they want it."

"Oh, I think that the Ethiopian ones will all be OK. I do have some doubts about the ones for Sudan and maybe for Somalia but I will go and see them all again before they get the pipes to lay out their pipeline. I'll just try and check that they have got some idea of levels. I know that I did originally suggest that a lot of it could go underground but that also there could be a need for some structure to suspend the pipes in places to get over the problems of large valleys. I'm fairly confident that with a constant pressure on the water as it starts its journey, Since the storage tanks themselves will be giving them some head, (The tanks had been designed so that the take-off to the pipe line was at the very bottom of the tanks and an 'inner lid' inside the top of the tanks tanks permitted compressed air to be put down into the tanks to pressurise the water and force it into the pipes) Then, as one of the pumps (at exit from the tanks) will be putting even more pressure down onto the water that will feed away from the tank, and all of this will give a good pressure on the start of the journey, the next pump though will then increase the pressure that will put quite a force onto it and that in itself will help to overcome some minor variations in levels."

"I didn't know that you had been studying any of that on hydro-technology?" Hugo said. "Very impressive and yes, that should, with a little bit of luck keep the water going since there is no pressure ahead of it, will just want to take the easy forward motion, won't it?"

"Well, that's more or less what I thought as well, Hugo," Jack said. "Mind you, I did ask one or two people about some of these things before I started to spout a bit about it. I just hope that what I picked up is enough to do the job. You see, the seventy-five-mile take-off points also have their pumps to start to push again and, if you remove some water from the pipe, it leaves a gap, the water behind it, as far as I can gather, rushes to fill that gap and the top up pump just gives it a bit of a boost. It was also suggested that I should have reduced, just a little, the diameter of the pipe at each takeoff point because they seemed to be suggesting that when the water coming from the larger pipe goes into one that is slightly smaller in diameter, it can increase, somehow, the onward flow. I didn't hear about that at the time though so that hasn't been done. Anyway, once we've got it all in place if we haven't got quite enough force, we could always put in one or two more of the larger pumps, couldn't we?"

"I'll believe you," Hugo said, with a little laugh at his boss, and friend. "Let's face it, if it needs another few pounds sterling to get the water where you want it, no doubt you will find that, won't you?"

The manager of the supplies had listened to all this with some interest and he said that he had followed what Jack had been saying and he said that although he wasn't a water technologist, it did sound to be so very feasible. He had also been a little surprised at just how close the friendship of Hugo and this very, very wealthy man was. He was just pleased himself that he had got the job there which was to simply ensure the continuous supply of materials, whatever they were, for this wealthy man, to send the materials to wherever he wanted them to go.

"So, Jack asked, "Has a ship been booked to take this lot of stuff? Have we got the transport arranged to get it all to the docks as well? I take it that you will be able to see to that, won't you Hugo?"

"Yes," Hugo replied, "The ship is booked and we have a stream of heavy goods vehicles picking things up from various places, including the ones from out of these old buildings of ours. That was a good idea though, Jack, to think of using those old buildings."

"Yes, well I had another idea with that as well, you see Hugo," Jack said. "You see, when Stewart Robinson came down to see us that time he did ask about the possibility of storage for some things. At that time, he meant outside space for anything that didn't need a mass of protection, but I thought that those buildings were only an extension of how his warehouse worked, anyway, weren't they? By the way, are you using any of Stewart's business to move some of the stuff? You must remember that I am also a director of that company as well, so I may as well look after my own interests as well at the same time that we are trying to solve some problems out in Africa, don't you think?"

"Very clever, Jack," Hugo said again with a laugh, clapping Jack on the back as he said so. "Come on, you doing any work is going to put us normal mortals out of work, isn't it, Paul?" he said to the department manager. "Let's get you your dose of coffee, eh? We'll see you later, Paul." And then Hugo and Jack left that office and made their way back up to the flat, and the kettle that was well worked in that flat.

They each got their coffee (Along with Jennifer who had just happened to be in the kitchen when they arrived) and then, off the three of them went to see Alec and Ray to put them into the picture that the materials were now starting to be shipped out to Ethiopia, or more correctly, to Djibouti, for the more detailed construction work to move forward.

"Tell me, Alec," Jack asked, "Do you start to get bonus points once we had agreed to do the work or do you have to wait until the project is up and running before you get them? I know that it has nothing to do with me, really, but I was just curious. I mean, if it is from when we agreed to donate the money, does that mean that the bonus points for the money for all five countries' donations have already led to some bonus points being given? Of course, there is additionally that extra million quid that we gave for some food for Ethiopia, isn't there?"

"You are a curious one, aren't you, Jack?" Alec said. "I understand that the bonus points do start once you have made the public announcement of the donations. Of course, they may say that the bonus points are now there, but not issued to anyone until the jobs are done. I'm not sure about that. Anyway, the points for the extra million that you gave I understand have been issued, so we are now getting some of them."

"Alec, Jack asked, very seriously, "Once the bonus points have all been issued, as you call it, does that mean that you and Ray will just go up to a better level right away? I know that I, and I think that Jennifer and Hugh think that you both deserve to get to that better level but, will that mean that we wouldn't see either of you in our office anymore? Yes, I do want you both to get to that level, but as we now regard you both as our good friends, will it mean that we won't see you anymore? That is like losing a friend and we don't like to lose our friends, do we?"

"That is so kind of you to think of us like that Jack," Alec replied. "As far as I know, and you must remember that I don't know a great deal more than you do at the moment, but it is possible that once we reach that higher level we may cease to know people that we have met while at this level. However, Ray and I have been talking about this anyway ourselves and we do both hope that we may be able to apply for some kind of special permission for us to keep our contact with you and the friendship of all of you in your world, a world that used to also be our world."

"Crikey, Alec, and you as well Ray," Jennifer called out, "They must give you that permission. It would be so unfair for us, and also for you if we couldn't meet and talk now and then, wouldn't it? I suppose that Jack's old friend Peter will have moved up at that time as well won't he? After all, it was he that made the start to try and got it all going, wasn't it?"

"I can promise you this, all three of you here," Alec said, "As we do discover what may happen, we will keep you all well informed. As you may gather, in the world that we are now in, there are no detailed sheets to advise what may or may not be going to happen. All that we can go by are the rumours that keep getting passed about. Both of us are hoping, as are you three, that we will get some permission, but nothing at all is ever guaranteed. Just do keep talking to us while you are getting the projects completed and we will let you any news that we do get."

"Well, as we've told you now, the next lot of stuff will be leaving either this week or next week and that should get the Ethiopian work well on its way. As that is the case, I had thought of going out to Ethiopia myself, taking Jennifer with me, of course, just to try and check in some way that the progress that we have all hoped for has been achieved. I may not be any kind of expert, but if they have laid the pipeline that is a fairly good indication, isn't it? Oh, by the way, Hugo, I know that I haven't mentioned it to you, but when we do go, do you think that it would be sensible to take a couple of security people with me, perhaps Manuel and Javier? I shall of course be asking the President of Ethiopia for some security anyway but I would certainly take your advice."

"Yes, of course, Jack," Hugo replied. "I'm sure that the President will be providing some security for you but yes, I will see Miguel and ask him if he will let Manuel and Javier go with you. It does seem to me to be a sensible decision to go and check on how things are progressing anyway. You will, on this occasion, only be going to Ethiopia and Djibouti, won't you? It is just my opinion but, for Somalia, I think that it may be a good idea to try and get the Prime Minister to go with you again as well. Yes, I too had some reservations about the people from Somalia. The others, Sudan and Eritrea could I imagine be somewhat safer for you. What do you think then of Jack inspecting the work progress, Alec, and you Ray? Let's face it; you two have somewhere in your lives seen some similar sorts of things and you may perhaps have better judgement than we have. Obviously, things do need some kind of inspection but the only thing that I was wondering was, should it be Jack, or should someone else be sent out to do some checks? As Jack has said, he's no expert on these kinds of things so would it perhaps be better to get some kind of surveyor of our own to go out and carry out any checkups? I'm not meaning for the Ethiopian work, that President did seem to be a much more reliable person, didn't he?"

"Thanks for still worrying a bit about me, Hugo," Jack replied. "Yes I did get a good feeling myself and have some confidence in the President of Ethiopia, but I have said all along that I wasn't too keen on the chap from Somalia. I do like the idea of sending some good, qualified surveyors out though, Hugo, particularly for the other countries. In view of the amount of money being invested in this project it would only be reasonable to do that, wouldn't it?"

"Of course, it would be reasonable," Hugo replied, "I would say that it would be expected that some checks would have to be carried out when they are being given this amount of money and aid. You know, they may even begin to feel that there was some catch if some checks weren't carried out. You have had the equipment checked at this end, their installation of the pipeline can be critical and if they haven't done the joints between the pipes properly then the water will be gushing out more or less at every joint, won't it? Yes, I think that you do need to appoint some surveyors to go out and check on the work being done. If they were in fact trustworthy, and who is to say that they are not? They may well have employed someone who has some qualifications to do some checking just to make sure that they can't be criticised for not doing the job correctly. If they have done that work correctly; good, then your mind can rest a little easier, can't it? The pipeline though is important and we should have had the Ethiopian line checked anyway. It is still all empty of water until we get the desalination units and pumps in place so it can still be checked. They may just use air to pressurise the pipes to check, but it can be done, I would have thought. I'll get on to that when I get downstairs. That doesn't mean that your visit wouldn't be worth a lot to the entire project though. If those countries do believe that you are likely to be visiting them yourself and if we send out surveyors ourselves as well it will make them try just that bit harder, won't it?"

"I hadn't realised that we would be going out to Addis Ababa again," Jennifer said. "We didn't see much of the city when we went before, did we? Do you think that we could go and have a look at some parts of it? I know that I may not be able to go and do any shopping as such, but it would be interesting to have a bit closer look at the place. All that we did the last time was drive through in that convoy of cars with the military and the police all around us. You could ask, couldn't you, Jack, if we could just have a little bit slower drive when we go around the city to see some of the things there, that would be nice, wouldn't it?"

"As I shall be speaking to the President, I could ask him," Jack replied. "Jennifer, just don't get your hopes up too high yet. Even he may think that it is a risk too many to do that. Let's be guided by what he says, eh?"

"And will you mention to your own Prime Minister that you are going to be making a visit to check on the progress?" Ray asked. "The Prime Minister may be a bit miffed if you don't include him in some of what you are doing. Yes, he will want to get some kudos from being involved, even slightly, but he will also know that if he only had the one visit, that wouldn't be much but, if he was also going out on some subsequent visits, that could be good news for him. Just have a thought about it all, Jack."

"I hadn't thought of telling him and making it a big outing for everybody," Jack said, "But I can see what you are implying there, Ray. Yes, I'll give him a call, or maybe I could call Norman Brooks, and at least that would just put them in the picture and then I could give them an invite if they want to pay another visit to that country. I will stress though that on this occasion it is just Djibouti and Ethiopia that we are going to. I can let them know that the bulk of the equipment is now on its way out there and that we are getting towards the final leg of the Ethiopian and Djibouti project. It lets me update them as well about all of that for the rest of the other three countries that have now been ordered and that all the pipes have been dispatched anyway so that their pipelines can be started to be laid and be ready for when the remainder of the equipment gets there. Yes, that seems to me to be a damned good idea, Ray. I'll get on and do that today."

"Look, I'm going," Hugo said. "I can see Paul, in our ordering department now and see if he has any details of any surveyors on hand (or if he knows of some somewhere) and then I could get the surveys put underway for the other countries, couldn't I? I'll see you all later."

"Look you lot," Jennifer said, "I do have some things that I want to get done myself so I'm going down Jack. If you want me, you'll find me in the lounge I think. I want to finish off a bit of that book that I've been reading. Once I've finished that there is some housework to do you know, don't you? Cheerio Alec and Ray, I'll see you both later." Jennifer then went down to get her book, and hopefully get to the end of it!"

"Oh we are getting to be a busy little crowd, aren't we," Alec said with a small laugh. "It's good though to see this amount of work, excitement and progress being achieved. It just now seems that the idea that Ray and I had of being able to get a scheme to get us bonus points was a good one. Yes, I know, we did rely on Peter at first and I suppose that we used him a bit, but he is also going to benefit himself, isn't he? I do know that Ray and I have enjoyed doing it all. Before, it was just an idea in our heads but at last, it is getting somewhere much nearer to fruition, isn't it? Mind you, a lot of the success of it all has been down to how you and we have all worked together wouldn't you think, Jack? You might say that it has been a common aim for a very uncommon kind of project."

Jack went back down to see Jennifer and, just to be a good husband he made her a cup of coffee and found her in the lounge area, reading the book that she had taken a liking to. Jack only liked reading his travel log and sometimes a travel brochure. He knew now though that anywhere that he saw in the brochures he could so easily manage to go and see the places in reality. The more that he looked at the brochures now though, the more that he thought of the pilot's licence that he was well on the way to getting. That, when he had finished it he felt quite sure, would let him choose when and where he wanted to go to, never mind just the brochures. His helicopter licence he had now managed to get and although he hadn't yet bought a helicopter, he had seriously been looking at some different models that interested him. Jennifer had told him that she wouldn't mind going for a ride with him in either the helicopter, or the jet if he ever did manage to get either, but she had insisted that she wouldn't want to try and get a licence herself.

Jennifer finished off the book and put it down, picking up her coffee and she looked at Jack and said, "So, I thought that you were going to ring that Norman Brooks, weren't you? Or was it the Prime Minister? If you are going to be making the trip to Ethiopia and Djibouti as you said to Alec and Ray, you had agreed that you would see if the Prime Minister may want to go out with you again. It's no good you just mooching about and thinking about that damned helicopter. You haven't even decided which kind you like, have you? The trip to Ethiopia is something that you do need to do, isn't it?"

"Yes," Jack replied, quite resignedly. "I know that I would like to get one but there seem to be so many variables and I just can't manage to decide. But, that apart I suppose that I ought to get it done with and ring the Prime Minister, oughtn't I? The other trip though, the one to Somalia, that one does worry me. I think that it is that one, more than any of the others that is making me hesitate so much. I feel quite sure about the visit to Ethiopia and Djibouti and I believe that I've become resigned somewhat to doing the Eritrea and Sudan visits, but, that man from Somalia, he did worry me quite a bit. Didn't he worry you at all Jennifer? I suppose that I could do it all with Hugo's way and just send out some surveyors to check on the pipeline there and then the rest of the progress, as it happens. Then I suppose that I would only have to go to see it when the line is switched on in each country wouldn't I? For each of the countries, that really is going to be something, isn't it? I believe that I really want to be there when that happens for them all. The thing is, I'd like to see it at both ends. When we do start to pump the water; and at the other end of the pipe when the water starts to pour out and it begins to make a start on creating the inland lake for them. Oh, come on, I'll give Norman Brooks a call and see what he thinks. If he thinks that the Prime Minister will want to go then that will be that. If he doesn't seem to want to go then we could go by ourselves, couldn't we?"

"Jack," Jennifer said, "This one to Ethiopia and Djibouti is only going to see how things are progressing, isn't it? You've said before that he will probably want to be in at the end, you know, to see the water gushing out at the end of the pipe, haven't you? That does make far more sense. Just think; if you were in his position, would you want to waste two or three days just to go and check that some progress has been made? I doubt it, and I think that if you're honest, you would agree. Yes, do let them know that you are going to check the progress but don't start to expect that they'll want to be going out there with you. The two of us could go out, three if you think that Hugo should go as well. You can always ask him if he wants to go. He may say that just for that, he'll leave all that to you. You do feel fairly safe with Ethiopia anyway, don't you? If you do that one, it is the first project, isn't it? The other countries will then presume that you may, I just say may, possibly, go out and check their progress. Yes, they may well expect you to go and see the final job as it is switched on and for that, you could possibly get a lot of world coverage by the press so don't think that you can hide from the publicity on that one, can you? Now, are you going to, just for the sake of good manners, call Norman Brooks and let him know that you are going to pay a visit to Djibouti and Ethiopia just to see the progress? You can tell him that all of the pipelines should be in place and that the rest of the equipment should be with them within a couple of weeks. Then it will be just a case of getting everything in order for it all to start up. How long do you think that will take? I would imagine maybe a couple of months or so wouldn't you? Well, go on then, give him a call and then you can go back to looking at some brochures of helicopters. Once you have decided on which one, you could then let Hugo get some people in place to build some kind of hangar for it, couldn't you? I don't suppose that that will take very long, but it will need to have some cover of some kind, won't it?"

Chapter Twenty-Three

Jack did make the call to Norman Brooks and he, in turn appeared to welcome the fact that Jack had troubled to keep them in the picture. Jack had also explained that he was now sending out surveyors to check on the quality of work on the pipelines in all of the countries as they were being laid. He had told Norman that the rest of the equipment was being shipped for the Ethiopian project and he hoped that it would be with them within two or three weeks. Then, he had said it would just be a case of them being able to get the equipment all assembled and working before the big switch on took place. He suggested that that could be in about three months but that he would let them know as soon as he knew himself. He also asked if they had heard anything of the situation in Somalia (since he knew that Norman was already aware of his doubts about that one country and the President that he had met). Norman told him that all that he had heard so far was that yes, there was some kind of unrest in that country, but that there was nothing in particular that he had been able to discover that was of any great importance. He did assure Jack that when he did hear anything, he would let him know.

Jack left the phone, fairly satisfied that he had informed the Prime Minister and that he was now quite confident that he wouldn't have politicians with him on this trip. He gave Hugo a call and asked if he would want to go with him and Jennifer to Ethiopia and Djibouti. Hugo didn't answer that directly, instead, he asked Jack if he wanted to take him with them on that trip, or did they want to try it by themselves. He did though tell Jack that when he had decided what he wanted, he would also be getting Miguel to assign Manuel and Javier to go with them for some security. He said that would be a normal and expected thing but that he too believed that the President of Ethiopia would, no doubt be making sure that he would have security for the visit.

Jack called out for Jennifer and as she came through to see what he wanted he asked her, "Do you want it to be the two of us for this trip to Ethiopia or do you want me to ask Hugo to go with us?"

"Don't be daft, Jack," Jennifer said. "When we go somewhere, we go together. We don't need to have Hugo with us all of the time, do we? I know that we may have to have some security people, but we can live with that, can't we? Just let him know that we are going, that's called good manners and then you could see about contacting the President of Ethiopia and setting up a date for us to visit. You could let him know that the equipment is now being shipped out and if you say that you would, ideally like to just see that at least some of their pipeline out there is completed properly, I'll bet that he'll be pleased with you and then, he'll make the arrangements for you at that end, you just see if he doesn't. Jack, it is you who is giving them a lifeline to protect their country. You will be the hero once the system is in operation. When you've done it all, do let us know when we are going. Oh, it may also be an idea to see about booking a 'plane to get us there and back, don't you think?"

"Jennifer," Jack said, with quite an offbeat, bored kind of tone in his voice. "You must think that I'm totally incompetent. I have got most of that in my mind. I just wondered if you thought that it would be better if Hugo was with us. I had thought about the rest of it. I may also ask the President if he could clear things with Djibouti and also if we could have a look at some of Addis Ababa while we are there. Go on, you do your cooking, I was only trying to be polite and involve you in what we were doing."

Jack then picked up some of the brochures from the table that was close to him. These though, weren't the travel brochures; these were the brochures with some details of helicopters! Jack had seen one or two that he liked the idea of but in the main, he had settled on either a Robinson R66 4 seat helicopter or a Bell 206B. He knew that for what he wanted one for it didn't need to be the fastest and most powerful. It didn't need to be new, although he was quite aware that with the amount of money that he had got, that cost was only an arbitrary thing. Both of these machines appeared to him to fit the bill for what he was thought that he was wanting or needing it for. He decided that before he did make any decision he would again ask his friend, Hugo. Hugo had once told him though that he hadn't got a pilot's licence but he had said that Miguel had got one so he thought that perhaps if he asked them both he may get some advice that would suit what he wanted. That, he decided was what he would do, he would get them both together and see what their joint decisions were. In the meantime, he decided that he would try and contact the President of Ethiopia and try and get that job sorted.

The President had given him a card which had both a private telephone number for him and also an email address. He thought that maybe an e-mail would be better for him and then he would have a full copy of what he was doing. First of all, he gave Hugo a call. Maybe Hugo wouldn't want to go but Jack just felt that it was correct to ask him if he did or not.

Hugo had answered Jack's call straight away and Jack had asked him if he would like to pop up and he would give him a coffee while they talked. Hugo said that he would be there within five minutes. Just to be ready, Jack went into the kitchen and put the kettle on. Jennifer was already in the kitchen by then and so he told her that he had just asked Hugo to come to see if he wanted to go to Ethiopia or not and that he was also going to get some advice on a helicopter, if he could, from either Hugo or Miguel.

Hugo arrived and, as soon as Jack had given him his coffee, Jack asked straight out, "Hugo, I'm planning on making that trip out to Ethiopia to see how things are there. Did you want to come out with us or not? Jennifer has told me that you probably have enough things going on here without going there, but I just felt that you should have the choice?"

"Jack, my old friend," Hugo replied, smiling at his friend. "You know that I have quite a lot of work on at the moment so unless I am needed, can I miss out on this? By the way, as you know,

I was talking to Paul to find out what he thought of some surveyors for going out to all four countries to check the pipelines and he has got me some names of people who he says are both reliable and reasonable and are probably available. I was going to get them to cover all five of the countries, starting with Ethiopia and Djibouti (since they have had the pipes there far longer and, with luck, they should be more or less all finished). If you go out to Ethiopia; that will just be icing on the cake, so to speak. Yes, I think that it will be a good idea for you to go and see them. That is a goodwill thing, that's all. It will be they probably who get the 'switch on' first anyway, won't it? For that, I believe that a visit would be essential for you, just to complete it all. If I stay here, I can work well with Paul and I think that between us we could be pushing some of the other suppliers quite a bit to get a move on. Those old buildings, are now becoming an almost essential storage warehouse for us, Jack. That was a good idea of yours. Anyway, I'll get back down there and do some work again. There wasn't anything else, was there?"

"Yes," Jack replied, "I was hoping to get your opinion on a helicopter for here, for me if you like. I have narrowed it down to two different ones. There isn't a massive price difference, they both have four seats and they both carry some luggage. I can let you have a look at the brochures later if you like. Also, I knew that you told me that you hadn't got a pilot's licence so you told me that Miguel had got one so I was going to ask him as well. This is just being polite, Hugo. What do you think? Oh, another thing. Why don't you see about getting your pilot's licence as well, for both a jet and a helicopter, whichever one I settle on? It could be a help to have that flexibility, couldn't it?"

"OK, Jack, I'll think about it," Hugo replied, "But as for asking Miguel as well, that makes a lot of sense so get him to get dual licences as well, why don't you? Right, now I've been here long enough and I do have some work to do, I'm off. I'll see you later"

Jack rather resignedly got up and went to his small computer (not the main one in the office where Alec and Ray were working) and he began by preparing an email to the President of Ethiopia. He told the President that he and his wife would like to pay a visit just to see how the progress was going on. He said that the balance of the equipment was now on board a ship and should be with them at Djibouti within about two weeks' time. He told the President that they had sent surveyors to all five countries and that they should either have seen one recently, or that one would be there soon. He said that he would appreciate it if when they did visit the President, if he could arrange things with Djibouti for his visit there. He also went on to say that although it may not be usual for such visits, his wife had expressed an interest in seeing something of Addis Ababa when they did visit. As usual, he completed it with some very complimentary greetings (unusual for Jack, but he realised that he may have to learn to start using some flowery phrases at some time!). He pressed the send button and thought that at least he had got that part underway. He wasn't keen on booking a 'plane until they had a firmer date from the President. With his work then done he gave Miguel a call and asked if he could pop up to see them and he said that he would get him a cup of coffee.

It didn't take Miguel very long to get to the flat and, as promised, Jack had made him a cup of coffee. He took him into the lounge and explained that he was thinking of buying a helicopter and that Hugo had previously told him that Miguel had got a pilot's licence and he would appreciate his opinion on the helicopter that he was thinking of getting. He handed the two Brochures for the helicopters, one for the Bell 206B and one for the Robinson R66 helicopter. He also asked Miguel if he did in fact have a licence for a helicopter but Miguel said, no, he had only ever got his licence for a twin-engine jet. Hearing that, Jack suggested that Miguel also try to get his licence for a helicopter and he said that he would appreciate his advice when it came to getting a small to medium-sized jet. Miguel was quite taken aback at all of this. He agreed that he would try and get some training for a helicopter and he said that any advice that he could give when it came to getting a jet, he would willingly do his best for them. Jack, of course, told him that any costs in getting his licence, he would pay for. Miguel was quite over the moon at hearing all of this and he went back to his work once again a very contented young man.

Jack knew then that all that he had to do now was wait. He had to wait to get back a response from the President of Ethiopia. He couldn't even try and book an aeroplane until he had heard back from the President. He had to wait, once again, for Jennifer to finish her work in the kitchen before he could get her to give any input to his decision about what kind of helicopter to get. He would have to wait now to see if Hugo could manage to pull forward any other deliveries for the other three countries. Jack wasn't good at waiting but, he did know that he could go and talk to his ghostly friends in the other office, the special office! He went there and, as usual, this time it was Alec who was sitting at the computer with his hands moving above the keyboard and it was Ray who appeared to be making notes on his pad.

"Hello everyone," Jack called out to the two of them. "I just thought that I'd pop in and see how you were doing. I have at present hit a dead spot. Oops, sorry, I didn't mean that as a pun or anything, sorry to both of you. No, at the moment I'm having to wait and I don't seem to be able to do anything. I have emailed the President of Ethiopia to suggest that Jennifer and I need to pay them a visit just to see what is happening, I've told him that surveyors have been appointed and are travelling to all five countries to carry out a few tests. I told him that the balance of the equipment had now been shipped and that we couldn't do anything more now until it had started to get there. I've asked Hugo if he wanted to go, but he said that he was too busy. I've suggested to both he and Miguel that they both get some pilot's licences for both a helicopter and a twin-engine jet and they are thinking about it. Of course, Miguel has got his licence for a twin-engine jet, for him it was just the helicopter, but at least he did like the idea of doing that. Jennifer has been working in her kitchen again so I'm afraid that it looks as though you two are stuck with me for now. How are things going here, anyway? I don't suppose that there are any major problems, are there? The fund hasn't gone all haywire again, has it?"

"Well," Ray said, looking up from his pad, "Alec has been saying that we could certainly do with getting some more money paid out soon. Yes, the stuff that you have ordered is all mounting up to a good total, but quite a lot of it is on credit to you so the total isn't going down quite as we had hoped that it would. Do you think that you can manage to find somewhere to make a few more donations? It would help but if the worst comes to the worst, Alec can manage to lose some more money. Neither of us likes to do that. It just isn't the way that things are done. You do realise that anyway, don't you?"

"I suppose that I could call up that Norman Brooks again and ask if he has got some more potential crises that could do with some help. I'll give it a try anyway but we do appear to be covering most things now. I'll go and see what I can do and I'll be back as soon as I can."

Jack left that office and made it back into the kitchen where Jennifer had just finished her work and was making them both another coffee. They took their coffee into the lounge and Jack began to tell her of his day and how Alec and Ray were again getting concerned about the fund total. He told her that he had said that he would try Norman Brooks again but Jennifer said no to that, quite definitely.

"Jack," She said, "Just consider what you would think was happening if someone kept coming to you saying that they just wanted to give away some more money. If you do that they will all start to say that there is something wrong when you do that. Yes, we can have another look at the old laptop to find any more crises, but let's keep it between the two of us." Jennifer moved out of the lounge and went to the small cupboard where they kept the old small laptop. She took it back into the lounge and turned it on. "Right," she said, "What did we look for the last time? Ah, I remember, I think, Crises in the World that cause loss of life etcetera. I think that it was something like that, anyway, now let's see what it brings up for us."

The screen lit up with quite a list of events and occurrences. Most of them were comparatively minor and didn't seem to have anything like the relevance that the East African ones had had. "Maybe we just have to keep trying, more or less every day," Jack said. "It doesn't follow that there will be major crises every day, does it?"

"Right then," Jennifer agreed, "Yes, we'll do it every day and let's set a time for it. I know, let's make it as soon as we can after midday every day. It doesn't follow that we'll get them each day, but if we get one now and then, that may be enough to keep Alec and Ray happy, don't you think?"

They just finished talking and the phone rang. Jack picked it up and said, "Hello, can I help you?"

"Is that Jack Dawkins?" the voice on the phone asked, "This is Norman Brooks. I know that we spoke earlier but I hadn't got much for you on that occasion. Apparently, though, there has been a Tsunami that has hit some parts of the southern coast of Sri Lanka. The news is just coming in now and I know that the Prime Minister asked me to keep you abreast of any crisis that we heard of. I shall be getting some more details soon. If I may, I shall keep calling you as I get more news. In the absence of the Foreign Secretary, I am in some way having to do what I can to help that department. As it happens, the Foreign Secretary is now starting to recover so hopefully I can pass it all back on to them then. In the meantime, I'll keep getting what I can for you. By the way, did you arrange the re-visit to Ethiopia? I'll bet that will be interesting. You will keep us updated, won't you?"

"Hello Norman," Jack replied. "I didn't recognise your voice but yes, do please keep us updated about the Sri Lanka incident and please, let me know if there is anything at all that I can do. Yes, we have contacted Ethiopia and I'm waiting for the President to get back to me hopefully to suggest to me any convenient dates for him. We have also now instructed surveyors and they are going to be going out now to check all five countries to see that things are being done how we wanted them done. That should be a big help. All of the equipment and materials for the Ethiopian and Djibouti projects are now at sea and should be there within a couple of weeks. Then there will be the installation completions and the start of the water to the inland area. Yes, I shall certainly keep you informed. And perhaps for the big switch-on the Prime Minister may wish to be in attendance, do you think?"

"Oh, I'm sure that he will," Norman replied. "We must keep in touch though. There seems to be so much happening at the moment, doesn't there? I'd better get back to my desk because my other phone is ringing now, cheerio, until later."

"Well," Jack said, "That has given us another crisis, hasn't it? And did you hear that about the Foreign Secretary having made a recovery? That's such good news, isn't it? Oh, I'll just pop in and let Alec and Ray know that we have got another crisis on our hands now, haven't we? I'll just bet that they'll be so pleased with that. I don't mean pleased that there is a crisis, but pleased that there may be somewhere else that could need a good conation."

Chapter Twenty-Four

Alec and Ray were pleased when Jack did get to the office and tell them. "At least that's saved me from losing a lot more money just to bring the total down," Alec said. "Just make sure that it is a fairly good-sized donation though. Just for the short term though, I can't imagine what you could do, other than simple cash donations, do you?"

"When there have been Tsunami before," Jack said, "Quite often the people have lost their homes, their properties and any number of things. Some of the homes seemed in some cases to be little more than some type of almost pre-fabricated building. For something like that I may be able to donate a few hundred of those small type of mobile home sort of things as well as some cash for immediate aid, don't you think?"

"All that I can say," Alec replied, "That seems to be faster thinking than I have been this time. Yes, that sort of thing could help to make a start, couldn't it? You just do your best Jack. We'll keep our fingers crossed, won't we, Ray?"

"Don't forget," Ray added, "Putting some mobile homes there is one thing but for them to be much good at all they'll be needing some water, some drainage and maybe some kind of power as well, Jack. All of those kinds of things can make their lives a little bit better after such tragic losses that they've had and it does help to make the donation a good bit more, doesn't it?"

As they were all talking, Jennifer went to the office and, she heard some of the latter pieces of advice from Alec and Ray. "Don't you two think that he has enough on his hands at the moment with all of these things that he's getting done in East Africa," She said. "You two have done a good job in getting a large enough total in the fund, there's no denying that. But, you two both promised when the allocator went and Jack needed some advice on crises around the World. You said that you would get yourselves and your cronies to do some searching, didn't you? What have you done exactly on that front? Now, just because the fund has gone up a little bit again, you seem to think that it is down to Jack to get it down each time by him making more and more donations. Yes, he does like to do that, but what exactly have you two been doing to help? Yes, we do regard you as friends, but come on, let's see you doing some work as well, besides just moving money about. I think that you are good at getting the stocks and shares to work to make money alright, but you haven't tried very hard to find ways to get the money to be sent out, have you? Come on, let's be hearing exactly what you have done to find any crises?"

"Oh dear, Alec," Ray said, "It looks to me as though we've upset the lady again, haven't we? Yes, we did promise that we would start to chase things up from our end and, being honest, we haven't found anything at all, have we? These two dears have done a lot for us. Yes, I believe that she has every right to be having a go at us. If you would just try and lose a billion or two more Alec, with what you have been doing in Africa things could get better. In the meantime, we should be also trying to find some crises for Jack to try and help with. Usually, Alec, you have quite a lot to say, don't you? Where's your voice at the moment?"

"Yes, Ray," Alec said. "We did promise to get some people doing some searching for some things. No, we haven't done what we said that we'd do. I'll lose a couple of billion and then the pair of us can go back and put the word about that we want to know of any crises anywhere in the World. I think that I can say sorry, quite honestly from both myself and from Ray, Jack. You'll see, once we get going on it we shall find some other things. Some may be quite small, comparatively speaking, but all of the bits will add up, won't they?

"That's sounding a little better, both of you," Jennifer said. "The present cost of this present thing at the Horn of Africa hasn't yet been evaluated. There will, no doubt be quite a few more things that are needed so that could quite easily almost double from what Jack has said so far, couldn't it? If it does double, that then that could get it up to four billion pounds, couldn't it? Let's get some sense into what we are all doing and give my husband a chance. I'm going take him now to get another dose of his coffee so you two just get going, will you?"

Jennifer then, very determinedly took hold of Jack's arm and led him out of the office and back to the kitchen where she pushed him onto a stool. "Now listen, you," She said. "I know damned well that you feel some obligation to help them to get their bonus points but when you agree to do things to help them, you do try to do that. So far, you've done damned well, haven't you? I know you have, you know that you have and if they would be honest, they know that you have. It's quite some time now since they promised to try and help you by finding crises in our world through their efforts, in their world looking forward in time as well to get some things that could help. At the moment, Jack, it's you who has done all of the finding and all of the donating. Yes, they did get the fund up high enough but now it's down to them to control the fund as they have to. They have told us before that if it gets a bit too high they can deliberately make some bad investments so that it loses some money. That is their kind of work so, if it has gone up a bit now, let them lose a bit until it gets back to what it is supposed to be. You do agree with all of this, don't you?"

"Oh, Jennifer," Jack said, "I've been so blind, haven't I? Yes, they did promise to find crises in their world and they haven't done a thing on that front, have they? Yes, we've done it all and it is still going on, isn't it? This Tsunami thing, yes, I can soon get something going for that. I'll get Hugo and Paul to start buying up all of these mobile homes that they can get and I can get them shipped out, can't I? Paul can soon get some people and some equipment so that they can install drains and get some water and a power supply to them. Yes, I think that we can soon do something to help them. I'll call Hugo now and get him to make a start on buying up all of the mobile-type homes that he can get. Paul is getting to be so good at getting the shipping organised that he'll soon get that dealt with."

"Look, Jack, here's your coffee," Jennifer said. "You just settle down and enjoy that and I'll give Hugo a call. I'll even make a coffee for him. That'll soon get him here, won't it?"

Hugo did appear within a few minutes, rather anxious-looking since he didn't know why he had to get there so fast. Jennifer did indeed have his coffee waiting for him as he walked in.

"What is it," Hugo said, "What's gone wrong, Jack? I thought that we had more or less got everything covered. It sounded urgent when you called for me Jennifer."

"The problem is Hugo," Jennifer said, "Jack received another phone call from Norman Brooks, you know who I mean, the Prime Minister's aide. Well, the Prime Minister had asked him to keep Jack informed of any major crises that did happen and apparently there has been a large Tsunami that has hit the Southern coast of Sri Lanka. It has caused an awful lot of damage. Houses and other buildings lost, they don't know yet how many people, but they think that it is in the hundreds and maybe in the thousands that have been lost. Anyway, Jack has decided that he wants to try and help with that as well. He came up with the idea of buying up as many of those mobile type of homes that he could get hold of, enough machinery and people to do some work to lay drains, water and power supplies to them and to get some aid going out as quickly as we can. He told me that he has a lot of faith in Paul knowing how to get hold of things and how to get things done. Can you pick it all up from there and chase it for him? I have been giving him coffee as he now seems to almost be in shock."

"No, I'm not in shock," Jack said. "Yes, I am upset that these kinds of things can happen and I just thought that we could help if the mobile homes are only a temporary home of sorts, it would be something for those people, wouldn't it? Will you have words with Paul and ask him to try and get things started? If he needs to employ more people, just employ them. You know the system, don't you, Hugo? That wasn't all that it was either Hugo. I had been to tell Alec and Ray about the Tsunami and they told me that the fund has been going up again and that I would have to find more crises to let me make more donations. As they were telling me to find more, Jennifer came into the office and she has had a good go at both Alec and Ray. Some long time ago, when we were trying to find something to donate to, they had said that they could get that kind of information from their world about what was going to happen in our world. Well, they haven't ever bothered to find anything at all and Jennifer gave them a good telling off and they accepted that and they have now gone off to see if they can find anything else that looks like a crisis. Now you can see what is bothering me. We now seem to be getting crises coming at us from all directions and we still have the East African things to finish off anyway, don't we?"

"Crikey," Hugo said, "You two do seem to have been having a time, don't you? So, Alec and Ray have admitted that they let you down as well, do they? Well, that'll be a good one to remember, won't it? Yes, I'll get onto Paul right away and get him to start buying up as many of the mobile-type homes as he can get. It'll need water pipes, drainage pipes, a lot of cabling and a lot of people who can kind of put those kinds of things together, won't it? I suppose it will also mean that they will need another load of diggers as well to make trenches and everything, won't it? What about sewage disposal itself? Do you want me to see if I can get hold of a number of septic tanks or something? At least we can't let them have a problem of waste sewage that could cause even more problems, couldn't it? Yes, I'll get going now, cheerio." With that, Hugo dashed out of the flat, making his way back to talk to Paul in the supplies office.

"Does all this make you feel any better then," Jennifer asked Jack. "You know that Hugo will now get things moving, don't you? I honestly expect Alec and Ray to be there with some information for you the next time that you see them as well. I think that it hit home with them that they had promised, and they have done nothing about that. Anyway, have you checked your emails today? You may have one from the President of Ethiopia and if that is in then you are going to have to get a move on at making some arrangements to 'pop out' to see how things out there, aren't you? Oh, you are going to be so busy now. I think that you'd better forget for a time anything about ordering that helicopter, don't you?"

"Oh, heck," Jack said, "I'd forgotten about that. I'd better get to it now and see if he has replied already, hadn't I? I'll go right away and see what there is there."

"Look, don't panic now about that." Jennifer said, "Remember that he'll probably be far more nervous than you are. It's you who is paying a lot of money to make his country that will become fertile to help the people there. When it's all done, you will have paid for it all but he will go down in their history as being the person who was President and did the negotiations to get it done. It will be his record, don't you see? As that is the case, he will now be terrified in case he upsets you in some way and you withdraw from doing it all. I know that you won't withdraw, and you know that you won't, but he doesn't know that, does he? Yes, respect the man and let him help you but also remember that at the banquet, just to help his people at that time you quite glibly gave them another million pounds to feed the people, didn't you?"

"The way that you put it, Jennifer," Jack replied, smiling a little more now, "They must all have been waiting for those damned ghosts to get around to making me wealthy. Oh, I can see that you may be right, but it just seems that there is now so much to do. I have to go to Ethiopia; I know in myself that he has probably answered and that I will have to go. And then there are all of the other countries to get watered properly. I know that I have some misgivings about Somalia. I may be completely wrong about that man. The other two, well, I'm not too bothered about them. We've got the surveyors checking now so they'll probably all be OK by the time that we have to put water into the pipes. Yes, I'm just being a bit stupid, aren't I? Peter always used to say that I was the daft one amongst us when we were young. Now I'm just proving him to be right, aren't I?"

Jack got up and went to his small computer to check his emails. Yes, there was one from the President of Ethiopia, thanking him once again for all that he was doing and saying that he would ensure that he was free whenever Jack wanted to go next week. That made Jack hesitate but only for a moment and then he went to find Jennifer. Jennifer had said that she was hoping that when they go again she may be able to see some more of Ethiopia, and particularly of Addis Ababa. Jack wanted to know just when she wanted to go next week! He hadn't expected it to be quite as sudden as this, and he didn't think that Jennifer had either. As usual, he found Jennifer in her beloved kitchen and he told her that he had received the email from the President and he wanted to know when next week they would like to go there.

As it was now Thursday for them, Jennifer suggested, "Look, if we fly out on Monday and then if you took a couple of days to see some of the pipelines that you need to in Ethiopia, that's Tuesday and Wednesday. If we fly down to Djibouti to see the starting base for both Ethiopia and Djibouti on Thursday, that would leave Friday for me to be shown around Addis Ababa and then we could fly back home on Saturday, couldn't we? You see, Jack, it is so easy to plan things when you want to, isn't it? It doesn't matter much about what you see of the pipeline anyway, does it, not when you are getting an experienced surveyor to go out and do a more detailed check of it all? You see, that is sense, isn't it? I'm not as bothered about going into Djibouti to see the towns and cities there. I would imagine that they will be fairly similar to any that we see in Ethiopia anyway, won't they?"

Jack had to agree with the 'logic' that she somehow applied to how they conducted a visit to this Middle Eastern country. He had a thought about how he should word his answer and then began to put it all into an email. He did cut short just a little some of Jennifer's tour of Addis Ababa by suggesting a half-day tour of that City and then them making a Friday night flight to get them back to England. Being very polite (and somewhat nervous about upsetting his wife by shortening some of her visits) he called Jennifer to see the email that he was going to send. In it, he had also informed the President that there would be he and his wife plus two of his 'aides', (him using the term 'aides' to cover that they were his two security men that Hugo had recommended that he take). He also suggested that if perhaps the President could advise the hotel where they had stayed the last time he would like the same apartment for him and his wife plus two adjoining apartments for his aides. Being fair to the President though, he did suggest that if the hotel would e-mail an invoice to him directly, he would settle that since he did not want his visit to be a costly imposition on the country. He also asked if the President could arrange suitable vehicles for while they were there to transport them about and possibly a helicopter to get them down to Djibouti and back. He had shown it to Jennifer and then, just to make sure that he was doing things properly, he called for Hugo to pop in and see him (just so that he could also get his approval of his arrangements). Hugo did come and he had quite a detailed look at the email and then he gave Jack some good compliments for his tact and diplomacy in suggesting that they would pay their own hotel bills. He said that he was also pleased to see that Jack had asked for two of the adjoining apartments on that floor for the security men. Jack had, of course, remembered how Hugo had in Spain insisted that with security men on their floor, they had mounted a guard of the clients (this time, the clients were to be Jack and Jennifer). He suggested that the President may ask that they be allowed to settle the hotel bill but he suggested to Jack that he insist on them paying for their own hotel bill. "If you are paying a fortune to get their lands to be fertile and capable of supporting their agriculture," Hugo had said, "How can they possibly afford to pay for the hotel bills?"

Jack liked the irony of a comment such as that (which did often seem to be the way that Hugo thought of things) and he simply sent out the email that he had prepared.

Hugo was also reporting that Paul had already sourced seventy-eight new mobile-type homes and was making arrangements for them to be got to the docks to be stored while waiting for any more that he could find before shipping them out to Sri Lanka. He had sourced some fairly large septic tanks from a company called Klargester that could be taken out with the Mobile Homes to provide some kind of sewage control for wastewater. Paul had also managed to find some plumbers, electricians and general fitters to work on the mobile homes as they arrived. In total Jack was extremely pleased with the way that things were moving along. Just to try and get the job completed, he telephoned Norman Brooks (the Prime Minister's aide) and when Norman answered, Jack said, "Hello Norman, I wasn't sure how things were going with the problems with Sri Lanka but I think that I have got my people to make a start on things already. You didn't say exactly how many houses had been destroyed, or how many people had been lost. I think that you just said that it was a lot of people and a lot of property didn't you? Well, my people have already sourced seventy-eight new large Mobile Homes. They have also got some large septic tanks, they are made by a company called Klargester and the ones that we have selected can cope with ten thousand litres each and they can handle the effluent from about fifty or more people. We believe that nine of these should cover all of the houses adequately so (If they believe that they need more, let me know and we can adjust the order), they can go out with the homes plus I have some electricians, plumbers and general fitters to get the homes up and running for the people there. I can only ship the Mobile Homes out, but I'll fly the workmen out to Sri Lanka when the arrival time comes about for the homes. If someone from our end could possibly negotiate with their authorities to find and have permission for the Mobile Homes to be erected and fitted out, I think that we may have solved some of their problems, don't you?"

"My goodness, Jack," Norman replied, "You don't hang about, do you? I shall be seeing the Prime Minister in about half an hour, I'll let him know what you are doing and I'm sure that someone will get the necessary permission for the Mobile Homes to have a good site."

"Oh, I don't know if I told you," Jack said, "But the bulk of the materials for the Ethiopian and Djibouti pipelines have now been put on the water and they should be there within two or three weeks, hopefully. I am personally going out with my wife and a couple of aides next week to Addis Ababa to check on the progress but the details and reports will be coming in soon from the surveyors that I have sent out to check it all. Oh, by the way, could you ask the Prime Minister when you see him if it may be possible for me (for security reasons) to get the jet that I am going to use to take me to and return me from Northolt airport again? I didn't think that the Prime Minister would want another visit out there yet, that's why I'm not suggesting that, but perhaps when we switch the water supply on, he may want an RAF jet do you think?"

"It must get a little hectic for you and your office with the way that things seem to get moving. It is most admirable that you can get so much done sir, well done. Yes, I'll ask the Prime Minister about you using Northolt aerodrome. I'll now go and try to find the Prime minister." The line ended and Jack knew that the next ones that he would have to talk to would be Alec and Ray.

Jennifer had been by him as he had made the last call and she too knew that Jack would now be able to report back to Alec and Ray. Together they went to the office and yes, there was Ray, sitting with his notepad and Alec had his hands moving above the keyboard. "Good day to you two then," Jack said. "I take it that you have told your friends in your world to get their fingers out and find some more crises for me, haven't you? Oh, by the way, I have had one more crisis from the Prime Minister and that was concerning a Tsunami that has in particular hit the Southern coast of Sri Lanka. I have got our people working already to try and get some help. My people have already sourced seventy-eight of the Mobile type of homes; some septic tanks to service them; plumbers; electricians and some general fitters to try and replace some of the lost homes out there. So, I have done something but I would be interested to hear what, if anything you two have done?"

"Jack, we have got a lot of our people looking now to try and find anything," Alec said. "The thing is, none of us in that world seem to know how to try and find out a lot about what is happening in this world. They are still trying, and we did promise, so we shall carry on trying to find anything that we can. That sounds to be a large crisis that you have heard of out there in Sri Lanka, doesn't it? Those kinds of things can cause so much loss and suffering, can't they? I don't suppose that you have got any idea of what that aid is going to cost yet, have you?"

"No, I haven't had a breakdown of the cost yet. I will probably be getting some idea of it before the day is out. Oh, by the way, next week, Jennifer and I won't be here, we are going to pay another visit to Ethiopia. We have spoken to the President in Addis Ababa and that is now arranged. As we hear more, we'll let you know what is happening. I won't interfere here anymore but do make sure that your people do keep trying to find things or we may start to feel that it is a bit 'one-sided', you see." Jack took hold of Jennifer's hand and they left the office and went to get some more coffee.

They got their coffee refills and just as they started to settle down in the lounge to drink them, Hugo appeared at the doorway. "Hello," he said. "It looks like I just made it at the right time, didn't I? I'll go and get one and then I can fill you in a bit on some of the costs of this latest job." He moved off to the kitchen and after a short time, he returned with a cup of coffee in his hand.

"Paul has done a good bit of hard negotiating, Jack. The Mobile Homes that he has got so far were initially being offered at just short of sixty thousand pounds each. In general, they do have two bedrooms and they are, I suppose, reasonable places to live in. Anyway, he did quite a bit of negotiating and he got them to reduce their price for a bulk purchase to forty-two thousand pounds. That then has the cost of the septic tanks to be added, plus the cost of plumbers, electricians and general fitters times to be added on and that comes close to three million five hundred thousand pounds. There may of course be one or two more bits and pieces to add on, plus the shipping costs, of course so I would imagine that it will end up more like four million five hundred thousand pounds or so, or it may even get to five million pounds I suppose. That is a lot of money, Jack. I know that, and although it will keep Alec and Ray Happy, I'm not too happy myself at spending your money like that. How does it seem to you? Have you heard how many homes were lost yet? Was that too many that Paul has bought, or was it still not enough?"

"Hugo," Jack replied, "We haven't had any further advice yet. Norman Brooks was going to speak to the Prime Minister and I hope that he'll come back to me when he hears something. If it is too many, then the powers that be in Sri Lanka will be able to use the spare homes to house some poor people from their country, won't they? If there aren't enough houses to do the job, then we can give Paul his head, can't we? Oh, Norman is going to get the Prime Minister to talk to their government people in Sri Lanka to try and arrange for them to find suitable sites for the homes and to aid the installations. I would imagine when it is an emergency like this they will be only too pleased to get aid that they will co-operate. I have also asked Norman to ask the Prime Minister if we can use Northolt for me going to and from Ethiopia to aid our security problems. If we can't, then I suppose that Heathrow would make some effort to work with us, wouldn't they?"

Chapter Twenty-Five

Monday arrived and, Norman had got back to Jack to tell him that the Prime Minister had had some words with some people and they had indeed been given permission to use Northolt as their aerodrome for the trip out to Ethiopia. Miguel had arranged for Manuel and Javier to be the guards accompanying them as aides and he had also arranged that Alvaro was to be their driver to get them to Northolt (and hopefully to be the one to bring them back). They did seem to prefer it when the security guards that were assigned to look after them were some of the ones that they knew. Miguel had considered putting two more cars onto the duty to provide a full security run but Jack said that he thought that it was 'going over the top a bit' to do that. Strangely, on that occasion, Hugo had agreed with Jack. It had always been Hugo's way from when they had first seen him in Spain to put a car ahead and a car behind them to give a fairly good cover of their celebrated occupants. However, on this day it was just one car and they arrived at Northolt in good time for their flight. On this occasion, Jack hadn't just booked a chartered passenger jet to take them but had instead ordered a nice luxury twin-engine private jet that was well capable of travelling the distance that they were going to cover and it did have a good turn of speed when needed. Just to provide the comfort that they may need on the journey, the luxury jet came with the stewardess to serve them teas and coffees as they wanted them, along with the occasional snack, again, if they wanted one. They knew that it would be a long flight but, after all, by now they were quite seasoned travellers. They knew that give or take a little bit of time it would be an eight-hour flight to get them there. The pilot told them that from the weather reports that he had had so far it was possible that they may be having a reasonable tailwind so they may be able to clip twenty to thirty minutes off of that time. Jack had done some negotiating of his own with the company that owned the little jet that they were flying on and he had told them that he would pay for the accommodation of the crew and attendants for the period while they were in Ethiopia. He had also asked if, because he was now well into his pilot's training, could he, at least for a part of the journey, travel with the pilot, just to get the feel of it. The company had agreed to that, as had the senior pilot himself.

Jennifer was quite settled in the very comfortable seats that they had on the jet and she decided that if, when Jack had got his licence, if he was going to buy a jet for their personal use he should see about getting something like this one. The stewardess also found which particular coffee they liked and was very attentive to their needs, and Jennifer, she found that they had happened to get a stewardess that she could get on with for this long flight.

Jack did for a time go to the cockpit and, at least for some of the time he did have a go at flying the 'plane (with of course the senior pilot sitting next to him and carefully monitoring his every move). Jack too decided that he liked this particular model (which happened to be a Cessna Citation X model which had ten seats) and he decided that once he had got his licence he thought that it would be nice to buy one like this for their personal use and pleasure. Once back in the seats in the body of the 'plane, he said as much to Jennifer and, although she did agree that she liked the 'plane she did raise one or two objections for him to consider.

"Look," she said, "Yes, I do rather like the plane and all the comfort that goes with it but why don't you look at it another way? If you did want to buy one, why would you want to buy a new one? For the amount of time that you would be using it; the 'plane would be getting to old age before it had got to a point that makes it just as nice as this one is. Ask the captain just how old this one is. So, if this one is something like what you want, why pay the extra for something that you don't need? Before you had got all your money, you wouldn't even have thought of doing anything as daft as that, would you? Right, now you like travelling in it, flying it as well, maybe. So, why not hire one like this just when you want to fly one? If you did that then you would also be hiring the services of some cabin crew who could look after me. Margaret there, (our stewardess on this flight) has been a little darling at getting us some coffee that we like and anyway, I like her and can get on well with her so if you were flying, I'd have someone to chat with, wouldn't I? Margaret and I have had quite a few chats while you've been playing at being a pilot. Yes, I like her and if you have to hire one you could ask that they assign her to us. How's that then? Now, you go on and make your case for going out and spending all of that money to buy a new one just 'cos now you are rich. You think about it, Jack, it just doesn't make any sense, does it?"

"I think that you have just shot down my little dream there, haven't you madam," Jack said, laughing as he gave Jennifer a playful little punch. "Yes, it does make a lot of sense to just hire one when I want one. If I bought one, I'd have to get somewhere to store it, pay for it to be serviced and looked after, pay lots and lots of insurance money out. No looking at it how you just did, I think that I'd tend to agree with you."

The pilot came onto the intercom to the passengers and informed both of the passengers that they were now approaching Addis Ababa and would shortly be getting into position for landing. Then, surprisingly (to Jennifer) he said, "If you wanted to come to the flight deck now Jack, if we are careful how we do it I could let you have a try at landing us. I would have to be here to correct anything if you did do anything wrong but, come on, you have had quite a few lessons now and you should be able to land us. One day, you will have to do this if you want to complete the pilot's course and get your licence, won't you?"

"Do you think that you can do it, or even dare to do it?" Jennifer asked a somewhat stunned Jack.

"Yes, of course I can, I've done it a few times already while I have been having lessons. Here goes, I'm going to go to the cockpit to land us. You just get Margaret sat here with you while we land and then ask her what she thinks of the landing."

Jack got up and went through to the cockpit to get into the second pilots seat. The captain just told him to take things easy, not to panic and to try and remember all that he had been doing during the training. Jack was ecstatic that he was actually going to land a beautiful little aircraft like this. Yes, the captain was there, and watching his every move, but at least it was giving him a real chance, wasn't it?

Jennifer called Margaret over and suggested that they could sit together while the 'plane landed. It was quite a smooth landing and the Pilot came over the tannoy system and asked the passengers if they would like to give some applause for a perfect landing done by Jack Dawkins. Both Jennifer and Margaret did as requested and gave Jack quite a bit of applause.

Jennifer had been telling Margaret that Jack, who was partway though his training for his pilot's licence now wanted to get a 'plane like this one. Margaret then mentioned to Jennifer almost exactly the objections that Jennifer had raised to Jack. Yes, she had said, it could be very nice to have a small plane to go to places but, the storage and inspection costs as well as the insurance, fuel and services turned it all into a very expensive hobby. Margaret was aware that Jack was now regarded as being a very wealthy man who, she understood, was some kind of diplomat doing things sometimes for the government, but she had also heard about some of the things that he was trying to oversee, like he was on this current visit to Ethiopia.

"Oh, as well as all this at the horn of Africa," Jennifer told Margaret, "He has now been asked to try and do something for the people of Sri Lanka where there has been another of those massive Tsunamis. He has already got almost eighty of those mobile type homes ready to be shipped, along with a lot of workmen to try and help out, out there. He does feel that for him having the opportunity to travel is almost an accident since he started out with very little, but he does try to help whoever and whenever he can. This visit though is just to see that things have been done properly so far. He has arranged for all of the other parts for this project to be moved and it is being shipped out now. I'm just having a half day to see around Addis Ababa. The President is going to be arranging something for me, I believe. Jack likes to travel but he doesn't have any real longing to see too many old buildings, as he calls them."

"That must be marvellous," Margaret replied, "I do hope that you have a nice trip when you do your tour. I don't know where you are going to be staying at. I think that we will probably be staying in some smaller hotel that the company book us into until Friday and then we have the flight back."

"Oh no, Margaret," Jennifer said, "You won't be staying in some small hotel that the company want to book you into. Jack has insisted that you will be staying in the same hotel that we are in. Mind you, we just happen to have got the rooftop apartment, so maybe we'll get you up there to look at it. If we are having dinner in the restaurant, why don't you and the others of the crew, come and join us? Jack would like that, especially since he has been allowed to land the 'plane."

Jack and the crew came through from the cockpit so that they could get ready for the cars that they could see arriving.

"Jack," Jennifer called across, "Margaret here has been telling me that they have been booked into some small hotel in the town. You said that they had to have rooms in the hotel that we are staying in, didn't you? And, I've suggested that they should all come and have dinner with us at the hotel as well. They must have a table large enough for all seven of us, mustn't they?"

"Yes, they are all staying where we are staying," Jack replied. "I told them that when I booked the flight, so that's settled and dinner together would be great, especially with my second teacher here being with us. You don't mind Manuel and Javier do you? Miguel won't complain, will he? If he does, just tell him that I'll see him later. Well, the cars are now waiting so we may as well make our moves to the hotel. Captain, you do know where our hotel is and I take it that you know that you are supposed to be there with us. If there are any doubts at all, do please let me know now and then I will deal with it all."

"Yes, Jack" The captain replied. "I know that the company had told us that they would book us into another much smaller place, but then we were told that you had insisted that we be booked into your hotel. We thank you for the dinner invitation as well and look forward to seeing you this evening. I'm afraid that we shall have to settle the 'plane down first and then we shall all be following you on later together."

They all moved to the doorway to get out to the waiting cars, Manuel and Javier making a quick scan outside before allowing Jack and Jennifer to get off of the aeroplane. They moved to the cars and got in, their luggage having been brought out and that was all loaded into the boot of the car that they were in. The cars set out and once again, they were in Addis Ababa. As they got to the exit to the airport, several police and military cars and motorcycles joined them and they were both led and followed with a military and police escort.

They arrived at the same hotel that they had been at before and, once again, the manager and, with an ample display of staff, were all waiting for them. They were escorted up to their apartment and, just before they went in, Manuel said that he had better do a quick sweep or Miguel would never forgive him. Javier remained by their side while Manuel did his check inside the apartment. Manuel then checked that their rooms were indeed on the same floor and he said to Jack that Miguel had instructed them that they had to mount a full night guard at the outside of their room. Jack just smiled and thanked him, knowing that all of this had happened before when they were in Spain.

Once in the apartment, they both began to relax once again. The phone rang and Jack went to answer it. It was the President, "Good day to you Mr Dawkins, or Jack if I may call you that, I do hope that you have had a good trip out. I gather that you are going to have dinner in the restaurant this evening and I have arranged for some guards to be assigned, just to make things safe for you. If I may, I would also like to attend the dinner with you as well tonight. The next couple of nights are going to be rather hectic for me so I would want to have at least one social meeting with you before we go out to see the pipeline tomorrow."

Oh, that would be grand, Mr President," Jack replied. "Yes, please do call me Jack. Just as a matter of interest, since on this occasion I have used a private airline to get us here, and since their Captain was good enough to let me have the controls for the landing we have invited the small air crew to attend the dinner as well. I do hope that this will not inconvenience you sir. We have arranged to have the dinner at seven o'clock this evening. Then, we shall all be able to have a decent night's sleep before we get out tomorrow morning."

"That is perfectly alright Jack. So, you are now trying to get your pilot's licence as well then, are you? That will be very useful for you, I'm sure. Well, until this evening then; and then we can have a little chat then, can't we?"

Jack put the phone down and told Jennifer that the President was hoping to join them for dinner, that the President had also arranged for some guards for the dining room and that he had told the President that the 'plane's crew would all be with them for the dinner.

Jennifer was pleased that he had done all that and said that if the crew realised just how he had got them to the same table as the President of Ethiopia it was probably going to get Margaret, their stewardess, to want to talk about that on the flight back home on Friday evening.

They both had a short rest since it had been quite a long journey. For Jack it had been a rather special one as well in that the Captain had allowed him to take control their jet in taking it in to land at Addis Ababa. It wasn't long after that and they both decided that it was about time that they got themselves ready for the dinner, again with the President, but this time with the crew from the aeroplane and their two security guards.

The time came for them to go down for dinner and as they left their apartment they found Javier waiting outside the door. It had been his shift to stand guard. Manuel had done the shift before so Javier gave Manuel's door a knock and Manuel joined them for them all to go down for dinner.

In the restaurant they found that the aeroplane captain, the second pilot and Margaret the stewardess were all waiting when they got down there and, of some surprise to Jack and Jennifer (although the President had told Jack that it was going to happen, there were several official guards near the walls of the dining area, quite obviously watching for anything that could be of any risk whatsoever to the honoured guests). Jack and Jennifer went to the table and just as they got there, the President of Ethiopia walked into the restaurant. The aeroplane captain appeared to realise who it was, the other two didn't look as though they had a clue. The President came up to Jack and they shook hands as old friends and Jack invited the President to take a seat, ensuring that Jennifer was with him, Jack sat himself next to the President and keeping Jennifer on his other side. Jennifer had motioned to Margaret to go to her and she got Margaret sat next to her with the rest of the diners spread around the table but the captain, as it happened became in the position sitting at the other side of the President.

Jack already knew the name of the President (from when they had met before) but to try and keep things just a little more formal he informed all of the other diners who their guest was, the President of Ethiopia. Jack thought that he heard a couple of little gasps but he could have been mistaken (and so it appeared had the President) and the meal began. Jennifer spoke quietly to Margaret and told her that Jack had built some relationship with the President since he had begun to try and arrange some aid to that country. She quietly pointed out that the President had arranged for the guards around the dining room (which Margaret hadn't noticed before).

Jack and the President, as the previous time that they had been sitting having a meal (that had been at the banquet, after the meeting when Jack had been introduced to all of the leaders of the countries involved) began to chat quite amicably.

"I don't suppose that you'll know or not if any of my surveyors have been out as far as your lines to check them, do you?" Jack asked. "I thought it better to ensure that all of the lines were checked in all of the countries a few times anyway but my surveyors have been covering all five sites. In the case of yours though, since the rest of the equipment is now so close to getting here it is hoped that all is well. Once the ships with the equipment on them arrives, one would presume that within perhaps three months, we should all be meeting again for the big 'switch on' when we start to get the water pumping out to the interior of Ethiopia. That is going to be a marvellous day, isn't it?"

"Oh yes, of course," The President agreed. "We are so looking forward to that day. I know that there are many of our people who believe that you have been sent from the heavens above to help us. Your tremendous efforts in getting us the water that is so valuable to us has been a gift beyond belief. I don't know if your surveyors have been to see our lines or not yet, but there again, I don't suppose that they will necessarily need it to be known where they are at any particular time, will they? By the way, Captain," The president said to the aeroplane captain sitting next to him, "On Thursday we need to get to Tadjoura Airport to see how the work is progressing at the start of our project. Will it be possible that you would be able to carry us down to the airport at Tadjoura? To travel by road can at times be sometimes rather difficult and it is quite a distance, something like almost six hundred kilometres."

"That should be no problems whatsoever, Mr President," the Captain replied. "Our 'plane does seat ten people so provided that we do keep the numbers to that it should be fine. I have never been to that airport before and I am presuming that it will have most facilities and size for us to land safely."

"Oh good," The President replied and, turning again to Jack as well, he said, "Yes, it is quite a nice little airport and perhaps tomorrow you could contact them to make you feel safer that they do have all that you need for your aircraft. I also feel sure that we can manage to keep the numbers to quite an acceptable level, can't we. There would, of course, be you, myself, your wife, and your two aides and perhaps I may have a couple of guards and then that should be quite adequate, wouldn't you think? I have told them to get a helicopter to the airport so that we can fly directly to the new sea site. The President of Djibouti has said that in view of the distance from the airport it may be better to travel that by cars and, naturally, he would like to attend so he will also be coming and he is now making arrangements for vehicles to carry everyone. Once again, the roads in that area are not quite up to a good standard for travelling but as it is a short distance, I'm sure that we shall manage I understand. On the Friday, Mrs Dawkins," The President said, speaking across to Jennifer, "That we have arranged for a good tour of Addis Ababa and we should be able to cover many interesting things. In ensuring your safety though, we will show you a lot of sites but at some of them, such as the market in particular, it would perhaps be safer for you to remain inside the cars. The markets in Addis Ababa are in themselves so very impressive, but of course, in the case of both of you; your safety is of paramount importance to us. By the way Jack, I have arranged for a car to come and pick up you and your lady wife tomorrow morning at nine o'clock. I trust that that will be satisfactory?"

The meal progressed quite amicably with all of the diners being served some excellent foods and there was some chatter amongst those who were there. Margaret and Jennifer had begun to get on so well together that Jennifer had even suggested that when they got back to Britain that Margaret should go and visit them at their estate and, if security allowed, they could maybe go out for a visit to the local town. Margaret also seemed to think that it would be a wonderful idea and she agreed that once they returned, she would give Jennifer a call.

With the dinner over with Jack said goodnight to The President and they began to make their ways back to their rooms. The Captain caught up with Jack and said, "I know that I agreed to fly you and your party to Djibouti on Thursday, but I shall have to make a call back to the UK to get permission to do that. I could hardly say that in front of the President, could I? I'm sorry if that sounds to be a bit wimpish of me but as it isn't somewhere that is on my list, I do have to get permission to fly there from them."

"Oh, that's fine," Jack said, "You can tell them that I didn't know that you were going to be asked to do that either but whatever it costs, just tell them to put it on the bill. By the way, I forgot to mention that we were going to have the President with us for dinner, but at the time it didn't even occur to me. I do hope that you didn't mind?"

"No, that was no trouble at all sir, In fact, it was quite a surprise and no matter who we are flying around, we don't usually get a meal served with guards all around us while we eat. That is another thing to remember for the grandchildren, isn't it? Anyway, if we can do the trip to Djibouti I can then make sure that we are refuelled for the flight back on Friday afternoon, can't I?"

The following morning they were both up in good time and as they left their apartment they once again found one of their guards waiting for them. This time it was Manuel who was the guard and as he saw them he knocked on Javier's door to get him to come and be ready for the day's work. They all went down and had a quick breakfast and then went out to find the official car waiting for them with once again several army and police cars waiting to act as an escort for them. They got into the car with Javier in the front seat beside the driver and Manuel took a rear seat.

The following morning they were both up in good time and as they left their apartment they once again found one of their guards waiting for them. This time it was Manuel who was the guard and as he saw them he knocked on Javier's door to get him to come and be ready for the day's work. They all went down and had a quick breakfast and then went out to find the official car waiting for them with once again several army and police cars waiting to act as an escort for them. They got into the car with Javier in the front seat beside the driver and Manuel took a rear seat.

The car left the hotel and, with the escort (again it seemed all with flashing lights) accompanying them they drove to meet the Presidents large limousine and once they were there, the two cars, fully escorted, began the drive to see the pipeline that was the nearest to the Capital city. Jack had known all along that he wouldn't be able to manage to see all four of the pipelines but to see this one did demonstrate his interest. He knew that this one as well was a good bit shorter than the other pipelines. The president had told him about this since some areas needed a longer pipeline and they had used the excess from this one to extend the other ones to get nearer to where they.The pipeline that they were going to see was apparently a good few miles outside of Addis Ababa and so they relaxed as they were driven across some land that was obviously itself rather dried up and didn't look to be good for much growing of crops, or other herbage to feed animals. Jack had, to some extent expected some of this but he had presumed that the main parched land was much further away from the Capital city. That, the President had told him was true, but that they did also have land nearer to Addis Ababa that was believed to be useful if only they could get irrigation to it. As they were driving, Jack thought that the President was probably correct, even this land, with some fairly regular water supply could be made to be capable of growing something. He thought that when they stopped he would ask the President about how much land they did have like this. Jack had been given the name of the President but it had been suggested to him (by both Alec and Ray) that he should just call him Mr President rather than try to pronounce a name and maybe get the pronunciation wrong and create an insult to the leader of this country.

Eventually, they could see what appeared to be a work area ahead of them. There were quite a number of Lorries and other work vehicles and some stacks of pipes, obviously waiting to be laid. The car stopped by the stack of pipes. They got out of their car, as did the President who got out of his car and came to join them. Jack and Jennifer, now flanked by Javier and Manuel, also moved towards the President.

"These are the final pipes that have to be laid on this line," The President said. "It can sometimes take a little while to get things going as they apparently are carrying out some kind of pressure testing of the pipes that have been laid to ensure that there will be no leaks on the way. If they don't pass the test, they have to go back to the last lot of pipes that had been tested and check all of the joints once again. It does sound to be quite laborious but my people have said that there is no point in laying the pipes if they aren't going to be able to carry the water to where we want it to be. This last load should have been laid by tomorrow morning and then we have a few bulldozers creating a large depression to create the base for a large lake. A lake like that, of course, is something that is unknown of in Ethiopia until now and we are hoping that from there, we shall be able to install some more smaller pipes to create lines going further and further out. That, I understand is also going to happen at each of the 'take off points' that you suggested so that some other areas can also be irrigated and that will then permit us to grow a lot of crops and, even if is just some kind of grass or other herbage, it will enable the animals to be able to graze, won't it?"

"These are indeed the kinds of things that I had hoped for," Jack said. "On the way here from Addis Ababa, the ground there was also very dry. Cannot some pipeline be directed back towards that to help to maximise the benefits for agriculture?"

"Those areas," The President continued, will, we hope, receive some water supply from the streams and the rivers that we believe will feed out from the lake that we are creating. We are doing these kinds of things on each of the pipelines so hopefully, we will have some large inland lakes and quite a lot of small streams and rivers to irrigate more and more areas as we progress. If the improved irrigation and agriculture do work to improve our country's economic status, we may even invest in more pipelines in the future if we find that we need them."

"This is all so very impressive Mr President," Jack said. "I only hope that your neighbouring countries are taking quite as much care as you are. Do you speak to any of the other leaders to find out how their work is progressing? I know that your lines start in Djibouti so, have you heard how they are doing? The President from Somalia I did feel had some rather different ideas to those that we had been expecting, but he may know better than us what is needed for his country? Do you speak to the leaders of the Sudan and Eritrea?"

"Yes, Jack," The President replied. "The President of Djibouti and I have had quite regular conversations and he does appear to believe along very similar lines to what we have been using. Of course, he doesn't require quite as much water as does our country and he is just making the best possible use that he can of what is available to him. I believe that Eritrea and Sudan are doing something along similar lines to our own, but no, I haven't spoken to them. I understand that the Sudan intends to extend considerably beyond the initial pipeline but how far that is, I'm afraid it is something that I do not know. Somalia, ah, now there is a puzzle. Their President does appear to be somewhat of a conundrum to many people. I believe that he does have some good intentions for his country but, as the saying goes, 'He plays his cards close to his chest'. I would imagine that he would take the advantage of your very generous donation but how he would achieve the end result is something of which I know nothing at all. Shall we just walk up here to see the end of our pipeline so far? You may be able to see some of the bases of the lake that the bulldozers are now excavating. Some people have said that I have started to create a lake that is far too large but it is only time that will tell, is it not?"

"Mr President," Jack replied. "What I have seen so far is very, very impressive and it does seem to generally follow along what I had been thinking of. As for the lake, there is a saying, isn't there, that 'what will hold a lot will also hold a little'. That being the case, perhaps you are correct and your critics will all be proved to be wrong in the long run."

"Do you know when the wind turbine will be ready then, Jack? "The President asked. "I only ask since that is obviously going to be a major point. If we do not have the power, we cannot desalinate the water and we cannot pump the water, can we? I know that we should be able to use some solar panels but perhaps they would be of much more use for some local things, wouldn't they?"

"Yes, they are more use as a local source," Jack replied, "There will be quite a number of solar panels on the shipment that is on its way now, along with pumps, the desalination units, the storage tanks, some more small pipes and everything else that you will need. The Wind Turbine has already been made and is being shipped separately, most of it is already assembled and the last that I heard was that they were negotiating to get permission to bring it through the Suez Canal. I would imagine that it could be here any day. I am hoping that both that and the ship with everything else on should be here within at most two weeks time, probably quite a lot sooner. We are already making headways on getting the parts ready for the other three countries. After that, well, I'm not sure what will happen. I know that I have had to put some people onto some other work to try and help those poor people in Sri Lanka."

"What is that then, Jack?" The President asked. "I wasn't aware that Sri Lanka had any shortage of water? What are their problems then, Jack?"

"Oh, I had presumed that you may have heard, sir. There has been another gigantic Tsunami and it has hit the Southern Coast of Sri Lanka. It has caused many, many problems, a lot of people have lost their lives, many, many homes and businesses have been lost and it is itself now a disaster area. I have had my team initially secure Seventy-Eight mobile homes and they, along with some septic tanks, some electricians, plumbers and general fitters are to be shipped out there by me. It was the least that I could do to help them."

"My goodness, Jack, is there no end to the good that you are seeking to do?" The President said. "You have already with our countries on the Horn of Africa done so much to prevent future loss of life. To now start immediately to try and aid Sri Lanka like that, I must say that I have been given a great privilege to be able to meet you, sir."

By this time they had reached the edge of a massive depression that stretched away into the far distance for some considerable way. Far, far away, Jack could see some bulldozers pushing mounds of soil up to create some banks. This obviously was the lake area that the President had been talking about when he spoke earlier. Jack was amazed at the size of it. Once the lake had been created of course, the President intended to install some smaller pumps and slightly smaller diameter pipes to pump water further to irrigate even more lands. This was marvellous and he congratulated the President on this achievement.

"Oh, it is my intention that there will be a similar lake at the end of every pipeline, that we get installed, Jack." The President explained. "From where we shall use the smaller diameter pipes and some smaller solar powered pumps and this, we hope, will extend our irrigation to almost all parts of Ethiopia. I do not wish to hear of any further droughts and famines such as those that we have had to suffer in the past."

They had a look at the various parts that were being handled and moved about, the men in charge of the operation explaining as fully as they could to Jack, despite the slight problems of language between them, the President acting as interpreter where needed.

"And where is the next pipeline going, in relation to this one?" Jack asked. "I am merely asking since I would gather that it is some long distance way from here. You would hardly want to be getting two lakes of that size close to one another, would you? Is it possible that we shall be seeing another pipeline tomorrow?"

Chapter Twenty-Six

"If you wish to see another pipeline, Jack, we can most certainly go to see one but the next nearest one is about a hundred and fifty miles more or less in an Easterly direction. If you do wish to see that one, I can most certainly make some arrangements for that."

Jack turned slightly towards Jennifer and said, very, very quietly, "Do we need to see another pipeline? We have got the surveyors going around them all and from what I've seen here I believe that things in Ethiopia are being done just how we wanted them to be. What do you think?"

"Just like you have said," Jennifer replied. "You have seen almost a model of what you wanted to happen. I think that it would be a waste of our time and that of the President to go and look at another pipeline."

"Mr President," Jack said, "I've just asked my wife, Jennifer what she thinks and she too agrees with just what I have been thinking. From what we have seen here, you have got things sorted so well here that it would be a waste of your time and ours in going to see another pipeline. Perhaps when we have seen the work being done at Djibouti it is going to fill all of our hopes for you and your country."

"Oh, I do assure you that they shall all be to the same rigorous standard, Jack. It is after all my name as President at the time that these that are being installed now, shall remain in our history, with of course, the name of our most generous benefactor who has enabled us to get our land to become useful to us all."

"Will it be possible then to bring forward a day the visit to Djibouti Mr President? Jack asked. "If that is possible it will shorten our week by a full day and then when I get back home I can see how we are getting on with our other works, can't I?"

"Oh, of course, Jack," The President replied. "I will have a word with the President of Djibouti when we get back and make the necessary arrangements. Would it be possible for your aircraft captain to be informed also? Now, one thing that we didn't mention was that of the cost of the hotel where you are staying. I do know that you felt that you would cover that cost but please, after all of the work and input that you have put into our country so far, it would please both myself and many in our government who I feel sure will feel that we are insulting you by letting you pay for such costs."

"Mr President," Jack replied, "As you are aware, my wealth came to me rather suddenly and yes, I too have known of harder times in the past. For us, the money that it costs for us to stay here in your country and in such a beautiful hotel, it would be petty on my part to even consider letting you foot that bill. Both Jennifer and I have enjoyed our visits to your country and it gives us the greatest of pleasure to be able to give the small help that we have done so far. Please, do forget such trivial sums as those for the hotel. We would be pleased to know that anything that we have done has in some way provided a comfort to you and your people."

"Jack, Mr Dawkins," The President replied. "It is refreshing to see your attitude to life and all of your humility and ways of offering aid to those who have hit some unfortunate times. I can assure you that your name will be held in the highest esteem in our country's history. Thank you so much for all that you have done and are continuing to do."

They had by then walked back towards the cars and they got into them and began the drive back to Addis Ababa. Jennifer said quite gently into Jack's ear, "You see, you can be a diplomat and you can be a marvellous speaker. I thought that the way that you got around the hotel bill was quite classic. I wish that I had tape recorded it for some to hear it when we get back home. So, I take it that we shall be having our tour of the city on Thursday now and then it may be Thursday afternoon to fly back home. Is that what you have planned?"

"More or less, my dear, more or less," Jack replied with quite a huge grin on his face. "I also gather that you and Margaret are planning on some outings of your own as well? She seems to be a nice girl. You'll probably have to get Miguel to check her out for security though, won't you?"

"I'm not letting Miguel get anywhere near Margaret," Jennifer said, quite firmly. "From what I've heard from some of the other security lads, Miguel has got quite a reputation with the ladies.

You've already heard what some of their family got up to with some of the Royal ladies, haven't you? No, if he's good, I may let him meet her, but he'd better be on his best behaviour if I do."

"I've not heard of any bad reports about Miguel from anyone," Jack said. "Who have you been talking to start hearing some bad stories about him?"

"I'm not talking of any misbehaving as far as his work goes, clot," Jennifer said. "Just ask Javier who is sat next to you about Miguel's reputation with the ladies?"

Jack turned to Javier, who was sat next to him and he said, have you heard any stories about Miguel then, Javier, I mean of him and any ladies?"

"Look boss, Jack," Javier said, "I don't want to get into any trouble but yes, Miguel does have quite a reputation with the ladies. I mean, I wouldn't let him get introduced to my sisters, I know that. It's not that he hurts them, oh no. It's well, that he can soon get them running after him and then, once he thinks that he's caught them, he just looks for another lady to chase after. Don't just listen to me, you ask Manuel; he's known him a lot longer than I have."

"Manuel," Jack said to the other security man sat in the front seat. "Have you heard stories like this about Miguel and the ladies?"

"Yes, boss, Jack," Manuel replied. "He has got quite a reputation, he always has had one and sometimes he seems quite proud of it as well. As Javier says, he doesn't actually hurt them, as such, he just gets them to be all keen on him and as soon as they are, he well, he just keeps them hanging on waiting for him and he will go and find another girl somewhere else. I'm sorry if I'm speaking out of turn, Jack, but he does have quite a reputation."

"Oh," Jack said as he sat back in the car, deep, no he was very deep in thought. This was going to be quite a touchy problem for him but if Miguel was like that perhaps Jennifer had been right to say that she didn't want Margaret to meet Miguel. "Maybe I could have a word or two, on the quiet of course, with Hugo," he said to Jennifer. "Maybe that would solve it. Hugo would know what to do, wouldn't he?"

"Are you sure that you are thinking quite straight Jack?" Jennifer asked. "I mean how long have you known Hugo? No, don't bother answering that, but just think back to when we were in Spain and we met up with our new 'security team'. You had mentioned about them coming back and Manuel and Javier wanted to talk things over with their wives before they decided, didn't they? You then asked Hugo if he was married and he told you quite definitely, no. With his families past reputation and with his wealth, don't you think it a bit odd that he hasn't found a lady yet? I think, but I may be wrong, but, could it be that both Miguel and Hugo may have similar types of blood in their veins and similar ways of living? I wouldn't worry too much about it at all, Jack. I can invite Margaret to come and see us and people don't need to get security clearance to come and see me. I'm damned certain of that. You look after your good works and I'll have my own little circle of friends. Since we got married and moved into the estate I haven't seen any of my old friends, have I? I may invite one or two over to see us and we'll take it from there."

They arrived at the hotel and they all got out of the car and went in, once again to be greeted by the manager and several other members of the staff. They were just going to go to their apartment and Jack realised that he needed to speak to the Captain of the 'plane. He asked the manager if he knew if he was in, or had the crew gone out into Addis Ababa.

The manager said that as far as he was aware, they were all still in the hotel and were probably in their rooms. He gave Jack the telephone numbers to contact them in their rooms and then they went to go to their apartment.

"Jack," Manuel said as he was standing close by to him with Javier also looking a trifle nervous. "We won't be in trouble for saying anything to you about Miguel, will we? We have both just been wondering if we could be in trouble for 'speaking out of turn' so to speak about our boss, sir."

"No, of course not," Jack replied. "You simply answered my question and as my wife had heard these stories before, all that you did was to confirm that what she had heard was probably correct. I won't say anything about where I have heard the stories from. Us married blokes have to stick together, don't we?" Jack laughed as he and Jennifer went towards their apartment.

Once they were in their apartment, Jack picked up the phone and dialled the number to get hold of the Captain. The Captain answered almost straight away and Jack asked if he had contacted the company that owned the 'plane about going to Djibouti.

"Yes," The Captain answered. "They told me that as long as you were aware that you would have the additional cost of any fuels and landing charges that would all be O.K. Is something wrong?"

"Yes, and No," Jack replied. "We went out to see one pipeline today and it has all been done so well (and I believe that when they say that they are operating to the same standard on all of the pipelines that it is correct) so we won't be going to Djibouti on Thursday but we thought that we would go tomorrow and then, on Thursday, my wife can have her tour of Addis Ababa and we could get off home again either on Thursday afternoon or Friday morning. To our mind it seemed to be a more sensible solution all round, wouldn't you think? They have even made a big start on digging an absolutely gigantic hole to make a lake and the President has told us that he is doing the same at the end of each pipeline so to our mind that was near to being perfect. So, how does tomorrow suit you for going to Djibouti?"

"That's fine. The co pilot is still in the hotel so I'll let him know and, as far as I know, Margaret is also still in the hotel so I can tell her. The 'plane has already been refuelled and it has been checked over so we can be ready whenever you want."

"The President said that he'd have cars here at nine o'clock am, so we can make a start then, can't we? By the way, Jennifer has asked if Margaret could pop up to see her sometime. They seem to have hit it off together, you know, so I don't know what they've got planned."

"Oh, trust the ladies to make their decisions, Jack. I'll pass the message on to her for you and may be we'll see you for breakfast."

"If you all would like another dinner, I can soon get that set up," Jack said. "After all, hotel rooms can be quite boring can't they? If you would like that, say seven o'clock again, eh?"

"Thank you very much Jack," The Captain replied. "I'm sure that the other two would like that, and so would I. Yes, seven o'clock will be fine."

Having done that, Jack opened the door and saw Javier moving about. "Javier, can you tell Manuel that we are all having dinner again at seven o'clock. I don't think that the President will be sending any guards, but I would imagine that we will be OK, wouldn't you? The management here will want to keep their reputation, won't they?"

Jack was just going back into the apartment when the elevator door opened and Margaret walked onto the foyer. "Jennifer said to the Captain that she wanted to see me so I have just popped up to see her."

"Come on in, Margaret, I think that Jennifer just wants to show off this apartment a bit. She has been telling me that you may be popping down to see us after we've got back. I'm sure that she'll find plenty of things to show you."

Jennifer appeared and she took Margaret off to show her what their rooftop apartment was like. Jack just went and started to complete a few more pages on his travel directory that he always carried with him. This one though was volume number twelve! He hadn't a clue how many volumes it would be by the time that he decided that he had finished it.

Dinner that evening was quite pleasant and with the only guards present being Manuel and Javier. The air crew found this new client passenger to be something rather special to work with. Besides everything else, it looked to them as though they may be returning home a day or so earlier than they had believed was the case.

Chapter Twenty-Seven

The following morning, breakfasts were enjoyed by Jack, Jennifer, his two 'aides' and the aircrew and promptly at nine o'clock, cars arrived at the hotel to take them all to the airport, once again, surrounded by both police and army escort vehicles. At the airport they found that the President had already arrived and the aircrew very smartly got to the aircraft to ensure that it was ready as soon as the passengers had met up and cleared them to depart.

"Jack," The President said, as he greeted Jack and Jennifer. "I have now been hearing of that terrible disaster that you told me of yesterday at Sri Lanka. It has been confirmed on the news that you are now in the process of shipping out new homes for some of the people who lost everything. Our lives to appear to be taking some strange turns, don't they, Allah must have some strange thoughts to cause such chaos to those people. And then, it was you again that is being named as the saviour for so many people out there. You do appear to be doing some marvellous things within the life span that it allotted to us all, and we too have been amongst those that have benefited from your work."

"Mr President," Jack said, "In all of life, things can go wrong for anyone and surely it is down to the remainder of the people to offer what succour they are able to. Come, I do want to see how the base unit is set up. I feel sure that after what I saw yesterday that you will have again managed to create a worthy edifice to your Presidency that will hopefully last for many, many years. Shall we board now? I believe that the crew have by now got everything in place for our journey today."

They did all get on board, Jack, Jennifer, Jack's two 'aides', the President and he too had brought two 'aides' plus one secretary to make notes about anything that the President felt needed reporting. The doors were closed and the pilot asked on the tannoy system for the passengers to please fasten their seat belts. The engines had started and the jet began the taxiing to get it to the main runway. In minutes, the 'plane was up and heading for their next destination of Djibouti. Margaret, the stewardess now had time to serve any that wanted it with a drink that pleased them. With Jack and Jennifer of course it was once again coffee!

The pilot began the approach to Djibouti but since they could see the five pipelines leading away from the main units at the coast, Jack had asked the pilot to try and follow the pipeline going to Djibouti a little way to see more or less how it had been laid. He did indeed do that and they saw that the one pipeline that was feeding into Djibouti did carefully skirt the more urban areas and from the height that they were then flying at, they could see what appeared to be a large depression much, much further inland. Jack, on seeing this, realised what he thought they were trying to do here. They had built yet another depression for an inland lake, as he had seen the day before and he imagined that they would then be taking off smaller pipelines to get to the land that they wanted irrigated. He was quite impressed and the pilot brought the 'plane around to make a sensible approach and landing at Djibouti airport.

On landing, the jet taxied to the area where, once again, a cavalcade of cars were waiting to take these visitors to see the site for the water processing and pumping operation. They began to leave the aircraft and, as they stepped down onto the ground, the President of Djibouti came forward where once again the hand shaking began once again for Jack, Jennifer, and the two Presidents. (Initially, Jack had felt quite awkward at the number of times that he had to shake hands, that had started on his previous visit with the Prime Minister and Jack wasn't at all keen on it, but he knew that it had to be done.) They were taken to the cars and Jack and Jennifer (along with his two aides) got into one car while the President of Ethiopia (along with his secretary and his aides) got into another car and the President of Djibouti, again with aides and helpers, got into a third car. Once again they were to have a military type escort to get them to the site. It wasn't a long drive though and they soon pulled up close to the new site, with the sea looking a beautiful blue from where they were standing.

The site comprised of one quite substantial building at one end and then there were five more buildings that did look to be quite permanent buildings erected almost in a line moving away from that main building of the operation. The two Presidents came across to join Jack and Jennifer and between them they began to explain what the buildings were and how they understood that things would work. First of all it was explained, where the operation was based was within almost a 'sheltered cove' to protect from any substantial storms that could at times hit that area close to the Red Sea junction with the Arabian Sea.

The explanations were that the large substantial looking building was to be the offices and the workshops for any ongoing maintenance that was needed. It would also be used as the 'receptor' area for the cables that were brought ashore from the sea bound wind turbine (when it arrived) and the electricity could then be allocated from there to where it was needed. There was also a large open space beyond the substantial building that had been reserved for solar panels to be erected as they were needed. These, if needed, would themselves be protected and were, in any case, capable of being moved comparatively easily if any weather forecast suggested any unusual activity that could put them at risk. The five other units they were told were to be used as the receptors for the water lines being taken from the sea. They would also house Pumps, the desalination units, the storage tanks (with their internal compressor units built into them) and they were the starting point for the five pipelines planned to start from these points. One single pipeline had been laid to feed into Djibouti and, if ever a further pipeline was needed, that would be constructed alongside that existing pipeline unit. The four other pipelines were seen to be going generally in the direction of

Ethiopia and, as they moved further away they were being taken underground in the main and then they would each divert to take the four pipelines out to four further areas within Ethiopia that did so badly need water and irrigation.

The President of Djibouti asked Jack when he thought that any of the rest of the equipment, including the wind turbine would be manufactured.

"Oh," Jack replied, "I should have explained to you earlier, that all of the pumps, storage tanks, desalination units and the other equipment that they needed (including a good stock of solar panels) have all now been made and was shipped out early last week so it should be arriving here either later this week or early next week. The wind turbine has been completed and is also being shipped and it is hoped that they will get permission to bring it through the Suez Canal and if that is achieved, that also could be here by next week. Then, I believe there may be a period of about two or three months of hard work in connecting and putting things where they are most appropriate and then, the desalination and the pumping can begin. I do hope that within three months I shall be able to return to see the start of the irrigation systems for your two countries to be completed. Gentlemen, I am quite impressed with what I have seen so far that has been developed here and we did notice on our flight to get here, just taking a small diversion, we did note that you too appear to be creating a large inland lake much further North. This is no doubt with which you plan to take off other smaller pipelines to areas more in need of that water. If indeed, you do later find that you need a second pipeline for Djibouti, do please contact me and we shall make every effort to help to get that underway.

As Jack just finished talking, the President of Djibouti's secretary's phone rang and they answered it and then, turning to their President said, "Sir, I have just received a telephone call that the first ship with goods needed to complete the pipeline operation is now approaching the docks, sir. It looks as though everything is happening at once, sir."

The President looked shocked almost and then he turned to face Jack again and said, "Did you hear, Mr Dawkins, the first shipment is now arriving. We are now so much closer to getting these pipelines working, aren't we? I wonder if the wind turbine is also following now."

"I'll just give my people a call Mr President and see if I can get an update on the wind turbines progress across the water, I know that they should be getting nearer now," Jack said and he took out his mobile phone and called through to get Hugo to see if they had any news. It took a few minutes and Hugo said that he would make some enquiries and he would get back to them in a few minutes. Jack told the two Presidents that they were now trying to discover where the wind turbine had got to and that they would be calling again in a couple of minutes.

There was almost a pandemonium amongst the people gathered there. Some of them were saying that they wanted to rush to the docks and others asking why it had taken so long to find out what, if anything was happening. Then, Jack's phone rang. He answered it and yes, it was Hugo. Jack pressed the end call button on his phone and then turned to speak to the two Presidents, "Gentlemen, the wind turbine has been cleared to come through the Suez Canal and it has passed there and is now in the Red Sea. It looks as though it should arrive later today or perhaps early tomorrow morning. Gentlemen, you and your people now have a lot of work to do, don't you, if you are to be able to get this system operational. I think that as things have now progressed to this stage we could leave here. I'm afraid that I have no idea about how to install these things that are coming, but I do have some other things to deal with. Would it be possible for us to leave here now so that these people can then prepare for the arrival of the rest of the equipment?"

"Mr Dawkins," The President of Djibouti said, "This event is far too urgent for you to leave now. I will get food and accommodation for you to stay here to see it arrive."

"Mr President," The President of Ethiopia said, "I don't know if you have heard of the disaster that has hit Sri Lanka. It apparently was a gigantic Tsunami and there has been a massive loss of life and houses and business premises. Mr Dawkins here has already started to provide aid for them. Obviously, you were unaware of just what this young man does do with his life. I agree that he isn't able to erect any of the equipment so I think that we should let him leave. He will, no doubt be back to see the start of the operation once everything is done and completed."

"Oh, Mr Dawkins," The President of Djibouti said, "I had no idea that you were also trying to help those people as well. Certainly, let us get back to your aeroplane and then you will, we hope be able to return to see the successful outcome of this venture for you."

They all began to move to get back to the cars and the cars started their drive to get them back to the airport. Once at the airport, as Jack, Jennifer and his two 'aides' got out of their car to get onto the 'plane, the President of Djibouti almost ran to shake his hand once again and to wish him good fortune with his other enterprises. The President of Ethiopia and his aides had already made it onto the aeroplane so Jack and Jennifer followed them and got on for the flight back to Addis Ababa.

It wasn't a very long flight back to Addis Ababa, about forty five minutes, but during the flight, the President said that he had arranged what he believed was a good and quite comprehensive tour of Addis Ababa for Jennifer the following morning at nine o'clock am again. On this occasion, as they were coming into land, Jack left it to the Captain to land the 'plane. Their cars returned (along with their now standard police and army escort) and they were once more returned to their hotel. The Captain and the rest of the aircraft crew told Jack that they would get back to the hotel after they had seen to the 'plane being re-fuelled again and dealt with to get it ready for them for when they did leave.

It was by then mid-afternoon and Jack suggested to Jennifer that if she wanted, he would arrange another dinner or did they just want a simple meal in their apartment. That, to Jennifer, appealed far more than yet another dinner so they planned on doing that, telling Manuel and Javier to do whichever they wanted but that in any case, it was Jack who would be paying the bill. Jack also contacted the Captain after they had returned from the airport and he explained to him what they were doing but he told the Captain that they could do whichever they wanted but that again, it would be he, Jack that would be paying the bill. The Captain thanked Jack and said that he would tell the rest of the crew and let them decide.

The following morning, Jack, Jennifer and their two 'aides' plus the Captain and his crew were down for breakfast. Jennifer had asked the Captain if Margaret could go with them for the tour of the City being organised by the President. The Captain, appreciating that there appeared to be some bond developing between the two ladies said yes, as they wouldn't be flying, they wouldn't require a stewardess. He did remind Margaret though that when they returned she would need to change and get her uniform on for the flight back. He said to her that friend or not, the Dawkins family had paid for a given quality of service and that the service of a stewardess was a part of that package.

Jack, Jennifer and Margaret appeared outside the hotel on time and saw their car approaching, once again surrounded by a number of military and police cars and motorcycles to act as escorts for the important visitors. Jack had spoken to Manuel and Javier and asked if they particularly wanted to go on the tour, or would they prefer to have a day off around the hotel. The two 'aides' knew that while they were on the tour there was going to be a surfeit of security for the tour so they chose to remain at the hotel. Jack knew that he would have to tell Miguel that it was he who had said that they could stay behind and he felt that Miguel would understand, considering the amount of escort that was being provided.

The car stopped and they all got in. The driver was wearing a face microphone and said that he had been chosen by the President to take them on a tour of Addis Ababa and, as far as he could, he would like to give them a commentary to describe the places that they would see. He said that the President had suggested that in view of the security needed for these guests of their country, he had been advised that they should view the tour from within the car but that he would, whenever he could, answer any questions that they may have.

The cars started out, quite slowly, but the escort cars all appeared to know just how to fully surround this car and they began to move away from the hotel. The driver began to tell them, "Addis Ababa is the capital city and the largest city in Ethiopia. There are quite a number of religions within the city as you may notice during the tour. The city has a population of about three million people and in general, it has quite a nice climate. July and August in Addis Ababa can sometimes be very rainy, and from October until January, we have little rain at all. Temperatures are remarkably constant from month to month. The average highs are between 17°C and 22°C. The average lows are between 11°C and 14°C. The warmest months are from February to May. The temperatures and climate though can vary due to elevation. Due to the altitude of the city, there is a huge day-to-night range of temperature: It is often 27°C at lunchtime and can be as low as 3°C at night. Many people do say that for the evenings in Addis Ababa always take a second layer of clothing with you. Addis Ababa is generally regarded as a very safe city to visit and to get around you can, of course, travel by car and we do have some rather wonderful trams that are very popular, plus there are the local taxi services. There are of course some parts of our country that do not have quite as favourable a climate, as does Addis Ababa, but I am sure that you may appreciate that from your recent need to provide such magnificent aid for some of our people who live in those parts of the country."

He took the car towards one building and said, "On your left, you can see the Ethiopian National Museum, (it is situated b*etween Arat Kilo Avenue and the University of Addis Ababa Graduate School*). Although the museum is unknown to most, the Ethiopian National Museum is a world-class museum; truly a hidden gem! Remembering that human form is believed by many to have started somewhere close to Ethiopia, if not in Ethiopia itself (and of course near to Addis Ababa). The most famous exhibit is the replica of Lucy, an early hominid, but the museum offers much more. With Ethiopian civilization being one of the oldest in the world, the artefacts within the museum span thousands of years, including some from its earliest days. As I have already said, it is believed that it was in the area of, or close to Ethiopia that the human form evolved first in the world so the replica of Lucy is so appropriate here. There are a wide variety of artefacts featured in the museum, from sculptures to

clothing to artwork. Both traditional and modern art are featured."
The drive continued a little way.

He slowed the car and said, "On the right-hand side you can see the Red Terror Museum, This is on Bole Road (*very near Maskal Square end*). This is a must-see to learn about the horrors of the Derg that led to the well-known famine of the 1990s. Most of the employees are survivors of the regime themselves and will tell you stories about facing torture at the hands of those who still run today free." Once again he slowed the car a little and said, "Straight ahead of us you can see Africa Hall, (*located across Menelik II Avenue from the Palace*). This is where the United Nations Economic Commission for Africa is headquartered as well as most UN offices in Ethiopia. It is also the site of the founding of the Organization for African Unity (OAU) which eventually became the African Union." He turned a corner and then said, "On your left now you can see the Parliament Building, (*Near Holy Trinity Cathedral*). Built during the reign of Emperor Haile Selassie, with its clock tower, it continues to serve as the seat of Parliament today. Down the road a little you will see Shengo Hall. This was built by the Derg regime of Mengistu Haile Mariam as its new parliament hall. The Shengo Hall was the world's largest pre-fabricated building, which was constructed in Finland before being assembled in Addis Ababa. It is used for large meetings and conventions."

The drive continued a little way and then he said, "Here is the St George's Cathedral, (*North end of Churchill Road*). It was built in 1896 to commemorate Ethiopia's victory over the Italians.

The cathedral is a circular building that does not look very impressive when you approach it. As you walk around the building, you will notice people praying beside the walls, but it is unlikely that you will find an entrance. The Cathedral houses a small museum and close to it, inside, you will often likely meet one of the archdeacons of the Cathedral. The interior is beautifully decorated with huge paintings and mosaics and will make any trip to it worthwhile. It is sometimes worth visiting the museum with a guide as well to see ceremonial clothes and ancient manuscripts."

The drive again took a few turns and eventually, he said, "Ahead of us again is the Anwar Mosque. This is in the Mercato district, which happens to be the largest market in Africa. It's quite impressive. Walking into the market, can sometimes appear to be a little chaotic, the Market is known here as Merkato and is just to the West of Addis' centre, it can be equally as rewarding as it is exasperating. You may discover there the most eloquent aroma of many spices and herbs for which the area is well known. As I mentioned earlier, The President has asked that I try to ensure for your own safety and security that you remain in the car. Those aromas I am afraid are something that I know of and which I can only tell you about, since you may not go to sample them yourselves."

He drove a little more and then paused near another large building, and he said, "This is the National Palace. Formerly known as the Jubilee Palace, built to mark Emperor Haile Selassie's Silver Jubilee in 1955, and it is now the residence of the President of

Ethiopia. As we progress along here, you will be able to see on your left, the Ethiopian Ethnological Museum. (It is located on the campus of the University of Addis Ababa) It is a fascinating museum with exhibits relating to the history and culture of Ethiopia. There are many displays of the various ethnic groups found in Ethiopia with information about each of their lifestyles. A large number of ethnic outfits, instruments, tools, and other artefacts accompany each ethnic exhibit, making it one of the most interesting museums in the city! Close to it on the same side of the road is the Addis Ababa Museum. While the national museum houses artefacts from all over Ethiopia, this museum focuses solely on artefacts and exhibits from Addis Ababa itself. The building itself was once a palace where Ras Biru Habte-Gabriel, a former Minister of War, resided. Moving on we can see Netsa Art Village. This has authentic and interesting art in a beautiful park across from the French Embassy. Unfortunately, the Netsa Art Village is no longer active, according to some reports that I have recently been given. Next to it is Holy Trinity Cathedral. It was once the largest Ethiopian Orthodox Cathedral. It was built to commemorate the country's liberation from the Italians, and many victims killed by the Italians during the occupation are buried here. The locals call the church Haile Selassie Church because Emperor Haile Selassie's body was moved here in 2000. Quite close to here is the Gola St. Michael Church. This is comparatively quite close to the centre of the city (*Next to the Federal immigration office*). Under normal circumstances, it can be a very interesting place to visit and it is one of the many old churches found in Addis Ababa. One can see old paintings painted by many Ethiopian celebrity artists. In addition, the church has a museum displaying church articles given by many famous people of the country including the emperor Haile Selassie and his Empress."

The driver took the car down towards the centre of the City again and said, "Since I have been told to try and make the tour interesting but because of the security I had to ask you to remain in the car I believe that we have gone as far as I am able to do and I shall now return you to your hotel. I understand that the President is also arranging for some cars to collect you for your return to the airport. May I please on behalf of the President (and the people of Ethiopia) give you our best wishes for your visit and hope that you all have a very pleasant journey home."

The car then pulled up again outside of their hotel. As they got out of the car they saw the manager of the hotel and his staff coming out to them again to attend to their needs. It didn't take long then for them to get back to their apartment, change and collect all of their luggage and return to the ground floor where they found the Captain and his crew, (all once again smart and in their uniforms). Jack had telephoned and made arrangements for them to have two cars again and they arrived, once again with a lot of army and police to give them an escort to the 'plane.

The drive to the airport didn't take very long (especially as the police escort was clearing the way for them as they drove). Back at the side of the 'plane, the Captain told his crew that they should get back on board and Jack saw that another car was arriving. It was the President, and, as the car stopped, the president got out and came across to Jack and Jennifer, he shook their hands and wished them a safe journey and asked if the tour had been satisfactory. He apologised for his instructions to the driver for them not to get out of the car but he insisted that, although Addis Ababa is normally quite a safe city to be in, due to their current position in life, such security was a case of being sensible to their honoured visitors.

They got onto the 'plane and they knew that it could take a few minutes for the Captain and crew to get everything in order (and receive clearance for a take-off) so they just took their seats and Jack and Jennifer thought that on this occasion they had done quite well. It wasn't long though before the captain announced on the intercom for them all to please fasten their safety belts and that they were now going to take off.

Chapter Twenty-Eight

Their flight back to England was quite straightforward and Jack used his mobile to call Hugo to give him an approximate time of arrival. Hugo did remind Jack that nowadays it was Miguel who was in charge of security and it was he that should have been called. He agreed that he would pass on the message and he asked how they had got on with their trip to Ethiopia.

"Oh, fine," Jack replied. "In fact, I went out with the President to the end of just the one line and they had some certificates that they are keeping to show the pressure testing that they have done as the pipeline is extended. At the end of the pipeline though, Hugo, they must have had four or five bulldozers creating an enormous depression that will form the base of a lake. From there they are going to be installing some smaller pumps with a slightly smaller diameter pipe, all powered by solar panels. That will then pump further out in several directions to irrigate more and more of their land. Yes, it was impressive. Up to the time that I got there, they hadn't seen the surveyors so I suppose that once they have been there as well we should have all that we need to say that it is being done well. At Djibouti, while we were there at the starting point, they received a call that the ship with the next lot of equipment was just arriving. It shouldn't be long now Hugo before it has all been done. Anyway, I'll see you when we get back, won't I? Oh, how's the work going on with the Sri Lanka problem? Have you been updated by anyone? Will they need more homes than those that we have got ready? Oh, the questions just keep coming, don't they? I know that you'll deal with whatever is happening, won't you?"

The Captain had obviously radioed forward to get clearance to land once again at Northolt and they arrived very close to the time that he had predicted. As they were going to be landing at an RAF base (Northolt) he didn't invite Jack to take over and land the plane this time. As they got off the 'plane, Alvaro was there with a car and the other two security guards (Manuel and Javier) got the luggage and put it into the car boot. Jennifer stopped near the door of the jet and called Margaret over to have a few words with her before they departed. Margaret had apparently promised that she would come out to visit them at their estate soon and see the flat that they had there. Jack thanked the Captain and said that he too would be welcome if he wanted to visit them at their estate and he passed him a very generous tip for him to share amongst the rest of the crew.

Alvaro got them all into the car and then they started their drive to get back home. Jennifer knew that she would have to pop in and see her Mum and Dad to tell them of all the wonderful things that they had seen and the places that they had been to.

Jack was just thinking that he could pop through and give a full update on his visit to Ethiopia to Alec and Ray in the office. He also wondered if they had done anything at all to find any crises for him to start working towards. He also would have to speak to Hugo to see if there had been any further developments with the work for Sri Lanka. One way or another, he knew that he would be having a fairly busy day when they got back home.

The drive wasn't very long and they drove into this estate that they all now regarded as home. Yes, they both knew it was home, but it did still seem to be strange to be living on an estate like this instead of living in a house on a street, like many more houses, amongst many more streets. They both now liked their home on the estate, but neither of them could really contemplate or give any reason to the many strange things that had brought about these strange happenings to their lives. Yes, they were quite happy, but they had both found that they were in so many ways isolated from their friends that they had known for many, many years. At least in the case of Jennifer, she was now trying to build at least one new friendship with Margaret and she really believed that Margaret would come out to see them soon.

Back at the estate, Alvaro drove them to the doorway to the main entry for their flat and they began to get out of the car. Manuel and Javier went to the car boot to get their luggage for them and they carried it in through the main doorways and to the elevator doors where they put it down. They just weren't sure, even now, if they were permitted to go into that elevator, but in any case, Jack and Jennifer didn't need people to do such basic things as carry their luggage for them.

Jack and Jennifer got to the elevator door and Jack thanked Manuel and Javier and said that they hoped that they had enjoyed their trip and that now, they would be able to tell their families some of what they had seen while they had been away. Jack had pressed the button for the elevator and he moved their luggage into it. As Jennifer also got into the elevator he pressed the button for the second floor and they were on their way home again! Once on their floor, they went more or less straight to their flat, pausing only as they went to give a call to both of their parents who had a flat each quite close to the pair of them. They would get them all into their flat as soon as they were ready to come through, they could give them some tea and they themselves could have some coffee. Then they could just let them know how their trip away had been. Their parents were obviously pleased to see them both back and they quite willingly agreed to pop in for a quick cuppa and some stories about their trip.

It didn't take long for Jennifer to get the kettle filled, along with both her Mum and Jack's Mum who were both quite eager to hear the stories of their travels, what they had seen and who they had met. Jack went with his Dad and Jennifer's Dad into the lounge where they could get some nice seats. Jack was quite keen nowadays on getting his comfortable seat and even though the hotel apartment in Addis Ababa had had some nice furniture, it wasn't quite like being sat in their own chairs. Yes, he had liked the seats on the aeroplane but these chairs just seemed to envelope you and give you a feeling of some kind of security.

Jennifer brought the teas and coffee in on a tray for everyone and once they were all sitting comfortably they began to tell their parents all that they had seen, where they had been and, in the case of Jennifer, she was telling her Mum and Dad that she had found a new friend who had happened to be the stewardess on the 'plane that they went out on.

Both sets of parent were now well aware of their ghostly visitors in the office and they knew some of the things that had been happening and so, they wanted to know how things were progressing at keeping their ghosts happy with their trip this time. They also wanted to know what else Jack had arranged for those poor people in Sri Lanka. They said that they had heard quite a lot more, and seen a lot on the television about when that Tsunami had struck their land. They said that it had appeared to them to be a horrendous experience and what else could Jack do now to help those people.

Jack filled them in with all that he had done and (from the reports that he had had from Hugo by phone while they had been away) what else they had done to try and give some kind of help and aid to the people of that island.

The tea and coffee sessions ended and both of their parents left to go back to their own flats and Jack and Jennifer decided that they should just go and tell the ghosts what they had seen and done in Ethiopia. In the office, they found Alec sitting at the computer moving his hands above the keyboard and Ray sitting quite near and with his notebook in his hands.

"Well, we're back," Jack called out, just a little relieved to see that things hadn't changed much at all while they had been away. "We went out to the end of one of the pipelines, the one nearest to Addis Ababa and, to be honest, we were both quite impressed with what we saw being done. You know how we had been concerned that they may have made some poor joints between the pipes, well, they have even been insisting on having a proper test done for each joint and they had kept the written reports of those tests for us to look at. They were excavating a tremendously deep depression beyond the end of the pipeline to create a lake and they were going to use some smaller diameter pipes and with some smaller pumps, pump water out to even more remote areas to make the land fertile and useful for the people there. We saw the point at the coast where the desalination units and everything is going and it looked really good. We are both looking forward to the next time that we go when they start the process working. That will be some achievement, won't it? Of course, we are not waiting for the surveyor's reports on what has been happening in the other countries with their pipelines. The surveyor reports for them should be with us soon, I imagine and I think that if they are OK then that should be enough, shouldn't it?"

"You have been busy, haven't you," Ray said. "And what did you make of the President this time? We were aware that you were quite impressed with him the last time weren't you? Did he look after you? Has he spoken to any of the other countries that are near to him? That will be necessary to keep things good out there, you know. If they get their land to be useful for them will they be happy with that or will they decide that they want some of the other land that is now being productive? No, I suppose that only time will give us answers to that, won't it?"

"How have you two gone on then," Jack asked them both. "Have you managed to get any of your people to start trying to find more crises for us to look at? I think that we have done fairly well so far, haven't we? You did both give us your word that you would get some of your people to start looking, didn't you? How is it going then?"

"Some of our people are now trying to find a way that they can to discover anything that may be useful but so far, we haven't had a great lot of success at that. We have managed to get your fund to stabilise, more or less and we are both happy with that. We will keep on at our people to try and find more crises. Eventually, I think that we may find a way but at present, no, we haven't done a lot yet. For that you do have our abject apologies. We shall keep on trying though."

"Yes, I know that you'll keep on trying," Jack said, "But until then it looks like it's down to us two to try and find more things, isn't it? Anyway, we haven't caught up with Hugo yet so we'll leave you two and we'll go and try and find him."

They both left the office, returning, of course via the kitchen, so that they could again top up with some more coffee.

As they finished off their coffee, Jack said, "I had better give Hugo a call, hadn't I? He'll want to know a bit more about how things have gone on, won't he?" he took out his mobile phone and dialled through to get Hugo. "Why don't you come on up and have a cup of coffee, Hugo?" Jack asked. "I know that I should have called you earlier, but we did have our parents to see to first, didn't we? Anyway, I expect that Manuel and Javier have been filling you in with all that we've done and what we've seen, haven't they? Anyway, the kettle is going on mate if you can make it up here."

It was literally only a few minutes later and there was Hugo, smiling broadly at seeing his old friends. "Come on, I wasn't with you this time," Hugo said, "So I need to have a full report of what you have seen, what you have done. Mainly though, more to the point was it worth the trouble of going all that way?"

"Yes, you already knew a good bit about it, didn't you? Jack replied, smiling broadly at his friend. "I did give you a brief outline while we were out there. The way that they are making those huge lakes at the ends of the pipelines is quite impressive. From the way that it was explained to me, the smaller pipelines that they will now extend from the lakes should give them an awful lot of irrigation to their very dry lands. When we had the tour of Addis Ababa, the driver told us that Ethiopia does have some good lands and although rain isn't all that common in all months, it seems to be mainly in July and August when Addis Ababa gets its rain. The temperatures as well do seem to be strange. He told us that it can have a daytime temperature of twenty-seven degrees but that it can then drop to about three degrees at the same night. That does seem weird, doesn't it? He also said that although that was the case for Addis Ababa, some parts of their country don't have such a favourite climate. Thank goodness for our rainy climate in England. At least we don't get droughts like that, and the famines that follow, do we? Anyway, I was generally impressed with what we saw out there. How are things going for Sri Lanka? Have you heard anything else? Our Mum's and Dad's have told us that they saw some shots of it on the television and that it looked to be a horrible experience. Have those mobile homes been shipped out yet? I suppose sending out the plumbers, electricians and the other workers can wait until the ship gets nearer, can't it? Have we been asked to do anything else?"

"Yes, from what you have seen and heard of in Ethiopia does sound to be good, doesn't it? We have had some surveyors reports in for Eritrea and Sudan and they all seem to be quite good reports. They were doing a similar kind of testing at the joints but the Somalia report suggests that they haven't been doing enough testing by a long shot. I think that either you, or someone else, will have to talk to them. It will probably be better if it is you. After all, it is you that is putting up the money to do the job. Perhaps a good word to that President and say something like 'get the joints tested' or you won't get the rest of the equipment. A deal is a deal and it is for the whole deal that you are putting up the money, not just so that he can bask in having a pipeline there when it won't work because of a lack of testing. I'm sure that if you make it a hard call, he'll respond. Why not give it a try? As far as your other work goes, I haven't heard a lot about the Sri Lanka work. Yes, the homes are all now at sea and must be well across the Mediterranean Sea by now. Maybe another ten days or so and they should be there. Once again, maybe if you give your friend Norman a ring, he may be able to update you a bit more."

"Yes, maybe a call to Norman would be a favourite one to try," Jack said. "I'll try that first and then I'll try and call the President of Somalia." Jack picked up the landline phone and dialled for Norman Brooks at Downing Street. It didn't take many minutes and the voice came back of Norman Brooks.

"Hello Norman," Jack said, "It's Jack Dawkins here again. I'm now back home from Ethiopia and things are moving on quite well out there. I would imagine that within about three month or so they should be ready for the big 'switch on'. Maybe at that time, the Prime Minister would want to be there to show the flag, so to speak. We are detecting a little bit of tardiness in Somalia and I'm going to call that President about what they need to be doing. The Mobile Homes that I got for Sri Lanka are now well across the Mediterranean and we now think it will maybe another ten days or so to get them all there. What else has happened there? We have heard nothing. Are the authorities going to get some land available for the homes to be put onto? Is the seventy eight Homes enough for what they need? We do need to be kept informed and no one else but you seems to bother. Can you find out anything else about what is happening? I have electricians, plumbers and some other workers ready to ship out once the homes reach Sri Lanka but we do need some information. Is there anything at all that you can do?"

"I'm sorry, Jack," Norman replied, "Someone should have been keeping in touch with you about it all. Yes, they have got some land for the homes to go onto. They have also got some diggers that can help to put in some kind of foundation and other holes, for pipes I suppose they mean. They should have spoken to you. I'll call them again and I'll tell them to keep talking to you. It sounds as though the seventy eight houses are pretty close to what they needed. I believe that they told us that it was eighty five families that have lost their homes. That only leaves them with seven more homes to find for their people, doesn't it? I think, no I can say quite certainly that the Prime Minister will want to be able to get there for the big switch on in Ethiopia. Are you OK at ringing the President of Somalia, I could get the Prime Minister to call if that would make it easier for you?"

"Thanks a lot for all of that update, Norman, when we finish talking I can see if I can get my people to look and see if they can get hold of another seven of those homes if you like. Let me know if they have found another answer to the shortfall or not then I can get my people to make a move to find some if they do want them. As for Somalia, I think that it may be easier if I have a word with him. He did seem to be the kind of person who may need some 'firm talking to get him moving'. I can tell him to toe the line and do the testing of the joints or I won't send any other equipment at all to them. I think that that may have a better effect, don't you?"

"Crikey, Jack," Norman replied, laughing a little, "At least when you aren't a politician and a diplomat you can do things like that. After all, you are the person who is paying the bill to get them what they want so yes; that would be a far better way of dealing with him maybe. Do keep in touch though and let me know what he says when you tell him to do the job. I suppose that it is a case of 'put up or shut up' isn't it? I haven't heard of any other crises that are going to be worthy of your attention, unless you have a magic wand to cure a lot of illnesses. No, that would perhaps be unfair for a while yet, wouldn't it?"

"Maybe for now, Norman," Jack replied, "But you never know exactly what my mind may turn to next, do you? Anyway, I'll go and see what else I may be needed for here. I'll talk to you later, bye." He put the phone down and went to find Jennifer once again.

Chapter Twenty-Nine

"Jennifer," Jack said, when he at last found her. She was as usual in her kitchen once again. "I've just been talking to Norman again and he said that he hadn't got any other crises that he knew about at the moment unless I thought that I could maybe cure some disease or something. Him saying that well, it just made me think. Do you believe that if we need another crisis, to invest in some kind of research would satisfy the need to donate to worthy causes? I mean, with that they may or they may not find a cure for something. If they do find a cure then it is a worthwhile donation but if they don't, well I'd have just been throwing the money away, wouldn't I? What are your thoughts on it? You know that you quite often seem to have a better sort of 'weighing it up' sort of mind for some things, don't you?"

"That can soon develop into a lot of things, Jack," Jenifer replied. "If you decided to donate or invest in a cure for one disease and you chose as a 'second thought' sort of thing perhaps another disease and if that did work, it would be fine. But if you decided to invest in another disease and then the one that you had thought about first was a success and if your 'second thought of investing in one came to nothing, that would just be a waste, wouldn't it? Oh, I think that that is far too complicated for me. Now, the things that you have so far put your money in are things that are happening more or less, at the moment and that can quite easily be dealt with by cash, their easier to go for, aren't they? With that kind of thing you know that you should get some success, even if you have to spend a little more than you thought that'd need to be spent at first, shouldn't you?"

"Yes, Jennifer," Jack said. "I think that you've really hit the nail on the head with that. I'll stick to more or less what we've been doing that does seem to work. In the meantime, I'll give that President of Somalia a call and tell him to get his act together or that I shall have to withdraw my offer of aid to them."

"Yes, dear, I think that you should do that," Jennifer replied, smiling at him, "But, before you do, just get Hugo to be near to you when you call him so that he can hear what you are saying."

Jack gave Hugo a call and said that he wanted him to be there when he tried to sort out the Somalia President about the poor work that they had done on their pipeline. Hugo was up with him within less than ten minutes and he had a sheaf of papers with him when he found Jack, as usual, sitting in the lounge, drinking coffee. "I've brought some of the surveyor's results with me, Jack," Hugo said. "You will need to have the evidence of what and where it has not been done properly, won't you? Well, this gives the actual readings done by your surveyor and their efforts at reading provided by their surveyor that shows a determined attempt not to comply."

"Thanks a lot, Hugo," Jack said with a huge smile on his face. "Do you want to get a cuppa and then I'd like you to be with me when I make the call to their President. I just feel that now is the time for us to start to show our muscle to them. They must realise that they either play ball with what the conditions that we have given them or they just won't get the goods. That's fair, isn't it?"

"Oh, yes, that's fair, Jack," Hugo replied. "In fact, let's face it, if they don't do the testing that they have been asked to do then it would just be a waste of your money in doing anything else with them, wouldn't it? Let's face it, with leaking pipes the water wouldn't get to where it is supposed to be going, would it? I'll just get my coffee. I shan't be many minutes."

Hugo returned with his coffee in his hand and Jack picked up the phone to start calling the President of Somalia. He pressed the button to turn on the loudspeaker from the phone. The phone rang for a few minutes and a voice answered, and it didn't sound like the voice of the President so, Jack said, "Is the President of Somalia there please? I was given this number for whenever I wanted to contact him".

"No, I'm sorry, he is here but he is rather busy and he doesn't take calls from just anyone who rings this number. If you need to contact him, please write a letter and it may be dealt with by the appropriate department."

"I see," Jack replied, "So he doesn't want to speak to me then by the sounds of it. My name is Jack Dawkins (which you never troubled to ask) and if he doesn't come on the line within the next two minutes I shall withdraw the entire donation that I was going to give to get your dried areas of Somalia some water. I was told that this number was a direct line to the President and I am now, not at all impressed. Now, put him on the line immediately."

"I'm sorry sir, I don't know your name and I don't know what you are talking about so could you please put it all in writing. If we do eventually get some meaningful letter from you the President may, or may not reply at his convenience."

"Tell the President that the offer to get water into Somalia has now been withdrawn and he may keep those pipes that he has got, but he will now not be receiving any wind turbine, any desalination units or any other kind of aid and assistance from me. Good day to you sir, If he changes his mind tell him that I too can be quite unforgiving." Jack put the phone down and looked across at Hugo. "Well, what do you think then, Hugo? That was the correct way to handle them, wasn't it?"

"It was harsh, Jack, yes, but it had to be done like that," Hugo replied. "I believe that whoever it was who you were speaking to on the phone will convey your message to the President quite quickly and I would imagine that he will be calling back here very shortly. Maybe we'll just have to wait a few minutes, don't you think?"

"That man, the President," Jack said, "He gave me that number as a personal number to contact him with at any time. The person who answered I don't think that they were even passing any message to him, do you? I just wonder if after that they will even bother to relay my final message to him. You don't think that it could be that we have just hit a time when there is another some kind of 'takeover' going on in that country and that they didn't know anything about the pipelines'. I mean, that is a possibility, isn't it? Do you think that I should get hold of Norman to see if he can get our Prime Minister to contact them to see if he has had the message or if they are in some other kind of turmoil out there?"

"Personally, Jack, I think that you need to wait for a little while and see if someone is going to call you back," Hugo said, "I think that they will call back, and quite quickly as well."

They both continued drinking their coffee with neither of them saying anything for a good few minutes. The finished their coffee and Jack said. "They haven't rung back, Hugo. Do you think now that I should call Norman to try and get some political people to talk to them?"

Jack had hardly finished speaking and the telephone rang. He picked up the phone and pressed the loudspeaker button and made contact, "Hello," he said, "Who is calling please?"

"Mr Dawkins sir," the voice on the phone said. "I have just heard from a rather worthless secretary that you called and wanted to speak to me, I am the President of Somalia and you just called on this number. I apologise for that worthless persons replies to you. How may I help you Mr Dawkins?"

"Mr President, the person who answered the phone knew full well who I was and what I represent. I believed then and still do, that you were present when I made the call. I believe that you are now starting to demonstrate some extremely unreliable and unworthy characteristics. I had called you today because, when I spoke to you before, I had made it quite clear that the pipelines had to be properly checked after each joint in order to ensure that there could be no leakages. I now have before me the reports of your workpeople and also the reports of my own surveyor who visited your site. My surveyor's reports show that your testing had been totally inadequate. That was a condition for me getting the rest of the work done. You, sir, have failed to satisfy my conditions so the answer must be to withdraw any more support to your country since that pipeline would be useless for the purposes for which it was to be used. It would leak at almost every joint. In view of that, I called today to tell you that as you have been unable to meet the rather basic requirements, I shall have to end any further donations to aid your country. All of the other countries that were going to benefit from my aid have all complied. Yours is the only country to have failed to do so. I can see no point in continuing this call so, good day to you sir." Jack put down the phone and looked across at Hugo.

"I know that it is your decision, Jack," Hugo said. "But that was a very harsh decision to make, wasn't it? It sounded to me as though it was a very definite and terminal decision to make as well. The people of that country will suffer Jack. Are you sure that you want to simply end your aid like that? Can you get them to re-open the dialogue by using your own politicians?"

"I'm not sure Hugo, not sure at all," Jack answered. "From the first time that I met that man I didn't like him and I didn't trust him. He just gave off an aura of being someone who would need a lot of watching. Why should we have to be the police, to have to watch over someone like that when it is they who are the persons causing the problem, the distrust? Yes, the people of that country may lose out, but my impression was that the people would lose out anyway when they have a leader like that. After all, they must have elected him, mustn't they? If he is deposed or is changed for a more reasonable person then that could change things. I believe that you do agree, inside yourself, don't you?"

"I am glad that it is you who has to make these decisions Jack," Hugo replied. "Yes, I can see some of your reasons. Yes, you did say after your first meeting with him that you didn't trust him. The people in his country need the water Jack. Maybe he will be deposed but if he isn't then they will still get famines from the droughts that they get, won't they? Let your politician try and get him to see some sense. Just to back you up on it all, Jack, I'll get the recordings of all of those calls and I'll keep a tape of it for you. At least it will be some evidence of their behaviour, won't it?"

They were just getting up to leave and the phone rang again, Jack, once again picked it up and pressed the loudspeaker button to make the call. "Hello," he said "This is Jack Dawkins here, how can I help you?"

"Oh, Hello Jack," Normans voice came out of the phone. "I've just heard from the people doing the work in Sri Lanka and they say that yes please, if you could get them some more of the houses for them. They are all saying thank you, Jack, I think that everyone is doing that. I'll let you get on with that then, shall I?"

"Norman, before you go off line," Jack said, "I did call the president of Somalia and it wasn't a pleasant experience. At first although the number that I dialled was the one that he gave me for a direct line it got someone who didn't want to listen and then later, I got the President and he was just as objectionable as before so I said that I was going to now withdraw my aid to their country. I told him the reason; that the pipelines have not been all checked as they should have been. If politically he can be brought back to the table but only if he is willing to get things done as we said in the first place I would continue with the aid. I trust you to get thing done Norman. Can you have a go?"

"Yes, I'll try and do that and I'll let you try and get another seven of those houses for Sri Lanka as well."

"Norman, I have been thinking about all of those houses as well and I think that I will make sure that there are some solar panels available for all of them, and that includes for the ones that are already on the water to there, and, whoever is the power or energy supplier out there, I will donate one hundred and seventy thousand pounds to ease their energy bills for the first year or two for the supply to the houses that we are supplying; that will be twenty thousand pounds per house (or family, won't it?), But I'll donate it via their energy companies, (not to the house dwellers themselves), so that it covers that aspect. I wouldn't want them to think that it was just some gambling cash that they could spend. Can you let them know?"

"Oh, thanks, Jack," Norman replied. I'll get onto them right away with that news. Some of those people out there have lost all of their money and their possessions. That will be invaluable to them. Thanks a lot, Jack." Norman ended the call.

"That was a good one, wasn't it," Hugo said. "I never expected that one at all. Well done and I'll go and see to the other seven houses and get hold of a load of solar panels for you." Hugo left and Jack was once again in a kind of limbo. He knew that he had just had some coffee so, instead of getting more coffee, he went try and find Jennifer. He looked but he couldn't find here anywhere in their flat so he went to her parents flat and knocked on the door. Jennifer's Mum came to the door and he said that he was just looking for Jennifer.

Jennifer appeared from behind her Mum and said, "What is it Jack, I can see by the look on your face that you are a bit lost again, aren't you? Come on; let's get you home and then maybe we can sort out what we can do, eh?"

They got home and Jack began to explain all that had been happening. He said that he hadn't wanted to do that with Somalia but that the President there had been so awkward and unhelpful that it seemed to be the only way to do it. He told her that Norman was going to see if they could open some political doors for them and he told her about the other bits about Sri Lanka. She was pleased with all of that and said that as he had done all that, why didn't she make them both a nice cup of coffee? Just having her with him though did seem to lift some of the gloom from him and so he agreed to another coffee each.

It was quite a lot later that day when the phone rang again and when Jack answered it and it was Norman, from Downing Street. "Hello, Jack," Norman said. "I told the Prime Minister and he has already spoken to the President of Somalia and he believes that that President is now almost begging for you to give them another chance. Maybe if you leave it until tomorrow you may be getting another call from Somalia. I don't think that you need to ring them. It is they who now have to make amends, isn't it? It sounds as though he has now realised that unless he gets you to agree to help them, theirs is going to be the only country in the Horn of Africa that doesn't get the water supply that they want, and need. The Prime Minister also asked me to thank you for all that you have done to help the people in Sri Lanka as well. He was quite impressed with all that you have done, and the speed that you did it with. I'm afraid that the buzzer has gone and he needs me so I'll speak to you later, cheerio."

Jack had told Hugo about this latest news from Norman and he said that if he happened to be about in their flat tomorrow morning he may be there when the President called from Somalia. Hugo agreed to that, now wanting to see just what the outcome of their boss and his discussions with the country that didn't want to toe the line.

It was mid morning the following day when the phone did ring. They had had quite a quiet day and had been on the point of ending their waiting so, the ringing of the phone was something of a relief to them both. Jack answered it, pressing again the loudspeaker button. "Hello, Jack Dawkins here, how may I help you," he asked.

"Hello, Mr Dawkins," Came across the voice of the President of Somalia, "I do believe that we have had some rather crossed lines recently and I would like to apologise for any misunderstandings that may have caused us to stop talking. I understand that your surveyor's report and our reports don't quite match as they should do? I do apologise for any discrepancies and I can assure you that all tests will be redone and if your surveyor could give us perhaps a couple of weeks before they re-check them, I feel quite sure that everything will be in order. I am not sure why exactly they were not done properly the first time but I do assure you sir, that on this occasion they will all be thoroughly tested and checked. Any joints that do fail will, I assure you, be completely resealed again to make them proof against any water leaks. I do hope, sir, that you will consider reinstating your aid to our poor country. It is so important for us to get our lands well irrigated."

"Yes, Mr President," Jack replied, "Your country does need the irrigation as well, doesn't it? Now, from what I have seen already in Ethiopia and Djibouti and have heard that it is being done in Eritrea is that some very large land depressions are being created to form lakes at the end of the lines and they are also making a start on the addition of a number of smaller lines to extend beyond those lakes. I would expect some similar actions to be taken by your country as well. If you can give me some assurances that that is the case, and provided that the next surveys do not find a mass of errors, I shall reinstate my offer of aid to your country. That offer will, I assure you depend on the compliance by both you and your people to the demands to get the work done properly. Can I have you agreement Mr President?"

"Oh, yes, Mr Dawkins, certainly we shall make every effort to comply with all that you ask for. Thank you so much for your benevolence to our country sir. Farewell for now." The phone went dead.

"Well, I still don't entirely trust the man," Jack said, "But he did agree to get the work done, didn't he? What did you think of him, the way that he said he'd do things? You maybe have a better feeling than I have, but somehow, I just don't trust him at all."

"Jack, I believe that you have hit the spot there." Hugo replied, "No, I wouldn't trust him either but, he has promised and we do have a tape of that so that is all that we can do. I will give him a week or so and then I'll get the surveyors out there again and we can also see if they are making any movement to make the lakes that you saw the other people doing. We shall just have to wait, Jack."

Jack was quite aware that he could do no more and so he reconciled himself with the fact that the man had promised to get things done. However, he knew that he would have to rely on Hugo getting the surveyors reports to him as they came in and then he would make the decision about continuing with the work for that country or to remove them from the list of countries that he would be prepare to help. The entire problem did worry him quite a bit and he knew that he was the only one who could make the final decision on this.

Hugo could see on Jack's face the great doubt that he was feeling. "Look, Jack," Hugo said, on this matter I can advise, but I can't make the decision. You obviously know that, don't you? Why don't you concentrate your efforts on the thing that you have been doing that do seem to be working? The Ethiopian project must now be getting well underway. Why not give that man a ring and lift up your own feelings with some good news? Maybe the Sudan and Eritrea are now getting closer to getting their other equipment. I'll go and find out what progress there has been on each one for you, how does that sound?"

"Hugo, I reckon that I'd be more or less lost without your help. Yes please, do go and see if we can get a complete list of how each lot of things are progressing. That, I think will be something to raise my hopes beyond belief."

"Jack," Hugo replied with a little laugh, "I already have some lists that are detailing the progress of the various things that we are doing. We update these quite regularly so that we can have some idea of what we have and at what point it is at; where it is being held; potential delivery times etc. That is more or less what you want, isn't it?"

"Yes, that's more or less what I am starting to need more and more. Do we have a date for when the wind turbines are to be delivered for Eritrea and Sudan? Do we know some approximate dates for the delivery to those countries of the Desalination units and the tanks, more or less the full kit for each of them? If you have, that will help me a lot. I'm going to talk to the President in Ethiopia and see what the progress is there. They have had some time and they may be getting to a point when they may have a potential date for the start of the system. When we get that date, the Prime Minister wants to go out with us also; do you want to go as well? You know that you would be welcome and you have played a big part in it all, haven't you?"

"Yes, I'd love to go out for the big switch on but I'd better go and get those other lists that you have asked for. Let's keep everything moving. By the way, I also have the potential dates for the wind turbine and the desalination units etc for Somalia. Do you want them as well?"

"Yes please, Hugo, that would be very useful," Jack replied. "Especially if I should be getting any more sudden phone calls from that man and his strange ways of not complying."

Hugo left and Jack went to see Jennifer to let her know how things were progressing again. He told her that he had better also put the ghosts in the office in the picture about what he had been doing. They went together to see the ghosts in the office and as they got nearer, Jack called out, "Ahoy in there, we now have some more update news for you. I'll bet that you thought that we'd forgotten all about you two, didn't you? Well, I have had to threaten to pull out any aid to Somalia as they hadn't done any checks on the pipelines for the joints. At first I was just going to tell them off a bit but then, the person on the phone seemed to want to pretend that he didn't know who I was and he said that the president was too busy. I told him that I'd stop it all and then later, the President came on and said that bit was the secretary that had got it wrong. Anyway, he was still quite horrible and I told him that I was going to pull out of helping them. I then passed that information on to our Prime Minister and he then more or less got the President to call back and agree to what I said. I've told him that I am going to send out surveyors again and that if everything is OK I will finish the job but that if it isn't that I shall withdraw completely. For the Sri Lanka job, they have asked for another seven homes, Hugo is now getting them all ready to go. I have also said that I would supply solar panels for all of the houses and that I will pay their energy supplier one hundred and seventy thousand pounds, that's two thousand pounds per house to be used to help them to stabilise their lives for a year or maybe two, if they're careful. Hugo is now getting me the lists of when all of the other countries things will be ready and I am going to contact Ethiopia to get a potential date for a switch on and then the Prime Minister wants to go with us (and of course, Hugo is going as well). Well, that more or less updates what I've done so far. Is that all OK for you two? I take it that everything is fine here with you two, isn't it? The fund is still behaving and staying fairly stable, isn't it?"

"Yes Jack," Ray replied, "It is all stable here, apart from the odd jump now and then compensated with the odd loss now and then as well. We expected that. We have heard as well that some special permission may be given to us for this work and from what you have achieved so we may be able to pop back now and then to see you after we have moved upwards a bit. We were pleased at that bit of news, I can tell you."

"Yes," Alec said, "And that extra seven houses, the solar panels and the payment to the energy people is all going to work towards out bonus points isn't it? I must say that you have done us proud Jack. I can quite honestly say that it has been a pleasure to meet you. It is just a shame that we couldn't meet while I still lived in your world. If we had, I'd most certainly have bought you a damned good whisky to celebrate a bit in advance. You are doing fine with the odd one jump now and then on the fund but that is all getting things to level out just how we expected. If you do happen to make a large donation of a couple of billion, that still won't upset it now. Well done mate."

"Well, I will keep you updated," Jack said, "But Jennifer and I again need our regular top up of caffeine again so we'll see you later, cheerio."

Chapter Thirty

They both went quite happily back to the kitchen area and Jennifer said that she had heard from Margaret and that she was going to come over to see them for a few days next week. Jack said how pleased that she had got herself a friend again. He had noticed how she had in some way missed out on that since they moved onto the estate. He had asked her before why she didn't get some of her old friends over, but Jennifer had told him that somehow they had all seemed to be a bit nervous of coming out to see them there on the estate. It was shame, but if this new friendship with Margaret got her one friend, things may develop more as time passed, maybe they would start to meet some other people as well.

Hugo rang and said that he had got the list, did they want to see it. Jack said that of course he did and to bring it up straightaway. Jennifer was more or less as excited as he was. This was going to give them some idea of the completion dates for a lot of the projects and that meant that Alec and Ray would be getting their actual bonus points once they started the projects going. He arrived and he was able to tell them that the surveyors reports for Eritrea and Sudan had all been good and he showed them on the lists that their wind turbines and other equipment would be getting somewhere near the bottom end of the Red Sea by the end of next week. That meant that with a little bit of luck they may have all of these projects operational within another three or four months time from now.

Jack then made the call to Ethiopia and asked to speak to the President to see if they had managed to get some idea of when their switch on day would be. The President said yes, they had got an approximate date and it would, in all probability be within the next two weeks. Jack explained to him that the wind turbines and the other equipment for both Eritrea and Sudan could be arriving next week and he asked if the President would be inviting their leaders to come to see the switch on ceremony in Ethiopia. The President said, somewhat hesitantly that yes, he would invite them if Jack thought that he should. Jack asked why the President was so hesitant about it and the President then told him that over the years there had, at times, been some discord between these other countries. He said that they weren't at present at war with them but that that there was quite a lot of ill feelings still.

Jack, being Jack simply said, "Wouldn't this be a good time then for you to start to build some bridges between your countries when you are all going to benefit from water like this."

The President replied to Jack, "Perhaps there is some diplomat hidden away inside you Jack. Yes, you may be right and maybe we should try to build bridges as well as lakes. Yes, I will invite them and, hopefully they will come, but I will then ask that you make the announcement that you expect us all, now everyone has the water, which we have needed for so long, that we must now begin to work together."

Jack was stunned at this, but Jennifer and Hugo were just laughing at his shocked expression. "Mr President," Jack said, "I'm afraid I hadn't expected that. I don't regard myself in any way as a diplomat but, if I am in any way capable of causing an end to any enmity between your neighbouring countries then I will do that, especially for you, my friend. All of your countries have so much in common that the unity of you all would make you all an invincible pact wouldn't it?"

"From you, Jack, to call me friend, means far more than anything else," The President said. "I shall start to make the calls today and I do hope that you and your Prime Minister will also attend."

"That has all more or less been arranged sir," Jack replied. He is just waiting for me to give him the exact date for the visit and he says that he would not want to miss this for anything."

"Thank you Jack, and your good wife Jennifer and we shall give you a more exact date within the next day or two. Farewell now then, until we do met again."

"Jack," Hugo said, "Presidents and Prime Ministers seem to be falling over one another to give you honours. As I told you before, before it has all ended you will be offered a Knighthood in England and some similar Honour in the Horn of Africa. You have done too much for it to end in any other way. Just you wait and see, you agree, don't you Jennifer?"

"Jack," Jennifer said, "I know that you don't seem to like publicity but like it or not, Hugo may well have a point. If they did decide to offer you a Knighthood, or some other honour, would it not be very churlish of you if you chose to refuse to accept it? It won't make you any different to me and I don't think it would to Hugo, either, would it, Hugo? It is just some things that countries do when they feel that someone deserves that little bit extra to show that they are respected, isn't it Hugo?"

"Yes, I'd agree with that Jennifer but more importantly to me is that I'd still like to be able to say that it was the same Jack Dawkins that was my friend," Hugo replied. "No matter what happened you would still be Jack Dawkins, wouldn't you? But to refuse any such honour when it is offered is more or less an insult to your country I would think. You would still be Jack within the estate and outside the estate you would still be sought after as the richest man in the World, wouldn't you? That kind of publicity is something that I would avoid if I could, but you can't avoid that Jack, that is a fact and that is something that you are now going to be stuck with for many, many years to come."

"Maybe we are all jumping the gun anyway," Jack said. "No one has said anything to me about any Honours or Knighthoods so we can just live our lives as we do, can't we? I think that I'd better get in touch with Norman and put him in the picture about Ethiopia, hadn't I? I know that Norman said that the Prime Minister wants to go but he will need some warning of the date, won't he? I wonder if Ethiopia will bother to invite Somalia to attend. I just didn't like that man (and I still don't) but it is a neighbouring country, isn't it? I don't want to suggest yes or no for that, since that isn't my place, is it? You will want to go, won't you Jennifer? I know that I asked Hugo and I just presumed that you would. You would want to go though, wouldn't you?"

"Yes, you clot," Jenifer said, giving him quite a slap to reinforce her point. "I'll be there and I wonder if we will be going in an RAF jet or will it be the private one that we went in do you think, Jack? If it's the private one then maybe we could ask for Margaret to be our stewardess, couldn't we?"

"Who the heck is this Margaret then?" Hugo asked. "That's a new one on me. I must have been asleep when all this happened. Who is she? How have you met her as well? I didn't think that you had been out at all lately. Oh, of course, I'm a fool, aren't I? You went out to Ethiopia and you hired a private jet. So, was Margaret the stewardess on the plane that you went on? If she was, I don't think that the RAF would let her be the stewardess on one of their planes. If you have the Prime Minister with you it is fairly certain to be an RAF plane that you will go on as well anyway. But you did seem rather keen on getting her to be the stewardess so it was someone that you got on well with, was it?"

"I'm afraid that I'm telling you nothing at all about her Hugo," Jennifer said. "She may be coming to visit me here but from what we've heard about you, your reputation with the ladies does mean that you won't be introduced to her."

"I do beg your pardon Jennifer," Hugo said, quite hurt at the rebuke. "It sounds as though my name has been blackened somehow by someone. Why on earth should I have a reputation with the ladies? I am usually very careful in what I say to any ladies. You don't mean that about my ancestor's do you? I mean, that was them, and not me. I have rarely had any time for any ladies in my life. When you are an officer in the army in Spain it is far better to stay clear of any commitments at all. I have never seen a lady while I have been working with you so, do please let me know what I may have done to get such a reputation."

"When we met Margaret" Jennifer explained. "I invited her to come here and I think that it was either me or maybe Manuel who said that as she could be a potential security risk I would have to get it cleared by Miguel and then I was told that if Miguel was going to clear her to come here then she was more or less doomed because of his reputation and his way with the ladies. Then I said that I would then get her cleared by you but I think that it was either Manuel or Javier who said that that was equally as bad since your reputation was even worse than Miguel's was."

"So, I see," Hugo said. "It was those two again, was it? Just wait until I see them. They have all made up all kinds of stories at times between them. Oh, they even started one story that I was Gay. No, I've never found out what it is with those two but no, I am not Gay and I do not, as far as I am aware, have any reputation with the ladies. Usually, I am far too busy to start to have a private life. Yes, I have occasionally gone to a dance and I may have danced with a girl on some occasions but that is as close as I have ever got to any ladies at all. Oh, those two, I don't know what makes them think of me like that. I believe that somehow it does go back to that business with my ancestors. None of them know the full story, as I told you, but they do put it about that I am in fact Spanish Royalty and related to the present King. I am not, and I do wish that they would stop doing this to me. I will talk to them, no, I won't get hard on them, but I don't like it when they put stories like that out about me. It's the same I think with Miguel. Yes, he is slightly related to me so he has, I believe, been tarnished with the same business of my ancestors. Please, do believe me when I tell you that I do not have a reputation like that"

"Oh, I'm sorry Hugo," Jennifer said. It was just that they made it all seem so very believable. I apologise and alright then, I will introduce you to her when she comes to see us next week. Maybe you will like her. I get on well with her and, since we moved here I have in some way lost all of my old friends so, we both got on so well together and so I invited her to come and stay with us."

"I promise that I shall not ravish your friend Jennifer," Hugo said, with a little laugh. Yes, I can imagine how you would lose some of your friends when you moved here but I'm surprised that some haven't asked to come, just out of curiosity. I would like to meet her. She does sound to be quite charming in the way that you talk about her."

"My apologies to you then Hugo," Jennifer said, smiling a little more. "When she does come I shall give you a call and I will introduce you to her. Now there, how's that then for an apology?"

"Apology accepted madam," Hugo said, laughing at the way his ancestors reputation seemed to be still tarnishing him. "Now that I have, I hope, put a stop to such damaging remarks about me (and my reputation), I will go and just chase up on the other eight homes for Sri Lanka. I believe that they should be at the docks by tomorrow but it is just as well to check, isn't it?"

Jack, himself being now quite excited picked up the phone to make a call to Norman at Downing Street again. Norman answered and Jack said, "Norman, I have just heard from the President in Ethiopia and he has told me that they expect the switch on day to be within the next two weeks. He said that he would get me an exact date as soon as he could. Oh, he did ask if the Prime Minister would be attending and I said that I believed that he would. I had also asked him if he would be inviting the other leaders in to see the switch on and in some way there I put my foot in it. He says that there has been a lot of bad feeling between several of them for some time so I told him that perhaps this was a good time to start bringing them together and he has asked that I make a statement like that at the switch on. Norman, I'm no politician or a diplomat and that does worry me. If I have to do anything like that, I hope that the Prime Minister will be there. If he is there with us, it may just give me a bit of confidence in what I'm doing."

"Jack," Norman laughed at his friend, "You may not have the title of being a diplomat or a politician but you are already bringing lots of people together who haven't been friends for a long time. Yes, I'm almost certain that he'll be there with you but I don't know why you worry, you are the big benefactor to them all. That could be the lynch pin that is needed to get them together properly. Yes, I understand that there have been some disagreements in the past, but they haven't had a war with one another or anything like that for a long, long time. You'll be OK, you just wait and see. Just you get me that date as soon as you can, OK. Sorry, the bell has gone so I'm wanted again; I'll talk to you later."

Chapter Thirty-One

The following week, everything seemed to start happening all at once. Margaret, Jennifer's new friend (who was a stewardess for the private air line that they had used) arrived and she did seem to be quite impressed with both their flat and the size of the estate itself. She and Jennifer seemed to have to do a lot of exploring together as Jennifer did want to show off the many things that they now had in the estate buildings. They did have a trip into the town to see the shops, but of course, to do that they had to have two security guards to accompany them (and, at Jennifer's suggestion, someone to carry some bags for them). At first, Margaret started to find it strange in the amount of security that they had to have but Jennifer did give her a brief explanation that it was more or less the risk of kidnapping that they were guarding against (as she had often been given by Hugo and the men). With that, they both seemed to get on really well and were enjoying their time both on the estate and in their shopping. Also, following the remarks that had been made to Jennifer about Hugo, Margaret was introduced to Hugo and there were no further comments made by anyone about him and his 'reputation'. In fact, Hugo and Margaret did seem to get on quite well together, whenever Hugo had any spare time, which nowadays did seem to be very rare events.

The first shipment of Mobile Homes had arrived in Sri Lanka and were all being transported to the proposed site, along with the septic tanks that Jack had supplied, and the solar panels for the homes. The government out there had made arrangements for a team of people to get the ground prepared and then, as the homes got to the site they were being fitted with electricity, plumbing and sewage to make them into nice little homes for those people. The second shipment of the remaining seven homes was due to arrive the following week so that, time wise, did seem to have been fortunate anyway.

The surveyor's report had come back again about Somalia and that informed them that all of the pipes now had been tested and found to be adequate for the work that they had to do. With Jack giving the go ahead, Hugo saw Paul and they made arrangements for the rest of the equipment needed for Somalia to be started on shipping. They said that they estimated that roughly that it would take about two to three weeks for it to get to its destination.

It was also late in the following week when the President of Ethiopia did contact Jack to let him know that they had fixed a date for the big switch on. It was going to be in ten days time and, with the date firmly fixed in his mind, Jack got hold of Jennifer, Hugo and both of their parents to let them all know the good news. He knew that he had to let Norman know so that the Prime Minister could make some arrangements to attend.

The Prime Minister did call him again within a very short time and said that he was so pleased to hear the news and that yes, he would like to attend and, would Jack and his party like to go with them in an RAF Jet to get to the event. Jack did, of course agree to that since he was on this occasion going to be taking Jennifer, Hugo and both his and Jennifer's parents with them for the event. He had also, after asking Hugo if it was a correct thing to do, he had said that he would like Paul to go, (he was the manager of the spares people and who had made many of the arrangements for the equipment to be got together). Hugo had then asked Paul, who was delighted to be given such an invitation. After asking Jennifer if she thought that Margaret would like to go with them, Jack included her in his list of people who would be attending. He called the President and confirmed that there would be quite a party of them and asked if he would be able to get eight rooms booked for them at the hotel that they had gone to before. Six of the rooms were for Jack and Jennifer, both sets of parents, Hugo, Paul and Margaret with another two rooms for the security men (since they would probably at Miguel's insistence probably do a night shift and rotate who was sleeping. He said that he presumed that the Prime Minister would make his own arrangements for accommodation.

The entire estate was getting excited at the prospect of a major world shattering news break that would come when the switch on occurred. Some of them had had little to do with any of the work, in fact, there were very few that had been involved in a lot of the work.

Jack and Jennifer had of course been to the office to see Alec and Ray to update them on the progress that they were making and, of course, of the now proposed date for the big switch one of the desalination units and pumps. Jack, when talking to Alec and Ray had told them about him having suggested that the President should invite the other leaders to the 'switch on'. They said that they had been aware that there had been some kinds of ill feelings between some of the countries in the Horn of Africa but they agreed entirely with the President's request that Jack should now, at the switch on event, try to get them to unite much more as they all now had common reasons to unite. Whether it would work was in the lap of the Gods but they said that it was possible, due to his now exalted position in the eyes of many of the people of those countries for the aid that he had provided, he may possibly just be able to bring them all together. While he was with Alec and Ray on this occasion, Peter appeared and, to Jack, he appeared to be much more introverted than the Peter that Jack had always known.

"What's wrong with you then, Peter," Jack asked, "You look like you've just lost all of your money on a silly horse bet. What is it that is troubling you now, my old friend?"

"Jack," Peter replied. "I knew that it may happen but we had so many good times when we were young. I do remember some of them, as I'm sure that you do. It was suggested that I could perhaps contact you and get you to go along with a daft scheme to get bonus points for us in our world. Well, I did all that and, during that time, it has been good to see you again but now, well, as you have now achieved what we asked of you, I shall be moving up a bit and I shan't be seeing you ever again. Just take care of yourself Jack, and

I'm sorry for any bits that I may have done daft, but I was always like that, wasn't I? Cheerio, Jack." Then Peter just disappeared.

"Alec, Ray," Jack asked urgently, "What is happening? I thought that you said that you had had some special permission to be able to see us now and then. Didn't that include Peter? If it hadn't been for Peter then none of us would have done anything, would we? You wouldn't have made me rich. You wouldn't be getting bonus points. Why isn't he included? Can't you have some words with whoever it is that says what happens in your world?"

"I'll try again," Alec said, "But they said that it was just the two of us that had made the fortune. You do have a very valid point and can I say that you expect him to be able to contact you now and then as well? That may well help. I'll try to get him approved again, honest I will. I'll go now and see what I can do." Alec and Ray disappeared.

Jack turned to Jennifer who had this time gone to the office with Jack. "You were correct there, Jack," Jennifer said. "If it hadn't been for Peter none of it would have happened, would it? Let's hope that they do get him some approval. Come on, I'll make you some coffee, if Margaret hasn't already made you some."

They got back to the kitchen and yes, there was Margaret and there were three cups of coffee for them to take into the lounge area. "You see, when you work as a stewardess on an airline, you do get quite good at making coffee. Oh, by the way Jennifer, Thank you for the invitation to go with you to Ethiopia again but the company have rung me and want to know when I'll be back at work. By the sounds of it I may have to get back before the Ethiopia trip."

"Like hell you will," Jack said. "I'll give them a ring and they either agree to you staying for a good bit longer or I'll just buy out their company and then you can be the stewardess on our little jet. I'll get my pilot's licence soon, you'll see."

"Jack, Thank you so much for all that you are trying to do," Margaret said, "But it is my job and I do have to have a job to live, don't I? I'll have to go back but I should be able to come another time, shouldn't I?"

"No, Margaret," Jennifer said, "Jack is right this time. This event is going to be world news and you will be a part of it. They must have another stewardess who can stand in while you have this trip, mustn't they? Jack, why don't you put in an offer and buy them out. Then we can decide when Margaret has to go, can't we?"

"It's ever so sweet of you to talk like that and to try and get me to stay," Margaret said. "But I do have to work for a living and I do enjoy that work so I will have to return. I'm sorry about this but let's face it this is life, isn't it?"

"Just you wait, Margaret," Jack said. He went to his little directory and found the number for the private airline company and took out his phone and rang them. There was an answer quite quickly and Jack said who he was and he wanted to know how many 'planes they owned and how many crews did they have.

The person on the end of the line became very cautious at answering things like that and for little or no reason.

Jack then asked how many stewardesses they had got in the company. The man answering said that they always had plenty of stewardesses since it was such a nice job to get.

Right, Jack said, I would like to speak to the Chief Executive of the company please, right away. There was a short pause and a man came on the phone and asked what it was that he wanted to know.

"Look, Jack said, "My name is Jack Dawkins and I have used your airline before and on our last trip your stewardess became very friendly with my wife and she is at present our guest. She has been invited to accompany us on a trip to Ethiopia, along with the Prime Minister of Britain to be present at the switch on of the water pipeline for Ethiopia. That is a very great event and I do take it that you have heard something about it? Well, she has now been told that she has to return to work so either she is given a further extension so that she may visit Ethiopia with us or I shall have to purchase your airline and then make yourself redundant. As you are no doubt aware, I am comfortably able to afford to buy your little operation. Now, I would like your answer. Does she have an extension for the period of this visit or do you wish for yourself to be made redundant?"

"Mr Dawkins," the man said, "I am quite aware who you are and if she requires a small extension then she may have one, by all means. She is quite a valued worker in our small operation and no, she will not, in any way be punished for taking the extension."

"Thank you sir," Jack replied, "And I may say thank you for the service that we received on our last trip. I shall of course be using your services again as and when I need any air flights." With that done he closed the call.

"There you are Margaret," Jack said. "You see, their big boss did agree to you having an extension, didn't he? I did mean it as well when I said that I would use them again. You see, I had been thinking of getting a 'plane like that aeroplane that we flew on with you but for the hassle that there would be of storage, services and everything else, it just isn't worth it. I can so easily just book your company, can't I?"

"This just isn't a real world that you two live in, is it?" Margaret said with a laugh. "If anyone heard you they would think that it was time to get out the straightjackets. I mean; you even said that he had to agree or you would just buy the company and make him redundant. It is a crazy world that you live in, but wonderful for all that. Yes it is nice to come and visit you but I think that if I was here for too long I could so easily start to lose my mind as well, couldn't I? I'm glad that you hired that plane that I just happened to be working on. Thank you all so very much for the kindness that you seem to give to everyone."

As they finished their coffee, Hugo walked in and said to Jack. "The shipment of all of the equipment for Somalia is now on board and has left the port. Our estimated time is still correct."

"That's good Hugo," Jack said. "I think that we must now be just about up to scratch on everything that we are supposed to be doing at the moment, aren't we? By the way, Margaret's airline has now given her an extension of her leave so that she can go with us when we go to Ethiopia. She thought that they wanted her back before that trip. They were wrong, weren't they," he asked everyone.

"Oh, well in that case I may, with your permission, of course, invite Margaret to the dance that there is being held in the town this weekend. I know that it is difficult for the rest of you to go to anything like that, but us two simple people can occasionally do things like that, can't we Margaret?"

"Yes, we can," Margaret replied, with a huge smile, "And I would love to accept your very kind invitation to go to the dance. Are you sure that you can't go as well Jennifer? It seems to be such a shame, doesn't it?"

"Margaret," Hugo replied, "They do both know that they can go if they wish. Miguel would let them go, but he would insist on having some security guards inside and outside of the dance hall. The guards would all be wearing civilian clothing, so they don't stand out. Jack, I know, is now very nervous because of what we have described as potential risks. You went shopping with Jennifer, didn't you? Did you particularly notice the guards that were with you? I suppose that the only thing that you did notice was that they would probably have been quite willing to be bag carriers for you ladies. Now, it is really down to you two, isn't it? Do you want to go out to a dance, to have some leisure time as you used to know it?"

"Yes, I'd like to go," Jennifer said. "And you'd better get yourself ready as well Jack. I'm not asking you now. I'm telling you that we are going to go out. There, that's done it, hasn't it? We are going to try living an almost normal life just for once."

"It looks like I don't have any option, do I?" Jack said, quite resignedly. "I suppose that it will make a nice change anyway, won't it? Who will we get as guards then Hugo? I don't suppose that you'd want Manuel and Javier again, would you? By the way, did you speak to them after we had our little chat the other day? Oh, you can tell me later what they had to say, can't you?"

They all went away to try and get ready for this (what was to Jack and Jennifer) very special night out. Hugo and Margaret were grinning at the way that Jack had been writhing at the idea of having to go out, and with security people with them as well!

They did all go out to the dance at the local village centre and not many people noticed them (or even knew who they were) and the security men did blend into the crowd at the dance. It did come near to the end of the dance and the time for the raffle to be drawn came (and of course, Hugo had bought some tickets for himself and also some for Margaret). It was drawn and the MC for the night announced the winners, one of them being Margaret and she collected her prize and carried it back to the small group that they were. The MC then announced that the profits from the raffle were all to be put along with the main fund to carry out the long overdue repairs to the roof of the building, a sum that they had been quoted for as being almost a hundred thousand pounds. Jack, on hearing this nudged Jennifer and said, "Shall I then? I mean, it is another worthy cause, isn't it?

Jennifer nodded her agreement so Jack stood up and called out to the MC and said, "We just heard what you said and I would like to help the centre a little so I would like to donate the sum needed so that the roof could be fully repaired."

There was quite a silence for a few minutes and then someone said, "Can we ask who you are sir? At present we don't know you but we do need to get the fund up high enough to get the job done. You wouldn't just be having us on with a statement like that, would you?"

"I'm sorry but we do live in the area but we just aren't able to get out as much as we would like to. My name is Jack Dawkins and we bought the estate at the end of the village that many of you would know. I do assure you that I am not joking and we are the same people who have just donated enough money to get a good water supply into Ethiopia, Eritrea, Djibouti, Sudan and Somalia. There have been a few bits in the press lately about that and well, we would like to be considered to be locals to you all. I'll get a cheque sent over to you tomorrow for a hundred thousand pounds."

Jack sat down and there was an enormous cheer from the rest of the people in the hall. The MC came over to speak to Jack and said that he apologised for not recognising him earlier.

Jack then said, "Look, we can't get out very often because of who we are but it has been a super night out for us tonight and we would just like to thank everyone for not recognising us at all. We just want to be some of the normal people of the village. We will now though have to go home I think, won't we, Hugo?"

Hugo nodded and he began to lead them through the people in the hall, all of them wanting to pat Jack on the back and say thank you. They got out and to the cars that were waiting and they drove back to their flat where they could all have some coffee together.

They got sat in the lounge of their flat and Hugo said, "I do believe that this man sitting here near to you Jennifer is the same man that said that he didn't like or want publicity, isn't he? It is my opinion that a man like that is very surprising when he just goes to a local dance and then says, '*Oh, by the way, I'll pay the full cost for your roof repair*'. It is the same man, isn't it Jennifer?"

"Yes, it is the same man Hugo, but there again; it was a long time ago when he started to sing that song wasn't it? He has made one or two slight changes since then, hasn't he?"

"Yes," Margaret said, "But that is quite a lot of money for them to get as a one-off donation, isn't it? I mean, that can mean so much to a small place like this, can't it?"

"Yes," Hugo said to Margaret, "But you do have to realise that that was just a drop in the ocean for him. Jennifer has explained anything to you about who he is, hasn't she?"

"Well, no, what explanation would there be? I have just gathered that he is someone quite high up in the diplomatic corps or something. That he does quite a bit of work for the government. I had presumed that for the way that they received him in Ethiopia and everything."

"Oh, my dear," Hugo said. "Do you never follow newspaper stories or television news stories at all Margaret? Jack here is called Jack Dawkins, as you heard back in the hall. No, he isn't in the diplomatic corps or anything. He is now classed as the richest man in the world and the reason why he was in Ethiopia is that it is he who said that he would donate two billion pounds as a starter, to get a good water supply to the dry areas of Ethiopia, Djibouti, Eritrea, Sudan and Somalia. I think that that may now have risen to three billion pounds. His wealth is far greater than the entire monetary value of many countries. That is why the Prime Minister wants to go out with us all when we go to Ethiopia this time. It is to switch on the new water supply. He is basically, getting the sea water, taking out the salt out of the water and creating huge internal lakes. I had presumed that you knew about him. Jennifer," Hugo said to Jennifer, "You have been keeping quite quiet with your friend, haven't you? Margaret will still class you as a friend, even if you are married to that man there."

"Oh, my goodness," Margaret said, quite shocked at what she had just heard. "So when you spoke to my boss and told him that you would buy the airline, you meant that you could do that then, didn't you? Oh, dear, I hadn't realised Jennifer. I'm sorry if I have butted into your life like this. Maybe it would be better if I did get back to work. I can pack and perhaps I could get a taxi tomorrow."

"NO," Jennifer said. "When we moved here, when Jack bought the estate, all of my friends seemed to leave me, they won't come and see me. They're scared of coming for some reason. I thought, and still believe that I have found a new friend and I'm going to hang on to any friends that I can find. I can tell you that. You cannot go tomorrow Margaret. We are all going to go out to Ethiopia and we may have a few parties to go to as well and I want you to be with me as my pal. You don't object to that, do you?"

"Oh, Jennifer," Margaret said. "Maybe I can see what you mean and yes, I have enjoyed doing some things with you, but you have to have security when you go out. How can you live like that? Oh, I do like having you as a friend as well, but this is quite a shock, I can tell you that for nothing."

"Look, Margaret," Jack said. "I was just an ordinary bloke who worked in a local warehouse getting stuff ready for moving here and there and then one day, well I just happened to buy a lottery ticket and I won the lottery. With that, I started to play at investing in stocks and shares and somehow it just all snowballed. I didn't know about stocks and shares but somehow I just got lucky and did well with it all. We are just ordinary people but in some strange way I just happen to have a lot of money so I try to give it away to worthy causes. You'll see as you are around us as time goes by. Yes, Jennifer needs her pals and for some reason, her old pals from where we did live seem to be scared of knowing her now, or it seems like that because they won't come here to see her. You just live here, if you like and you can be her pal and, if you want I can pay you the money that you got as a stewardess for pocket money. I don't care, but I don't want her to lose any more friends. Now can you see what I mean?"

"OK, I'll hang around a bit but I do still like my work and I would like to try and keep that job, if I can but I could still keep popping out here to see you all, couldn't I?"

"Yes," Hugo said, "I'd like it very much if you decided to stay as friends with Jennifer and Jack and came here now and then. Maybe I would then be able to take you to some more dances, wouldn't I?"

Hearing that, Jack and Jennifer glanced at one another and they both had some large smiles on their faces. Yes, those two had got on well at the dance, hadn't they?

So, it was generally agreed that Margaret wasn't going to leave, just like that and she was going to stay to go on the Ethiopian visit with them all.

As the time passed, getting much nearer to the time for the Ethiopian trip, there was no doubt whatsoever; Jack, Jenifer and their families, plus Hugo, Paul and Margaret were all becoming very excited at the prospect of the forthcoming event.

Chapter Thirty-Two

At last, the day came around for their trip out to Ethiopia. The Prime Minister had again agreed that they would use an RAF Jet and it would depart from Northolt aerodrome. Miguel had been trying to organise everyone so that he would have some comfortable, but secure passengers from the estate to Northolt. He had had words with Hugo and had said, quite plainly, that, as it was now he who was responsible for the security during the journey. He said that he expected Hugo to play his part and to oversee their security once they went to Ethiopia. He had in the first instance arranged for a mini coach to be delivered which would hold Jack, Jennifer, both of their sets of parents, Margaret, Hugo and Paul. Two more cars were going to be driven, one ahead and one behind with security men in them. Three security men would be travelling with them, making Jack's party a total of twelve people. This was slightly more than he had anticipated, but he knew that unless there were any major incidents, it should be enough to make it a sensible party to see the switch-on ceremony and then, hopefully after a short flight back to Addis Ababa they would be all driving out to the end of that first pipeline and, hopefully, to that lake that the President had been having created.

The Prime Minister also had his small party to travel with them and he assured Jack that they had, he believed, now covered most parts of the visit. He also complimented Jack on the quality of the homes and work being done in Sri Lanka to aid the victims of that Tsunami. He said that Norman had been keeping him fully informed of all that was happening and he said that it was, to say the least very, very impressive to see the precise way that items were being delivered and then having people on hand to complete the tasks. He had asked Jack if he was now happy with the actions of the Somalia people and Jack said that as far as he was aware, they had corrected all of the joints on the pipelines and how much Somalia did after the water got to the end of the pipeline was something that he didn't think that he was capable of controlling. He had, of course, described the giant lakes that he had seen being created in Ethiopia (and a similar one in Djibouti when they flew over it).

The flight began and they all were aware that once again, it was going to be a long flight. The President of Ethiopia had reserved the rooms that Jack had asked for and they settled down for that long journey. Margaret, of course, felt that she was now in her own element and she also tried to assist in getting and serving refreshments to those on the trip. The Prime Minister was quite astonished that one of Jack's party was taking such an active part in doing this and he mentioned it to Jack.

"Ah," Jack said, "When we came out the last time, we hired a private jet and we had this wonderful Stewardess on board and it just happened that she and Jennifer have, over the time since that flight, become quite close friends and that Margaret now spends quite a lot of time at their estate. Indeed, since she has become such a regular visitor we have given her one of the flats in our main building so that she can know that she does have some independence. As far as the stewardess work goes though, she just loves that kind of work and, given the opportunity she just gets stuck in whenever she can."

"My goodness," The Prime Minister replied, "That is really showing people how to enjoy their work then, isn't it?"

Some of the people tried to sleep, some played some games but no matter what they did, the journey, they all knew would be long and quite tiring. They were all aware that when they arrived in Ethiopia, they were going to get a night's sleep at the hotel (possibly after they had yet another dinner there) and then the switch on ceremony would be on the following day. The President had heard of some of the other work that Jack was involved with (like the Sri Lanka problem) and had accepted Jack's decision that after they had been out to see the end of the pipeline, they would all, once again be boarding the jet for their flight back home. Jack had though, promised the President that he and Jennifer would return later as visitors to see what reaction the water had made to the lives of the people of those areas where the drought had hit in the past.

Eventually, the pilot did announce on the tannoy system that they were now approaching Addis Ababa and asked everyone to please fasten their seat belts. The landing was then once again, quite smooth and, as they taxied to the unloading area, once again, Jack saw the military band waiting and the large quantity of cars waiting to carry the people and their luggage to the hotel. There was also a good-sized fleet of army and police vehicles also stood waiting, ready to provide the escort for these honoured guests.

The time came for them to leave the aircraft and Jack suggested to the Prime Minister, that as he was indeed the most senior of the British visitors he should precede everyone down from the 'plane. The Prime Minister already was aware of Jack's aversion to being in front of anything that attracted publicity: so he led the queue of people leaving the plane. Once on the ground though, the band began to play, of course, there was the British National Anthem and some other music of which Jack had little knowledge. The President was there, of course, to greet his guests and he too, knowing of Jack's aversion to publicity, shook hands first of all with the Prime Minister and then Jack. They were all shepherded out to the waiting cars and Jack and Jennifer's parents were quite amazed at the way that they were being treated by the people in this country. Yes, of course, they knew that Jack had donated enough money to try and resolve the problems of the ongoing droughts and famines, but they just hadn't been prepared for such a reception as they were getting today.

The cars started out and then both the army and the police escorts took up position to escort them all to their hotel. At the hotel, of course, Jack was by now quite used to the manager, along with a number of his staff, standing there waiting just to greet these honoured guests. Jack and Jennifer guided their parents, plus Hugo and Margaret and Paul to the elevator that would take them up to their rooftop apartment. As it happened, although Jack and Jennifer had got the largest apartment on the rooftop, their parents also had some rooftop apartments that were quite amazing to look at. Hugo, Paul and Margaret, along with the security guards had been allocated rooms on the floor below the rooftop apartments. The guards knew from the instructions given by Miguel that there were two bedrooms (that just by chance happened to have two beds in each room) and the reason was for them to have one person sleeping while two would take up sentry duty, rotating so that they would all get enough total sleep.

The Manager had already spoken to Jack and had told him that there was to be a dinner in the special dining room that evening so he, in turn advised his and Jennifer's Mum and Dad plus Paul, Margaret and Hugo. The guards, following Miguel's instructions would not be in attendance at the meal but would have meals delivered to their rooms.

After such a long flight, they were all quite tired and by choice, Jack would have liked to decline the dinner but he was starting to learn, and he knew that they would have to go to it. The Prime Minister (along with his party), he had been told, had been taken to another hotel and they would not be joining them for the dinner.

The time for the dinner came around and they did all manage to get down to the special dining room for that special dinner. As they went in, they saw, once again, that there were guards all the way around the room and the President of Ethiopia had already arrived. They took their places and the dinner began. Fortunately, the

President was quite aware of how tired his guests would be after their long journey so the dinner was kept quite quiet with only a minimal amount of conversation going on. Jack, along with most of the other guests also appreciated this acknowledgement of how tired they all were. The President told Jack that cars would be at the hotel at nine-thirty in the morning to collect them. They would then be going back to the airport to get back onto the plane for the short flight down to Djibouti so that they could get in position for the switch-on procedure timed for midday.

With the dinner over with, they did all retire to their rooms all of them with the knowledge that they would be starting out again at nine-thirty on the next morning. Breakfasts they had been told would be available from seven o'clock in the morning.

Both Jack and Jennifer were so excited that neither of them really wanted a breakfast but, with both of their Mother's there, they were told that they must have something, even if it was only a piece of toast with some coffee. Everyone was ready though and they all trooped out to the cars that were waiting for them. Once again, they saw the police and the military escort vehicles taking up position and they were driven to the airport where, once again they got onto the aircraft for the comparatively short journey of about forty minutes to get them to Djibouti.

At Djibouti, once again they saw a fleet of cars waiting for them and also quite a number of police and military vehicles to give escort to them as they went to the coast site where the equipment was based.

They got into their cars and once again they set off to drive to the start point where they found many, many more vehicles and people waiting for the big event. By that time it was about eleven-twenty-five and they had been told that the 'switch on' had been set for midday. Time does drag when you know that something important is going to happen. For Jack and Jennifer, this was very, very important.

It was still nicely ten minutes or so to the 'start time' and they saw near the main units some lights starting to flash. That, Jack thought, would be the desalination units warming up. Once they had warmed up, they would have to get the pumps started to get the water into them before they could turn on the main pumps that would start to pump any water into the pipelines. It was almost noon and the voice of the President of Ethiopia came out across the area from the large loudspeakers that they had fitted for the occasion. He welcomed everyone and began the countdown from one minute before midday. That time seemed to drag even more and then, as the President said the word zero, everyone could hear the noise of the pumps really starting up. The water further out in the sea was churning and Jack realised that would probably be the action caused by the suction of so much water to get it to the desalination units. The main pumps then began to pick up the desalinated water and it began to be pumped into the pipelines. Everyone could hear the noise of the water being forced into the pipes and some of the pipes even started to vibrate at first, but then they settled down as the pressure became more constant. They had started the process, and now it would be a case of how long it would take for the water to start coming out of the pipeline near to and into that massive lake area. That, they were aware was something that they wouldn't know until they got there to see it.

Everyone started to move back towards the cars so that they could get back to the airport. "How long do you think we will have to wait when we get to the end of the pipeline for the water to come out?" Jennifer asked Jack.

"Oh, I don't think that we'll match the water for speed, not on this run," Jack said, quite excitedly. "At the force that the water seemed to be going into the pipeline it will be there at the lake well before we get there. We may just be there to see the lake starting to get its fill started."

The Ethiopian President had been standing fairly close as Jack said this and he said to Jack, "Do you think that it will move as fast as that then Jack? I had been presuming that it could take at least two or three hours to go anywhere near as far as that."

"Well, Jack replied, "With that force of water and that diameter of the pipe, I may be wrong, but I would have imagined that the water would be going at some considerable speed. Remember as well that it is going, more or less, in a straight line. We are going to drive to the aeroplane now, and then we have to fly to Addis Ababa, and then we have to drive to the end of the pipeline. Now, if we estimate twenty minutes to get to the airport; say one hour to get the plane into the sky and then about another forty-five minutes flight. From Addis Ababa I would think it will be almost an hour to drive to the pipeline, won't it? That gives going on for almost three hours and I believe that the water will move faster than that. We'll see when we get there, won't we?"

"Yes, I'd agree that you could well be correct as well," the Prime Minister said as he joined in the conversation as they went to the cars. "I think that the water could be moving at quite a tremendous speed and that is a constant speed as well, isn't it?"

They got to the cars and once they were all in, the cars started and drove them back to the airport. There were by then several aeroplanes in a holding bay with their engines running. Obviously, there were going to be quite a few other people who wanted to get to where the water came out of the pipeline. Jack and his group (including the Prime Minister and his party) got onto the aeroplane; they all got into their seats and started to fasten their seat belts even before the Captain had asked them to do so. With the 'plane loaded, they began to taxi to the runway and then, within a very short time, they were again in the sky and flying back to Addis Ababa. The flight was, as Jack had estimated, about forty-five minutes. The 'plane landed and taxied to the unloading bay and they could see the collection of cars with police and military escort vehicles all waiting for them. It didn't take them very long to get off the 'plane and into the cars (they were all by this time very excited at just what they were going to see).

The cars started out for the main gates and then onto the road that would take them to the pipeline end again. It wasn't a bad road, but it wasn't a road that was in any way suitable for any high speeds and once again, Jack's estimate wasn't too bad and it took them just over an hour to get to where they would have to park the cars and then walk to be able to see where the pipeline ended.

Everyone got out of the cars and made a rush to get into a position so that they could see into the large land depression and to about where they thought that the pipeline ended. As soon as they got there, they could hear a tremendous jetting noise as the water came out of the pipe almost as a jet itself and it was soaring across the depression and then falling down into the depression itself. It was already collecting quite a small lake there, and that lake, even then, was growing at a reasonable rate.

"Jack, you were right," a few people were shouting. "What's going to happen when the water has filled the depression though?" someone else said.

"Look," The President said, "You can see some smaller pipes situated further away along the edges of the lake, they are now waiting for the water to start reaching there and then, once those pipes are covered, the small pumps will be switched on and the additional pipes will take that water to the other areas that need the water. If that isn't enough to get rid of it, as Jack had told us from the start, we could have some rivers developing to carry water across the land and back towards the sea again. I am so delighted at what I am seeing here. Of course, if we ever thought that there was too much water we could of course turn off the first lot of pumps just for a little while to let things settle down, couldn't we?"

The leaders from the other countries had arrived and were marvelling at what they were seeing develop. An internal lake was being created. The additional pipes to start the smaller pipelines were at that time still empty and waiting for the level of the water to rise so that they too could play their part in helping to irrigate some very dry lands.

The President of Ethiopia called everyone to a halt and then said, "Would everyone here, who like my country, are going to benefit from the ideas of this man standing by me, Mr Jack Dawkins, like to put their hands together and say thank you for his idea and his funding for our countries. I know that we have been fortunate enough to be the first, but I understand that all of the countries that he said that he would aid do now have their pipelines in place and their equipment is arriving so that everyone can enjoy similar benefits. I give you Mr Jack Dawkins everyone." There was a tremendous amount of applause and it went on for some time and then the President again held up his hands and said again, "May we ask Mr Dawkins if he has anything to say to us all?"

"Well, everybody," Jack said, quite loudly, "Yes it started as a dream, a dream brought about by a nightmare. The nightmare was seeing the people of Ethiopia who were starving due to a drought and then a famine caused by the drought. Yes, I did have some money that I have been very fortunate to acquire over some time and to me, the obvious way was to spend that money to try and prevent any more future disasters of this kind. All of your countries, The Horn of Africa countries are a tremendous area in themselves. Now, you are all going to be getting your irrigation. That should help your people to prosper. In the past, I have heard that there has been enmity between some of the people of some of these countries and to me that is a shame. Now you can all prosper, why can you not begin to talk and unite in your common aims to make your Horn of Africa the point of envy for other parts of Africa and of the World? United and with boundless opportunity can we not, in the rest of the world, see you talk and cease such pointless enmity? Let you all remember that you can all become just as successful as a good water supply can be to each of your countries. Please, can we have genuine peace between all of your countries, trade and wealth for all of you? Thank you, everyone, I am pleased that this has worked how I had hoped that it would. Please let the peace that I imagine between your countries also become a reality. Thank you, everyone."

Jack stood back a little and once again there came a massive cheer that seemed to be from everywhere within the crowd.

"My Goodness Jack," The Prime Minister said to him, "Perhaps the next step for you should be to become a politician. That was a good and marvellous little speech that you gave just then and it seemed to be so 'off the cuff' so to speak and I do believe that it has hit home to a lot of the people here. Well done Jack, well done."

The Ethiopian President gave Jack a little slap on the back and said, "I told you that you could do it, Jack. I just hope that the fervour that we have amongst the people here will continue and develop to create the peace that you have asked for."

The crowd did begin to disperse a little as they made their way back towards the cars. Each of the leaders of the other countries though made a point of coming to thank Jack for what he had done (including the President of Somalia, who in some ways appeared to Jack to be a slightly changed man, somehow, slightly more humble!) and they all said how they believed that what he had suggested of them all uniting much more was such a sensible idea for them all and could improve all of their futures.

Jack and his parties all got back into their cars and they all made the drive back into Addis Ababa and once more to their hotel. The President had agreed with Jack that since it had been quite a long day it may be more sensible for them to leave their return home until the next day. Jack believed that all of his party agreed that that was far more sensible.

Chapter Thirty-Three

The following day found them all once again going out to get into the cars (again at nine-thirty in the morning) so that they could make their way back to the airport to begin their flight back home once again. Everyone on the 'plane had made their comments about just how well the project had worked. This, though for Jack had been the first. Yes, there had been two countries that benefited this time, Ethiopia and Djibouti and the fact that they had now both got some inner lake created from what they had done did seem to have achieved more or less what everyone in those countries had hoped for. For Jack though, there were still a further three countries that would have to have a 'switch on' as soon as they had managed to get their equipment into place and working. Jack had said to both Jennifer and Hugo that if he could just get some reports of a successful pipeline working that would be enough for him. He didn't see a need or particularly want to have to go to the opening of each one. It had been necessary to see that first one, just to know that the idea had worked and it appeared to have worked out very well. Hugo had already confirmed to Jack that all of the rest of the equipment for the other countries was now 'on the water' and should be with them within days. The Prime Minister had also complimented Jack on all that he had done. There was the water that he had taken to five countries but there was also the work that he had done for the country of Sri Lanka. Jack was just longing to get back home again.

Hugo had telephoned forward when the pilot had given them an estimated arrival time and as Hugo's message was passed on to Miguel at the estate he was then able to make arrangements for some transport to collect them from Northolt and to drive them back to their estate.

Once again, the arrival at Northolt was on time and as they taxied around to the unloading area they could see a mini coach and a couple of cars waiting for them. Well they were almost home, weren't they?

Once off of the plane they got themselves sorted into the mini coach and with the security men in the two cars they began their drive back home. It seemed to have been so long ago now, but it had only been about three and a half days, perhaps four if you took the hanging about as well as part of that time.

They arrived back at the estate and were dropped off at the main doors. The security men made sure that they got everyone's luggage out of the car boots and into the main doors by the elevator door. They soon got up to their flat and Jennifer knew that the first job for her would be to get the kettle on for some coffee. Hugo and Margaret had joined them in their flat to have some coffee and Jennifer knew that Margaret would be leaving the next day to go back to her work as a stewardess on that private airline. Hugo would soon have to be sorting out what else was needed, along with Paul, in their 'ordering department' while Jack and Jennifer would once again be wondering just what to do with their time. Jack did know that he had another lesson due for his pilot's licence (which he did enjoy) but Jennifer had nothing other than some more work in her kitchen to occupy her.

Once Margaret had left the flat, Jennifer knew almost for certain that Jack would be going to the office to update their friendly ghosts in there. Those ghosts sometimes seemed to rule Jack's life as far as Jennifer was concerned. Yes, they did owe them a lot for all of the things that they had got them but it does seem to be a strange kind of thing when your main interest is talking to some ghosts, friendly or otherwise.

They thought that they had by then settled down from their journeys and the phone rang. Jack answered it and it was Norman Brooks from Downing Street. "Hello, Jack," He said. "I've just received a request from the President of Sri Lanka and they are asking if you would care to visit them since they do feel that you have done so much and so quickly to help their people. They have left me their contact details which I am now forwarding to you by e-mail but I did explain that you had only just returned from a rather long and tiring journey. He said that he could appreciate that but could you please consider their request? I just agreed that I would pass on their feelings and maybe you would give them a call when you had managed to recover a little. By the way, the Prime Minister was speaking very highly of the way that you have made some of those people in the Horn of Africa think more about getting together to unite their common interests instead of talking about a battle or two. Well done, sir. There doesn't seem to be any end to your skills, does there? I won't take too much of your time right now but, well done in all that you have achieved so far and cheerio for now."

Jack put down the phone and realised that, despite all of his misgivings about publicity he was probably going to have to go out to see these people. He was feeling a little lost but then he just thought that he should also report to Alec and Ray who had done so much for them. And that he and Jennifer (with Hugo's help) had also done quite a lot for all of them in their world. He strolled around to the office and peered in. Yes, there, sat as was usual with his hands floating above the keyboard was Alec while Ray was sitting there with his notebook in his hands.

"Hello then, my two friends. And how are you getting on? Did you miss us when we were away then? Yes, we have been out to Ethiopia and we saw the big 'switch on' and we even went out to the end of the pipeline that is only an hour's drive from Addis Ababa. That of course was the shorter of the main pipes that were installed. They used the pipes left over from that three hundred miles worth. They used that pipe work to extend some of the other lines. That was all so very impressive. They are starting to create the lake that I told you that they had planned and they already have some smaller pipes (with another lot of pumps). Those pipes are just waiting for the water to rise enough in the lake and then they will be pumping water out to quite a few other areas where there is a distinct lack of water. They knew that they needed a bit more than three hundred miles for some areas. Even these other lines will have lakes at the end of them as well, yes, and again some of the smaller pipes to get the water further into the land. It should irrigate quite a lot of Ethiopia. We were all impressed, as were the leaders from the other countries and since their pipelines are all now ready and waiting they should soon get their own 'switch on' events, shouldn't they? All of the equipment for the other countries has either arrived or is due there at them all within the next few days so I believe that the Horn of Africa should no longer suffer from droughts as they have done in the past. How have things gone on with you two then? I would imagine that you will now start to be getting your bonus points, won't you? After all, I made the donation and we have got the projects underway. We have got the ones in Sri Lanka underway and I even gave another hundred thousand pounds as a donation to repair the roof of the local hall where we all went to a dance. Yes, you should soon be getting the points, shouldn't you?"

"Yes, Jack," Ray replied, "We understand that the bonus points are now coming through fine. We have also heard, and have had it confirmed, that we two, and yes, Peter also, will be able to occasionally come back here to see you now and then. We have now got the fund to be quite self-serving and it can even now lose money when it needs to, and that is without us telling it how to do it. If the total goes down, it will automatically correct things and put the total back up again. You, our friend, will never have any less money than you do have now. When you have children, they will, no doubt inherit the fund and that should just carry on for them as well. I just hope that you do teach your children the need to keep donating and helping others. We don't know what will happen if you don't, somehow, the fund may just go mad and grow and grow and grow. We never meant it to do that either, nor did you, did you?"

"Yes," Alec chipped in, "And now that we have done our bit we shall be spending far less time here than we have in the past. You will still be able to call on any of the three of us as you did in the past by just calling our names three times. I don't think that you will necessarily need to call us too often. Just when you do get your Honours (and a probable Knighthood), do remember an old friend from your youth and a couple of old-time brokers who helped to make things work for you. We will wait for a little while, just to say cheerio to Jennifer and Hugo as well. Do please let them both know that we are about to be going away soon, won't you?"

"I'll go and get hold of them right away. Just you two hang on for a bit, will you?"

Jack went out of the office and went to the kitchen, looking for Jennifer and as he was doing it he was trying to get his phone to work so that he could call Hugo to come up to talk to their old friends. He found Jennifer and said, "Don't bother with the coffee yet, Jennifer; we have to go to the office. I've already called for Hugo. Alec, Ray and Peter are going to be moving on. They want to say cheerio for now to us all."

Hugo ran into the flat and called, "What's gone wrong, Jack? Your call sounded to be deadly urgent. Oh, there you are, and you Jennifer, You are both OK aren't you?"

"Yes Hugo," Jack replied with a huge smile on his face. "Alec and Ray want to see us all together to say cheerio for now. They are being moved up but all three of them can come back now and then to see us but they just wanted me to get you both so that they could say cheerio."

The three of them almost ran to get to the office and, once they got there they saw Alec and Ray standing there waiting for them and with them, there was Peter with quite a smile on his face.

"I'm glad that you got them here then," Alec said. "It has been a fairly long road but we've all got there, haven't we? All three of us, along with a lot more people in our world are now moving up a few levels so we just wanted to say cheerio for now. We will pop back now and then to see you all but we just wanted to say cheerio before we go. The three of you have done us all proud, I can tell you that. Thank you for all that you have done. We shall be back, but not for a few days yet I believe, cheerio to you all." With that, all three of them, instead of just disappearing as they usually did, they gradually faded away and left them with what now seemed to be an empty office.

So, at last Jack has managed to put the ghosts to bed, at least for a little while, hasn't he? At least he is intending to try and remain friends with them, just in case!

He has dealt with some rather serious incidents and he seems to have dealt with them well. He has built quite a reputation as well for being quite generous with some of his money. He has now, we presume bought his helicopter but how long is it going to take for him to get his pilot's licence for a twin engine jet aircraft? If he does get one, will Margaret go and be the stewardess on it? Who knows, but she and Hugo do seem to be getting on well together, don't they?

No doubt in time Jack will do all that he wants, or needs to do but in the meantime, if you have enjoyed reading about his rather different encounter with his old friend Peter then perhaps you may think about giving a short review saying what you did and you didn't like about the book. Authors, after all only write what appears in their heads, they don't know if their readers are enjoying it, unless of course some of those readers do send in some kind of review, perhaps leaving it on the Amazon website.

Thank you once again for being a reader and now, perhaps I too shall just fade away from your sight!

Regards to all readers,

Ralph Wilson
(N R P Wilson)

Printed in Great Britain
by Amazon